Black Roses Grow in The Dark

By
Natavia

SOUL Publications

Black Roses Grow in The Dark   Natavia

Copyright © 2022 by Natavia. Published by SOUL Publications. All rights
reserved www.nataviapresents.com This book is a work of fiction. Names, characters, places, and incidents either are the product of the author's imagination or are used fictitiously and are not to be construed as real. Any resemblance to actual persons, living or dead, business establishments, events, or locales or, is entirely coincidental. No portion of this book may be used or reproduced in any manner whatsoever without writer permission except in the case of brief quotations embodied in critical articles and reviews.

SOUL Publications

The Beginning

A thousand years ago there was a magical forest goddess by the name of Lyira. Inside the forest lived elves, walking trees, sparkling water, eagle-sized butterflies, two-headed birds the size of dragons, unicorns, giants, centaurs, and many other creatures. Lyira sat on a tree log near a pond while braiding her hair and humming a sweet melody to the birds as they flew around her head. The melodic sound of Lyira's voice caused a sparkling red rose bush to emerge from the ground. The forest was connected to her spirit and vice versa so whenever she ate, sang, danced, or laughed, a piece of the forest grew. If Lyira had a bad day, a flower would die or the sun wouldn't shine. But as long as the goddess was well fed and happy, so was the forest.

Her mate, the king of the forest, appeared in front of her with a basket of freshly killed rabbits. Lyira stopped braiding her full, coily, ankle length hair as her stomach growled at the sight of her dinner.

"My goddess," the king said, kneeling in front of her.

"Where have you been? You've been gone for some time now," she said. She noticed an uneasy look on her mate's face, he looked troubled.

"Amstid opened the portal again," he said.

Amstid was a warlock from the outside world but in Lyira's eyes, he was just a human with special tricks. She didn't want their worlds to collide since she was a creature and he was a human, but somehow Amstid kept finding a way to her world.

"Amstid still wants to join my world in exchange for what he calls black magic? I told you before, my love, and I'll tell you again, our kind doesn't belong with others. I don't know what black magic is but I know our magic is enough," she said.

"You appointed me as the king of the forest and I should have a say. I want to be able to protect you from danger, but I'm not worthy if I don't have the magic he offers," he said.

Lyira stood from the tree log to look in her mate's eyes. "There's no danger in my forest to be protected from and if there is, I will fix it since it's my forest. What did this black magic show you that makes you doubt yourself as the king, huh?" she asked.

"It showed me that this forest will perish if we don't join him. His magic gave me a glimpse of the future and in the future, our forest turned to ashes. Without access to the future, how can we determine our fate?" the king replied.

"Fate isn't supposed to be seen and that kind of energy doesn't belong in my forest. If you disobey me again, I'll disown you as the king. No king of mine will join forces with a human who uses magic," she said.

Anger flashed through the king's eyes. All of a sudden, the forest seemed too small compared to Amstid's world. He was obsessed with the warlock's world, especially the gruesome deaths he had witnessed.

"I won't bring this subject up anymore," the king said.

"I want him dead, my love. His ability to open portals to a forbidden world is a magic that doesn't belong here. I shouldn't have to fight while carrying a life inside my womb, so I trust you to handle it for good," Lyira said. She picked up the basket of bloody rabbits before heading towards her resting area. The goddess's resting area was inside a pond where the lily pads were three times her size. A young woman named Merci jumped from the top of a tree, carrying a nest of bird eggs to go with Lyira's dinner. "Can I clean this for you, my goddess?" she asked, reaching for the basket of rabbits.

"No, I enjoy cleaning my own rabbits, but I need something else from you," Lyira replied. Merci dropped to her knees, bowing her head at Lyira's feet.

"Yes, my goddess," she replied.

"I want you to bring me Amstid's head. The king said he'll take care of it, but I don't trust his words lately. He's *changing and it could be bad for the forest. If the king tries to stop you, take his head too. No mate of mine will become a traitor," Lyira said.*

"I'll do as you wish. Do you want me to gather the others?" she asked.

"There's no need. I want this to be done silently," Lyira replied.

While Lyira was giving orders to the warrior, the king was listening. At that point, he knew what needed to be done. He teleported to the portal which was deep in the forest where the sun rarely shined. Amstid and a small group of his clan members were patiently waiting for the king's word to join forces.

"The vision you showed me came true. The goddess wants me dead," the king said in disbelief. Amstid's warnings of Lyira's forest were coming true, causing the king to second guess Lyira as their true goddess. The king thought he could change destiny by joining forces with Amstid, a man who could cheat fate. Amstid pulled a crystal globe out of his lambskin knapsack, the purple beam lit up the woods. Amstid had promised the king the globe if he persuaded Lyira to allow his clan to live inside their world. Unbeknownst to the king, Amstid had destroyed many hidden worlds he'd discovered through his globe. He was the grim reaper of realms.

"You see this? It can be yours if you kill the goddess before she kills you. With her out of the way, you'll be the leader of the forest. We can teach your people sorcery," Amstid said.

Merci approached the men on a white unicorn. The unicorn's golden horn stood three feet tall. Amstid was so intrigued with the forest creatures that he wanted to own them and turn them into his personal weapons. Merci angrily jumped off her unicorn at the sight of the outsiders trespassing.

"I know Lyira sent you to kill me," the king said to her.

Amstid couldn't take his eyes off the tall Amazonian creature. He didn't see a need for the men of the forest, but the women could enhance their breeding rituals.

"You can join us," Amstid spoke out to Merci. Merci snarled at Amstid.

"The queen wants your head and I shall bring it to her," Merci replied. Amstid gestured for his men to attack Merci. Four of his men surrounded her. The king cowardly watched Merci as she fought them off with magical weapons that appeared in her hands. Amstid clasped his hands together in excitement.

"Your kind is truly a gift," Amstid said.

Merci back flipped onto a man's shoulder. The sound of his neck snapping echoed throughout the dark end of the forest. Amstid's men were what he called warlocks. One of his men used a wind-like force, knocking Merci off the dead man's body, sending her into a tree.

"I taught my little brother, Sheldon, well. Don't worry, he'll kill her," Amstid told the king. Sheldon took off his cloak, revealing his bald head and gruesome markings that were burned into his skin. It meant an innocent life was sacrificed to give him strength. Merci snapped her broken bones back into place to fight one on one with Sheldon. Sheldon raised himself off the ground, spinning his body to cause a strong wind. Merci's body was swallowed by Sheldon's wind; it sent her soaring her through the air.

"This isn't right," the king spoke while witnessing one of his people being tortured.

"Look into this globe and tell me what the future brings?" Amstid asked the king. The globe's glow faded away and was replaced by an image that filled the king's heart with rage. Inside the globe was an image that Amstid has been tormenting the king with for weeks in the hopes of him turning on the forest goddess. The king felt worthless while watching his mate have passionate sex with another man—a warlock. The warlock was giving his mate great pleasure, a pleasure that he didn't give to her.

"You aren't in her future so why not rule this forest by your hand? She doesn't love you and never has. Her loyalty doesn't lie in your hands," Amstid said to the king. Merci's body crashed into a tree with so much force the tree shattered into dust. Blood poured out of her mouth. "I'm not going to give up! I'll die for my goddess!" Merci weakly said while painfully pushing herself up from the ground.

"Stop your brother from hurting her and I'll take care of Lyira. By moonlight, you'll be able to join my forest," the king finally said.

"Back away, Sheldon!" Amstid ordered his brother. Sheldon backed away from the wounded elf. Amstid went into his knapsack, pulling out a bag of aged salt.

"What is this?" the king asked while taking the bag.

"The way to dry out a garden," he replied.

Since the beginning of time, when there's good, there is evil. When there's light, there's darkness...

Black Rose

May 5th 2036...

I tapped my long, pointy fingernail on the table as I stared in the face of the distraught human. She was hysterically screaming at me because my spell didn't work in her favor.

"You are an evil witch! I didn't pay you five thousand for this!" the human screamed. Her blonde hair was stuck to her wet, tear-stained face and her cheeks were redder than a cayenne pepper. I burst into a fit of laughter as she screamed obscenities at me—she looked pathetic.

"You wanted your husband to stop his love affair, therefore I granted you your wish."

"I didn't want him to die!" she screamed.

"Well, how else was he gonna stop cheating on you? I told you before that he didn't love you and only wanted to marry you because of your family's wealth!" I said, standing from the chair. I was inside my client's home to collect what I'd come for after granting her wish. Her husband's soul belonged to me. Collecting souls through make believe love spells was how I survived and kept my appearance youthful. Emily cradled her husband's dead body in the middle of the kitchen floor. He had died from the black rose I had given Emily to give to him. Silly rabbit thought the scent from the rose would make him love her. She looked up at me with pain filled eyes as I approached her.

"Please bring him back! We have children!" she sobbed.

I kneeled next to the body. Emily's eyes grew big as saucers when I pulled back the black lace hoodie of my gothic, form-fitting dress to reveal my real identity. My jet black eyes and pointed ears with gold tips frightened her. The markings embedded in my skin turned into real rose stems which covered my body.

"You are a…you are a monster," she said.

"Call me what you want but you sealed his fate the moment you came into my shop looking for a potion to cure your miserable marriage. Didn't your parents ever tell you to be careful what you wish for?"

Emily got up from the floor, she grabbed a butcher's knife from her knife rack.

She charged into me. "You are dead!" she screamed.

A three foot rose thorn shot from the palm of my hand, piercing through Emily's chest. She dropped to the floor on her knees with blood spilling out the corner of her mouth.

"Love is a weak emotion, my child, but don't worry, at least you can die with him," I chuckled. I withdrew the thorn out of her chest, her body crashed onto the floor next to her husband. Blood flowed from her body creating a puddle of blood.

"Til' death do us part," I mimicked the human's wedding vows.

I pulled out my rose shaped, golden wand from the knapsack sown to my dress. I waved the wand across the bodies, happily watching their bodies shrink and vanish. After their bodies disappeared, two rose seeds appeared. I picked up the bloody seeds, placing them inside my knapsack.

A little girl who looked to be six years old came into the kitchen, holding her stuffed animal. She was dressed in pajamas. She looked a little discombobulated, perhaps she'd just woke up. I stood over the puddle of blood, letting the train of my dress shield it from the eyes of the child. In my eyes, children were pure. I quickly transformed into her mother while she rubbed her eyes.

"Mommy, I had a bad dream," the little girl said.

"I'll be upstairs in a minute, honey," I replied, imitating Emily's voice.

She looked around the kitchen. "Okay, where's Daddy? I thought he was in the kitchen too."

"He's in the basement, but go on, go upstairs."

The little girl went upstairs; I breathed a sigh of relief. I left the kitchen, heading to the front door to return to my cabin in the woods.

****

I took off my clothing, before entering my world of serenity. My garden room was full of onyx colored plants, roses, butterflies, and sparkling hummingbirds. I inhaled the scent of the room, it reminded me of a forest from the past. The garden was created from the many souls I had collected over the centuries. In the center of the room was a pool of crystal green water, full of lily pads. I dug my nails into the rich soil in the floor, then dropped the two rose seeds into the hole. Afterwards, I grabbed a water pail filled with human blood. I sprinkled a few drops over the soil and seconds later, the two roses were already sprouting. Unlike many gardens, my garden didn't blossom from sun or water, but from blood, death and darkness instead.

"Come out, Silver! You can go hunt now!" I called out while heading towards the pool.

The bushes rustled; Silver's legs came out of the bush as she stretched her front legs. She was a silver fox, which was why I called her Silver. Her jet black coat had traces of white hair which looked silver at night. My black rose symbol was engraved on her ears to let others know she belonged to me. Her tail wagged as I pet her. It was midnight, Silver's favorite time to go outside and hunt.

"You may go now, but don't go too far," I told her.

Silver happily ran out of the room to go outside to hunt. Black butterflies landed on my head as I stepped into the pool water. I closed my eyes after I sat on the metallic green stones at the bottom of the pool. As soon as I was ready to drift off to sleep, the door to my garden room opened.

"You have someone here to see you," Majestic said.

"It's past midnight, business is closed, now please, let me rest," I replied.

"The client is offering twenty thousand," she replied.

I opened my eyes, sitting up in the pool. Majestic's purple eyes glowed as she smiled.

"I knew I would have your attention," she said.

Majestic was wearing a black sheer robe showing the markings of serpent scales covering her deep and rich brown skin. The way her markings were created, looked like she was wearing a snake-skin catsuit. Her bald head was covered with reptile scale prints but many thought they were tattoos. I created her with blood from a serpent I had killed seven hundred years ago, and even though she was my creation, I still looked at her as a sister.

"These silly humans are handing me their souls on a silver platter. What is it now? Love? Heartbreak? Cheating?" I asked.

"Actually it's a female werewolf," she replied.

"A werewolf needs my services? Aren't they mated for life? And besides, a werewolf's soul can't help me. I only deal with human sacrifices, not immortals."

"She wants the spell to be against a warlock," she replied.

"I'll be up once I finish my bath, and tell that bitch not to sit on my couch, she might have fleas."

"You've been grumpier than usual lately. Maybe you need to get laid," Majestic said.

I rolled my eyes at her. "I don't need the distraction of a man right now."

"There's nothing wrong with having emotions," Majestic replied.

"Emotions will ruin my garden. I collect souls better without feeling anything so please, leave me be."

"Yes, my goddess," Majestic said. She pushed open the door to go upstairs.

I bathed in my pool for ten minutes before getting out. The water caused my thick hair to shrink and now my natural braids stopped in the middle of my back. A black dashiki was hanging off the branch of my blueberry tree. After I got dressed, I teleported to the living room area of my cabin. Majestic was sitting on the couch drinking a glass of wine while flipping through a jewelry magazine. A pregnant woman was standing by the front door of my cabin. I noticed she was holding a flyer that Majestic had passed around the inner city. The flyer was an advertisement for my business of fortune telling and love spells.

"Hi, my name is Jetti and I really need your help. You are the only witch who can help me," she said. She extended her hand for a handshake but I didn't take it.

I'm not a witch!

"Um, oh okay. I guess you aren't a friendly witch," she giggled to lighten the mood.

"You interrupted my bath."

"I didn't mean to, it's just that I'm really in trouble," she said.

"Follow me," I replied.

I walked down the hallway of my cabin, pushing past wooden beads that hung from the top of the doorway. We entered my make believe psychic room decorated with historic artifacts that I had collected over the years. Behind my table was a glass case filled with fake potions inside of crystal bottles. It have the illusion that I really sold love potions.

"Have a seat."

Jetti looked around my room in awe. "Wow, this looks like it came out of my child's father's mansion," she said. She took a seat at the table across from me.

"I must say, you look so young. Wow, you are so beautiful. I was expecting an old witch living in this cabin in the woods. With your looks, you can marry a rich man," Jetti said.

"Rich is a mindset but a dead soul is worth more than gold."

"I don't know what that means," she said.

"Don't worry, my child, you'll see soon. Now, what can I help you with?"

"I need an escape from my pack and being with my son's father, Akea, is the only way out, but he thinks I betrayed him," she said.

I chuckled. "What's so special about this man where you want to betray your pack? I thought it was in werewolves' nature to roam in packs."

"That is true, but Akea can offer me a better life. He's rich and handsome," she said.

"A woman who wants everything but love. This is the first."

"It's about survival for me. My pack is poor, living in the swamp of the woods where there's barely food. Akea gave me money to survive until I have his son, but my pup is coming. After he takes our son away from me, I won't have much left," she said.

"And something tells me he knows you are after his fortunes. After all, he is a warlock and could possibly see right through you. This is gonna cost more than twenty thousand."

A low growl escaped her throat as her eyes glowed yellow with a hint of brown. Her canine teeth expanded from her gums—I had pissed her off.

"This is all I have left! I'm gambling with my life!" she said, banging on the table.

Majestic rushed into the room with her dagger, shaped like an eagle's claw, in her hand.

"Are you okay, Rose?" Majestic seethed, wanting to attack Jetti.

"Yes, I'm fine. Jetti's hormones are just out of hand right now. You can leave us," I replied. Majestic reluctantly left the room.

"If you want your child to remain safe, I suggest you calm down that beast. Majestic shifts into a twenty foot serpent and I doubt you want her to swallow you."

Jetti burst into tears. "I can't go back to my wolfpack! Please just help me! I beg you," she sobbed.

"Tears don't move me, Jetti, so less crying and more talking about what you can give me for doing you this favor. My work is top notch and twenty thousand nowadays won't last more than a month," I lied. The trick was to keep upping the prices to see how much the client was willing to pay, but I was already sold since a warlock was involved.

"I've met witches who had more of a heart than you. How can you not feel anything for my situation? Do you know how hard it is for us females trying to survive in a poor pack? There's barely any food, but Akea's land has plenty of deer. I can stay full while sleeping in a massive king-size bed," she said.

I tapped my fingernails on the table while leaning back in the chair. Her actions were so desperate that I was beginning to get a kick out of it.

"Can you change my appearance? Get rid of this identity and make me look beautiful like you? Akea is a sucker for a beautiful woman. I really need your help and I won't leave until I get it, even if you have to kill me. My son will be here tomorrow and this is my last resort," Jetti begged.

"Would you sacrifice your child to be with his father?"

"Yes, I can always make more children. Do you want my baby? I heard most witches are infertile. It has to be awful not being able to feel a life inside your womb," she said.

"I have many seeds to grow. Children are the least of my worries, but I have something for you since I'm beginning to feel sorry for you. I'll be back."

I teleported to my garden room and picked off a few leaves of my wolfsbane plant. Poisonous black mushrooms grew from the floor near my pool and I grabbed a few of those too. After I made my rounds through my garden, I collected everything I needed for the ancient potion.

The snide remark she had made by assuming I couldn't carry a child, was an unnecessary low blow. "The bitch won't be able to feel a life inside her womb ever again after I'm done with her," I chuckled to myself. I dropped the flowers into a gold mixing bowl, afterwards my wand appeared in my hand.

"After darkness she rose so they called her Black Rose," I sang. I zapped the contents with my wand, and it turned into a purple remedy.

"Now all I need is a potion bottle," I said aloud.

A potion bottle appeared on the table next to the mixing bowl. After my remedy was complete, I returned back upstairs. Jetti was still sitting at the table crying her eyes out. I sat across from her, placing the potion on the table. She immediately reached for it, but I grabbed her hand.

"Aht, you might want to hear the rules first," I warned her. She sat back in her chair, crossing her arms as if she were annoyed.

"What is it now?" she asked with an attitude.

"It's a potion that'll change your identity. You said you didn't want Akea to recognize you therefore he won't. But you must drink every drop after you give birth, it won't work while carrying a child."

She clasped her hands together in excitement. "Thank you so much! I'm so happy that you understand how important this is to me. I was wrong about you, you really do have a heart," she replied.

I smirked. "Majestic will walk you to the door."

She left the room leaving the bag of money behind. I grabbed the bag, dumping the money on the table to count it. Seconds later, Majestic came into the room. We were sitting on millions of dollars after years of tricking humans with my spells.

"What kind of potion did you give her? You usually don't make potions," Majestic said.

"Let's just say, you have to be careful what you wish for," I replied.

"That is true," she laughed.

Majestic helped me carry the money to the safe that was behind a picture on the wall. It was just one of my many safes.

Nine hours later...

I sat on the couch to pour a glass of snail and honeysuckle wine. It wasn't a good concoction to most, but I was addicted because it perked up my mood. Majestic walked into the house, she'd just come back from passing out more flyers.

"Don't you have to fill in for your sister? It takes almost an hour to get to the city and your father wants you there no later than eleven," Majestic said.

I rolled my eyes at the mention of working for my father. He owned a cab company that was struggling and no amount of magic could help the business.

"As if he's going to make any money, but I'll be leaving shortly," I replied.

Majestic sat my flyers on the coffee table before she sat down. She kicked off her shoes and laid across the couch. She yawned. "I'm so tired, Rose. Can I stay here instead of going to work with you?" she asked.

"Sure, I'll only be gone for a few hours anyway. Circa's got it all wrong if he thinks I'll be working all day so go ahead and rest up."

A second later, Majestic was balled in a fetal position, lightly snoring. I finished my wine before getting off the couch to change out of my dashiki and black silk hair wrap.

"Damn, I hate wearing jeans!" I said aloud.

I was standing in the mirror while getting dressed. My natural braids reached my knees and almost got caught in the zipper of my jeans. The doorbell rang while I was putting my arms through a plaid button-up shirt. My pointed ears vibrated at the tip, letting me know it was one of my people at the door. Telekinesis was one of my many abilities; I unlocked the door and it opened from where I was standing. My father's messenger had to bend to walk into the house because he was so tall. His head almost touched the ceiling. He looked like a wizard. He had long white hair with a long beard, but most of the men in our clan had a lot of white or silverish hair. He had pecan colored skin and one white and gray eye. He wasn't blind, he was just born that way.

"What brings you here?" I asked Findis.

"I'm here to relay a message from your father. Tonight we will attack Sheldon's clan at their covenant," he said.

"We finally found his hiding spot after all of these years?" I asked while buttoning my shirt.

"Yes, he has resurfaced. We will be ready at midnight, by the lake near Old Farm Woods," he replied, staring at my cleavage.

"I know I'm way shorter than you and you don't have a choice but to look down at me, but don't disrespect my presence ever again, Findis. You may go now and hurry before I tell the leader that you have wandering eyes," I said, feeling disgusted. Findis grinded his teeth while clenching his jaw in frustration for being put on blast. Not even a second later, he was out of my cabin.

"Old fucking pervert!" I yelled out as the door slammed.

I stepped into a pair of black tennis shoes before heading towards the door. I flipped over the *We're Closed* sign of my home then vanished, teleporting to my father's cab.

****

"Move over, bitch!" I yelled at another cab driver who was blocking the entrance of a hotel. He gave me the middle finger before pulling off, almost side swiping the front of my cab.

I blew my horn. "You are dead the next time I see you, asshole!" I shouted.

The Annapolis streets were busy since it was rush hour. I parked in front of the busy hotel, hoping to make a sale for my father. While I waited, I listened to the soothing sound of jazz playing from my busted radio. I tapped my fingernails on the peeled steering wheel of the old yellow and black Malibu car, mouthing the lyrics to take my mind away. A second later, a man came to my window.

"Is this taxi available?" his deep and soothing voice asked. I'd been around for many years and no man's voice has ever sounded better than jazz music until him.

Today is my father's lucky day, this shitty old cab is finally taking someone somewhere.

I didn't respond, I kept my eyes straight ahead as I unlocked the back door. The man got in the backseat. He rambled off his address as I pulled into traffic; his voice gave me chills again. The tiny hairs on the back of my neck stood which had never happened when I encountered a human. Out of curiosity, I looked in the rearview mirror. He was cradling a newborn baby.

"Just born, huh?" I asked, adjusting the mirror to get a better look at him. His normal brown eyes flashed ice blue when he looked into the mirror. My eyes changed too, turning jet black. We were reading each other, by staring into each other's eyes. It was something witches and warlocks did, however what he envisioned of me wasn't real. I had a way of manipulating minds, letting people see whatever I wanted them to see.

So, I finally get to meet Jetti's man. This world is getting too small for us!

"Yeah," he finally said, looking away.

"Nile is a nice name, Akea."

"How do you know me?" he asked, caught off guard.

HA! He must've thought I couldn't read him.

"Let's just say we're one in the same, if you know what I mean."

"You're from the bayous in Louisiana and your name is Keisha but they call you Black Rose? I guess we can both read minds," he said.

Wait a minute! What I showed him wasn't real so how does he know my real name?

I laughed it off but I was caught off guard too. "I beat you to it. You were so distraught that you didn't know who was driving you. Your son's mother is a shifter and you took your son from her because of her family. You made the right choice. No need to beat yourself up about it."

"Do you have any kids?" he asked.

"No. I'm a workaholic. I'm too busy for kids. I do fortune telling in the mornings, clean schools during the evening, and drive a cab at night," I somewhat lied. What I really wanted to tell him was that I was a witch hunter but since I was curious as to why Jetti was so distraught over Akea he was safe...for now.

"How old are you?" he asked.

"A woman never tells her age."

"You look to be my age," he replied.

He's a charmer and his voice is so soothing.

"I'm older than you of course," I said, turning onto a highway.

"You have a beautiful voice, Black Rose," he replied.

The way my name rolled off his tongue was enough to cause a woman to cream in her panties. Akea was a young warlock, but he had old fashioned mannerisms.

"Thank you. Is your son a warlock too?" I asked, making small talk.

"No, he's a human child, but it'll come when he's older," he said.

Babies are innocent despite what they become. How could Jetti offer up her baby that way? I can't wait until the bitch drinks her potion.

Five minutes later, I approached the address Akea had given me. I stopped at a gated mansion. He put the back window down to punch in the code to the gate. I was in awe of how big the castle style mansion was compared to anything I'd seen in my thousand years of life.

"Beautiful home."

"Thank you. We just moved in not too long ago."

The gate opened, I pulled up around the circular driveway and a group of young adults were waiting for him.

"See you around, Akea," I said when he opened the back door, stepping out of the cab with his sleeping baby wrapped in a blanket. Our eyes locked again since we were face-to-face. Akea's strikingly handsome face almost caused my heart to skip a beat. His eyes glowed; he was smitten by my beauty as well.

"Can I have your number?" he asked.

"You know my number. You know a lot about me."

"Can I call you?" he replied.

The people standing in front of the mansion were growing impatient. I figured they had come out to greet Akea's newborn son.

"You know the answer to that, too. I'll see you later," I said, before pulling off.

I didn't have any plans on seeing Akea, since my kind didn't mix with his kind. If he would've seen my true life when he read me, he would've known that I was deadly to his kind.

I can't wait to get home and tell Majestic that I ran into a charming warlock. Wait, I can't tell her that! She might think I like him.

I drove away from Akea's mansion, thinking about our encounter and I must say, it was a short and lovely one.

Midnight at Old Farm Woods Lake...

I admired the twinkling stars and bright full moon above the lake as I followed my father's clan deep into the dark woods. We were heading towards the Amstid's witch clan covenant. For centuries my clan had hunted witches. It started when a warlock destroyed our enchanted forest and killed many of our kind to steal their magic. Our clan was called the Yubsari Warriors. There were only twenty-five of us left because of the many wars we had encountered.

"Are we almost there?" I asked my sister, Nayati.

She looked down at me with a smirk. "Are you in a rush? Do you have a date with that werewolf again?" she asked. I rolled my eyes at her for bringing that up with our father just a few feet ahead. Sometimes Nayati was an asshole and always wanted me to get in trouble.

"Don't fucking temp me to cut your eyes out of your head. What I do is none of your business. Besides, that was a month ago," I gritted.

She chuckled. "I'm sorry, Tinkerbell," she giggled.

I was short, standing at five feet even while the others were tall. My father was seven feet and my mother and sister were a little over six feet.

"Whatever, but just know big things come in small packages and my strength is unmatched. Keep talking and I'll bring you down to my height," I threatened.

"No need to get angry, little one," she said.

Majestic slithered past us in her serpent form; her purple eyes shined like gemstones. She was always near, blending in the night whenever we were on a mission. She was a fierce creature that I had created with magic.

"I know you two aren't bickering while we're on a mission," our mother scolded us.

"She started with me," I replied.

"If I hear anything else, just know you two will have to hang upside down from a tree until the sun comes up," she said. It was her way of telling us we would be punished.

"I mean that's not a bad idea considering we're creatures of mother nature," I replied. She pinched my arm with her sharp black nails, drawing blood. The vine-like veins underneath my skin, covered my arm to heal the wound my mother had given me.

"Let that be the last damn time you talk back to me!" my mother scolded me. I didn't respond, I rolled my eyes at her instead. It wasn't a secret that I was her least favorite child. I hated my mother and wanted to kill her but even with a heart like mine, I didn't have it in me to kill the bitch. She was the queen of our clan and despite her beauty, a honey badger had a better attitude than her. She and Nayati resembled each other a lot, both had dark gray skin in their creature form, white sparkling eyes and high cheekbones that were so sharp, their faces looked sunken in. I almost had the same characteristics, except in my creature form, my eyes were pitch black and my skin was the color of graphite, covered in silver markings. The tips of my ears were pointier than theirs with rose symbols on my earlobe. Maybe being cursed had made me different from the rest.

"Black Rose...come up here!" my father's deep voice resonated through the woods. The clan separated so I could walk through to get to my father.

Look at them, moving to the side so I can get through as if I'm a fragile human child. I can find my way to my father, assholes!

"Hi, beautiful," Blizzard said, winking at me. Blizzard was my sister's husband's younger brother and he had a crush on me. He was easy on the eyes but it wasn't enough to have him in my bed.

"Yes, Circa," I said to my father.

"Scope out the cave to let us know how many witches are inside," he ordered.

"I'll go with her," Blizzard spoke up.

"Go," Circa replied.

I walked off with Blizzard behind me. He grabbed my hand, swallowing my hand in his. "I heard what your sister said so you better be nice or else I'll tell your father that you fucked a werewolf," he said.

"And you'll die."

Blizzard smirked, showing off his sharp canines.

"I just love your little feisty ass. You got me so hard right now. When will you let me in?" he asked, playing with one of my braids. I was about to respond with a snide remark but a werewolf howled from the top of a cliff where the witches' cave was located.

"They must be the witches' guard dogs," I said. Majestic hissed, she was ready to eat but the werewolves were too big for her.

"Calm down girl, those beasts are out of your league. You can eat the witches after I sucked their souls dry," I told her.

"I'll go, wait here," I told Blizzard.

"Don't test me, Rose. Do you think I can't handle those beasts?" he asked with a raised eyebrow.

"Whatever, you are on your own. Come on, Majestic."

I walked away, leaving Blizzard behind. Majestic slithered up a tree to meet me at the witches' cave. A few tree branches fell from Majestic's heavy body.

We're supposed to be quiet, Majestic! You are gonna get us caught!

Suddenly out of the darkness of the woods, a giant furry animal jumped out the bush, tackling me to the ground. The beast's sharp teeth and claws ripped through my skin as it's canine teeth locked on my neck.

"GRRRRRRRRR!" the beast growled, while slinging my body through the dirt.

The vines underneath my skin protruded out, protecting me from the werewolf's teeth. A black dagger, the shape of a rose, appeared in my hand while I tussled with the beast. The beast howled when I drove the dagger into its neck, the smell of burning flesh filled the air from the poisonous dagger. The beast's body went still, I crawled from underneath the werewolf and watched its body turn into ashes.

"What the fuck happened?" Blizzard asked, running towards me.

"The witches knew we were coming!"

The howls from the werewolves echoed throughout the woods, coming from where my clan was waiting for me to return. Blizzard went into his knapsack, sliding on his spiked brass knuckles. They were infused with wolfsbane poison strong enough to kill a dragon. In a flash, he took off running towards our people. I ran behind him, as my body began transforming in a crouching position. Brown and black hairs pierced through my skin like thorns, big paws expanded from my hands, and my face stretched into a snout, imitating a beast. The spell was only temporary, so I had to move fast before turning back into my human form.

We made it to the center of the woods, my clan was outnumbered by witches, warlocks and their werewolves.

"End it, Circa! Your war with us must end now!" A warlock named Sheldon said. Sheldon was the leader of what was the last of the Amstid Clan. I stood next to my father, growling at the ten werewolves that were with the Amstid Clan of over fifty witches and warlocks. We were outnumbered and surrounded—it was a trap.

"We won't stop until your head joins your brother's," Circa replied.

Sheldon took off the hood on his cloak, revealing his bald head with symbols and piercings etched into his skin. "My clan has grown, Circa, and it's more of us than what you see here. For centuries, we've hid from your kind but not anymore. Trust me, a war isn't what you want to start with us. For the last fucking time, I'm not responsible for your forest disappearing or your endangered species," he said.

My sister pulled out her ancient spear from underneath her hooded robe.

"You witches are a bunch of lying pieces of shit! You got your magic from our ancestors, and we want it back!" Nayati spat.

My mother elbowed Nayati. "Shut up, this is between him and your father," she gritted.

A brown owl with golden wings landed on Sheldon's shoulder. "My eyes have a very far reach," Sheldon said, referring to his owl.

That's how he knew we were coming. His bird has been watching over us.

"My favorite witch hunter, Black Rose. I don't know how I've missed you," Sheldon chuckled.

"Don't talk to her like that!" Blizzard said and I rolled my eyes at him. I hated when he openly claimed me.

"Look here, muthafuckas! We came to kill you all so enough of the goddamn small talk!" I said.

"Bring it on, bitch!" Dyika said. She was one of Sheldon's head witches. I had tormented her years ago and executed her mate right in front of her eyes.

"Don't end up like your lover, sweetheart. I spared you once, but I won't do it again!" I replied.

"Your karma will come soon, demon," she replied.

"We won't fight tonight, so everyone calm down!" Circa said to his bickering clan who was standing behind us. I looked up at my father who looked defeated, which wasn't like him. He fought under any circumstance, but not this time.

"This has never happened to us before, Father. Why are you backing down from a weakling like Sheldon? This is what we've been waiting for so our lives can be complete," I said to him. He shot daggers at me with his eyes.

"This is my clan so don't you dare question me!" he barked.

"We are guarded by the Anubi kingdom. The new king, Akua Uffe, has the blood of a warlock and werewolf, so now the witches, warlocks and werewolves worship him together. So, if you go against us, you'll be at war with Anubi," Sheldon said. A pack of werewolves growled at us to scare us, but I found humor in it all.

I burst out laughing. "A wolf god?" I asked.

"Laugh now, dark flower, but your father knows exactly who I'm talking about. Anyway, enough of the small talk, we have to pray to our great god. Stay away from our territory and our people and all can be forgiven," Sheldon warned.

"Til' next time," Circa replied.

"Of course, but just remember, you can't win it all, Circa. Not even your little magical flower can help you," Sheldon said.

"Don't sleep on my daughter, Sheldon. She has never failed me," Circa replied.

"Yes, that may be true, but my vision has never steered me wrong. Love can either be a blessing or a curse. Black Rose will pick her own medicine," Sheldon warned.

He and his clan of witches and beasts fearlessly walked past us, heading back in the direction of their covenant. They bitched us and were going to live another day to talk about it.

"What in the fuck, Circa! We're more powerful than this!" I said to him once the Amstid Clan was out of our sight. Circa backhanded me, sending my body towards a tree. Quickly, I teleported, appearing back in front of him before my body could hit the tree.

"Don't you ever question me! Are you stupid, Black Rose? Do you have a brain the size of a pigeon now?" he asked, mushing me.

"I'm sick of this bullshit! Why do you always patronize me as if I'm some weak bitch? In case you all forgot, I don't need any of you! Y'all assholes need me!" I screamed.

"We don't need you!" Nayati screamed back.

"Everyone hush!" Circa yelled.

Majestic slithered down a tree then around my feet to comfort me—I was angry. Whenever I experienced anger, I went off the deep end.

"What are we going to do, Circa?" Blizzard's father asked.

"We're going to figure out a way to cut off the connection between the Amstid Clan and Anubi. If we don't, they will be able to wipe us out. We are weak when they are stronger," Circa replied.

A woman in our clan named Zelda spoke up. "I know the wolf god's twin sons. I bought my necklace from their jewelry store, A & K jewelers, a few months ago. If we steal his warlock son's magic, we can defeat them. Especially if he has magic like his father," she said.

"What are their names?" Circa asked.

"Akea and Kanye," she replied.

I knew I would eventually have to slay Akea, but I didn't think it would be this soon! Damn it, why didn't I know he was the son of the Anubi king? When I looked into his eyes earlier and read him he must've shielded that part of his life, the same way I had shielded mine. Seems like we both played each other.

"Are they both werewolves and warlocks?" my mother asked her.

"If their father is a beast and warlock, one twin will be a beast and the other will be a warlock. Hybrids never pass both genes to one offspring, it's either one or the other," Circa said.

"Who will lure him in? We don't need a whole clan for one warlock. It'll look suspicious. We have to do it quietly without Sheldon's clan knowing," Nayati said.

I'll lure him in!

I kept quiet about my run in with Akea and while everyone was discussing who was going to lure him in to steal his power, I focused on the hare out of the corner of my eye. My stomach growled, thinking of rabbit stew. At that moment, nothing else mattered to me but food. Since Circa had slapped me, I didn't want to be around them anymore. I left them to catch my meal and Blizzard jogged after me. The hare was prepared to run off; my body went invisible to catch it. I hurriedly snapped its neck, to put it out of its misery.

"Go to your clan, Blizzard, and leave me be," I told him as he watched me. He was leaning against a tree with his arms crossed. I sat on a rock to skin the rabbit with my nails.

"Why do you feel superior to the rest of us?" Blizzard asked.

"Because I am. Am I supposed to appear weaker to make you all feel better? I would rather die than downplay my role on this earth."

"What you did back there to Circa was not the way to go! You made him look like a weak leader," he fussed.

" I might tolerate you all's bullshit because of the respect I have for this clan, but no one will ever see daylight if they put their hands on me again. Matter of fact, leave me alone so I can enjoy the trees, the lake and the stars!"

"This conversation isn't over," he said. I remained silent as he walked away.

I hate my loyalty to this fucking clan! I should've been left!

Circa and his clan left the woods, leaving me to myself. Majestic shifted into her human form, joining me on the rock by the lake.

"I hate how they treat you," she said.

"What doesn't kill you, will make you stronger."

Majestic licked her lips as her eyes glowed at the hare. "I'll find another one," I said, passing her the skinless animal.

"Are you sure, my goddess?" she asked.

"Yes, you haven't eaten all day. Take it."

Majestic took the rabbit from me, her mouth stretched wide enough to swallow a small dog. She dropped the rabbit down her throat.

"Gosh, that was tasty and now I feel bad that you haven't eaten anything," she said.

"Don't worry about me. I have bigger shit to stress about," I replied, sliding off the rock.

"You created me so that I could serve you so that's what I must do," she said, standing up. Majestic towered over me too, she was a tall and slender yet shapely creature. I named her Majestic because of her striking beauty.

"No, Majestic, I created you so that I could have someone to protect me."

"I'll bring you a fat hare later on," she said.

"Come on, let's go home."

We vanished out of the woods, reappearing in my three-story cabin. It was located so deep in the woods that if a human got lost, they'd be lost forever. I was a creature of nature, therefore I stayed far away from the city. Majestic went into the kitchen while I laid across the couch, staring at the black roses that covered the ceiling of my home.

Akea is the son of a god? Why didn't he go with his father to their world? At least he would've been a tad bit safe. Ugh, why can't I stop thinking about him? Damn it, I hate how the universe works. The first warlock I have ever been smitten over turns out to be an enemy after all. Why does he have to be the son of a man who is protecting the Amstid Clan?

Majestic came out of the kitchen with a gold urn full of wine. I had made it from fruits and plants.

"Are you thinking about that warlock Zelda mentioned?" Majestic asked.

"Why do you think you can read me?" I replied, sitting up.

"We're in sync so I will always feel what you feel," she said.

"Fuck it, I met Akea earlier. He was my first and only customer today. As much as I hate his kind, he had this aura about him that spoke to me. Oh, and he's a charmer. I've known this clan for centuries, but still connected more with him than anyone other than you in just a short period of time. His presence alone was more soothing than jazz."

"And now you have to kill him? Damn that suck, maybe you should save him," she said.

"I'm cursed because of a man like Akea. Nothing good will come to this clan if I save him. Killing him is the only way."

I picked up the urn, taking a sip of the fruity but piney wine. It was a strong concoction and a few sips of it could put a human into a deep drunken sleep.

"I'll be right back," Majestic said.

She ran upstairs then came back seconds later with a magazine in her hand. Majestic handed me the magazine; Akea and his twin brother were on the cover wearing high quality jewelry that was worth millions.

"Wow, they are beautiful," I said, opening their magazine. It was a catalog of their jewelry selection.

"Which one is Akea?" Majestic asked.

Black Roses Grow in The Dark   Natavia

I looked at the black and white picture of them standing in the woods wearing white linen clothes. The picture looked vintage, and I was impressed with their jewelry. I studied the two brothers to see if I could point out which one was Akea. The brother leaning against a tree with his hand in his pocket really caught my attention. His diamond frame glasses, and pose made him appear less menacing. He was also leaner while the other brother looked more muscular.

"This is Akea," I said, pointing at the twin with the glasses.

"He looks mean like a beast. Are you sure it's not this one?" Majestic asked, pointing at the other twin who had his arms crossed.

"No, that is the werewolf. His physique and jawbone give it away. Werewolves have more chiseled jaws because of their teeth. If you look closely, you can see his canine teeth are showing more, which is the sign of an alpha," I said.

"Wowww, you know your shit," Majestic replied.

"I've hunted every creature known to man, I know a lot," I bragged.

"And they are also filthy rich," she said.

"I know that, I saw his castle earlier."

"He *does* look like a charmer," she said, taking the magazine from me.

I took another sip of wine. "What are you doing with that magazine anyway?"

"They have a serpent necklace that I like. See, it's right here," she said.

The gold serpent necklace with diamond fangs and red diamond eyes was a magnificent piece.

"A quarter mil' for that?" I asked in disbelief.

"It's worth every dime. It's soooo beautiful," she said.

The tip of my ears tingled, alerting me that someone was in my garden. I vanished from the couch, appearing in my garden room. My father, Circa, was inspecting my garden as he dragged his gold scythe across the ground. His eyes glowed as he balled up his fist in anger. A plant had died since my emotions were connected to the garden.

It's because of Akea. I'm feeling regret of having to kill him. The sooner I kill him, the better.

"This isn't a good sign," he said.

"You need to leave my house."

He snarled, showing off his gold canines. Circa was almost two thousand years old but looked no older than forty in human years. His skin was the color of coffee beans, and his hair was platinum which he kept in long braids that reached his knees. Gold beads decorated his hair and he had gold rings on the tip of his ears. Circa's beauty was undeniable; he could pass for a woman with strong features.

"I saw the look on your face when Zelda mentioned that warlock's name. You don't know it but your body tensed and you grew quiet as a field mouse. I felt your aura, Rose, and you felt...sad," he said.

"You are getting old, Father, you felt nothing because I didn't tense up but then again, if I did, it's because you fucking slapped me."

Circa nodded his head in agreement. "I came here to tell you that Zelda will take care of that warlock she mentioned. I want you to stay away from him and that's an order. Matter of fact, for that stunt you pulled in the woods, you cannot come on any missions with us until I say so," he said.

That bitch Zelda ain't me!

"You can't go a day without pissing me off!"

Circa smiled at me in a teasing manner. "Good night, my rose," he replied. He vanished from my room, leaving me seething in anger. Who was he to tell me I could no longer fight with them?

I left the garden room, going back upstairs to the living room. I angrily kicked the coffee table over and the wine flew across the room. The wine was about to soak Majestic when she came out of the kitchen, I held out my hand, freezing the wine so it wouldn't splash her.

Majestic looked around at the mess I'd made. "Whoa, what has gotten into you."

"My father wants Zelda to handle Akea. Since when the fuck does Zelda do anything alone? Ughhhhh, why does everyone keep me trapped like this, huh?" I asked, pacing back and forth. Majestic grabbed my shoulders to get me to sit down. Rose thorns came through my shoulders when she touched me.

"Ouch," she said, snatching her hands back.

"I'm s—"

Majestic quickly covered my mouth. "Ssshhhh, don't apologize. A plant might die," she said.

The jewelry magazine on the floor with Akea's face on the cover was drenched in the spilled wine. I picked up the magazine, staring into the face of a natural born enemy. Sheldon's words flooded my thoughts….

"Love can either be a blessing or a curse. Black Rose will pick her own medicine."

"You said you wanted that necklace, right?" I asked, Majestic. She was picking up what was left of the tenth coffee table I had broken in the past week.

"Yes, but it costs a lot," she replied.

"We're rich, Majestic. I think it's time we stop being so modest and go shopping for jewelry."

"Let me go pick out our outfits for tomorrow and don't worry, I'm not going to make you look basic," she replied, in excitement. Her joyfulness warmed my heart. My days would be gloomy if I didn't have Majestic in my life.

Akea

Later that day...

"Yes, Akea! Fuck me right there! Go deeper, babyyyyyyy!" Lameda said. She was bent over the table, with her ass tooted up while I rammed my dick between her tight folds. Her twin sister was on her knees, suckling on my testicles. I smacked Lameda's soft ass while pulling her hair.

"Come in me, Akea! Come now!" she screamed out.

"I'm going to fill this pussy...up baby," I groaned.

I gripped her hips, slamming further into her. Her pussy exploded. "Taste me, Akeaaaaa. Come on, baby! Taste your creation!" she screamed out.

"BRO!" My brother knocked on my bedroom door.

Lameda and her twin sister disappeared into thin air like they were never there, which they really weren't. I had the ability to create and feel things as if they were really there, such as freaky porn star twin sisters. It was a way to sexually satisfy myself since I was staying away from women that only wanted my life and not me. I got dressed before opening the door. My twin brother, Kanye, walked into my bedroom with blood dripping from his mouth. He'd just finished hunting.

"You doing that freaky shit again, aren't you? Come on bro, talk to me. Why aren't you with a *real* woman?" he asked. He sat on my bed, putting blood stains on my white silk sheets. He plucked a huge chuck of deer fur from the side of his mouth, getting it on my carpet.

"Bro, really? You know I hate when you mess up my room," I said.

Kanye was a werewolf and I was a warlock. At times we clashed and it had taken a lot for us to build a brotherly bond, but when we got older, he became my best friend. I went to the bar in the corner of my room to pour myself a shot of whiskey.

"I'm stressed out, bro. I can't believe I took my son from his mother soon as she gave birth to him," I said, gulping down the liquor.

"Bro, I got you. You had to do what you had to do. Her pack is dangerous and that isn't a safe environment for your son," he said.

"I never imagined myself having a kid by a woman that I only fucked one time. You did it the traditional way, you have pups by your mate. I'm telling you, bro, I'm never fucking another woman again, especially a werewolf. If I have to get my rocks off by imaginary women, so be it."

Kanye smirked. "So, what's up with that beautiful ass woman that dropped you off yesterday? Didn't you get her number?" he asked.

"I was caught up in her beauty but I'm not fit to be with anyone right now, especially with a newborn. You know how much I believe in fate so if it's meant to be, it'll happen."

"Yo, I feel bad that you have a kid and not a mate," he said.

"I'm not tripping about that right now."

I took a shot of liquor over to him so that he could wash down the rest of the deer he had consumed.

"I'll go into the store today since your mate will need help with the pups," I told him. Kanye's mate had given birth to a boy and girl pup on the same day my son was born which was yesterday.

"Appreciate it and we will look out for Nile," he said.

"I owe you."

Kanye stood from my bed. "You owe me by getting some real pussy, bro. It's been like two months. Release that beast," he said.

"Yeah, right. I have zero beast gene in my blood," I chuckled.

"I'm not talking about that, bro. I'm talking about smashing pussy, pile driving to the deep end. I promise you, it'll relieve some stress. Hit up the witch girl you met yesterday. You always said your next woman will be a witch instead of a werewolf anyway," he said.

"Bro, I'm telling you, stop feeling bad for me. I'll be cool."

"Alright, I'll leave you alone," he said.

We gave each other a dap hug before he exited the room. While he was leaving, my housemate named Baneet came into my bedroom, holding my son. She was a werewolf and I had been around her my whole life because her father was my father's pack brother. Everyone who lived in the house was the offspring of my father's pack. His pack brothers and their mates were also in Anubi which was a kingdom in an immortal realm.

"So, I hear that you can create women for sexual pleasure. Your magic never ceases to amaze me," she giggled.

"Who cares? Why is everyone in my business about how I masturbate?" I asked. I went into the bathroom to wash my hands before holding my son. Baneet leaned against the door, cradling my son like he belonged to her.

"I think it's wrong how you took him from his mother, Akea. Jetti isn't as bad as you think. I mean she's a little rough around the edges, but I know she would've been a decent mother," she said.

"She lives in a fucking swamp! Why would I have my son living in filth when we're damn near billionaires? And let's say I give her money to live a lavish life, she'll share with the wolfpack she roams with. She can see him, but he's staying with me."

I dried off my hands after I finished washing them. Baneet gave me Nile who was half-awake. I held him close to my chest.

"I didn't mean to offend you, but I lost a child two months ago before I met Jasiah so I know what it's like not being able to hold your baby. I'm still not okay from it," she said.

"Alright, Baneet. I get your point, maybe I overreacted because she trapped me for money. She could've at least told me she was in heat when we had sex. She knows damn well I don't know when a werewolf's body is ready to mate."

"I just know how traditional your family is when it comes to mating. Maybe you should look past that so Nile can have two parents under the same roof," she replied.

"Enough of this, you may leave so I can get ready for work."

"I can take him while you get ready. I like holding him," she said.

"I'll bring him to you before I leave."

Baneet left the bedroom, closing the door behind her. I slid open a door next to my bed, it led to my room where I practiced my spells and meditated. It was also a place to keep Nile safe as he slept without a demon lurking over him. Demons preyed on infant warlocks, sacrificing them allowed the demon to gain strength. I laid Nile in his wicker bassinet so I could prepare his formula.

He screamed at the top of his lungs, maybe I was taking too long to make his formula from scratch. I poured dried cow's milk into a mixing bowl along with whey protein.

Kanye wants me to date when I have a day-old infant to look after. Would it be wrong for me to date with an newborn?

Two hours later...

I slammed on my brakes when I pulled up in front of the jewelry store in Kanye's black sports car. It was the closest car in the driveway and since I was running late to open the store, I took it.

"Goddamn it! My nose!" Tiko said, holding his nose. I must've slammed on the brakes too hard.

"My bad, bro. I'm not used to driving sports cars."

"I can tell. Hell, warn me next time," he said.

A handkerchief appeared in my hand; Tiko took it. He was sent from Anubi with his brother to help protect Kanye's pack. He also was a salesclerk at the family's jewelry store. Tiko was single like me, matter of fact, the two of us were the only single men in a house full of couples.

"I hear that you can make women appear. Is that true?" Tiko asked, referring to my magic.

"Kanye told you?"

Tiko smirked. "I'm just saying, next time don't leave me out. I've been celibate for a week," he said.

"A week?" I repeated.

"Women took care of me every night when I was in Anubi. A week is too long," he replied.

"If you don't want any offspring, that's a good thing but stay away from the werewolves here. The women aren't the same as the women in Anubi. The werewolves here only want money so they'll do anything to get it."

"Damn my brother, you really sound hurt about Nile's mother," Tiko said.

I cut the engine off. "Yeah right, I'm just giving you a heads up."

We got out of the car and luckily nobody was in front of the building waiting for the store to open. I went inside my pocket to get the key card. Our jewelry stores had a high security system since a piece of ours had been stolen before. I was about to swipe the card against the keypad but the door of the store opened.

"Well, look what the wind blew in," my grandmother, Naobi, said.

I hugged her. "Hey Grandma, what are you doing here?"

"I told your father I'd be checking in, and luckily, I did because you have two customers in the waiting area. You look so handsome, you're almost dressed like your father," she replied, squeezing my cheek.

I was dressed in a navy-blue suit with a white silk shirt underneath. The necktie had white, brown and navy-blue polka dots. My loafers were also brown and my socks matched my necktie.

"Thank you Grandma, but you didn't have to go through the trouble of opening the store."

"I actually like the idea of filling in," she said.

"Good morning, Queen Naobi," Tiko said, bowing his head.

"Blessings, but my son's mate is the queen now. You can just call me, Naobi," she replied.

"You are still a queen while in my presence so forgive me," he said, bowing again.

"You have the charm of an Anubi warrior," she laughed.

I walked into the jewelry store and two women were sitting in the waiting area drinking the self-serve wine on the coffee table. Their backs were towards the door but there was something familiar about the lady wearing a black hat. A delightful rose fragrance crept in my nose. I followed the scent trail as it led me to the woman I'd been thinking about off and on.

Black Rose's eyes glowed. "I guess luck is on our side," she said.

Standing still like a deer caught in headlights, I observed her beauty. Black Rose stood from the chair wearing tight fitting black bell bottom jeans that hugged her full curves. Her scent was alluring, but her face alone was enough to make a man drop to his knees. Black Rose wore a black, lace, vintage style blouse. It had long sleeves and dipped low revealing a nice amount of cleavage. I hadn't realized how short she was since she was sitting down when I met her.

"You look gorgeous on this beautiful day," I finally said.

"You don't look bad yourself. I'm feeling this grown and sexy look you have going on. I'm sorry, where's my manners? Akea, this is my sister, Majestic; Majestic, this is Akea," she replied. The woman she was with stood from the couch to shake my hand. Her hand was cold with an odd texture which reminded me of reptile skin.

"This store is amazing," Majestic said.

"Appreciate it, do you need a tour or did my grandmother already show you around?" I replied.

"Grandmother? I wouldn't have guessed that," Black Rose said.

"Yeah, well you know, we age gracefully in the immortal world," I joked.

Tiko elbowed me then cleared his throat. Black Rose had my full attention; I forgot all about Tiko coming to the store with me. I introduced Tiko to Black Rose and Majestic.

"Maybe you can show me around," Majestic said to Tiko. She looped her arm through his; his eyes lit up like a kid's on Christmas. Majestic was tall with a slim physique. She resembled one of the female warriors from my father's kingdom—Tiko was in heaven.

Black Rose and I walked into the showcase room, leaving Tiko and Majestic behind.

"What brings you by? I know you didn't come here to see me," I said.

Black Rose chuckled. "I actually came here to buy this."

She went inside her purse and pulled out a picture that was taken out of our magazine. "I wanted to give this to Majestic," she said. It was a serpent necklace from our Pharaoh line which was on the top floor.

"Follow me."

I headed towards the red velvet curtain; Black Rose's heels clicked across the floor while following me. I had to stop walking to watch the movement of her hips. Her eyes glowed at me when she caught my gaze. Usually, I was shy around women, especially women who looked like Black Rose, but her aura was relaxing.

"It's funny that I thought you were shy," she smirked.

"Usually I am, but there's something different about you. Is that why you call yourself Black Rose? It's because you are rare?"

"You can say that," she replied.

I pressed the button on the wall for the elevator. Black Rose's scent crept in my nose again, causing me to get an intense erection. It was embarrassing that I couldn't control my hormones around her, and my erection wasn't a small one. I grabbed a magazine off the stand near the elevator to hide the bulge.

"What kind of fragrance is that?"

"I bathe in the pool inside my garden. It's a natural scent," she replied.

The elevator door opened, I gestured for Black Rose to go first while holding the elevator door. Her ass was so curvy, I thought I was a werewolf for a second, wanting to sink my teeth into the flesh of her ass. I stepped in with her; the doors closed trapping in her fresh garden scent. I pressed the button to the third floor.

"Are you okay, Akea?" she asked.

I adjusted my tie as sweat beads formed on my forehead. She slipped her hand into mine. "Relax, I don't bite," she said.

I hurriedly pulled my hand away from her then cleared my throat. "I'm straight, it's just a little warm in here."

"It's okay to be sexually frustrated, it happens to the best of us," she replied, looking at my erection. The magazine I was using to hide it didn't do any justice. Black Rose seductively licked her lips which were covered in red lipstick. I was so caught up in her pulchritudinous face that the elevator door opened to the third floor, but I was still stuck in her presence.

"Shall I follow you?" she asked.

"Don't take this in the wrong way, but I can't stop staring at you. I hope you don't think I'm a pervert."

Black Rose started to blush, but she paused.

Maybe she thinks I'm a perv.

Her face got serious. "Can you show me the necklace I came for?" she replied, in a cold tone.

Damn she's ice cold.

Black Rose walked off the elevator, I was right behind her.

"I know you came here to see me, why the cold shoulder?" I called out to her.

Black Rose stopped walking. Her eyes were pitch black when she turned to face me. Her aura wasn't welcoming—she was angry.

"Did I piss you off? I apologize if I made you uncomfortable."

"Excuse my mannerisms. I've been having a bad day," she said. Her voice was filled with emptiness all of a sudden. I stepped closer to her to look into her eyes, but she was blocking me out.

Black Rose stepped back with a smile plastered on her face. "Are you trying to read me?" she asked.

"I was trying to see who I have to fuck up for giving you a bad day."

"I didn't take you for a bad boy. I thought you were a lover, not a fighter," she replied.

"I have my moments, but I'm definitely a fighter. You are delicate so I feel like I should protect you."

Black Rose cracked a smile. "I'm far from delicate. Piss me off and you'll see a monster," she joked.

I playfully surrendered. "You win, I don't want to fight," I chuckled.

I walked away, leading Black Rose down the marble floor hallway towards the golden double doors with hieroglyphics drawings.

"This place looks like a museum instead of a jewelry store," she said, walking past a mummy casket behind a red rope.

"My father has ancient Egyptian roots so everything in here is antique and a part of history. I guess you can call it a museum too."

Black Rose looked around and I could feel her energy, she was still sad but with a hint of joy. I didn't want to pry but I wanted her to let me see her past instead of blocking me out. Black Rose was hiding something, and I wanted to help her. Her mood was so strong that I was beginning to feel down too. I pulled open the black latches on the double doors.

"Wowww," Black Rose said, stepping into the room.

The room was filled with tall statues of Egyptian rulers, carved out of the wall and in their hands, were glass jewelry cases of our top-of-the-line jewelry. In the center of the room were glass cases of weapons with gemstones. Black Rose's eyes lit up when she saw a rose gold sword engraved with rose stems and red diamonds.

"How much is that sword?" she asked, circling around the glass case.

"It's two million."

"Can you hold it for me?" she asked.

"Swords are very old fashioned, aren't they?"

"Swords will never go out of style," she replied.
I grabbed the lock on the lock case and a jolt of electricity shot from my hand, popping open the lock.

"I've never seen a warlock with that before. Where does it come from?" Black Rose asked, referring to my powers.

"Think of my brain as an electric generator."

"What else can you do?" she curiously asked.

"I'll have to tell you over dinner, but since I'm on the clock, we're just here to discuss business, remember?"

Black Rose leaned against the glass case, crossing her arms underneath her full breasts. "Who said anything about dinner, Akea?" she asked sternly.

I was taken back. "I can't take you out on a date?"

She giggled. "Yes, but I prefer a picnic in the woods under the moonlight. Can you handle that?" she asked.

I massaged the back of my neck; me in the woods with Black Rose alone wouldn't end well for me. My mind kept drifting to dirty thoughts such as fucking her against the tree until her pussy exploded.

"Uhhh, I don't think that's a good idea. Maybe some other time."

"Are you afraid that you'll get another erection?" she asked, putting me on the spot again.

"I've been raised by werewolves so sometimes I feel beastly when I'm in the woods underneath the moonlight."

Black Rose chuckled. "So, do you fuck like a werewolf?" she asked.

"I can fuck like anybody you want me to, beautiful."

"I'll keep that in mind," she replied.

I picked up the sword and the red diamonds beamed, giving the room a red and golden hue.

"Wowww, I think I'm more impressed with the sword than the serpent necklace," she said. I passed her the heavy sword which was too big for her height. She looked so innocent but her personality was slightly questionable. Her beauty had me curious and her scent was driving me insane. She took me by surprise when she wielded the sword with precision. She could no longer hold back her smile.

"You can have it," I blurted out.

Black Rose paused. "What's the catch? Our kind never gives anything for free," she said. She walked over to me, with her heels clicking against the floor. Every little thing she did aroused me. She grabbed my neck tie, pulling me down to be eye level with her.

"Do you want to make love to me in exchange for this sword?" she asked. Black Rose licked my bottom lip, a deep groan echoed throughout the room. In my twenty-one years of life, nobody had ever had me that aroused. As much as I wanted to slide between her slit, I couldn't. What I wanted was deeper than that. I wanted to read her but she was blocking me out.

"I want to look into your soul, but you have a shield up," I finally said.

She released me. "I would rather pay for it because my life is my business," she replied.

"That's true, but I can feel your energy and it's depressing. Why not let me help you? I used to be like this until I realized I could drown in sorrow."

She put the sword back into the case. "Your words are too kind and I hate it. I'm not the only one who is hiding something, you are hiding a lot. Why must I reveal myself to you when you aren't ready to do the same?" she asked.

"You came here for me, Rose, and I want to know why. We can do this all day, but you need me for something and with your age, I'm sure you know what goes on in the dark comes to light."

Tiko and Majestic walked into the showroom. I wasn't finished with her, so I grabbed her. We both vanished.

****

"What the fuck, Akea!" Black Rose screamed at me when the gold portal behind us disappeared. I took her to a place that humans didn't know existed. It was a rainforest, surrounded by crystal blue water. She closed her eyes when the breeze from the waterfall kissed her cheek.

"How can you bring me to a place like this and with magic?" she asked.

I grabbed her hand. "There's no place on this earth where a portal can't open for me."

Black Rose took off running through the forest. "Come on, Akea! You brought me out here so now we have to play!" she screamed in excitement.

I was trying to be romantic! Not play like a damn child! But it's cool as long as I can see her pretty smile. Now, I have to change my clothes, I can't play in a suit.

My suit quickly turned into workout clothes with tennis shoes. I ran after Black Rose who was like a lightning bolt, zooming between the trees. All I could make out was a black shadow. My feet raised from the ground, the energy inside of my body, carried me through the forest. I went invisible while searching for Black Rose.

Black Roses Grow in The Dark   Natavia

Where the hell is she?

Minutes had passed and Black Rose wasn't anywhere in sight, but I heard a noise I hadn't heard since coming through the portal. I followed the sound of the chirping birds. A banana fell through me, coming from above my head. When I looked up, it was a capuchin monkey shaking a banana tree. There were many of them high up and they seemed to be heading in the direction of the singing birds. I trailed behind them and they led me to a bright red rose near a pond, it was surrounded by tropical birds. Black Rose was damn near naked, only wearing a bra and thong made out of black roses. Her nails were longer than they were moments ago, and her ears came to a point at the tip. Black Rose's jumbo braids reached the ground; her body was covered in vine-like markings that beamed underneath the sunlight. She wasn't aware of my presence, so I stayed silent. I was astounded when a bird flew on her shoulder and turned black seconds later. The red rose bush near her also turned black, along with the rest of the surroundings that were in her proximity. She sat on a rock, slumped over in sadness again.

"Darkness always falls on me, even when the sun is beaming on my face," she said, aloud.

She can't be a witch. Witches are never this attuned with nature or is she a different kind of witch? Damn it, I need to study more about my kind.

"I can feel your presence, Akea. You can make yourself visible now," she called out. She got up from the rock, walking deeper into the forest with me on her heels.

SOUL Publications

"Why did the trees, plants, roses and birds turn black? Are you poisonous? Wait, is that why you wanted a serpent necklace? Are you kin to snakes? What do your markings mean? Who is your god?"

"Stop asking me questions, Akea! We came here because you wanted to cheer me up and you are doing a poor job at it!" she said. I jogged behind her, scooping her up in my arms.

I cradled her close to my chest, staring down at her full lips. "I'm going to take your eyes away if you keep looking at me like that," she smirked.

"I'm spiritually guarded so that will never happen."

She crossed her arms. "I don't want you liking me because then I'll be a villain in your story. This moment will be our last moment together, Akea," she said.

I stared into her face to see if she was going to crack a smile, but she didn't. Black Rose didn't want anything to do with me.

"My father always told me that a warrior will come across many challenges and even if he fails, he'll still be respected because he never gave up. We might not see each other again, but you can't change fate."

Black Rose rolled her eyes. "What makes you think we're fated? I don't believe in that bullshit and neither should you! Is it because of my good looks? How about I fix it," she said.

Black Rose's face turned into a clown and she had a balloon-sized red nose. I chuckled when her clothes changed, turning into a bright yellow clown suit.

"Our bodies are only temples, it's the soul that holds the true beauty. I'm attracted to your face, breasts and ass, but your presence will always feel the same and your scent will never change. Do what you want, Rose, you can't break a man that's heavily guarded by great gods. In other words, I'm going to have you when the time is right."

She turned back to her normal self and remained quiet as I carried her through the forest.

Tiko and my grandmother can run the store while I enjoy a few hours with Black Rose. It may be our last day spending time together so I'm going to make it worthwhile.

Jetti

Meanwhile...

"*You're late!*" I screamed at Akea when he appeared in my hotel room. I had gone into labor three hours ago and Akea had missed the birth of our son. His handsome face was in a scowl as he disgustingly stared at me. Nile was wrapped in a blue blanket, peacefully sleeping against my chest. Akea took him from me; he pulled back the blanket to see our son's face.

"I can't believe you're taking my baby away from me," I sobbed once reality hit me. Akea had given me a nice lump sum of money and had me staying at a fancy hotel resort during my three month pregnancy. Since Nile was going to live with his father, Akea didn't have any more reasons to take care of me.

"You can visit but he's not living with you. What part don't you understand? Do I have to travel to the past to show you how many times I repeated that to you? Your pack is going to take food from his mouth to feed everyone else. They'll kill you if you leave them for a better house and not take them with you. Or I can get rid of them all. Which one is it?" he asked.

"I'll visit him," I cried because he was threatening to kill my pack.

"Your family has billions of dollars; it's in the newspaper. Yet you can't supply anything for her and your son?" my cousin, Gensin, asked him. She had been by my side throughout my pregnancy but I couldn't say the same for Akea.

"My son is not a fucking meal ticket! You can visit him in a few days," he replied.

My sadness turned to anger at how Akea was treating me. "Who will nurse him?"

"Human formula. I'll see you in a few days," he replied.

I burst into sobs when Akea left the hotel room with my son, taking my future away from me...

I sat on the broken step of an old cabin reminiscing about Akea taking Nile away from me. The bottle of potion the witch made for me was on my lap, but I was too afraid to drink it even though it was the answer to my problems with Akea. Gensin's gray, brown and white beast, was mauling a deer with her razor canines. Her oversized beast paw, pressed down on the deer's head as she shook the animal by the neck until the deer's neck snapped. I didn't have an appetite because I was depressed.

Gensin shifted back to her human form, blood from the deer dripped down her chin.

"Come and eat, Jetti. You gave birth a day ago so your body needs it's strength again," she said.

"I can't eat!" I screamed at her.

She growled at me as her eyes glowed; she wanted to shift and attack me. "Let Akea go! He doesn't like you! So, what y'all fucked one time, you got pregnant by him and now he's moved on. He lives in a mansion with his brother's pack! They will never accept you for what our pack did to them!" she screamed.

"We aren't with that pack anymore so it should be forgiven!"

A member from our old pack worked at Akea's jewelry store, but when they stole from him, it ruined what he and I could've had. Akea disowned me when he found out I knew about the stolen jewelry. We were only looking for a way to survive so we preyed on the rich werewolf family. Getting pregnant by Akea was another part of the plan. Of course, he didn't know I was in heat when we had sex, which made everything easier.

If I had known he had a very dark side to him, I wouldn't have gotten in on the plan. He wasn't as weak as we thought.

Tears fell from my eyes. "It's only been three months and I can't stop thinking about him. I wasn't supposed to fall for him, he was just supposed to be a way out for our pack."

"What about Mila? You haven't given a fuck about your other pup since you've fucked Akea! We are werewolves, Jetti! We can survive in the woods! We don't need expensive clothing or shoes since it tears anyway when we shift! I'm so fucking sick of you and this bullshit! Akea doesn't owe you a fucking thing!" she screamed.

"Shut up, bitch!" I growled.

I had left my three-year-old daughter, Mila, with her father's sister so Akea wouldn't have the burden of taking care of her too. Mila's father was killed by a rogue wolf before she was born, but I didn't miss him. Mila's father was crazy and abusive, but Akea was gentle and had never laid a hand on me, which was why I had to be with him. Nobody understood how safe and secure I was when I was with him. Gensin grabbed her clothes out of a basket to wash in a bucket. Gensin was older than me. She was born in the 17th century so living in the woods and doing things the old-fashioned way didn't bother her.

Gensin dropped her clothes inside the water to let them soak. "I'm joining Sheldon's clan without you. I've done everything I could but now you have the brain of a squirrel," she said.

"Sheldon's clan only wants werewolves as guard dogs! And since when have werewolves roamed in packs with witches?" I shrieked.

Gensin shrugged. "I told you that I have feelings for Sheldon and to get close to him, I will join that clan. Wait, don't Akea live in a house with werewolves? What in the fuck is the difference?" she asked. She squeezed her clothes inside the water bucket and I couldn't help but to feel disgusted. The only good thing Akea did was pay for my hotel room for up to a year so I could have a roof over my head. That's how I knew he loved me because he thought of my wellbeing.

I went into the cabin which had a hole in the ceiling. The floors were so weak that I had to jump over the loose boards to keep the cabin from collapsing. It had broken up wooden furniture and a rusted bed frame. I picked up a good chair, taking a seat at what was left of the table.

I sat the potion on the table. "Why am I scared to drink this?"

I really should stop procrastinating since I gave that witch the last of my money! It better work or else I'm going to snap her neck. After I drink this, I should be very beautiful like Black Rose. Welp, here goes nothing.

My heart was beating fast and my temperature rose. My hands trembled when I popped the wooden cork off the crystal bottle. The dark purple drink glowed when I brought the bottle to my lips. The strong plant smell almost made me puke.

Do it! This is your last chance!

I held my head back; I poured the nasty concoction down my throat. The taste was horrible like rotten meat and spoiled cheese. I urgently had to vomit but nothing came up.

"ARGHHHHH!" I screamed.

My stomach immediately cramped and my throat burned.

My body went crashing to the floor. The pain was worse than giving birth to a pup. Gensin rushed into the cabin.

"What happened?" she panicked.

"My...stomach!" I cried.

Gensin picked me up off the floor, since she was a werewolf, she had the strength of eight men. I coughed up blood.

"What the fuck did you do, Jetti?" she asked.

"I drank...I drank a potion."

"A potion? What fucking kind?" she yelled.

I couldn't answer her, my stomach was on fire and I was going blind in my right eye. Gensin burst through the doorway and part of the cabin collapsed from the impact.

"Hold on, Jetti. I'm going to get you help! You are bleeding from between your legs. What did you do?" Gensin cried.

I coughed up a chunk of gooey blood. Another cramp rippled through my body causing me to scream so loud, Gensin dropped me in a pile of leaves.

"I'm going to...die," I heaved.

Gensin shifted into her beast form. She picked me up by my sweater, tossing me on her back. Her large animal soared through the woods to get help as I clenched onto her thick fur coat. My body was getting too weak to hold on. I let go of Gensin's fur—I stopped breathing.

****

"Jetti," I heard Gensin's voice. I groaned in pain while opening my eyes. My head was spinning and throbbing.

"Can you hear me?" Gensin asked again.

I couldn't make out who was standing next to Gensin, but I could tell by the broad shoulders it was a man.

"Owwwwww!" I groaned as I sat up.

I thought I was going to vomit again. "Where am I?" I asked, trying to make out my surroundings. The last thing I remembered was being in the woods next to Gensin's getaway cabin.

"Why did you drink that potion, Jetti? What did you do to yourself?" her voice trembled.

"Do I look the same?" I asked, rubbing my head.

"No," she said sadly.

I was relieved that the potion had worked. If I could go through the pain again to get a new look, I would. A giggly feeling washed over me. I was so excited that I jumped out of bed, losing my footing. The man standing in the room caught me.

"I don't know what you're happy for, Jetti," the man said.

"What are you talking about? I'm beautiful."

"Sit her down, Sheldon. She's still out of it," Gensin said.

Sheldon helped me back into bed, I hated to admit it but laying on my back was soothing. My vision was getting a little better, but still a bit blurry.

"I can't believe you did this to yourself! Bitch, you've lost your fucking mind!" Gensin screamed. Her screams were giving me a headache.

"Feel yourself, Jetti, and do it now!" Gensin yelled. Her yelling was about to cause my ears to bleed.

"Let me rest. I need to save my energy so I can go to Akea."

Thinking of Akea wrapping his arms around my body, swallowing me in his embrace to protect me from the world gave me an arousal. When I felt something between my legs raise up, I touched myself. I hurriedly sat up and I had an erection.

"I hate to break it to you but you should go by Jetster now," Sheldon said.

"NOOOOOOOOOOOOOOOOOO!" I screamed.

I felt my breasts and they weren't there. My ass was gone and replaced by a muscular ass.

"What did she do to meeeeeeeee? That bitch tricked me!" I sobbed. My body trembled as I cried my eyes out. It had to be a dream, how could a witch turn me into a man?

Sheldon handed me a mirror, but I was afraid to look at myself. Since my vision was clearer, I could make out the room. The walls were stone and there were tables covered in what looked like remedies. I was lying in front of the fireplace on a bed with bearskin sheets. Weapons such as spears, daggers, scythes and shields hung on the walls. It was apparent that I was in Sheldon's cave and I couldn't believe he was still living like he did in the Renaissance Era. Everything was making me sick to my stomach. I was sick of seeing immortals live so poorly.

"Do you not want to see yourself?" Sheldon asked. He sat at the foot of the bed, clasping his hands together, waiting for me to look at what the witch had done to me.

Gensin snatched a bottle of liquor off the table and gulped it down. She was upset as if it was her life. I used to love her, but I was starting to hate her nagging mouth.

Gensin burped. "Go ahead, this is the moment you were waiting for!" she yelled.

"Calm down, furry one," Sheldon said to her.

Gensin angrily sat on a stool in front of the fireplace.

About time she listens!

I turned the mirror around to see my new face.

This can't be real! I'm having a nightmare!

"WHYYYYYYYY!" I bellowed.

My hair was grown out into heavy silver locks and I had a chiseled jaw bone. I had a hooked nose, thin lips and chin hair. There was nothing about my face that resembled my old one. Black Rose had turned me into a beautiful man opposed to a woman. My plan and money went down the drain. I had nothing and certainly wouldn't be able to get Akea.

"Black Rose is dead! That short-legged bitch tricked me out of my money and love life!" I tossed the mirror over Gensin's head; the mirror flew into the fireplace.

"Did you say Black Rose did this to you?" Sheldon asked with a raised eyebrow.

"Yes, she cursed me. I'm going to kill her and that snake she calls her sister. They will die."

Sheldon scratched his eyebrow as if he knew something. I didn't know what Gensin saw in him, he wasn't a ugly man but he was creepy. He had markings on his bald head and piercings in his face. Sheldon reminded me of a grim reaper with his hooded, wide-sleeved, black cloak that dragged across the floor. He wore a medallion shaped like a three pointed star with rubies in between; the star was the symbol of his clan.

"What do you know about this witch?" Gensin asked Sheldon.

"Let's just say, she's not a witch," he said.

I gasped in horror. Not only was I a man, but I had been tricked by an imposter!

"Then what the hell is she to cast this spell?" Gensin asked.

"Black Rose is a dark elf," he replied.

Gensin giggled. "She's a what? An elf? As in a short human that lives in a tree baking cookies?" she asked.

"She's a very dangerous creature and her spells are very dark and demonic. It won't be easy killing her, it's borderline impossible," Sheldon said.

"She's a creature?" I asked again for reassurance. I still couldn't accept the fact that I had been bamboozled by an elf. Hell, I didn't know they were real.

"Yes, a creature that needs death to survive. We call her the Goddess of Death and the Yubsari Clan wouldn't survive without her. Her magic caused us to hide in caves for centuries and she won't stop until every witch or warlock is dead," Sheldon said.

"Wowww, Jetti. Do you hear this? You've been tricked by a fucking monster!" Gensin said.

"Don't you think I know that by now, huh? Have some sympathy for me! I'm stuck like this for the rest of my fucking life!" I yelled.

"I'm going for a walk while you sit here with your dick still sticking up in the air. While you were sleeping like a prince, I watched you transform into what you are now! Your womb fell out of your pussy on our way here. I really wish you well because I'm done with you! I disown you!" she screamed.

Gensin snatched open the wooden door, disappearing down a hallway.

Sheldon poured a drink into a wooden cup. "Drink this to get rid of the cramping and headache," he said.

"I'm not taking anything else from a witch so please let me lay here and mourn my life."

"I serve a great god, Jetti. I will never trick you into doing something that will harm you, now drink this tea. It's natural herbs and blood worms. I made it for you," he said.

I snatched the cup from Sheldon. "So, you are the werewolf that trapped the wolf god's son, Akea? If you have to trap someone to be in love with you, you are screwing up their fate. The Anubians are firm believers of fate and you shouldn't mess with it. Leave it alone, Jetti, and walk away. Start a new life and live like an honest man," he said.

I tossed the slimy drink down my throat and to my surprise, it was tasty and I wanted more.

"Akea belongs to me, Sheldon, and as you know, I'm not a believer in Anubi nor their god."

Sheldon smirked. "You should be since your offspring has the blood of the wolf god flowing through his veins. But take heed to my warning, stay away from Black Rose and her clan. They are very dangerous and are the cause of The Three Arms becoming extinct. My clan is the last arm left of the star and I will do anything and everything to protect it," he said.

"The Three Arms?"

Sheldon held his medallion. "Yes; Black Rose and her people hunted down every clan member of The Three Arms and slaughtered them after stealing their magic. My clan has traveled all over the world to remain safe but this time we're tired of running. So, what I'm saying to you is that if you need to stay here, you better stay the fuck away from Black Rose and Akea. I'm a honest man, but if you fuck up my plan, I'll behead you," Sheldon threatened.

I was flabbergasted because nothing was going the way it should've. All I wanted was Akea and ended up getting caught between an evil elf and an ancient warlock quarrel.

The tears came back again. "What should I do now, Sheldon? Can you reverse this spell? I want to see my child!"

"I cannot reverse an elf's spell," he said.

He walked towards the door, leaving me drowning in tears of anger. How could I live my life as man? Sheldon closed the door after he left the room. I got out of bed, realizing how tall I'd gotten. My new body had to be well over six feet.

I paced back and forth across the cold stone floor. "I got to do something! I can't live like this."

I looked around the room to see how I could put an end to my life. Slitting my throat would be too painful. I couldn't go down another painful road after drinking that potion. My eyes landed on the table covered with medicine.

Maybe I can drink all of it before I slice my throat. That way I won't feel anything.

I scooped up the bottles on the table, and a few of them fell onto the floor.

"Shit!" I grumbled when a bottle fell on my foot.

Someone knocked on the door. "Is everything okay in there?" a woman asked.

"Yes! Now go away and leave me the fuck alone!" I shouted in a voice I wasn't familiar with. My voice was beginning to get raspier which was confirmation—I had to die.

"My name is Dyika and if you need someone to talk to, I'm here. I'm sorry that evil bitch tricked you, but she will pay for it," the woman said.

I tuned her out as I sat on the floor, twisting the tops off the bottles. When I brought a bottle to my lips, her soft voice spoke out again with much sincerity. "I can help you, Jetti," she said.

"How?" I asked.

"We are on the same side, just know that, but I have to speak to you privately," she said.

What else do I have to lose? At least I can hear her out. Maybe she can get this curse off.

I rushed to the door, snatching it open by the handle. "Oh wow, you look great," Dyika said.

Immediately I was jealous of the stranger. She was so pretty that I wanted to bite her face off. Her hair was styled into a dreadlock bun with a few strands falling down her face. She had a bullring in her nose with ear piercings and markings of her clan etched into her neck. Dyika's skin was the color of honey with freckles underneath her hazel eyes. She walked around my naked body, checking me out.

"This isn't a circus."

"You are a breathtaking handsome man, Jetti. I was curious to know the final look since you were still changing when Gensin brought you here. Can I touch it?" she asked. Dyika grabbed my dick, I smacked her hand away.

"Hey! We just met and you're already sexually harassing me. Back the fuck away," I growled.

"Whoaaaaa, your voice is getting deeper. I'm really infatuated with you," she said, staring into my face. I hurriedly closed the door when I saw two people wearing red cloaks, walking down the hallway.

"Come, have a seat," she said, patting the bed.

I grabbed a robe off the floor and put it over my head, but it was too small. It seemed like I had grown another two inches. "I'm going to kill you if you touch me again," I warned.

"I want to show you something," she replied.

She pulled a clear crystal globe out of her knapsack. My heart started racing. "Are you going to curse me? What are you going to do with that?" I asked, backing away.

"I want to show you what we're up against. You see, unlike Sheldon, I want to get revenge on the evil bitch that killed my lover. If you give me what I want, I can help you get closer to Akea," she said.

I walked over to her, sitting on the bed next to her. Dyika was giving me hope again and unlike Sheldon and Gensin, she understood me.

"Put your hand on this globe and you'll see her true form. You can trust me," she said. I placed my hand over the globe that sat on Dyika's lap. She spoke in a language that I wasn't familiar with. Whatever she said, caused the globe to beam with a purple glow. I closed my eyes because the light was too bright, but somehow, I fell asleep...

"Where in the hell am I?" I asked myself when I opened my eyes.

I was standing in the middle of a battle in front of a temple surrounded by an iron gate. It was caught on fire. The smell of burning flesh and blood permeated the air. A woman holding a lantern ran towards me. "Excuse me, what place is this?" I asked. She kept going. There was so much blood soiled into the ground that it seeped through the bottom of my white dress. Once I realized what I was wearing, I immediately felt my chest, realizing I was in my old body.

This must be a dream. It seems as if nobody can see me.

A sword went through me like I was a ghost while two men dressed in black cloaks were sword fighting. I was confused trying to figure out what Dyika wanted to show me.

What is the purpose of this dream?

"ARGGGGHHHHHHH!" a man screamed near the gate. A gigantic black serpent snake with purple eyes wrapped its body around the man. The crushing sounds of his bones resonated through the air. It was a sickening way to die. Blood was pouring out of the man's eyes, ears and mouth from being crushed to death. Afterwards, the snake swallowed the man whole. I'd been in a lot of battles against other werewolves, but it was never that deadly.

"You won, Circa! Your clan has defeated us so please leave our land!" A man shouted. He was wearing a brown blood-soaked cloak and I noticed he had the same medallion around his neck as Sheldon. A tall man that looked to be seven feet jumped off a horse with long silver braided hair, carrying a bloody scythe. His eyes glowed the same color as the moon.

"This war has just begun, Ryul. Now, you can either surrender your soul to us or we'll have to take it! Pick an option!" Circa said. Ryul looked around, watching his people being slaughtered by Circa's people. Dyika appeared next to Ryul, grabbing his hand.

Is that her lover?

"Leave us, Circa! Your sick elves have done enough to our village!" Dyika screamed.

"I'm sorry precious one, but it's too late for a truce. As you know, my orders come from my god, Yubsari, and he wants you all's souls! It's the way of fate," he replied.

"I'll never surrender to a group of murderous demonic creatures!" Dyika screamed. Two swords magically appeared in her hands. Her lover, Ryul, looked defeated.

"Let's just surrender to Circa. We'll die painfully if we don't," Ryul said. My heart was beating out of my chest. I was curious as to what was going to happen next.

"No, I won't!" Dyika said.

She rushed towards Circa with her swords pointed at him. "NOOOO!" Ryul shouted. Black Rose appeared in front of Circa with a gold wand the shape of a rose. A black flash shot from the wand; a cage appeared around Dyika trapping her.

"DEMON!" Dyika screamed. A thorn pierced her hands when she grabbed onto the bars of the cage.

Black Rose smirked, showing off her sharp gold canines. She took the hood off her cloak, revealing pointed ears and glowing symbols on her neck. Her eyes were the color of coal and her nails were about three inches long. She looked menacing, opposed to the beautiful youthful witch I had met.

Black Rose walked around the cage, stalking Dyika. "Surrender or I'll make you!" Black Rose yelled at her.

Ryul dropped to his knees. "Take me instead and let her live! Please just take me and leave my clan. I'm the one you want!" Ryul cried.

Black Rose stuck her hand through the bars of the cage. She held out her hand in front of Dyika's stomach. Black Rose's cheeks glowed with a golden hue.

"She's with child," Black Rose said. *I gasped, praying that she didn't kill Dyika's unborn child.*

"Kill her anyway!" *Circa yelled at Black Rose.*

"I will kill anything you want but I will never kill a child. We can let her go until later," *Black Rose said.*

"So they can give birth to more witches. I'll kill her myself," *Circa said. He charged towards the cage, but Black Rose stopped him.*

"I said leave her be! The baby won't survive anyway, but as of now, it's alive!" *Black Rose said.*

"I'll punish you for this," *Circa threatened Black Rose.*

"I'll take my punishment but if you harm her, I will be forced to fight you, Circa. Children are off limits!" *Black Rose said. Circa snarled at Black Rose, balling up his fist.*

"Don't you forget I'm the leader of this clan. This will be the last time you disobey me in front of the enemy," *he threatened her. Circa jumped onto his horse before vanishing into the night. Black Rose walked over to Ryul who was still on his knees.*

"Leave him alone!" *Dyika screamed.*

"Pleading will never save your kind so it's best that you save your tears for when you lose your child," Black Rose said.

"What did you do to my child? Did you curse her?" Dyika sobbed.

"I don't curse children. Ask your god why your child isn't worthy to live," Black Rose said coldly.

Ryul looked up at Black Rose as she towered over him. "Please spare my people, Black Rose. I'm sacrificing my soul and body so Circa can stop this war," Ryul said.

"NOOOOOO!" Dyika screamed.

Black Rose's wand turned into a weapon that resembled an ax. "Take me!" Dyika yelled.

"Your time will come soon!" Black Rose said. She raised her ax. "After darkness she rose so they called her Black Rose," she sang.

She brought the ax down on the back of Ryul's neck. His head burst into ashes; a dark and purple glowing cloud emerged from the neck of Ryul's body.

"What the fuck!" I screamed out but nobody heard or saw me.

Black Rose went into her knapsack pulling out a crystal bottle. As soon as she popped off the corkscrew lid, the bottle sucked up Ryul's spirit.

Dyika dropped to the floor of her cage and sobbed. "Whyyyyyyyyyy!" she heaved. Black Rose smirked. "You people are the reason why we're trapped in this realm! We won't stop until all of you are dead," Black Rose replied.

She walked away and I ran after her. "You lying bitch! You are a wicked being and I hope you burn in hell!" I said. Tears fell from my eyes after witnessing the dark creature take an innocent life...

When I opened my eyes, I was back to reality. Dyika was sitting next to me on the bed. Tears were still falling from my eyes. "Do you see why I despise her? She took my mate away from me," she said.

"She should pay for what she did to us, but we'll be punished by Sheldon if we go near her."

Dyika stood from the bed. "Sheldon's clan has been hiding from those elves for damn near a thousand years which is how long it's been since they killed my old clan. Since the wolf god has returned to his kingdom, Sheldon has come out of hiding to defeat Circa and his elves. The old fucker thinks he's protected under the wolf god, but I don't give a fuck about anything else but revenge," she said.

I rubbed my temples, feeling a headache coming on. It was still hard to grasp everything that was transpiring with Black Rose.

"If you want your old life back, I'll need the innocence of your child," she said.

Hearing that brought a sense of relief over me. "If I bring you my child, can you reverse the spell?" I asked.

Dyika nodded her head. "Yes; I must return to my room so I can figure out a way for you to get close to your child, but in the meantime, this stays between us. I'll be back with a plan," she replied. Dyika left my room quietly, leaving me pondering my thoughts.

My child or my old body? Which one is the most important?

Black Rose

"How long have we been here?" I asked Akea.

He looked down at me. "You want to leave me already?" he asked in that soothing voice of his.

We were sitting near a waterfall, leaning against a tree. I was still enjoying the beaming sun and singing birds. Akea wanted to know more about me. He was holding me hostage for information about my past, but I wouldn't dare tell him.

"I told you a thousand times, Akea. I cannot stay here with you. I've got things to do and you are screwing up my plans. You brought me here to cheer me up and now I'm happy, you see?" I asked, pointing at my fake smile.

"Those were my intentions in the beginning but now I'm realizing I needed this too," he said.

Akea laid next to the tree on his back, stretching out his long legs. He was only wearing pants; he had taken his shirt off moments ago because it was hot. His body was carved like a statue and his erection was pressed against his inner thigh. I was an highly sexual and experienced creature, but I was afraid to touch his shaft. Matter of fact, I was a nervous wreck around Akea. There was something foreign about his personality that had me so drawn to him but it also pissed me off.

"I'm serious, Akea. We need to leave."

"Give me twenty minutes," he replied with his eyes closed.

"If I tell you about myself, will you open the portal?"

Akea opened one of his eyes. His ice blue glowing eyes warmed my heart. I had been merciless for so long that I never had a chance to blush. I looked away, flicking one of my braids over my shoulder.

"Did you just give attitude?" he asked.

"I'm going to give you something else if you don't get me out of this forest. I like it too much and I hate liking stuff so please, respect my wishes."

"Tell me why your magic turned those birds and plants black. I got to know what I'm getting myself into," he said.

I looked back at him. "Getting yourself into? Nobody is asking you to do anything, Akea. Are you one of those rich spoiled kids that don't understand how life works? I don't like you and don't want to be here anymore, now take me back!" I demanded.

Akea chuckled. "Okay, I'll take you back. Give me your hand," he said. He held his hand out to me. When I reached out to him, he disappeared. I angrily slammed my hand onto the ground. "Fuck you, Akea!" I shouted. The ground cracked from the impact, causing a tree to fall.

"Come down here then I promise we can go back!" he shouted. His voice was coming from below the cliff. I went to the edge of the cliff and saw Akea standing in the pool underneath the waterfall.

He held his arms out. "I'll catch you," he said.

I really wish you could, Akea. I wish we could live here, make love, laugh and even horseplay in the water, but I have to kill you.

"Stop being so perfect!" I shouted out.

"I'm not perfect and neither are you. I've done things in my past that I'm not proud of but I've dealt with it and moved on!" he shouted back.

Maybe he'll really open the portal after this.

I jumped off the cliff; it was probably sixty feet above the pool. "Whooooaaaaa," I laughed from the rush.

"Your ass is dead if you don't catch me!"

"Don't insult my manhood! I got you!" he said.

I thought I was going to fall into the water once I got closer to the pool, but Akea caught me.

"You see that, Rose, that was trust. You feel safe around me which is why you can stay here a bit longer," he said. My cheeks were feeling hot from blushing for the hundredth time. I looked away from his stare and noticed fish swimming around us. Akea was right, it wouldn't hurt to stay for a little longer because when it was all said and done, it would be my last time having peace.

"I'll stay longer but I won't speak about my past," I heard myself say.

He grinned. "I can deal with that," he replied.

Akea's grip around my body caused my nipples to turn into cement. My pussy ached from my throbbing clit. A moan escaped my lips as I imagined him stabbing my G-spot with his thick shaft.

"Your body is getting hot," he said. His voice was deeper and huskier than normal—he was aroused too. I pulled his face closer to mine, eyeing his full lips. My nails sharpened and my body was fighting the urge to let Akea have his way with me. I got out of his embrace and swam over to a rock nearby.

Damn he's making me hot!

"An old witch like yourself shouldn't be afraid of a young warlock," he called out.

"Oh puh-leaseeee!" I giggled.

Akea swam over to me. He lifted himself up on the rock, kissing my thigh. "You must've forgotten how magical I am. I might be younger than you but I'm still a man," he said. His warm lips kissed my thigh again but that time, he used his tongue. I cupped his chin and we locked eyes.

"Show me, Akea. I want to see this magic of yours."

He turned me around, spreading my legs apart. I closed my eyes when he massaged my inner-thighs, kneading my flesh with his hands. I scooted closer to him as his hands got closer to my center.

"This feels so good," I moaned out.

My sweet nectar poured out the sides of my thong. Akea ripped off the rose thong. "I knew you wanted me," he said. He slipped his fingers through my slit; I wrapped my legs around him.

"Ohhhhhhhhh," I panted. I felt his warm tongue brush across my clit. My bra came off. A pair of hands were massaging my breasts while someone was licking my neck. My eyes shot open because it was just Akea and me in the forest but someone was behind me. I looked down at my breasts and could see the imprint of someone's fingers while Akea suckled on my bud. He was using his magic on me. Circa would crucify me if he knew I was bewitched by a warlock; I was under a love spell.

"Akeaaaa!" I cried out.

The squeezing of my breasts got intense. I was ready to explode.

"Ummmmmmm," Akea mumbled while his tongue flickered across my clit. His tongue had the speed of a lightning bolt. A feeling of lips on my nipples came over me followed by an imaginary person forcing me to fuck Akea's tongue.

"STOP AKEA!" I screamed out.

He entered a finger in my opening. "Fuck, you're tight," he groaned. I bit my bottom lip, drawing blood. His thumb rubbed my clit while he finger fucked me, easing in another finger. My body was still bucking forward; my pussy walls tightened around his fingers. A loud wail spilled off my lips as I exploded. While I was coming, Akea, suckled on my clit. His fingers went deeper, pressing my G-spot.

"AKEAAAAAAAA!" I trembled.

My pussy squirted onto Akea's goatee. "You're so sweet, Rose, and your pussy is so juicy. I can't stop tasting you," he said. He pushed my legs back, burying his lips between my folds. My back arched off the rock like I was possessed.

"Akeaaaa, babyyyyy! Akeaaaaaaa!" I cooed.

"How aroused…are…you for…me?" he asked between licks.

"I'm burning up, babyyyy. Ohhhhhh, I'm ready to come again!" I screamed. Akea slowed his tongue strokes and to my surprise, it intensified the orgasm. Tears welled up in my eyes and my body was as light as a feather. A wave of passion burst from my center, wetting Akea's chest. I lazily laid across the rock with my legs vibrating. Akea climbed on the rock, laying his naked body against mine. His dick throbbed against my center.

"Can I come in," he asked, staring at my lips.

"I'm yours until we go back, so please do whatever you want to me. You can either fuck me or make love to me and I'll still cherish the moment."

I brought his face to mine and kissed him. We locked tongues like two lost lovers. Kissing was too intimate for me, but I couldn't resist him. I wrapped my legs around him, urging him to enter my body. My nails dug into his back, breaking his skin. He gently rubbed the head of his shaft up and down my slit before pressing into me.

He tensed up. "Fuckkkkkkk, Rose," he groaned. My pussy latched onto the head of his shaft then squeezed him in. Akea eased the rest of his dick into my tightness. I could feel the ridges of his veins around his shaft. The blood flow in his body was overworking, causing him to swell and grow a few inches.

"Hmmmmm," he moaned in my ear while stirring his dick to the back of my entrance. He groped my ass to go deeper. Akea was in a place no man has ever reached, which was my womb. I didn't think I had any more essence left in my body until my pussy gushed, reminding me of the waterfall.

"Shittttt, Akeaaaaaaa. Arghhhhhhhhhh!" I wailed.

He pulled out, leaving the tip in before diving back in. His raspy moans were making me aroused. The pleasure was causing my body to transform to my true form. My rose vine symbols protruded through my skin, my ears grew into a sharp point. Akea's strokes got faster; he was pile driving my pussy as his eyes glowed.

"FUCKKKKKKKKKKK!" I screamed out, rotating my hips. My nails punctured his back when he played with my clit. Akea bit his bottom lip when I threw my legs over his shoulders. The sounds of my wetness echoed throughout the forest. Akea was rough and delicate, sending me into overdrive. I fervently thrust my hips, fucking him back like my life depended on it. Akea licked from my chin to my breast. Another major climax was coming, but it was nothing like the others. My stomach cramped, my legs went numb and my breath was knocked out of me. The rock cracked underneath us from Akea's vicious pumps. He massaged my clit again.

"Let it out, Rose! I want you to come before me, baby."

My body flopped like a fish out of the water as my clit swelled twice it's normal size. My pussy creamed like coconut milk while I kept climaxing on Akea's shaft. Akea fell onto my chest after he came. I was sprawled out and soaking in the nectar we had created from lovemaking.

Akea's heart was beating against my breasts while his head rested in the crook of my neck. I'd never cuddled with a man after sex. I usually disappeared but I couldn't leave Akea's portal.

"Did I hurt you?" he asked while kissing on my neck.

I smiled. "It was painful, but pleasurable. But, I have a question," I replied, pushing him off. Akea almost fell off the rock but he caught himself.

I sat up, crossing my arms. "Do you make all the women you've been with come like that?"

The moment was too special for it to have been shared with others before me.

Akea caressed my chin. "To be honest, I've made every woman come at least five times, but I will say you have the best pussy I ever had. No woman has ever made me come while just tasting her," he said.

I punched him in the chest as hard as I could. "Womanizer! I thought it was special but you mean to tell me, you shared this with other women?"

Akea was wincing in pain while rubbing his chest. "Shit, Rose. You pack a mean punch," he said.

"I pack a whole lot of other shit!"

Akea fell over in laughter. "I've fought warlocks twice your size before," I said, standing up. My weak legs caused me to fall right back into Akea's arms.

SOUL Publications

"You like me, don't you? Is that why you are jealous?" he asked.

"I will never like you, Akea."

He moved my hair out of my face. "Our souls connected when I was inside you and to be honest, I like you too. It might not matter to you but you are the first woman I chased. In the past, I was too shy to approach women first, but seeing you brought me out of that shell," he said.

I could hear the seriousness in his voice, but him being too honest saddened me because we could never be.

I rubbed his chest where I had punched him, it was my way of apologizing.

"Now, can I ask you a question?" he asked.

"Go ahead."

"What kind of witch are you?" he asked.

"I'm an ancient witch that comes from a forest. My magic comes from nature."

"I figured that out, but I was still curious. I didn't know there were different witches out here," he replied.

"You'd be surprised at what really exists now."

"That is true; are you still in a rush to leave?" he asked.

I pointed my finger in his face. "We aren't doing it again so don't even think about it."

"I know that, it's too swollen down there," he chuckled, referring to my pussy.

"HA! You are so not funny," I giggled.

"Let's go for a swim before we leave," he said.

Before I could decline, Akea threw himself off the rock and into the water with me in his arms.

Enjoy this moment, Black Rose, because you'll never get another like this.

"Can you carry me to the waterfall?"

He looked down at me. "I don't want to let you go so I'll carry you anywhere," he replied.

I rested my head on his chest as he carried me to the waterfall. The way he held me was as if he was sent to me to protect me. *Could a creature like myself need protection? What could he protect me from?* I asked myself. I closed my eyes and rested against Akea's chest.

****

"Where the hell have you been?" Majestic asked after Akea and I came out of the portal. I checked my surroundings and we had come back to the same exact spot where we had left.

Akea fixed his suit jacket. "We went sightseeing," he replied.

Tiko shook his head. "Looks like y'all did something else," he said.

"We've been waiting around since yesterday for you two to come back," Majestic yawned. She and Tiko looked exhausted.

"YESTERDAY?" I shrieked.

"Shit, I didn't think we'd be gone for this long. I have to get home to my son," Akea said. He hurriedly unlocked the glass case that had the sword I wanted.

"I hate to brush you off, but I've been away from home for too long. Can you meet me at the restaurant Blue Moon on Saturday night at ten?" he asked me.

"Okay, I'll see you there," I replied.

Majestic elbowed me on the sly. I looked up at her and she was smiling from ear-to-ear; I had a feeling she knew what we were doing inside the portal. Akea unlocked the cabinet door underneath the glass case, pulling out a leather sword case.

Tiko's stomach growled, sounding like a bear. His eyes glowed, turning into a goldish brown with a hint of yellow and his canine teeth grew out.

"Are you seriously about to shift?" Akea asked Tiko while wrapping up my sword.

"I'm starving! You know what happens when my kind doesn't eat. Soon, I won't be able to control shifting so can you please hurry up so I can hunt?" Tiko asked.

"I'm done now," Akea replied.

Akea handed me the sword. "I don't know what to say," I beamed. Having a sword reminded me of the old days when my clan battled the witch clans.

"Don't say anything, but I'm expecting to see you Saturday, Baccara Rose," he replied.

"Baccara Rose?" I repeated.

"Come on, Tiko. Let's wait outside for them," Majestic said. She pulled his arm towards the door. His body was going back and forth from mid-shift to human form.

Akea caressed my chin after it was just us in the room. "A Baccara Rose is a rare black rose with the meaning of true love, mystery and romance," he said.

"It's funny that I'm a witch of nature and have never seen one before. Are you making this up?" I asked.

"I'll bring you a dozen of them Saturday, but don't go snooping for it. Let me show you what they are. Can you wait for me to show you?" he asked.

Shit I'm curious! How come I don't know about this rose?

"I'm curious now. Ugh, Akea. I don't like surprises."

Akea chuckled then backed away from me. "Don't fuck up the moment. Can you just wait for me?" he asked while looking into my eyes. How could I tell a man like Akea no?

I quickly gave in. "Fine, I'll wait, so make it two dozen for my troubles."

"I'll do you one better and make it three," he winked.

"Fine, now let's go. I know my fox misses me," I replied, heading towards the doors.

"A shifter?" he asked.

"No, she doesn't shift into a human but her size changes if she comes across a threat. She'll leave the house and track me down by my scent if I'm away for too long."

"Let's hurry," he replied.

We walked down the hallway, heading towards the elevator doors. The tips of my ears vibrated—an elf was nearby. I stopped walking. "Are you coming?" Akea asked, stepping onto the elevator.

Did someone come here to kill him? Fuck! I'm not ready for him to die! Am I ready to go against my clan for a warlock I just met? Well, at this point, we're not even strangers anymore. I let him taste and enter my body.

"ROSE!" Akea's deep voice boomed from the elevator. He snapped me back to reality—my reality. I couldn't be with Akea the way I wanted because he was a natural born enemy to my kind.

I'll have to kill him Saturday. It'll be better if he dies by my hands and I'll make sure he goes peacefully. His magic can open portals. Maybe we can go to the forest he took me to, but why does my heart ache?

I dropped the sword on the floor, placing my hands over my chest. Akea rushed towards me. "DON'T!" I winced, stopping him in his tracks. I'd never experienced real pain since my body healed fast, but the pain in my heart felt like death.

"I'm fine, Akea. I guess I need...I need to eat too," I replied.

"Are you sure?" he asked.

I picked up the sword case, putting the strap over my shoulder. "I'm fine," I replied, mustering up a smile. Akea reached out to me to help me onto the elevator, but I moved away from him.

"Please just let me walk on my own," I begged.

"I know pain when I see it. Did my magic harm you? I know the portals can be draining sometimes," he asked. We stepped onto the elevator; I leaned against the wall to keep my balance. My chest was tightening up and sharp pains rippled through my heart. Akea watched me from the corner of the elevator as my body trembled from pain. The elevator doors closed, going to the main floor.

"You are shaking, Rose," he said.

"I'll be fine once I get home. I promise."

My ears tingled again. I was getting closer to whichever elf was in or outside the building. When the elevator doors opened to the lobby, Majestic was standing in the lobby, laughing with Tiko.

She doesn't look worried so maybe someone from our clan isn't inside the building.

"Do you want me to carry you?" Akea asked. I was walking slowly off the elevator. The pain was slightly wearing off, but there was still discomfort.

"I'm starting to feel better. Don't worry about me and hurry home to your son," I replied.

"There goes the two love birds," Tiko said when he saw us coming towards them.

"Glad to see you're still a human," Akea joked, slapping hands with him.

"We'll walk you two out," Akea said to Majestic and me. He and Tiko walked towards the main door.

"Someone from Circa's clan is nearby."

Since I created Majestic, we could telepathically communicate. We communicated that way to avoid listeners, especially other immortals who had advanced hearing.

"Well they aren't in here. We closed down the store after you and Akea vanished," she said.

"You must have forgotten their strength. They can get into a place like this, Majestic."

She shook her head. *"No, they can't. Tiko told me that this place is shielded once it's closed. Nobody, not even an immortal can break in. Apparently, Akea's grandmother is some badass witch from Ancient Egypt and her sorcery is unmatched,"* she replied.

"I didn't know she was a witch. I assumed she was a werewolf!"

"No, she's married to a tiger shifter so maybe it was his scent that I smelled on her yesterday," she said.

"Maybe we can kill her instead to spare Akea."

"If you do that, you might have to kill him anyway. He will avenge his grandmother's death, Rose. How about you not kill anyone and figure out an escape plan. I can tell by the way you two look at each other that love is brewing," she replied.

"I wish you knew it wasn't so simple."

"I know it isn't, but maybe you can get Akea on your side," she replied.

"At the end of the day, a warlock put this Black Rose curse on me. I have had a hatred towards them since I could remember. No matter what, Akea and I can't be together. It's a harsh reality that I have to face."

Majestic looked at me then rolled her eyes, but she was the one being naive to think Akea and I could ride off into the sunset happily ever after. Akea opened the door to let us walk out first.

"Where are you parked?" Akea asked when we got outside.

"Further down. Me and Majestic got it from here," I replied.

"I know but it doesn't feel right not walking you to your car. At least let me walk with you," he said.

"Me and Majestic have a few girlie things to discuss. You know how we can get," I chuckled. Akea smirked. "Gotcha. Have fun talking about a brother," he said.

"Of course I will. I'll see you soon," I said.

I pulled Majestic's arm so we could leave and she almost lost her footing. Someone was watching us and I didn't want to raise any suspicions.

"Wear a pretty black dress Saturday!" Akea called out but I kept walking. He was still standing on the sidewalk in front of his store when I looked back.

Shit! Someone could've heard him.

"Slow down!" Majestic said as I pulled her because she wasn't walking fast enough. I released my grip on her arm once we cut a corner and out of Akea's sight. My ears vibrated again; the elf was getting closer.

"I forgot to tell you I have the necklace. It's in my purse," Majestic said.

"Show me when we get home. We really need to get the fuck out of here."

My midnight, vintage, 1952 Rolls Royce was parked near a high-end boutique. I stopped in my tracks when I reached my car.

"There's humans out here so play nice," Majestic said to me.

Zelda was leaning against my car with her arms crossed. She was dressed in a short brown dress with brown high-heeled boots. Zelda was a pretty elf with a slender physique but busty chest and a nice round ass. Her deep brown hair was styled into a wraparound braid with gold charms hanging from them. Her skin was the color of chestnuts that glistened from the natural body butters she sold at the market her mother owned.

"You look very womanly today, but your beauty is still dull."

Zelda cracked a half smile. "I came here last night, hoping to catch Akea leaving the jewelry store, but he never left so I waited in the area and I discovered your car. I mean it sticks out like a sore thumb considering this car is almost a hundred years old," she said.

I wonder if she heard me and Akea talking outside his store with those big ass ears.

"That car is worth millions, but I'm not the type to brag about my fortunes."

"Great, because I don't care to hear about it. What I want to know is why you and that pet snake are stepping on my toes! Circa put me on this mission and here you are, fucking it up. You just can't stand to see anyone else prove their loyalty to their leader, can you? Are you the only warrior he has because last time I did the math, there were over twenty of us!" she said.

I walked over to Zelda; she quickly uncrossed her arms. She was frightened that I would harm her. "Don't come any closer," she pointed once I was in her face. I slapped her hand away; the impact caused her body to fall back into my car.

"Get the fuck off my car, Zelda, or else I'll snatch your eyeballs out of your head and feed them to my fox," I demanded. She hurriedly stepped away from my car; Majestic was giggling behind me.

"Circa will know about this, Black Rose, so beware of your punishment that's sure to come," Zelda threatened.

"Do as you wish but just know if you breathe my name out of your mouth, I'll haunt you. This isn't a battle you want with me, Zelda. I've killed many for way less. Now what you can do is move the fuck out of my way."

Zelda stepped away from my car. Majestic bumped into her on her way to the passenger's door. Zelda's eyes glowed with a silver tint as she evilly watched Majestic get into my car. Majestic stuck out her tongue, making a hissing sound. Zelda gave Majestic the middle-finger before she walked away.

"Don't forget my promise, Zelda! One word to Circa will send your soul somewhere dark…darker than my soul!" I called out to her as she sashayed down the sidewalk. I opened the driver's door, tossing the sword into the back seat. Majestic was staring at me getting into the driver's seat.

"Say what you have to say."

"For seven hundred years I've been by your side, living in the shadows of your father's clan and still, they degrade me every chance they get. I don't regret you creating me, but I wish you would have turned me into a likable creature. Your kind hates snakes," she said.

I started up the car. "I like you and that's all that matters. Listen Majestic, Circa ordered me to slay a serpent that was eating our rabbits so I did. I was young and didn't understand the meaning of survival so I did it with no questions asked. Anyway, I killed that serpent which was the last of its kind. It was the first time I cried for a creature different than me. Somehow I couldn't let go of what I did so I went back to the gigantic slain creature and took its blood to create you. You have my blood and a serpent's blood in your veins. Since we're connected through blood, you are just as equal as me and never forget that."

"You told me this story a thousand times," she replied.

"And I'll keep telling you until you stop letting them make you feel unwanted. You have to let it go and enjoy being the creature you are."

"Forgive me for being selfish," she replied.

"You haven't brought it up in a while so is it because you like a werewolf? You think a creature like yourself can't be with a beast?"

"Realistically, we can't. A snake and a werewolf? How can we even fuck?" she bluntly asked.

"Your creatures might not mix but the human forms can, but don't forget we aren't on their side."

"Can I at least fuck him once? I mean, you got yours so I might as well get mine," she said.

"Do your thing sister, just don't catch feelings."

I drove into traffic, coming to a red light. My ears vibrated, causing me to become annoyed. Someone honked their horn at me and when I looked, it was Nayati in our father's cab. She put her window down.

"We're on to you so stop while you can! We have our eyes on you!" she said. The traffic light turned green; Nayati sped off almost sideswiping a truck.

"Stupid bitch can't even drive," I said and Majestic giggled.

"So, how good was it?" she asked.

"How good was what?"

"The sex and yes I know you gave it up," she replied.

"I couldn't deny him and the sex was more than amazing. It was so good that I almost revealed my magic to him. He likes me because he thinks I'm innocent, but I'm a dark elf that possesses black magic. Akea is so pure that it pained my chest. Loving him would kill me."

"Or maybe it's a cure," she said.

I drove the rest of the way home in silence. There wasn't a cure for me and there would never be. I had tried everything to lift the curse, but once you were born cursed, it stuck with you forever.

****

I walked around my garden room and half of my garden was dead. My once black sparkling butterflies were lying dead inside my pool. Silver followed me around carrying a dead bird in its mouth while wagging her tail.

"I can't play, Silver. Mommy's garden is dying."

Dried rose petals crunched underneath my heels. My honeysuckle plants were withered, and the mushrooms were covered in mold. I didn't think the garden would suffer that much. Silver was digging in the soil of a dead plant to bury the bird she'd caught outside.

Majestic came into my garden room with a tray of my favorite wine. "Whoaaaa," she said, looking around.

"I can't believe one day of letting my emotions run freely would do this much damage."

"Maybe we should run a sale so you can get more clients. That's the only way you can heal this garden. Did Akea really make you this sad?" she asked. She sat the tray on the ground to pick out the dead butterflies in the pool.

"Yes, because I felt so much regret when I was with him. It truly saddens me that I like a warlock who Circa wants dead. Shit, I should've stayed away from Akea like Circa warned."

"Akea isn't the warlock that cursed you so does it really matter at this point? He also didn't destroy the world that you came from or kill any of your people. At some point, you are going to have to let it go and live your life," she said. Silver began growling and sniffing the air. She ran to the door and scratched underneath to get out of the room.

"Someone must be near our home," Majestic said.

The *Closed* sign was displayed in the front door, so I knew it wasn't a human coming to my home unannounced. My ears didn't vibrate which meant it wasn't an elf. Silver ran out of the garden room then up the stairs to the main level. I teleported to the living room. Silver was scratching at the door to get out. A werewolf howled from outside my cabin. I opened the front door, stepping out on my porch. My home was surrounded by a dozen werewolves and a naked woman. Majestic and Silver came out behind me. A werewolf growled at Silver and she growled back. The rose symbol on her ear glowed—she was about to transform to a larger body.

"Can I help you?" I asked the naked woman who was snarling at me without saying a word.

"You cursed my cousin, Jetti, and I want you to uncurse her! You were wrong for taking advantage of a pregnant woman and tricking her out of all of her money! Your kind doesn't even belong here! I'm a fair woman and I'm willing to work out a deal. We'll leave your property if you give us an antidote to turn Jetti back into a woman," the woman said.

"My curses are permanent, and I don't give refunds. I'm assuming you have never heard of me because you must be out of your poodle mind if you think this scares me," I said, scanning over her posse.

"Evil creatures don't belong here and, bitch, I know your midget ass is scared!" she shouted.

I walked down the steps in front of my cabin while my clothes transformed into a black lace dress with the train fanned out. The werewolves stepped back as the bone structure in my face sharpened, causing my eyes to slant upwards. Black rose thorns painfully pierced out of my head and formed into a crown; my gold, rose-shaped wand appeared in my hand. I was more than ready to battle.

"You still don't scare me!" Jetti's cousin screamed. The wolves behind her howled to intimidate us.

"Now, I'm going to ask you again, Black Rose. Do you want to give me the antidote or die?" Jetti's cousin asked again.

"I would rather die!" I shouted.

Jetti's cousin howled as she shifted into a werewolf; her heavy paws thumped across the grass as she ran towards me. My wand extended into a staff with hooked tips. I hurdled my staff through her torso when she leapt mid-air.

"This is too easy! Make this battle worthwhile!" I shouted. My staff came back to me like a boomerang. Her pack of werewolves ran towards us, sounding like a stampede. The ground rattled and the chimes on my porch shattered onto the ground. Warm blood splattered on my face when I slashed a werewolf's neck.

"I'm going to enjoy my fur coats with the shoes to match after I slaughter all of you!" I yelled.

Majestic shifted and Silver grew ten times her size, making her larger than the werewolves. The three of us collided with the pack of werewolves. A werewolf jumped on my back, sinking its teeth into my neck. Poisonous thorns popped out of my body, wounding the beast. The beast collapsed with blood bubbling out its mouth from the poison.

I swung the hook end of my staff across its neck, decapitating it. A wolf tackled me from the front; I dropped my staff. We rolled into a tree clawing at each other. My nails dug into the beast's snout while its heavy body had me pinned to the ground. A rose dagger appeared in my hand; I stabbed the beast in its neck until it stopped moving. Black blood seeped through my dress from the chunk of flesh snatched out of my shoulder.

Majestic's serpent was swallowing a werewolf while Silver was running through the crowd, slashing their bodies with her talon claws. I held out my hand so my staff could come back to me; on its way, it drove through a werewolf's head. Vines moved around my flesh wound, healing it immediately. I stuck the staff into the ground. The sun disappeared and a dark cloud shadowed the land. Silver jumped off a werewolf's back and onto the roof of the cabin; Majestic slithered up a tree to hide from the danger that was yet to come. Six werewolves were left alive, including Jetti's cousin.

"I'm not leaving without an antidote!" she said. She was holding her hand over her stomach. The veins in her body were turning black and her lips were blue—she was poisoned too. The werewolves backed away from my cabin when patches of the ground began sinking.

"Your black magic is going to be the death of you!" Jetti's cousin cried. She coughed up blood from her mouth and nose. A wolf howled when razor sharp, black, rose petals with stems for legs crawled out the ground like ants. I burst into a fit of laughter when the black rose bugs crawled onto a werewolf, eating his flesh. The werewolf ran around the cabin howling as he was being eaten alive. The rest of the werewolves dispersed, leaving Jetti's cousin behind.

"Go on, my children! Leave no flesh untouched!" I coached them as they ran after the werewolves. Jetti's cousin stood to run, but she collapsed.

"Don't worry! They won't eat you because your flesh is dying!" I called out to her.

"Sheldon's clan is going to destroy you! Do you hear me? He's going to put your evil ass in hell where you belong!" she cried. I walked over to her; she spat blood in my face when I kneeled next to her.

SOUL Publications

"So you are in cahoots with Sheldon?"

"Yes and we're protected by the wolf god!" she said.

"And where is he now?" I asked, looking around.

"In our hearts," she heaved.

"Your heart, eh?"

"YES!" she gurgled.

My nails drove through her ribcage, piercing through her heart. "Let's see if your god will save you now!" I gritted.

Black veins covered her skin; she convulsed while black blood bubbled out of her mouth. Her heart turned into ashes when I snatched it out of her chest.

I stood from the ground, staring down at her dead body. "Your god still isn't here. He wasn't even in your heart," I chuckled.

I stuck my staff into the ground and a wave of energy rippled over the land, causing the black rose bugs to disappear.

"Majestic and Silver come out! The bugs are gone!" I called out to them. Majestic jumped from the top of a tree in her human form and Silver came from behind the cabin with her tail tucked between her legs. She feared the bugs because she had been gruesomely bitten once.

"It's okay girl, come," I patted my leg. Silver ran over to me and I rubbed her chin. She panted while wagging her tail. "Go hunt," I told her. Silver happily ran off to find food.

"You took it easy on them," Majestic laughed.

"They weren't worth burning my energy. I hate getting weak."

"I was waiting for you to turn the trees into deadly warriors," she said.

"Only if someone pisses me off very much, but this was just a workout."
We walked up the stairs to our cabin. "Let's reward ourselves with a glass of wine for another winning battle. Me, you and Silver kicked ass."

Majestic sat in the love seat, rubbing her swollen belly. "I can't do anything until I sleep this off. I'm so stuffed," she yawned.

"Okay, good night. I'm going to relax in my pool."

"Good night," Majestic said with her eyes closed.

I teleported back to my garden room. Before stepping into the pool, I peeled off my dress. Out of nowhere, I heard Akea's voice.

"I'm here to catch you, Rose. Whenever you fall, I'll be right there," he said. I broke down in tears. My garden was already destroyed so it was useless holding in those hurtful emotions. I buried my face in my hands and wept. Even when I wasn't around him, I heard his soothing voice. My head was twisted up in confusion. The only purpose my life served was death so why was I craving love? Why now? Why me?

Akea

An hour later...

"*Am I dreaming? When did I fall asleep?*" *I asked myself aloud.*

I was standing in a magical forest with flowers the size of trees and colorful glowing butterflies the size of a newborn. A little girl with pointed ears and long braided hair ran past me laughing while a boy ran after her. They looked like they were playing tag. The pure air gave me a boost of energy. I kept walking, taking in the breathtaking scenery. No amount of magic could create the world I was experiencing. A woman wearing a dress made out of a tree leaf, climbed up a flower stem. She opened a petal and from where I was standing, I saw a group of children waiting for her inside the flower. The flowers were the forest peoples' homes.

A sweet and melodic voice resonated through the forest. A wooden door inside a tree opened; a tall dude bent underneath the door frame. He had to be around seven feet tall. He wasn't dressed like the others in the forest, he wore a white silk garment, and his hair was the color of platinum. I followed him as he followed the singing voice. Moments later, we came to a pond near a garden full of red roses. A woman was standing near a tree, singing while brushing her thick, jet-black hair with a comb made from sharpened sticks. Her back was facing me, but her body was like an hourglass. The leaf skirt she was wearing was too short, revealing a nice amount of her buttocks. Her skin shimmered underneath the sunrays and the tree branch shaped markings covering her body glowed. I was desperate to see the face of the woman. From where I was standing, I could tell she was beautiful.

"My goddess Lyira," the man called out to her.

She turned to the side to pick up a rose from a rose bush. I couldn't make out her face because the sunrays shielded her identity, but I noticed her swollen midsection. Her stomach was glowing with a golden hue, and I could see the silhouette of her unborn child inside her womb connected to the umbilical cord. The man sat the basket on the ground before he went to her, cradling her stomach. My curiosity got the best of me so I approached the couple. I was so close that I could reach her, but suddenly everything went black...

I was sitting on the shower floor with my back against the wall when I opened my eyes. The water was ice cold and I still had the soapy rag in my hand.

How long was I out?

"BRO!" Kanye called out while knocking on my bathroom door.

"Yeah!" I said, standing up. My head was pounding and I was wondering if I had hit my head when I fell asleep.

"You've been in the shower for two hours, bro, and I got to go to the store. Nile is sleeping in his crib," he said.

"I'm almost finished."

"You ain't in there doing that shit again are you? Tiko told me you got some at work so I know you ain't still masturbating!" he called out.

"Tiko doesn't know what he's talking about!" I winced. The ice-cold water was beating against my skin like shards of ice. I hurriedly washed my body then rinsed off.

"Aight, I'll see you later and you owe me. Nile cries too damn much, bro. Monifa tried to breastfeed him last night but he wouldn't latch," he said.

"Appreciate everything and I'll watch the twins for you Sunday night so you and Monifa can go out and spend time together."

"Good looking out. Oh yeah, Grandma is downstairs. She said she wanted to talk to you," he said. I heard the bedroom door close while I was getting out of the shower. Nile's cries cracked the bathroom mirrors. I hurriedly dried off then got dressed in sweatpants and a T-shirt. He stopped crying when I held him close to my chest, rocking him.

Someone knocked on my bedroom door. "Can I come in?" my grandmother asked.

"Yes!"

She appeared in front of me with her arms out. I placed Nile in her arms. "He's such a beautiful boy. You might need to change the formula. Maybe he doesn't like the milk. I was here last night, and he cried for hours," she said.

She sat in the loveseat next to the bed while humming a song to Nile. He closed his eyes, drifting back to sleep. I rubbed my temples to release some stress. Black Rose was heavy on my mind; the taste of her pussy was still on my tongue. Her beautiful eyes and mysterious personality were things I would never forget.

"What bothers you, child?" Naobi asked me.

"You know I've always been a thinker."

She smirked. "That is true but are you thinking about that creature?" she asked.

"No, I don't think about Nile's mother."

Naobi cut her eyes at me. "You know who I'm talking about. The young woman that came to the store yesterday. She introduced herself as Keisha," she said.

"She's a witch."

"I'm a witch, but that woman yesterday wasn't a witch. Her aura wasn't magnetic, usually we gravitate to one another but not Keisha. I overheard the pack talking and Tiko said that you spent a day with her inside a portal. Be careful showing outsiders your magic, Akea. You never know who is watching and wanting to steal your gift. You have many abilities that others would love to possess," she said.

"You sound like Father."

She chuckled. "Well I did birth him. I know you're grown and I'm a firm believer of fate, but I couldn't sleep last night, Akea. I get that feeling whenever something dark is hovering over my family," she said.

"I can't stop thinking about her. Since the moment I met her, I can't get her out of my head."

"Did you...did you bed her?" she asked.

I brushed my hand down my waves, embarrassed that I was having this kind of talk with my grandmother.

"Yes, we did the 'grown' up," I admitted.

Naobi threw her head back and laughed. Nile was about to wake up, but she quickly rocked him back to sleep.

"Oh child, you don't have to sugarcoat it. I know you miss having these talks with your father, but you can always come to me. I won't judge you nor yell at you, but Keisha's aura can't go unnoticed. Since birth bad energy latched onto you because of your magic. The prettiest roses have thorns. She might be beautiful and make your body feel good, but what good is she if she isn't good for your soul, huh?" she asked.

I sat back in my chair pissed off that my business was spreading through the pack like a plague, but I couldn't ignore Naobi's concern. She was an ancient witch who was rarely wrong. The pack had been through a lot in the past, dealing with demons and vampires.

"Saturday will be the last time I see her. I just want to give her the roses I promised her and I won't see her again."

Naobi stood from the bed. She laid Nile in his rocker. "I have a feeling your heart will follow what the mind wants no matter what, but whatever you choose, you must suffer the consequences," she replied. Naobi disappeared from my bedroom.

The doorbell rang and since my window was facing the main gate, I pulled the curtain back to see who was at the mansion, but there wasn't a car outside.

"AKEA!" Monifa yelled.

I teleported to the main lobby; Jetti was standing in the doorway with a scowl on her face. Monifa, Kanye's mate, growled at her.

"Umph, you better make sure she doesn't steal anything," Monifa said, still holding onto the door.

"Can I come inside, Akea?" Jetti asked.

"She's good, Monifa. I told her she's allowed to visit Nile," I said.

"You hear that? I'm allowed to visit *my* son. This isn't just your home, it belongs to Akea too," Jetti replied.

Jetti stepped into the foyer; she was dressed in unusual attire. Normally she wore eccentric clothing but not this time. She was wearing a white, crop sweater, tight jeans and a pair of pumps. She also had light make-up on her face with her hair pulled into a tight fancy bun.

She's trying to trap me again I bet. She has never fixed herself up like this.

Monifa closed the front door. "You know what, you are right. It belongs to Akea too, but guess who it will never belong to?" Monita asked with her arms crossed. She was a firecracker; she was a werewolf and a witch which made her high-tempered.

Jetti rolled her eyes. "Look, I don't want any problems. I only want to check on my newborn who needs me. Is that okay?" she asked Monifa.

"Umph," Monifa replied on her way to the kitchen.

It was just Jetti and me standing in the lobby. "I just realized how handsome and tall you are," Jetti said, walking around me. She wrapped her arms around me, feeling on my abs.

I pried her hands away from me. "Keep your hands to yourself if you don't want to be thrown out."

I walked up the spiral staircase and she followed. "Are you always this intense where you can't take a compliment? You don't have to be a jackass. Who pissed in your smoothie this afternoon?" she asked.

"I'm not intense, I'm exhausted from working and you are adding to the stress."

We walked up another flight of stairs then down the hallway. I pulled open the double wooden doors of my headquarters. Jetti took off her heels before stepping into my bedroom.

"Where is he?" she asked.

"Inside the rocker," I pointed.

She rushed over to Nile, picking him up. "I can't believe I get to hold a baby," she said. She sat in the love seat and pulled out her breast. I stayed in the corner of the room observing her. Nile latched onto her breast, and I was relieved that he didn't deny her.

"Here you are judging me as a parent but you can't even feed him properly. Look how hungry he is, he needs breastmilk whether he's a human child or not," she said. Nile's suckles echoed throughout the room.

"You don't have to stand there and watch me. Come have a seat so we can talk," she said.

"What's your agenda? You come here wearing make-up and tight clothes and now you actually seem happy about giving birth to him."

"I've always been happy but given the circumstances, I couldn't enjoy my pregnancy how I wanted to. I'm sorry, Akea, and I was selfish for doing what I did but now I see the importance of life which is being a loving parent. I don't want the money or the house, I just want to be with Nile," she said.

Jetti actually sounded sincere, but I was still skeptical. It could all be a ploy to get back in my pockets. However, she did seem to be at peace with herself.

"You can read me if you want to. I'm telling the truth," she said.

"Yeah whatever."

I went into the kitchen inside my room to make a smoothie with natural herbs. Natural herbs kept me from experiencing a lot of weakness after using magic.

"Can I have one?" Jetti asked.

"Damn, Jetti. What else do you need?" I asked, getting annoyed.

"Energy since I'm a nursing mother," she spat.

I grabbed the jars of fresh herbs out the cabinets. "Are you in college?" she asked, looking at the books on my nightstand.

"You know I'm a student."

"I mean, are you still going to school? How can you raise a baby, go to college and run a business?" she asked.

"I took a break from college."

I grabbed a pitcher of water out the fridge. "Can I come back Saturday?" she asked.

"I have a date."

Jetti shrugged her shoulders. "That's great, Akea, but what does that have to do with me feeding Nile?" she asked. There wasn't a hint of sarcasm or jealousy in her voice.

I think she moved on, which is good for her.

"You can't pump enough milk for three days?"

"I can but I won't. I'm supposed to accommodate your needs before Nile's? I plan on coming every day, Akea," she replied.

I didn't have a response. Jetti being around every day would confuse her into thinking we were a family. I dropped the ingredients into a blender; Black Rose's face invaded my thoughts again. She was heavy on my mind again.

"AKEA!" Jetti shouted; she snapped me out of my daydream.

"WHAT!" I shouted back.

"The smoothie," she said.

I looked down and was covered in a thick, gooey and sticky substance. Black Rose was destroying my focus; I couldn't do simple shit like putting a lid on the blender. Jetti laid Nile in his rocker. "I'll help you clean up," she said, fixing her shirt.

I took my shirt off, tossing it on the counter. "Just tell me what you want so you can leave. Do you need more money? This extra nice shit isn't going to get you far so keep it honest with me and tell me why the sudden change."

She leaned against the counter and crossed her arms. "You are right, Akea. I do want something but it's not your money," she admitted.

"Is it jewelry?"

She jerked her head back like she was shocked I had asked her that. "I want forgiveness and for us to start over. We don't have to be in a relationship, but maybe we can start a friendship," she said.

"I would rather give you money at this point."

She threw her arms up in frustration. "Who really hurt you?" she asked.

"YOU! What the fuck don't you get? I have trust issues, Jetti. Now every time a woman comes into my life, I feel like she has an agenda. You know, I would've respected you more had you trapped me because you simply wanted a baby, but you did it for financial gain. The shit is foul and I still can't get over it. It's taking everything in me to not wrap my hands around your neck! You sashayed your airheaded ass right into my house with a smile on your face as if you have a pure soul! Stop pretending like me and you can be friends. I fucking hate you."

"People do change but I won't bring this up anymore. Just know that I don't want anything from you but a friendship. You can hate me all you want but I'm still a part of your life," she replied.

She grabbed paper towels off the towel rack to clean up the mess. Someone knocked on my bedroom door. I usually liked to be left alone but I was ecstatic that I didn't have to be around Jetti by myself.

"COME IN!!" I said.

"Yo, Akea. Are you trying to smoke with us?" Zaan, my pack brother, asked coming into my bedroom. He looked at me then at Jetti.

"Want me to get Fiti to come up here and watch her?" Zaan asked. Fiti was his witch girlfriend.

"Yeah, send her up."

Zaan walked out of the bedroom; Jetti burst out laughing.

"I need a babysitter?" she asked.

I grilled her. "You damn right you do. You come from a pack of thieving wolves. You might steal Nile from me."

"I can't steal what's mine!" she shouted.

Fiti appeared in the room with a book in her hand. "Zaan is in the pool room," Fiti said.

I walked out of the kitchen to get a clean T-shirt from the dresser. "This conversation isn't over, Akea," Jetti said.

"For me it is and please don't go through my shit."

I put the T-shirt over my head before teleporting to the pool room. Zaan and Tiko were sitting on the lounging chairs while listening to rap music.

"Yooo, my bro. Did you get any rest yet?" Tiko dragged out with bloodshot red eyes.

"That's impossible," I replied.

I sat in the lounging chair and Zaan tossed me a fat blunt with homegrown weed.

"How come you never tell me shit?" Zaan asked me. I assumed he was referring to meeting Black Rose.

SOUL Publications

"Because your IQ is lacking, bro. You never understand shit we tell you," I chuckled. Zaan was a straight up pothead, he'd get so high at times he wouldn't be able to hunt so most times he ate raw meat from the grocery store. His brain cells were completely fried.

"There you go using big words. What's an IQ again?" Zaan asked Tiko.

"Bro, don't fuck with my high because your IQ isn't high," Tiko joked. Zaan waved him off.

"Are you finished with my botanical book?" Zaan asked.

"Not yet," I replied.

Tiko passed the lighter so I could light the blunt. Instantly a big ass fire erupted after I lit the blunt; the fire almost melted my lips. Tiko and Zaan cracked up laughing when I dropped it on the floor. Once the fire ceased and it began burning slowly, I picked it up.

"I call that TNT because when you light it...BOOM! It blows up," Zaan said. I relaxed my back against the chair, I doomed the blunt.

"Broooooo, be careful before you start seeing shit! I think that might be stronger than your magic," Tiko warned.

"I'm already seeing shit. I passed out in the shower and woke up in a magical forest with gigantic butterflies and people that lived in flowers that were the size of a small house," I replied.

"That sounds like a Disney movie," Zaan chuckled.

"The world was magical, and the air was the purest I ever felt. The sunrays shimmered like glitter and the scent of the forest reminded me of Black Rose. What bothers me is that there was a pregnant woman in the vision I had, but I couldn't see her face. Apparently, she was the goddess of that forest."

"Shidddd, give me what you had so I can see it too," Zaan said.

"Black Rose's pussy is what sent him there," Tiko chuckled.

"See, this is why I can't talk to you fools about personal things. Everything always has to be a joke," I replied.

Tiko put his hand on my shoulder. "Lighten up, brother, and enjoy the herbs," he said. I took another swig of the spiced rum before taking another drag from the blunt.

"I think I'm in love," I admitted.

"Give me this shit back!" Zaan said, snatching the blunt out my hand. Tiko was cracking up, holding his stomach.

"How are you in love already, Akea? Isn't it too soon?" Zaan asked.

"That's the cleverest thing you have ever said," Tiko told Zaan.

"Which means I'm right," Zaan replied.

"Y'all two just don't believe in fate. I think I came across Black Rose because she needs me. Maybe I'm her cure, the light that'll help her grow and blossom," I said.

"What in the fuck is he talking about?" Zaan asked Tiko.

"Shit, I don't know. It sounds like poetry," Tiko replied.

"I'm talking about fate."

"I hate to tell you this bro, but it sounds like you're pussy whipped," Zaan said.

"Or maybe the pussy was that good because she's meant to be mine. I can still taste her nectar on my tongue," I replied.

"Naw, you just ain't brush your teeth yet," Zaan replied.

"Actually, I did, twice."

"Hold up, Akea. Are you sure she ain't put the golden lake on you?" Tiko asked.

Zaan's eyes widened in shock. "You let her pee on you?" he asked.

"Not a golden shower, acorn brain. The golden lake is what women in Anubi used to trap a warrior. She'll bath in golden special flowers for a week to make her center extra tight. It snatches a man's soul when he enters her. Not only is the pussy very tight, but it's also wetter than anything you could imagine. I mean pussy nectar is just oozing out of her body. It's now forbidden in Anubi because it was cheating men out of picking their real mates," Tiko said.

"Don't get me wrong, I thought she put voodoo on me the way she gripped my girth, but it's above that. I was feeling this before we took it there. It was the reason why I had to have her. I'm usually a gentleman but I barely had restraint when I was around her. It's like she's the one for me. I was ready to give up on the thought of having a soul mate then she came along," I replied.

"This conversation is too deep for me," Zaan said.

"We know!" me and Tiko said in unison.

Zaan stood from his lounging chair. "I got to sober up a little. I'm taking Fiti shopping and the last time I fell asleep in the shoe department. I slipped into a coma," he said. He dived into the pool to swim laps.

"Did his parents drink Anubi's rum when they created him?" Tiko asked me.

"Uncle Elle is a wise man and so is his mate. Bro just damaged his brain cells from smoking so much."

Tiko passed me back the blunt Zaan had taken from me. "So, you are really digging Black Rose?" Tiko asked.

"Yeah, but Naobi said I have to cut her off. You know I respect my elders more than anyone. If I don't stop seeing Black Rose, I'll look like a betrayer. You know Naobi is barely wrong. She has a bad feeling about Rose."

"What do *you* feel?" he asked.

"I feel that Naobi could be right, but I still want her."

"We always want what we can't have the most. It's crazy how life works. But if Naobi says no, then you must end it," Tiko said.

"If my father and mother were here, they would tell me the same thing. I just have to get accustomed to being single."

"Bro, you can create a woman. Isn't that what your kind does, creating women from magic? You can make her beautiful, loyal and she can treat you like a king. I mean you are a prince since your father is a king. This house can be full of women if you want it to be," he said.

I took another sip of the rum before smoking the blunt again. "What are you going to do with Majestic?" I asked.

Tiko shrugged. "There's not much I can do if you have to stay away from Black Rose. My loyalty is to this pack so if Black Rose is a problem, so is her best friend, Majestic," he replied.

Zaan jumped out of the pool. "Who is Majestic?" he asked.

"You heard that?" Tiko replied.

"We're werewolves bro, we hear everything. Have you forgotten?" Zaan replied.

"Majestic is Black Rose's best friend. She's a serpent," Tiko answered.

"A serpent? Why does that sound familiar? Is that one of those big reptilian dinosaurs that breathes fire?" he asked.

"She's a snake, Zaan. She shifts into a snake," I said.

"A werewolf and a snake? What kind of offspring will you have? A Pokémon?" Zaan asked. I chuckled while imagining what the offspring would look like.

"She wouldn't be able to get pregnant from my sperm. We can enjoy ourselves in human form, though," Tiko said. Zaan grabbed another blunt off the table. I wanted to say that the purpose of him going for a swim was to sober up, instead of getting high again.

"I miss my father but I know it's traditional for the pack to follow their leader," Zaan said.

"Me too. It's been two months since my father's pack has been here, and it seems like forever," I replied.

"I have to admit how much I miss Anubi. I enjoyed being a warrior there but I'm grateful for being in a different world and being a part of Kanye's pack. This homesickness is hard at times, though," Tiko said.

"Someone is cutting potatoes," Zaan said because Tiko was getting emotional. He poured Tiko a drink and passed it to him.

"It's onions, Zaan. Goddamn, you are blowing my high," I said.

"You eat human food, I'm on a strictly meat diet. How would I know the difference?" Zaan asked.

"I'm cool now. I just had a little moment. This rum always gets to me," Tiko said.

I zoned out while Tiko and Zaan got into a discussion about Anubi's female warriors. The blunt and rum had hit me hard all at once; it seemed like my body was floating but I was still seated.

"Akeaaaa," Black Rose's voice echoed in my head.

She appeared in front of me wearing a sheer black dress with black rose patches. Her face was hidden behind a black veil but I could make out the deep red lipstick on her lips. I caught a whiff of her fresh garden scent on her wrist when she traced my lips with her fingernail. She straddled my lap and immediately she gave me an erection.

"This isn't real," I told her.

"I'm inside your head," she replied.

I looked around the pool room and it was just the two of us. Rose vines were sprouting out of the floor and walls, transforming the pool room into a rosarium.

"You can't leave me. You promised you were always going to catch me if I fall," she said.

"I don't think you're good for me. I've been through a lot and the last thing I need is to fall in love with a woman who is living a secret life—a life that can ruin mine."

Tears fell from her eyes. "You betrayed my heart," she said. She climbed off my lap and walked to the diving board. The pool water disappeared, turning into a fire pit.

"What are you doing, Rose? Get away from there!" I called out.

"I would rather burn in hell if you can't have me," she said. The train of her dress draped over the diving board, catching on fire.

This isn't real. This isn't real!

The fire was climbing up her dress and the smell of burning fabric was clogging my nose. I realized Black Rose standing on the diving board wasn't a dream when I began coughing from her dress going up in flames.

"ROSE!" I said, jumping up.

"You did this to me and now you have to live with regret. I'll never forgive you for lying to me. No one has ever told me they would catch me if I fall, but you did! You let your dick control your emotions. You only wanted my body, not my heart," she sobbed.

"That's not true, Rose."

She got closer to the edge of the diving board and the fire rose to the ceiling. She fell off the diving board. "ROSE!" I yelled. I teleported, appearing underneath her not caring about burning in the fire with her. Her body was badly burned when I caught her, wrapping my arms around her. The fire faded away with Black Rose as I fell into the pool water. Someone pulled me up from underneath the water.

"Bro, what the fuck!" Tiko shouted at me.

I frantically looked around and Zaan was stomping out a towel that was on fire. "What happened? Where is Black Rose? She was just here," I said.

"You zoned out, bro, then suddenly you jumped off the diving board while yelling for Black Rose. Are you sure she didn't curse you? You looked possessed when you were talking to her. This is out of hand now, Akea," Tiko said.

"Yeah! You smacked my blunt out of my hand and it almost burned down the house," Zaan said.

The burning towel must've been the burning fabric I was smelling and the fire I saw.

I felt a headache coming on while trying to piece it together. Black Rose burning seemed so real. I pulled away from Tiko, pulling myself out of the pool.

"I told you not to drink that rum," Zaan said.

"No you didn't, bro, so don't even lie," I replied.

Tiko handed me a towel but being soaking wet was the last thing on my mind.

"I'm tied to Black Rose somehow," I said aloud.

"Did you get her pregnant?" Zaan asked. Tiko slapped him on the back of the head.

"Witches can't carry children unless they were born human. If they were created from magic then you know they are infertile. Wait, is Black Rose a witch created from magic?" Tiko asked me.

"I don't know but I'd know if she was pregnant," I replied.

Zaan threw his arms up in frustration. "You sound like me, bro. You don't know shit," he said.

"This won't be good if she's pregnant. You know our tradition and beliefs don't believe in outside children," Tiko said.

"I'm not mated with anyone," I replied.

"Damn, that's true. But you might want to keep your dick in your pants," he replied.

"Bro's sperm can create an entire world. You might want to figure out how you can make your sperm infertile. Either that or you use a condom," Zaan said.

"What's a condom?" Tiko asked.

"And I'm the dumb one?" Zaan replied.

"It's a piece of rubber that a man wears to keep from getting a woman pregnant," I told Tiko.

"Isn't that cheating fate?" Tiko asked.

"In our tradition it is, but humans live differently than us. They even get this thing called STD's," I replied.

"You mean the test we had to take in school?" Zaan asked.

"That's SAT's and trust me, you never took that test. STD stands for sexually transmitted disease. A lot of humans used to get them after wild college parties," I replied.

"A disease from sex? Sounds like black magic to me," Tiko replied.

"You have a lot to learn about humans," I said.

"There's a library down the hall," Zaan said.

"How do you know?" I chuckled.

"I ran out of paper and needed something to roll up a blunt with. Y'all just don't think, but my mind is creative," Zaan replied.

Tiko yawned. "I'm about to go hunting then afterwards I'm taking a long nap. I can't hang anymore," Tiko replied.

"I'm out of here too. I had something to do but it's not coming to me yet," Zaan said while scratching his head.

Tiko shook his head. "Take Fiti shopping," Tiko replied.

"Oh yeah, well alright, fellas, the brotherly bonding session is over, back to our lives," Zaan said. He grabbed the urn of rum and his canister of weed before he left the pool room.

Tiko placed his hand on my shoulder. "And you, my brother, need to stay away from Black Rose. You scared the shit out of me yelling her name out just moments ago," he said.

We slapped hands before he left the pool room; I teleported to my bedroom. Jetti, Fiti and Baneet were surprisingly having a girl talk. In their eyes, I was probably a bad guy for taking my son away from her—they felt sorry for her.

"What happened to you?" Baneet asked because my clothes were still soaked.

"I went swimming. Isn't it obvious?" I asked and she rolled her eyes.

"Typical smart mouth Akea," she laughed it off.

Nile was asleep in his rocker and Jetti had made herself comfortable. She was wearing one of my robes. "Nile made a mess on my clothes when I changed him. I hope you don't mind," she said.

"I'll get going since Akea is back," Fiti said.

"Yes me too," Baneet said.

She and Fiti left my bedroom. I cleared my throat. "Aren't you going to join them?" I asked Jetti.

She crossed her legs and arms. "No, I'm not leaving until tonight. I have to feed him again once he awakes," she said. Her eyes fell on my dick print. I was somewhat still stuck on Black Rose so I wasn't thinking about the wet sweatpants sticking to my manhood.

"Don't even think about it," I warned her.

"We have soul ties, Akea. I'm never going to not think about it," she said.

SOUL Publications

I went into the bathroom, locking the door so Jetti wouldn't come in. When I walked past the bathroom mirror, I noticed something on my neck.

"What in the fuck is this?" I asked aloud.

"Who are you talking to?" Jetti called out.

"Your sister!"

"I don't have a sister!" she shouted back.

"She doesn't claim you either."

I got a closer look in the mirror; I had a black rose tattoo on my neck. It was sore when I touched it, it must've happened when I saw her on the diving board. Tiko was right, Black Rose must've cursed me when I slept with her. She was poisonous to my mind, body and heart.

Jetti

Midnight...

Sheldon's covenant was filled with witches, warlocks and werewolves. The center of his cave was where he practiced his rituals, the rituals he thought were going to protect his clan. I sat in the back row of his worshipping room, waiting for Dyika to return. She had gone to Akea's mansion, posing as me. I couldn't hide the jealousy I was feeling about her being near Akea with Nile like a family. What if he liked her version of me better? Dyika wasn't money hungry nor had she experienced the struggle. She was content living her life hiding in caves.

"The wolf god is a god of fate and we must not interfere with the fate that is laid out for us. We will receive great messages from him as long as we obey his rules," Sheldon spoke out to the crowd.

If he doesn't shut the fuck up!

The crowd was cheering, hanging on to every word out of Sheldon's mouth. A woman sat too close to me so I scooted over. She scooted close to me again.

"Excuse me but someone is sitting here," I said.

"I'll get up when they come," she replied.

She blushed, putting a dreadlock behind her ear. She was attractive with dark brown skin and doe eyes. She also had red drawings etched into her forehead. Sheldon's clan reminded me of vikings. They were stuck in time while the world was evolving. No wonder they stayed hidden far away from civilization.

"I hope you don't mind if I compliment you on your good looks. There have been rumors that Black Rose cursed a werewolf, turning her into a handsome man but I didn't believe it," she said. She was eye fucking me. It wasn't the first time a woman has approached me from Sheldon's cave.

"Get away from me before I bite your fucking head off," I gritted.

She placed her hand on my lap. "Meet me by the pond after the meeting is over. I promise it'll be worthwhile," she replied.

My dick formed a tent underneath my cloak. I wanted to burst into sobs because whenever a woman comforted me, I'd get an arousal. The curse was still transforming me. My voice was much deeper than earlier, and my dick was the size of an alpha's. The new body was taking control over me and soon I worried that Akea would be a distant memory.

"Do you not understand that I'm a woman?" I asked.

"We don't care. You look and sound like a man to us. It's not every day a very handsome man with a physique like yours joins our clan. You have the body of a warrior," she flirted. I removed her hand from my leg.

"I'll kill you, do you hear me? I'll fucking kill you if you don't get out of my face," I growled.

"You might as well get used to this because Black Rose's curses are permanent. She plagued one of our villages ages ago, killing at least twenty of us. The sooner you realize you are stuck this way, the better off you'll be. In the words of Sheldon's teachings, this might be your fate," she said.

"Are you saying that Black Rose killing your people was fate too?" I asked in disbelief.

"Every fate doesn't have a happy ending. We go when it's time to go. I believe that this new body of yours is a fate that you deserved," she said.

I jumped up from the stone bench. "FUCK YOU!" I shouted at her.

The cave grew quiet, including Sheldon. "Is there a problem, Jetster? Please enlighten us why you are disturbing our peace with our god," Sheldon said.

"This bitch is trying to come on to me! I'm still a woman and want to be respected as such. These dick hungry whores should be punished!" I said. The people in the cave snickered. I was more than embarrassed.

"Our god doesn't have any sympathy for sinners, so I apologize but we don't care about your feelings at this moment. The reason for your situation is because you tried to cheat life by tricking a man into being in love with you. How you feel right now is probably how Akea felt when you had your hand out, begging him for his fortunes. Being used is never a welcoming feeling, eh?" Sheldon said.

"Fuck all of you!" I yelled in a deep baritone.

"Take him to the dungeon until he cools off," Sheldon instructed the men guarding the doors. Four men began walking towards me. My beast felt threatened, and I couldn't control it. I howled as my body painfully began transforming into a much larger beast. My spine cracked and thick hair ripped through my flesh. I howled again when my body crouched over. The pain was unbearable like I was shifting for the first time ever. Sharp canines expanded from my gums and thick paws cracked the ground from the weight of my beast. I shook off the ripped material of the cloak after I transformed. The men circled around me as my beast snarled.

"Don't fight it, Jetster. You cannot take down my best men," Sheldon said. I jumped on the man closest to me, going for his jugular. One of his guards swung a spiked bat across my back, but the pain didn't stop me from mauling the man who I had in my grasp.

"RELEASE HIM!" Sheldon shouted while the man screamed. The tangy taste of blood was fulfilling. I hadn't had any fresh flesh in over a week. My beast tore a hole out of his neck despite three other men hitting me with weapons. The onlookers didn't intervene. I snapped the man's neck, instantly killing him. Suddenly, a strong wind knocked me into a wall. The wall cracked, causing debris from the cave to tumble on top of me. Sheldon floated across the room holding a gold sword etched with his clan's symbol. My beast howled in pain from being mushed to the floor. I couldn't move, my hind legs and ribs were broken.

"I hate to use my strength on those who aren't worthy of breathing the same air as me. Is this the thanks I get for taking you in as a new clan member? You killed one of my warriors!" Sheldon's voice boomed.

He pointed his sword at me. "Kill...me!" I begged.

"Everyone out! Return to your normal studies!" Sheldon instructed his people. Sheldon was stronger than I thought. He telepathically moved the debris by directing the rocks with his hand. Once I was free I turned back to my human form; I was covered in the man's blood. I groaned in pain from my broken bones; they would take time to heal. Sheldon held his sword against my neck.

"I'll forgive you this time, but the next time you disrespect my ceremony, I'll cut your head off then throw your body in the swamp so the vultures can rip your testicles off. I'm a fair man and I know what you did back there was out of anger, so I'll take it easy on you. You'll be locked up in the dungeon for thirty days," Sheldon said.

"Thirty days? How am I supposed to eat?" I asked.

He placed his sword inside his sword belt. "You'll get one small meal a day. By the time you get out, I don't want to hear shit about you being a man!" he replied.

"Why do you all take pity for Black Rose? She caused many deaths against your clan. She's supposed to be dead, Sheldon."

"Black Rose will be her own demise. She's no longer a threat to us," he replied.

"At least kill the others like her! You can't hide behind your so-called beliefs."

Sheldon chuckled. "You've been in my clan for one day and think you know so much about it, meanwhile you don't know shit! I've been running my clan for hundreds of years, keeping them safe and away from those evil elves. I'm supposed to drop my planning for you because you're angry about getting a hard on? Well, guess what hairy chest Jetster, I'm not doing a fucking thing you suggest. Stay out of my clan's business and enjoy your stay as a guest," Sheldon said.

Sheldon grabbed my arm, teleporting to a freezing cold dungeon with rats the size of weasels. The smell was rancid like a portable potty mixed with rotten corpses. The cell only had a bucket in the corner and a dirty holey sheet as a blanket. If my body wasn't badly hurt, I would've ripped Sheldon's face off.

"Will Gensin be able to come down here and see me?"

"Speaking of Gensin, she's been gone for a long time. She and a few others left hours ago to go hunting but haven't returned yet. I hope you didn't send her to do anything stupid. She joined my clan in the hopes of living an honest life, but I fear you put her up to something," he said.

He disappeared from my cell and reappeared on the outside. "Her blood will be on your hands if you send her to Black Rose," he said.

I began to panic, not realizing Gensin had been gone for hours. My thoughts were on Akea and Dyika. "I promise I would never do such a thing," I said.

Sheldon put his arms behind his back. "Well, enjoy your stay. I know it isn't Akea's mansion, but at least you have brick walls," he said, while walking away.

"Fuck you!" I shouted.

A door slammed then I heard it locking with a chain. Sheldon's dungeon had ten cells from what I could make out. There were only five candle holders inside the dungeon so it was somewhat dark. I leaned against the wall in agony. My body was drenched in blood and sweat and I needed a shower. Chills were settling in because I was losing a lot of blood from the wound in my leg.

"I heard what happened to you," Dyika said.

I perked up, looking around the dungeon but I didn't see her.

"Where are you?" I asked.

She appeared in front of me with a bucket of water. Those witches creeped me out, they rarely used doors or made their presence known. Dyika kneeled in front of me.

"I heard what happened and you can't cause trouble here. Sheldon has close eyes on you now, he doesn't trust you," she said. She handed me a rag and I snatched it from her.

"I'm locked in here for thirty days. You have to get me out of here," I said.

Dyika stood. "I can't do that, Jetti. I'm already risking my life for you," she replied.

"Bullshit. You only agreed to help me because we have the same enemy. Why were you gone for so long anyway?"

I hissed in pain when I applied the wet rag on my wound. "I need Akea to trust me so he can be comfortable with me taking Nile out of the house. You did a number on him, Jetti. He hates your guts and I'm the one who has to clean it up," she said.

"You don't have to do anything but take Nile without raising any suspicions. I can't be in this body for another day and I damn sure don't feel like being in this cult."

"I need more of your hair, Jetti. The spell only lasts for six hours, but if I get more, it'll last longer," she said.

"And he doesn't suspect you at all?" I curiously asked.

"He has a date coming up. Did you know he was seeing someone?" she replied. Tears fell from my eyes as I thought about Akea giving another woman what he couldn't give to me.

"Who is she?"

"I don't know but whoever it is has a hold on him. This will take time, Jetti, so I need you to be patient," she said.

"And your body produces breastmilk?"

"Yes, he took to it. My body turns into the body you would have if you weren't cursed. That's why I need more of your original DNA strand so that I can continue nursing him," she said.

"There has to be another way. I hate that you get to nurse my fucking son. I didn't think this spell would go that far. It's almost like black magic."

"You think pure magic would work on bad deeds? Of course, it's black magic. I'm going against everything I believe in to bring Black Rose to justice for what she has done to me, you and others. How dare you question my magic when you knew the plan," she spat.

"A plan that I didn't think all the way through but you really produced breastmilk when I can't?" I asked in disbelief.

"The death of Black Rose must come from the sacrifice of an innocent child. A child of warlock blood and you know this. I shouldn't have to repeat myself," she said.

I wiped the tears away. "How much time do you think you need?"

"A month. I promise a month is all I need to sway Akea," she replied.

She went into the knapsack around her waist for a pair of scissors; she cut a handful of my hair.

"This can make me a lot of potion. I'll check on you shortly," she said.

"Let me know if you see Gensin. I think she's missing."

"Will do but clean yourself up. You look like shit," she replied. She vanished into thin air leaving me unconvinced.

I hope she becomes me for good! I bet she'll find out the hard way it's not a walk in the park being me.

Black Rose

Two days later...

I'm here to catch you Rose.

I kept replaying Akea's words in my head while I sat at the end of Circa's feasting table, staring at the rare steak on my plate. Circa's feasts were once a week at his gothic style home. It used to be a mental asylum in the eighteen hundred. I looked at the numberless clock on the wall and it was six thirty in the evening. My date with Akea was three and a half hours away. His innocence and sincerity have been haunting me since the last time I'd seen him. I couldn't stop thinking about him especially with Majestic always in my ear about how I shouldn't see Akea as the enemy.

"Why aren't you eating?" my mother asked. My mother picking a fight with me was normal whenever we had a gathering. I looked up from my plate and she was staring a hole into me. I'd been at their home for an hour and nobody had said anything to me, not even nagging ass Blizzard who was sitting next to me.

"I'm not hungry," I replied.

"She might eat thousand-dollar steaks now since she went behind our backs and visited that warlock, Akea," Nayati said. She was sitting next to our mother. They were dressed alike in white, vintage style, button gowns. They were also wearing a crown on their heads made out of sticks, leaves and flowers. Nayati was the clan's "princess."

The clan members stared at me in disgust because of my run in with Akea. Blizzard scooted his chair away from me—I was now deemed a traitor.

I pushed my chair away from the table to be excused. "You better not even think about leaving while I'm talking to you. You've been quiet since you came here and I want to know why! I've spent hours butchering six cows for us to eat and you haven't touched anything!" my mother yelled.

I looked at Circa and he looked away, sipping his flask filled with goat milk wine. He still had a grudge against me for embarrassing him in front of Sheldon's clan.

"I don't have time for this, Merci," I replied, standing up. My mother banged on the table and a couple of dishes fell on the floor.

"Sit the fuck down and eat that steak, Black Rose. Everyone else is eating and you will do the same and don't you ever call me by my name again," she warned.

Nayati burst into a fit of laughter. "This freak always gets into trouble," she said to her husband.

I leaned over the table and blew into her face, sealing her mouth shut. Nayati dramatically wailed her arms because she couldn't speak. Her face was mouthless.

"Can't laugh now, bitch!" I yelled at her.

"Uncurse her!" Nayati's husband, Glendan, yelled at me. Nayati fell onto the floor, panicking because her mouth was gone.

"Pay me first! Nothing in life comes free!" I yelled back.

"Don't talk to Black Rose like that, just chill out. Nayati did start with her," Blizzard said to Glendan.

"Of course you'll come to her defense. Newsflash, baby brother, Black Rose fucks everything except you so pull your fingers out of her twat!" Glendan replied.

"Come on, Rose," Blizzard said. He grabbed my hand, pulling me out of the feast room.

"Bring your ass back here and uncurse my child!" my mother shouted from behind us. I snatched away from Blizzard once we were in the hallway.

"Did you sleep with that warlock and don't lie to me," Blizzard said.

"Why do you want to know, huh? There's nothing going on between us so let it go."

"Damn it, Black Rose. Can't you see how much I care about you?" he asked. Blizzard was pleading with his eyes but I felt nothing for him. He tilted my chin up so I could look into his eyes.

"Just one time, let me make love to you and I promise you'll feel our souls connect. I can't even look at another woman and I also can't control my composure when another man touches you," he said.

Circa appeared next to us. "Go back inside the feast room. You don't have to run after my daughter like a dog in heat. She's grown and can handle her own feelings," he said sternly.

"Yes sir," Blizzard said, bowing his head at Circa.

He went back to the feast room like a little boy. That was another reason I couldn't date my own kind. I would hate for my mate to cater to Circa and not stand up from himself.

"Tell me something, Black Rose. Why did you really go to Akea and don't lie to me," Circa said.

"Zelda already told you why I was there and the last time I checked, I'm free to go anywhere I want."

Circa's eyes glowed as he clenched his jaw. "Don't test me, Rose! Did you sleep with that warlock? Is that why your garden is practically dead? It saddens that black heart of yours that he needs to die? You fucked him, didn't you? I can sense when you sleep with someone," he said.

"You are starting to question me as if I'm your wife. My pussy, my choice!" I yelled at him. Circa choke slammed me into the wall.

"Go ahead, fight me back. Do it!" he said. The veins were popping out his neck and spit was flying out of his mouth—he was furious.

He squeezed my neck hard enough to cause my head to explode. I had never laid hands on my father before, but I could no longer take his weird obsession and anger he had towards me. I slashed his face with my nails drawing blood.

"Your breasts swell every time you fuck someone and you come around me with that filth!" he gritted. He raised me against the wall while I struggled to breathe.

"You've had that warlock's dick inside of you so don't deny it. I've always turned a blind eye to your loose ways but not this time. I warned you! I told you to stay the fuck away from him!" Circa shouted. I raised my leg, kicking him in the neck with the sharp end of my stilettos. Circa dropped me on the floor; blood spurted on the walls when he yanked my heel out of his neck. His scythe appeared in his hand and he raised it at me while I was still on the ground. Circa swung the menacing weapon but I hurriedly ducked and he hit the wall instead.

I jumped up, ready to battle. "You really want to fight me, Circa?" I asked.

He pointed his finger at me. "I'm not going to kill you, but you'll be seething in pain by the time I finish," he said.

He quickly snatched his weapon out of the wall, swinging it across my abdomen. Black blood leaked through the material of my dress, dripping onto the floor.

Circa smiled. "I made this weapon just for you in case you got out of line. It burns doesn't it?" he asked.

I fell against the wall with tears in my eyes. The wound burned into my skin like acid. I coughed up a glob of blood.

"I'm the leader of this clan and the messenger of our ancestors! Your magic is powerful, but it's me who is unstoppable," he bragged. The wound on his neck had already healed; he angrily paced back and forth pounding his chest.

"I'm the fucking leader, Black Rose!" he said with glowing eyes.

I pushed myself since my body was beginning to heal. The pain was still present but the loss of blood was diminishing. "You might be the leader, but we all know I'm a goddess of death! You might be unstoppable, but I'm untouchable and untamable."

"Goddess? So now you think you're above me?" he asked with veins popping out of his neck.

"YES! I am above you and everyone else in this clan!" I screamed. Circa rushed towards me. I teleported to the ceiling near the chandelier. He curiously looked down the hallway.

"I know you are close and I'm going to find you!" he said.

My nails sharpened, hooking into the wall to keep me from falling. Black silky hairs covered my arms and legs; my body swelled causing my dress to rip in shreds. A piece of clothing fell on top of Circa's head while I was transforming. By the time he looked up, I had shifted into a magical forest creature called, Barghest. Barghests were the werewolves of our magical forest but they had gone extinct when the forest died.

I jumped on Circa, sinking my teeth into his neck. My creature's nails slashed a chunk of his face off. He punched me in the ribcage with spiked knuckles but it didn't stop me. I flung Circa down the hallway; he rolled into a statue of an angel. His silk garments were drenched in blood.
Circa weakly got up from the floor. "You have to come better than that!" Circa said. His face was blemish free. I was ready to finish him off before I turned back to my human form, but the feast doors opened.

"ENOUGH!" Merci screamed.

The clan was standing behind her, observing the damages and the red and black blood splatter in the hallway.

"We heard everything, Circa. Tell me why you sound more like Black Rose's mate than her father? You want to fight her because of whom she gives her body to, huh?" Merci asked with venom in her eyes. I shifted into my human form, wearing a black dress and heels as if nothing ever happened.

"What I say to Black Rose isn't your concern. And since when does the clan interrupt my business with my daughter? You knew better than to come out here!" Circa yelled at Merci.

"Everyone back to the feast room," Merci said. The clan dispersed, heading back to the feast room. Blizzard came to me. "Are you alright?" he asked, inspecting my body for wounds. Merci was watching Circa while he watched me and Blizzard. She knew he was jealous over Blizzard's interaction with me.

"Yes, I'm fine," I replied with my eyes still on Circa.

"Head back like everyone else!" Circa said to Blizzard.

"This isn't right, Circa. Black Rose isn't your property," Blizzard replied.

A spear formed in Circa's hand; like a bolt of lightning he threw his spear at Blizzard. In quick reflex, I caught the spear. I crumbled the weapon until it turned to ashes. It was a shot at his ego because Circa's spears were too fast to catch.

"I'm leaving this clan. From now on, I'm no longer a Yubsari Warrior," I told Circa.

"You can leave this house but you will never leave this clan. I'll fight you till death before you leave," Circa said.

"Maybe she should go for a while. The clan needs a break from her. She cursed Nayati and she's always getting you angry! I'm sick of you paying more attention to her than me and I'm the one you share a bed with!" Merci yelled at Circa. He slapped Merci with so much force that her canine tooth flew down the hallway. Her jaw was twisted and detached from her mouth.

"SHUT UP!" Circa yelled at her. In fear that he'd strike again, Merci rushed back into the feast room holding her face in shame. I'd never seen Circa lose his control like that or hit Merci in that manner.

"I'll walk you home," Blizzard whispered to me.

"I'll forget the rules and behead you in front of your family if you leave this house with her. I ordered you to back away from her; do it now!" Circa shouted at Blizzard. Another weapon formed in his hand, it was an iron hammer with deadly spikes.

"I want to marry Black Rose and hopefully my bravery will grant me my wish, Circa. I'm willing to die right now if it proves that I love her," Blizzard said. Another hammer formed in Circa's other hand–he now had two hammers.

"I don't want you, Blizzard. My heart belongs to another man. Since everything is out on the table, Father, I fucked Akea and I enjoyed it. So everyone is right, I'm a traitor for screwing the enemy of our people and I want to do it again," I said.

"How could you go behind my back?" Circa asked with tear filled eyes. Blizzard stepped away from me. He silently went back to the feast room.

"Release me from this clan, Circa. I'm a traitor!" I said. I was practically begging him to release me. I could've taken the easy way out by killing Circa, but through it all, he was still my father.

"ZELDA!" Circa called out.

"Her death will be on you if she even comes near me," I warned Circa.

She appeared in front of him, kneeling. "Yes, my leader," she said.

"Go take care of that warlock. Bring me his head and cut out his eyes. I want his soul to be blind so even if he comes back in the afterlife, he won't be able to look at my daughter again," Circa demanded.

"I will prove to you that I'm a great warrior by bringing you his head," she said. My heart felt like it was about to explode. I tried to mask the pain but it hurt worse than it did the last time I saw Akea. I thought about killing Akea myself but hearing someone else willing to do it didn't sit well with me. Matter of fact, it was at that moment I decided my own fate.

"And I hear he has an offspring. I want his child's head too," Circa ordered Zelda.

"I'll do anything to please you, sir," Zelda replied.

Circa looked at me. "Your cursed heart can't handle love, Black Rose. Being in love will kill you. That's why I fight so hard for you to not fall for anyone because it'll turn you into ashes. Love is your death but death is your life. You either kill to feed that wicked heart of yours or fall in love and parish," Circa said.

"I've lived for a very long time, Circa. I'll welcome death with open arms if it means I get to feel Akea again."

"He cursed you and made you fall for him so quickly. That's what his kind does! How do you know if what you feel is real? What if this is their weapon to kill you? You heard Sheldon's threats. He said love can be a blessing or a curse. They are building an army against us right before our eyes. You've fallen into their trap! A great warrior puts the safety of their clan first. Sheldon resurfacing after all of this time only means he has a plan and that plan is you. Can't you see that?" Circa said.

A tear fell from my eye because what Circa said made a lot of sense. I was so blinded by Akea that I had forgotten there was a possibility that Akea was plotting against me. Sheldon's clan worshiped Akea's father. How could he not have any involvement? I was beginning to feel played again. I wondered why Akea had said all those sweet things to me. One thing Sheldon said was true, I had to pick my own medicine.

Circa's eyes softened. "Your silence means that I'm right. I'm willing to forgive you and pretend you didn't disobey me since you were blinded by his wicked magic," Circa said to me.

"I'll get going now," Zelda told Circa.

She stood from the ground, facing me with a snide smirk. "I will make sure I torture him for you, my leader," Zelda said over her shoulder to Circa.

I grabbed her arm when she walked past me. "I have to give you something that'll kill him faster," I told Zelda.

"I knew you'd see it my way," Circa said to me.

In the blink of an eye, I jumped on Zelda's shoulders, wrapping my legs tightly around her head. Circa's eyes widened in shock.

"The only way out of this clan is to kill a clan member and as a leader, you should honor those rules. I didn't want it to come to this, Father, but as you said, death is my way of life."

Zelda's nails were digging in my thighs to get me off of her. "Help me! I can't move!" Zelda said to Circa. A dagger appeared in my hand.

"NOOOOO!" Circa yelled.

I cut across my tongue with the dagger to draw blood. "I never liked this bitch anyway for how she talked to Majestic," I said.

I slit Zelda's throat, cutting through her flesh to take off her head. The poisoned tip of the dagger was melting her flesh as I cut, making it easier to slice through her neck. Circa dropped to his knees; not because he cared for her, but because he was distraught that I had exiled myself from his clan. I jumped off Zelda's body, holding her head by a braid. Blood flowed down the hallway, saturating Circa's knees after her headless body hit the floor.

"Her parents will have to mourn their child because you picked an enemy?" he asked in disbelief.

I tossed him Zelda's head. "I didn't pick Akea either. I picked myself," I replied before teleporting out of his home. I had a date to get ready for and I couldn't be late.

Akea

Two hours later...

Kanye knocked on my bedroom door. "Bro, you dressed?" he called out.

"Yeah, come in," I replied. I was standing in the mirror, trying to decide if I looked decent.

"What do you think? Too dressed up or under dressed?" I asked him. I was dressed in a black, silk dashiki with gold symbols, black silk pants and loafers.

"You look straight. Yo, I'm diggin' this look but where the jewelry at? You can't leave the house without dripping in Anubian diamonds," he replied. Kanye walked into my closet. He pressed his thumb against the monitor on the wall near my jewelry case. Two doors popped out of the wall, revealing my jewelry collection. Kanye grabbed a yellow diamond Cuban link chain with a matching bracelet.

"Can't leave without the glasses either," he said. He picked up a pair of gold framed glasses adorned in diamonds. I stood in the mirror checking out the finished look.

"Hold up, bro. I forgot something," he said.

He grabbed a black velvet box off the shelf. "I'm not doing that. You have your look and I have mine. This ain't for me."

"My father-in-law made these for you and you never wear them. Come on and pop these in. We all have a pair but you are the only one who hasn't worn it yet," he replied. I opened the box and it was a pair of golds with canines.

"Um, no, bro. I'm not doing this," I said, pushing it away.

"Aight, well at least wear the bottom one. It's just a bar that goes across your teeth," he said. I picked up the bar, popping it into my mouth.

"Whew, that boy is crisp. Now we're identical-identical," he said.

"That's not a compliment. I keep telling you bro, I'm cool with being different from you," I replied. I pressed a button on the wall to lock up my jewelry.

"Aight nerd boy, if you say so. Now when you break it off with her, don't be soft about it. Tell her you want to work it out with your son's mother. That'll keep her away for good," Kanye said. He laid across my bed to watch TV.

"I don't want to wish bad luck on me by lying about that. What if I just tell her the truth? I'm going to tell her that she's no good for me because of her voodoo. I don't care what anyone says, she cursed me."

Kanye sat up on the bed, fiddling with his chin hair. He seemed to be thinking deeply about something. "I know you don't want to break it off with her, bro, and all jokes aside, you should find out the truth before you assume she's cursed you. From everything you told me, this so-called curse hasn't harmed you. Besides that rose on your neck, what else has she done to you?" he replied. Kanye knew my feelings without me saying it and vice versa.

"I'm afraid to hurt that woman's feelings but if Naobi's assumptions about Rose are true, I also can't bring possible danger around my son."

"She felt the same way about her sister, Ula, because she was created from black magic. She thought Ula would harm us, but she didn't. Ula eventually found love and peace. Be up front with Black Rose and if she can't let her guard down, walk away," he replied.

I was about to respond, but Jetti came into the bedroom holding Nile with Fiti behind her. I had eased up on Jetti because for the past few days, she had stayed out of my way when she came over. We barely talked and I was cool with that too.

"You look handsome as always," Jetti said to me.

"Monifa is calling me. Yo, have fun tonight and let the chips fall where they need to be," Kanye said. He gave me a dap hug before leaving the bedroom.

"My limo should be outside so I'm ready to go," I told Jetti. I kissed Nile's forehead and he opened his eyes. His eyes flashed ice blue; he was trying to read me but was too young to understand.

"I think he's developing his powers already. He's not a human child like you thought. He's already tapping into his magic," Jetti said.

"That may be true but he doesn't understand it."

"When will you allow me to be alone with him?" she asked, looking at Fiti. Fiti was fixing Nile's sheets in his crib.

"You're a guest, Jetti. Only pack members can roam freely around the house or be alone with Nile," I replied. She laid Nile in his crib since it was his bedtime.

"Will you be staying out until morning? If so, I can stay here longer," Jetti asked.

"I won't be gone long so you can leave at midnight," I replied.

Jetti sat in the rocking chair next to the crib with her arms crossed. "You don't mind me walking alone at midnight? There's plenty of rogue werewolves that roam the woods. What about my safety? A nursing mother isn't as strong as the others because she has to share her nutrients with her offspring," she said.

"I don't want to go against your wishes, Akea, but she's right. The rogue werewolves have increased in the city. She's can't fight off a group of sex craved beasts," Fiti replied.

"You can spend the night in the guest house," I told Jetti.

"Thank you," she replied.

I left the bedroom and was already feeling nervous about seeing Black Rose after our last encounter. The Bentley limo was in front of the mansion waiting for me. Our driver, Simon, who was a sixty-two-year-old white man, was smoking a cigar.

"Good evening but I thought I was assisting Akea. Is he feeling alright?" Simon asked. I chuckled because the golds in my mouth must've thrown him off.

"It's me, Simon. I let Kanye add a little seasoning to my outfit," I replied. He opened the back door for me. "A little seasoning has never hurt anyone," he smiled.

I got into the backseat. "I have to make a stop at the florist shop to pick up an order before we reach the city."

Simon tipped his hat before closing the door. He got inside the limo, pulling off seconds later. Before I met Black Rose at Blue Moon, I had to pick up a special order which was the Baccara roses I had promised her.

Black Rose

Blue Moon Restaurant...

I tapped my nail on the table while sipping a glass of red wine; I was vibing with the atmosphere. The restaurant had a romantic vibe. It was dimly lit with Louis Armstrong's song What a Wonderful World playing in the background. I wasn't expecting a reservation, I thought Akea and I were only meeting up to have a drink. When I arrived, the waitress took me to a private room with a fireplace and lit candles. It was set up like a wine cellar. From what I was told, I could have any wine I wanted inside the room since it was all paid for. According to the clock on the wall, Akea was five minutes late. I tried not to worry, but I couldn't help it. Circa's words were repeating in my head, telling me that Akea was working with Sheldon to take me down.

Was I blindsided? Is this a trap? Did Akea set this sympathy dinner up for me because he knew he wasn't going to see me again?

I wore one of my best dresses which was a black 1950, off-the-shoulder, retro dress. It flared in the back but was cut short in the front, revealing a nice amount of my thighs. The high tie-up heels I wore had black roses stitched to the strings that Majestic had made for me twenty years ago. I was dolled up more than ever and wearing expensive jewels. A young Caucasian waiter came into the room with a tray of warm bread.

"Akea Uffe will be arriving shortly. Can I get you anything else?" he asked. His eyes lustfully gazed at my thighs while he sat the bread basket on the table. I curiously listened to his thoughts:

She's a high price whore I bet...most of them are. I can't wait to finish college so I can buy a freaky black woman and make her a slave. Yeah, that's what I'll do and send it to my frat buddies.

I glanced at his name tag and it read *Peter*. "Excuse me, what did you ask?" I asked him.

"Can I get you anything else?" he replied.

"Do you have a little dick, Peter?"

His cheeks turned red in embarrassment. "Excuse me?" he asked.

"I asked if you had a little dick. Is your dick that little whereas you are just going to college to get a good enough job to buy black women? Are you that much of a coward that you have to work this hard to shame black women?"

"I don't...I don't know what you are talking about," he replied.

"Do you know what I do for a living?"

He nervously fiddled with his fingers. "No," he replied.

"It's 'no ma'am'. You will address me as ma'am while you serve me. Now answer the question. Do you know what I do for a living, Peter?"

"No ma'am, I don't," he replied.

"I curse people who disrespects me."

I went inside my clutch, pulling out a licorice jellybean. Peter took a big gulp while he watched me in my elf form. My black eyes captured him—hypnotizing him.

"Eat the jellybean, Peter," I demanded.

"Yes ma'am," he replied.

He took the jellybean out of my hand. A smile spread across his face after he chewed and swallowed the poisoned candy.

"You can go now and don't come back to my section especially when you start feeling sick."

"Yes ma'am," he replied under hypnosis.

Peter walked away from my section in a daze. In an hour or less, he was going to die a painful death as his body decayed on the inside. I took another sip of my wine with my eyes on the clock. Akea was ten minutes late. He seemed like a punctual man but I guessed I was wrong.

Maybe Circa was right. He's going to stand me up. I should leave and save my dignity.

I finished the rest of my wine before grabbing my clutch off the table. The door to the private room opened when I was about to leave. Akea walked in holding the three dozen Baccara roses he had promised me. My heart exploded with joy but the roses weren't the only reason why. Akea looked and smelled so good that I quickly forgot about the roses in his hands.

"I apologize for being late. The roses weren't ready when I got there to pick them up," he said. He set the roses on the table. I knew he was caught off guard when I hugged him. He froze for a second before hugging me back. Akea's cologne was enticing and the glasses he wore gave him that schoolboy look that I loved. I pulled away from him and noticed a black rose symbol on his neck. The symbol was the size of a ring box. I touched the symbol and it felt fresh like someone tattooed it on his neck.

"When did you get this tattoo?" I asked.

"It's not a tattoo, it's a marking. It appeared out of nowhere," he replied. He gestured for me to sit at the table. I picked up the vase admiring the black roses with red velvet tips.

"These are really pretty, Akea. Thank you," I gushed.

"Anytime; you look lovely as always," he said.

"Appreciate it. I was beginning to think you were going to stand me up."

"I never break promises," he said. He picked up the dinner menu. "Do you know what you want?" he asked.

"Yes, the rabbit stew with extra meat," I replied. Akea looked up from the menu. "Your kind likes rabbits, right?" he asked.

"Yes, rabbit is our favorite but we do eat other meats."

"Does your kind also live in trees and gigantic flowers?" he asked.

Did he figure me out? Wait, did he know what I was the whole time?

"Yes, but something tells me that you already knew that."

"That's the thing, Rose, I don't know shit about you. When I looked into your eyes the first time I met you and read you, everything you showed me was a lie. The Louisiana accent you had that day is even gone," he said.

"Of course, I showed you what you wanted to see. I do that with every witch or warlock I encounter. My fake identity is twenty-two-years old Keisha Heron who was born in Louisiana. You don't have to hide behind an identity because unlike me, you were born twenty-one years ago. I'm wayyyy older than you, Akea, so what am I supposed to do?"

"Just be real with me, Rose. Am I in danger? Should my people fear your kind?" he asked.

"Did you ask me here to patronize me? Is this a date or a job interview because I'm not feeling you asking me this."

"I apologize if I'm coming off coldhearted. I have been having these wild dreams that seem real and this rose on my neck is a marking. Marking isn't a witch or warlock tradition, no matter what kind of witch they are. Something like this only comes from an animal or a creature," he replied.

I was clueless too because no other man had ever been marked by me. Being with Akea was opening a lot of cans of worms. I hated not being in control of the narrative of my life but I had nothing to lose anymore since I was exiled from my clan.

Maybe if I tell him my truth, he can tell me his.

"I'll tell you what I am after dinner but I also want you to tell me why you seduced me."

"I thought you already knew why but I'll tell you again after dinner. Now back to this rabbit, how does it taste? I've never had it before," he smirked. I noticed he had gold covering the bottom of his teeth. It looked damn good on him.

"It tastes like chicken but more gamey. I like it stewed or raw, but never grilled or boiled."

"Raw meat?" he asked with a raised eyebrow.

"My kind can eat raw meat."

"I'll try the stew," he replied.

The waitress came in with a bottle of cognac for Akea. "Where's Peter?" I asked her.

"He left early. I think he has a stomach bug. He can't keep anything down," she said.

"Ohhh what a shame. I hope he feels better," I replied. She leaned forward to place Akea's bottle on the table, but I could tell she wanted him to see her breasts. Seeing her act that way made me jealous.

"Would you like for me to put the flowers aside so you two can have space?" she asked. I listened in on her thoughts.

He's young and rich and can get any woman he wants. Why would he want this woman wearing that vintage clothing? My great grandmother had a dress like that. Maybe he's just caught up in her beauty.

"No, you can leave them there. The flowers complement her dress. I know I told you that you look good but I have to tell you again how breathtaking you look," Akea said to me.

I blew him a kiss. "Thank you, honey."

"What are you two having tonight?" the waitress asked. The waitress took our orders before rushing out of the room.

"You heard her thoughts, huh?" I asked.

"Yeah, I saw how you were looking at her so I figured she was thinking of something foul," he chuckled. Akea scooted his chair closer to mine. "I can't get you out of my head, Rose. I don't want to sound like an ain't shit dude that just wants to sweet talk you, but I smell, taste and feel you whenever you aren't around me. It's scary because it happened so fast. Almost like you put voodoo on me," he said.

"You'd be dead if that ever happened."

Akea smirked. "So your magic is like that?" he asked. I shrugged my shoulders.

"I mean you can say that I get a little carried away. But how you feel is how I've been feeling. I guess we're both nervous."

"I see that your attitude isn't cold towards me anymore. I told you these roses would bring a different meaning to you," he said.

"That may be true, I did get a warm feeling when I saw them but you have a bigger impact on my heart than these flowers. Maybe it's you that warms me."

Akea's smile widened. "I know I'm special," he arrogantly stated. I playfully pushed him away from me.

"You are too close so go back to where you were."

He chuckled. "There goes that fence again but okay," he said, going back to his spot. I only wanted space because his closeness would've had me straddling his lap. Thinking about his girth buried deep in my pussy was making me hot. I picked up my glass of cold water to cool off. My breasts were swelling and my nipples were poking through the fabric of my dress. I crossed my arms on the table to hide them from Akea who was staring a hole into me.

"Did I make you uncomfortable?" he asked.

"No, I'm just hungry, that's all."

Akea sipped on his cognac while his eyes glowed at me. He was observant and possibly had already realized I was burning with desire. My thong was soaked and so was the cloth of the chair.

"I think you're too close to the fireplace. You look hot," he said.

"You have to stop observing me. It makes me shy."

"How can I do that when I have your symbol on my neck? We're permanently connected. I can feel what you feel right now," he said.

"How do I feel?"

"Your aura feels better than it did the last time we were together, but it still has a sadness to it. You feel guilty for smiling when you're happy because you are confused about me being in your life. You also worry that I'm too good to be true, so you are waiting for me to reveal my hidden agenda. You are also more open to dying than living," he replied.

Tears fell from my eyes; I quickly wiped the tears away. What Akea described was a pitiful and dark being. I was a cursed soul and there was nothing I could do to change that. I was better off hating him for what his kind had done to me, but where would it get me?

"I could've been happy had you not made me sound so pitiful. Why did you remind me that your kind made me like this?" I vented.

"My kind?" he repeated.

"I was talking out of my head. Forget I said anything."

Akea didn't press the issue, he took a drink from his glass instead. Maxwell's song This Woman's Work played in the restaurant. Akea leaned back in his chair, I could tell that he was into the song.

"I see you love this song."

"It reminds me of my mother. She played it a lot on Sundays when she cooked for me," he replied.

"What did she cook for you?"

"Fried chicken, baked macaroni and cheese, yams, collard greens, pies and the list goes on," he replied.

I was stunned that Akea was raised like a human. I was expecting him to eat sushi, snails, caviar and other fancy foods.

"I wasn't expecting that. I never had those foods before."

"My mother grew up as a human with regular family traditions. She didn't know she was a jackal until my father came into her life and discovered she was his soulmate. They bumped heads a lot because she was more modern than him. But she listened to this kind of music, kept up with the fashion trends and cooked soul food," he said.

"A jackal?" I repeated since I had never heard of any jackal shifters.
"Yes, a golden jackal from ancient Africa," he replied.

"That's unique, not too many immortals can experience what you've experienced. Usually both parents teach their children with ancient upbringings. We tend to be very old fashioned and less modern, even in today's time it's hard to adjust."

"How about your parents?" he asked.

Emotionless, selfish and heartless with dark souls like me.

"They are different. I stay out of their way and vice versa."

"You'll tell me the truth soon," he chuckled.

His smile was contagious; I had to smile too. "Are you saying that I'm lying?" I asked.

"I told you, Rose. Your vibe speaks to me. I can't see your thoughts but I damn sure can feel your mood," he replied. I reached for the bottle of cognac on the table.

"I think you are too delicate for this grown man juice," he said, taking it away from me.

His protectiveness is so domineering. He thinks I'm delicate when I'm a savage creature of death.

"The wine me and Majestic makes is stronger than that. Don't underestimate me, now pass that over."

Akea gave me the cognac; I filled my glass to the tip of the rim. The date was going smoothly, and I let my guard down again. I wanted to enjoy my time as much as I could since I couldn't predict what would happen once I told Akea that I was a dark elf.

Circa

Midnight...

I paced back and forth in my study, not knowing how to deal with Black Rose's betrayal. My lieutenants, Findis and Lark, were waiting for me to give the order to take down Black Rose. I sent a gang of my top fighters to her house but it was reported back to me that her cabin had vanished.

"We need to do something now, Circa. Zelda's parents are questioning your leadership because you haven't given orders on our next move. Black Rose should be punished for beheading Zelda," Findis said.

"You both know that Black Rose cannot die. All we can do is hurt her, but death isn't the answer," I replied.

Lark's eyes angrily glowed at me while he bit the inside of his jaw. "I told you that your greed would do this. You should've left it alone, Circa. We had healthy air, clean clear water and a tribe of our people living. There were hundreds of us until you had a vision of this so-called new world. You let that warlock come to our land and make promises that cost us in the end. I'm tired of fighting,

Circa. Goddamn it, I'm tired!" Lark said. He banged his fist on the table, breaking it in half.

"We are slaves to our own hatred. Generations of our tribe are gone down the drain because of YOU!" Lark yelled.

"You speak with an enemy's tongue, Lark. I think you might want to lower your voice before I cut your head off and give it to your sons. And speaking of your sons, Blizzard needs to be on a leash for constantly sniffing up Black Rose's ass. He's lucky to be spared," I replied.

"I'll fight you to death if you hurt my son. I've stuck with you for years and held on to your secrets so you better pay me with respect," he replied.

"Now is not the time to fight. We need to put our personal issues aside and take care of that warlock Black Rose is sleeping with. If he's the son of a god, his magic will reveal the truth. She'll make rose seeds out of our souls if she learns of her past," Findis said.

Lark chuckled. "Maybe this is our fate, Circa. We might as well accept it because we created a monster that we can't control," he said. Lark got up from the chair and almost lost his footing because he was drunk.

"Take him to his room," I told Findis.

"Come on brother, you've had enough," Findis told Lark. Lark broke down in tears. "I hate that we've turned into this. Every day I feel like killing my family then taking my own life so we won't have to live in shame," he sobbed.

"Get him out of here and do it now," I told Findis.

Findis rushed Lark out of the room; I angrily slammed my fist into the wall, causing the ceiling to collapse.

"FUCK!" I yelled, picking up a table. I hurled it into the hallway. My wife came into the room holding a tray of raw meat and goat milk wine. She got on her knees.

"I'm here to serve you," she said.

Her face was healed from when I lashed out on her earlier and her tooth had grown back. My wife was someone I didn't love, but I used to cherish her. I was smitten by her beauty but no one compared to Lyira, who was the goddess of our world. Lyira's beauty was captivating and her scent was alluring. I used to wake up at the crack of dawn to hear her sing near her pond. The moment I lost her, I lost myself. Merci was supposed to fill the void my heart longed for, but no matter what she did, I couldn't love her.

"Get up, Merci. You look ridiculous."
I sat behind my desk and she closed the door. "We had to carve out a mouth for Nayati and now she's in great pain. Black Rose scarred her for life, Circa. Our precious daughter's husband won't even look at her because she lost her beauty," she said. Merci placed the tray on the desk before sitting across from me.

"Nayati isn't my blood child therefore she brought that on herself."

A tear fell down Merci's face. "Neither is Black Rose but you love her," she replied.

"Why are you here, Merci? I didn't tell you that I was in need of food or a drink. Do you think you can barge in on me whenever you feel like it because you are my mate? Have some dignity for yourself for once. You look weak and tired, get some rest."

"Come to bed please. I need you," she said.

She opened her robe to reveal her naked body. I picked up the goat milk wine; I would rather be drunk like a viking than lay with Merci.

"It's been five years, Circa. I'm in need of love," she pleaded.

"I can't get aroused. I don't want to get distracted and intimacy is a big distraction. We are warriors, members of the Yubsari clan, the last of our kind that's left. A leader doesn't think with his dick, he thinks with his weapons. He also thinks of death and bringing justice to those who deserve it. Now, can you please cover up your body and get out of my study?"

Merci closed her robe. "It's not fair to me. I can't even kiss you! Is it because I don't look as youthful as Black Rose? Should I wear black dresses and let my hair down for you to notice me? I'm practically begging you to make love to me," she said.

"You bring nothing to this clan other than food and you are worried about getting laid at a time like this? Does it look like I want to be intimate right now? Black Rose is gone and more than likely, she's with that warlock. We have bigger fish to fry."

"I guess I can continue to live in misery. Nothing has changed, right?" she asked, standing up.

"I tell you every day that you have access to any man in our clan. Since you are the leader's wife, you should take advantage of your position. No man in this clan will turn you down or they'll be punished."

"Can't you see this is unfair? Why not get jealous the same way you do with Black Rose?" she asked.

"Get out of my study before your spirit joins Zelda's. We lost our strongest warrior, and you are worried about sex! Get out and find someone to fuck!" I barked.

Merci walked to the door. I called out to her when she put her hand on the doorknob. "You can fuck him anywhere in my domain except for my bed and study."

"Yes, Circa," she replied before quietly closing the door.

I grabbed a piece of meat off the tray, washing it down with the bitter and tart wine. The clan was diminishing right before my eyes. I lost my grip and didn't have the energy to get it back.

A silhouette of a woman appeared in front of me while I guzzled the wine. I pounded my chest while letting off a burp. The silhouette turned into the creature I yearned for the most. Lyira, the forest goddess, stood in the middle of the floor, naked from head-to-toe. Green plants and blossoming pink and red roses sprouted from the floor and ceiling, reminding me of the old days.

"Come to me, Circa," she said with her arms out.

Her pointed ears were covered with small flowers and her body had a golden glow because of the shimmers in her smooth skin. Lyira's long hair was braided down to her ankles; she was wearing a crown made out of red roses. I got up, walking over to her. Her flowery, honey scent filled my nostrils, causing my erection to grow. I went to her, wrapping my arms around her; I inhaled the apricot scent of her hair to make sure it was real.

"I'm doing everything that I can to get you back but nothing I do is working."

Lyira broke away from my embrace. "You were always a clever liar. You've done nothing to reunite me with Black Rose. You are pushing her away and soon she'll discover what you did to the forest, me and my child. I'm disappointed in you," she said. I dropped to my knees to beg her for forgiveness.

"I'm afraid that Black Rose won't forgive me, but I know you will. She can't find out the truth, Lyira."

"What makes you think I'll forgive a liar? You betrayed me over something you already had," she replied.

"I was childish back then, Lyira. I did what I felt was right."

"Find Black Rose and bring her home. You are supposed to be protecting her, not turning her into an enemy!" she said.

"When will you forgive me for my sins?"

"I won't forgive you until you fix this, Circa," she replied.

I stood up to face her. She moved my hair away from my neck, exposing her red rose symbol. The symbol meant, love, beauty, romance and love at first sight.

"You hide this well as if I meant nothing to you. Look at you, Circa. You were once a beautiful man, the best in the forest. Now, you are aging and the only magic you have is in the weapons you create. How much will it take for you to realize that you are a weak leader? It was me who led our people the right way! It was my magic from the forest that gave us strength. You can't do anything but lead them to the pits of hell," she said.

"Even in death, you still look down on me. The difference is I'm still here and you aren't, my love."

"You are a brainless mushroom if you think I'm gone for eternity," she replied.

"I did everything to bring you back, Lyira, and guess what? You still haven't come back."

"Do you want me to find Black Rose myself?" she asked.

"You wouldn't dare step on my toes from your grave."

Lyira smiled. "I'll find a way to her and when I do, you will answer to her sword," she threatened. She turned into a cloud before she vanished. Her coming back to me was a delusion. The only time I envisioned her was when I failed.

I went to the mirror on the wall to see my reflection. My handsomeness was becoming dull like Lyira had stated.

"I'll find that little bitch myself."

A carving knife appeared in my hand. I braced myself for the pain I was about to endure. Black Rose could sense our presence because our ears were signals to the others. I grabbed the tip of my ear, quickly slicing it off to get it over with.

"AHHHH!" I bellowed, dropping the knife. I was losing a lot of blood, enough to cause me to faint. There was a candle on the table, I used the fire to seal the wound and keep my ear from growing back too soon. Findis barged into the room.

"What are you doing?" he asked, observing the blood on the floor.

"I'm going to get Black Rose myself and kill that warlock."

I cut off the other ear, quickly burning the wound to seal it.

"I'm with you every step of the way," Findis said, bowing his head to me.

I reached inside the pocket of my robe for my keys. "Because you know that I'm a great leader. You can close the door on your way out. I want to be alone."

Findis bowed his head before he left the room. I moved a picture from the wall behind my desk, uncovering a secret compartment. The door came ajar after I turned the key. Inside of a magical box was the head of Sheldon's brother, Amstid. I killed him a thousand years ago. I took the box out of the compartment and sat it on my desk. His eyes popped open when he coughed up a heap of dust. His eyes frantically looked around in horror.

"Circa?" he asked.

I sat in front of him. "Yes, it's me. It's been a while since I last awakened you. You look horrible," I chuckled. Amstid's face was loose from rotten skin, exposing the pinkness of his eye socket. He was almost toothless and the few he had left were rotten. His once black hair was gray in one patch on his head because the rest was bald. Amstid's nose was gone, only showing the skeleton of what used to be there.

"Take me to my brother and let him bury me," he replied.

"Sheldon will be dead soon. I told you a long time ago that everyone in your clan, even the innocent ones, will pay for what you did."

"You asked for that black magic in exchange for the forest. We had a deal! And because you didn't like the outcome, you blame me?" he replied.

"I offered a portion of our forest because your weaklings needed a power source to practice their spells! You blindsided me and now everyone will pay. Sheldon's clan is the only one left and for that, I'll make sure his head joins yours. He's out of hiding now so it's only a matter of time before I collect his soul."

Amstid coughed up slimy gray mucus. "You've turned into a bad man, Circa, and because of that, you will pay with your life the same way I did. I can't stop you, but I do know you will join me. You have to be careful what you ask for because you might get it ten times more," he said. A tooth fell to the bottom of the glass while he laughed. I gritted my teeth in anger that a dead man still had his arm wrapped around my throat.

"Laugh now, but Sheldon's head is next."

"Leave my baby brother out of this, Circa," he said sluggishly. He was about to fall asleep again since he couldn't stay awake past a minute.

"Nah, I can't do that. He has to die the same way Lyira did, muthafucka. The war might have been delayed but it's not over. Every witch and warlock must go."

Amstid closed his eyes, falling back into a deep sleep. I didn't have any time to waste. The clock was ticking and I needed Black Rose back because I couldn't take down the last members of Amstid's clan alone. Warlock boy, Akea, was in my way and he had hell to pay.

Akea

An hour later...

"I'm so stuffed. That rabbit hit the spot," Black Rose said, rubbing her stomach. I was holding her hand walking out the restaurant with the vase of flowers in my other hand. She was a bit tipsy after chugging down the cognac and wine.

"Dinner was nice. I'm stuffed myself," I chuckled.

"I don't want to go home just yet," she replied.

Simon was standing outside the limo waiting for me, but I wasn't going home yet.

"I'm going to stay back for a little while. I'll find a way home," I told him.

"Are you sure? It gets a little rowdy down here at night once the clubs let out. I don't want anyone to rob you," he said.

"Trust me, Simon. Nobody can or will rob me. I'll be fine."

"Alright, Akea. Don't forget to call me if you change your mind. I'll stay in the area in case you do," he said.

He looked at Black Rose and tipped his hat. "A woman that can put a smile on his face is good with me. You have a nice night too, ma'am," he said to her.

"Goodnight," she waved at him.

Simon got into the limo and I watched him drive off. We walked down the sidewalk. "Do you have housemaids too?" she asked.

"There's a cleaning crew that comes once a week, but we don't have humans working in the house. Too much shit goes down and it might scare them."

"It doesn't take much to scare a human, they are so fragile. But the night is young so what are we going to do next?" she asked.

"We can go somewhere quiet and have that discussion."

Black Rose smacked her teeth. "How about we hold off on that discussion and go somewhere quiet so I can show you my magic," she flirted.

"We have to talk about this symbol on my neck, Rose. I need to know everything about you since I'm stamped."

"I told you that I don't know. It has never happened to anyone else I've slept with," she replied.

A group of drunk people were walking down the sidewalk. "Awww those roses are so prettyyy," a girl slurred. She reached out to grab the flowers. "Can I buy these from you?" she asked. Black Rose grabbed her wrist, digging her nails into her flesh.

"Owww! Get off of me, crazy bitch!" the girl shouted.

"Keep your hands to yourself, wench, now go fuck off before I rip your arm off," Black Rose threatened. She shoved the young woman into the building. "That whore broke my arm!" she shouted.

"And I'll break your fucking jaw next," Black Rose replied. I wasn't expecting a woman of Black Rose's stature to be that aggressive. She was usually prissy and well-posed. Her pretty, mean ass gave me an arousal.

"Bro, put that crazy bitch on a leash," a guy said.

"The fuck you just say, fool?" I replied.

Black Rose pulled my arm. "Let's just go before we show them who we are," she said.

"Nigga, you heard me," he replied.

I gave Black Rose her vase of flowers. My father hated that word and it wasn't allowed in our house. I grew up seeing that word as an insult. I connected my fist with his jaw, knocking him through the glass window of a shoe store. The security alarm began to blare.

"Weak ass muthafucka!" I called out to him.

"Yo, get up!" one of his friends said. He was knocked out in the display window.

"The police is coming, we need to get out of here. Leave him!" a girl said. They scattered away, leaving their friend in the window.

"We need to bounce too," Black Rose said, pulling my hand. We cut through an alley while the police sirens were getting closer.

"I'm a bad influence, huh?" Black Rose asked.

"No, you just cherish your roses."

"That's not why I grabbed her arm. She was too close to you," she replied.
I caressed her cheek. "You were jealous?" I asked.

"Yes, very jealous; I could've killed her," she replied.

"You don't have to be, Rose. I only have eyes for you."

She blushed. "Your words are so perfect that they don't seem sincere," she said.

"You just never had anyone to capture your heart the way I did. You'll get used to it. Matter of fact, close your eyes."

"Is this another surprise?" she replied.

"Just close them."

When she closed her eyes, we disappeared from the alley to a quiet place.

Deep Creek Lake...

Black Rose's heels clicked across the wooden floors inside my cabin. I had bought this house a month prior because of its closeness to the lake and huge bay windows. It was quiet and miles away from the closest town and rarely had humans snooping around. It was a perfect getaway for me and Nile and a place where I could teach him how to use his magic.

Black Rose walked around the cabin, inspecting the rooms. "I love cabins. They are always in the center of nature. You have the trees, the lake, wildlife and a peace of mind," she said, coming out of a bedroom. I sat on the windowsill in the living room admiring her. Her curvaceous body in that dress had me thinking of doing sinful things to her.

"Skip the small talk, Rose. I want to know what you are," I said.

She blew me a kiss. "How about we get cozy near the lake. We can talk there," she said.

"I see that you are stalling."

"Only because I want to make love to you first," she replied. She kicked off her heels while making her way to me. The prowess in her stride was enough to make me forget about the conversation. She cocked her leg up on the windowsill, revealing her smooth, fat mound. Black Rose was laying it on me thick when all I wanted was for her to let me in her head. The flower and fruity scent seeping from her pussy was hypnotizing.

"My pussy has been throbbing all night while sitting across from you and you think I just want to talk. Don't be selfish, Akea," she said. She rubbed her center, drenching her fingers with her nectar. I brought her wet fingers to my lips, hungrily tasting her essence. My erection burst the seam of my pants; Black Rose seductively licked her lips at my girth. "Damn," she mumbled.

She reached in to kiss me, but I stopped her. She jerked her neck back. "Do you not feel how wet I am?" she asked.

I grabbed her waist. "Yeah, but I need to know what's up with you."

She climbed off my lap. "Come on, let's sit by the lake. Do you have anything comfortable I can slide into?" she replied.

"I have a few shirts in the master bedroom closet."

She undressed, tossing her dress on the coffee table before walking into the bedroom. Seconds later, Black Rose came back into the living room wearing one of my black button-up shirts. She left the top three buttons undone, exposing her round breasts.

"Lead the way," she said.

We walked out of the cabin then down the hill towards the lake. I sat next to a tree and she sat between my legs. With her legs stretched out, they didn't go past my knees. She put my arms around her while we sat in silence for a minute, listening to the sound of the waves in the lake.

"You don't know how much I appreciate this moment with you but you want me to ruin it by revealing myself to you," she said, breaking the silence.

I wrapped my arms tightly around her to make her comfortable. She let out a deep sigh. "I'm an elf from a magical forest who was cursed by a warlock while inside my mother's womb. So for a thousand years, since I could remember, I have helped my father's clan hunt down anyone who was affiliated with the man who cursed me," she said.

"Let me guess, you had some kind of resentment towards me because I'm a warlock too?" I asked, thinking back to the times Black Rose had given me the cold shoulder.

"Yes, I wanted to hate you but once I realized you gave me a purpose to open my heart, I let my guard down," she said.

"What kind of curse did the warlock cast on you? Maybe I can reverse it."

She shrugged. "I don't know what it's called, but I do know I'm different from the others of my kind. It's like I have to kill to live. I hate the thing that I am," she said.

She put her hands over her face before bursting into tears. "I just want to be normal instead of harboring this dark cloud over my head," she said. I turned her around to face me and noticed her skin was the color of granite, sparkling underneath the moonlight. Her symbols appeared on her skin with a silver glow. I pried her hands away from her face, so she could look at me. Her pointed ears glowed at the tips and I thought it was the sexiest thing known to man. I caressed her cheek, swiping a tear away with my thumb.

"Don't worry about shit else from here on out. All you have to do is stick beside me and let me love you hard enough to the point where you'll fall in love with yourself too."

"I'll try," she said with a half-smile.

"Do you know a goddess named Lyira? I saw her in my dreams and she was pregnant. Tonight at dinner when you ordered the rabbit stew, it made me think of her because she likes rabbit too. I think you and her must be connected. There wouldn't be any other reason why I would see her in my dreams."

"What did she look like? Maybe she's my real mother because I have no connection to my parents, especially my mother," she replied.

"The sunlight was blocking her face but she has the same figure as you. When I saw her, I felt a connection as if I knew her."

"What if it was just a dream?" she asked.

"My dreams are mainly connected to the past and future. What I saw was real, and the atmosphere was even more real. I saw a man with her, I think he was her mate. Maybe you can ask your father about Lyira."

"Me and him aren't on good terms. I exiled myself from the clan to build a new life. But since we're laying everything on the table, how close are you and Sheldon?" she asked.

"Sheldon? Who the fuck is that?"

"He's a warlock that is protected by your father," she replied.

"I don't know him. Never heard of him, but what's up with him?"

"He's the last of the Amstid Clan that has to die for what they did to my people. I thought you and him were working together to distract me since he's protected by your father. You came off as too good to be true, so I thought you had bad intentions," she replied.

"I can't picture my father protecting a man that's connected to black magic, but I'll find out the true story so don't worry."

Black Rose put her arms around my neck when she straddled me. I gripped a handful of her ass cheeks and she moaned against my lips. "I have a surprise for you," she said.

I kissed the nape of her neck. "Let me see."

"Count to a hundred before you come into the cabin. Don't come a second early or late," she said.

"A hundred is too long. Why can't you surprise me right here since you are already sitting on it," I replied, referring to my erection. She playfully pinched my hand.

"Don't ruin my flow so count to one hundred as soon as I disappear," she said. She vanished off my lap and I immediately began counting. When I got to the eighties, I started walking towards the cabin.

Ninety-one...ninety-two...

I walked up the stairs to the porch; the front door came ajar once I counted to one-hundred. The cabin was no longer there; I was inside a black forest. A rose scented black butterfly sprinkled a glittery dust on my nose. Instantly, I was feeling aroused like someone pumped Viagra into my veins.

She shouldn't have given me that stimulant. Now, I'm going to spend hours inside of her.

I walked deeper into the forest and a midnight-colored unicorn with a gold horn appeared in front of me. I have seen a lot being an immortal, but I never expected to see a real unicorn. It was twice the size of a Shire horse which was the largest horse breed. The mane was decorated in black roses. The unicorn kneeled so I could climb on its back. After I climbed on, the unicorn galloped through the forest.

"Slow down!" I shouted. A tree branch almost knocked me off the horse. Wings burst out of the unicorn's back after it leapt over a tree log. My stomach was still full from dinner and I was having motion sickness.

"Whoaaaa! Shit!" I yelled when it twirled in the air like a flying spear. I heard giggling echoing in the forest, it was Black Rose laughing at me. Moments later, the mystical creature landed in a black rose garden. In the center of the garden was a rose bed. I jumped off the animal's back; the unicorn faded away. Black Rose appeared in front of me naked.

"Are you hurt?" she asked, snickering.

I picked her up and she wrapped her legs around me. "You got a kick out of that, huh?"

"Not really, but you were damn sure loud. You said you wanted to see my magic, so here it is. I can't open portals, but I can create illusions as if they are real. We're still inside the cabin," she said.

I laid across the rose bed with her legs still wrapped around me. My dick was oozing pre-cum from her bare center being on my shaft. She ripped my clothes off, even my boxers.

She traced my lips with her finger. "Do you mind if I have all of the control?" she asked.

"Go ahead, Rose. Don't spare me."

I felt something wrapping around my legs and arms, it was vines strapping me down to the bed. My adrenaline was pumping and every drop of blood in my body shot to the tip of my dick, causing the head to swell twice its size. Black Rose slid down the length of my body; she wrapped both hands around my shaft before slurping the head of my dick.

"Fuckkk," I groaned when she wrapped her warm mouth around my shaft. She brought me to the back of her throat like a vacuum. I thought I died and my spirit went to the afterlife. She literally took my breath away when she made my dick disappear. I couldn't grip her hair to control her head movements like I wanted to.

"Ummmm," she hummed, sliding her wet mouth up and down my girth. Counter clockwise, she jerked me off with both of her hands. My dick was throbbing uncontrollably as I was on the verge of exploding. I held my breath to avoid coming too soon. She placed her hand between her legs, pleasuring herself while pleasuring me. I was jealous listening to the wet sounds of her golden lake splashing everywhere but on my tongue—I wanted to taste her.

She released my shaft. "Akeaaa, babyyy," she cooed while toying with her clit with one hand and jerking me off with the other.

"FUCKKKK," I groaned.

Cum was drizzling alongside my shaft after I came. She curved her tongue upwards, like a soup spoon and caught my spilled seeds. I exhaled deeply, pissed that I had come too soon, but I was still heavily aroused with my dick standing at ovation. Black Rose climbed on top of me with my manhood still in her hand.

"Sssssssss," she hissed when she placed her wet mound on my shaft. She tensed when I thrust my head at her tight entrance, bulldozing my way in her pussy. Her nails scratched my chest drawing blood, but it didn't stop me from stretching her walls.

"Ride this shit, Rose. I'm too hard for the patience you need."

"Don't size me up, Akea. Once I adjust, you'll be sucking your thumb afterwards," she warned. She placed her feet onto the bed in a squatting position. I was ready to bust again when she slowly rose her body to the tip of my shaft then wined down while twirling her hips. She sat still for a second, letting her pussy cream on my testicles before she repeated her hip movement. Her nipples were aimed at me like missiles and her breast had swelled. My dick print was in her abdomen, she was taking every inch of me as she promised. She aggressively put her hand around my neck, digging her nails into my flesh. Her sharp canine teeth sank into my bottom lip. The vines tightened around my limbs, keeping me restrained as Black Rose fucked me harder while her pussy clamped around my dick again.

"ARGHHHHH!" I jerked while shooting my seeds into Black Rose's womb. My dick was still hard. I didn't think there would be anything left. Her body trembled and her eyes rolled upwards from climaxing. I promised her that I would let her take control but I couldn't. Sex wasn't just about orgasms, it was like art. Anyone could have sex, but to understand the person's body was a skill. My eyes beamed, causing Black Rose to look away. Black Rose was startled when a pair of hands grabbed her breasts from behind. She looked over her shoulder in shock when she realized the extra person was a clone.

"What is this, Akea?" she asked but I knew she was more aroused by the way her pussy flooded my lower abdomen.

"You tied me up so how else can I please you? Your breasts are dying to be suckled."

My clone toyed with her nipples and kissed on her neck while she continued to ride me. She slowed down her rhythm, seductively rotating her hips. I stirred my dick while thrusting upwards, jabbing her G-spot. The clone hungrily stuffed her breast into his mouth; a tear slid out the corner of her eye. When the clone sucked harder on her nipple, I jabbed at her G-spot until she screamed out in pleasure.

"I'M CUMMMINGGGGG!" she screamed. The clone picked her up underneath her legs, pile driving her onto my dick. Her pussy exploded as she cried out.

"I LOVE YOUUUUUU!" she whimpered.

I wasn't sure if the sex had her confused or if she fell for me the same way I fell for her. Since I wasn't sure, I pretended not to hear it. Her essence poured out of her; she couldn't stop squirting.

"GRRRRR! ARGHHHHHH!" I growled. I busted a heavy load inside her, causing her lower stomach to slightly swell. She collapsed on my chest after the clone dissolved into what looked like ashes. The vines faded away too, freeing my arms and legs. Black Rose was breathing heavily on my sweaty and scratched up chest. I was feeling sticky from laying in our love juice. The forest background was gone and I realized we were on the bed inside the master bedroom.

"I hate to break up the moment but I feel like I'm coated in molasses."

Black Rose lazily lifted her head up while I ran my fingers through her wild mane. "You cheated," she said.

"How? I remained strapped to the bed."

She playfully smacked my chest. "It was my moment to shine and you just had to pull out your tricks," she replied. She climbed out of the bed with wobbly legs.

I sat up. "Where are you going?"

"To turn your jacuzzi into a garden pond so get up. You owe her some tongue action," she said, pointing to her pussy.

"Hell no, Rose. I flooded your womb with tiny Akeas. I'm not tasting my own seeds."

"That's why we're going to soak in flowers and herbs," she said. She left the bedroom with her meaty ass cheeks bouncing. I got out of the bed to follow her to the bathroom. She was twirling a rose shaped wand inside the jacuzzi until it resembled a pond with clear water.

"Is that honeysuckle?" I asked, trying to identify the different flowers.

"Yes, and we have chamomile, wormwood and mugwort," she replied.

She stepped into the jacuzzi and I joined her. My skin began tingling but in a therapeutic way like my body was detoxing. I sat across from her and watched her, putting the flowers in her hair. She hummed a melody that I'd heard before, matter of fact it was the same melody as Lyira's.

"You make me nervous when you stare at me like that," she said.

"I told you why I stare at you."

She came over to me, sitting on my lap. She picked up a plant leaf out of the water then mashed it up in her hands. After she made the paste, she massaged it into my shoulders. I was ready to doze off when she cracked my shoulder bone. She burst out laughing. "You have fragile bones like a baby," she joked.

"You are in no position to be making age jokes when you are the height of a child."

She laughed harder. "Oh fuck you," she said.

She turned around, with her back facing me. "Here," she said, handing me what was left of the paste. I moved her hair out of the way to massage her shoulders. Suddenly, I was getting lightheaded. I could feel my body falling against hers.

"Are you going to sleep on me?" Black Rose asked, but it sounded like an echo. Next, my eyes closed and I drifted off into another place...

Black Rose was standing on the edge of a cliff and there was a fire below. The smoke was burning my eyes and clogging my lungs. The train of her dress caught on fire.

"Rose!" I called out to her. She took a step closer to the edge; she was preparing to jump into the fire. I was about to run to her, but someone grabbed my arm. It was my son's mother, Jetti.

"Let her go, Akea. She has caused many deaths! What about Nile? Is her life more important than being there for your son? He needs his father! That evil creature will never be good for you! Why are you willing to risk everything to be with her?" Jetti cried.

Black Rose turned around and I noticed the fire was spreading up her dress. "This time, I don't want you catching me. Jetti is right, Akea. Your son needs you," she said.

"Do us a favor and die already!" Jetti yelled at her. I pushed Jetti to the ground to go to Black Rose. She got closer to the edge of the cliff once I was within arm's reach.

"Get out of here before you get hurt," she said.

"I thought we were happy, Rose? Why would you do this bullshit to us?"

"You were happy, but I was dying inside. I'm grateful for the moments we shared together, but I would rather die like this than to hurt you. You deserve a world that brings you nothing but joy. My world is filled with darkness so please let me go," she cried.

Tears fell from my eyes too because she was speaking nonsense. I thought we beat the odds, but seeing her give up broke me down. Black Rose was killing my spirit.

"If you leave me, I'll hate you for the rest of my life. This is betrayal, Rose!" I yelled at her.

"I rather you hate me, it'll force you to let me go!" she yelled back.

"I'm here for you, Akea! I'm the better half! Me, you and Nile can live happily but you have to let that evil bitch burn! She deserves every bit of pain she's going through," Jetti said.

"SHUT THE FUCK UP!" I shouted at her.

"Goodbye Akea," Black Rose said.

She fell into the fire and I rushed to the edge of the cliff that was collapsing. The fire coming through the cracks of the ground burned me but I didn't care.

"ROSEEEEE!" I shouted out to her but she was gone...

"AKEA! WAKE UP!" Black Rose yelled while slapping my face. I hurriedly sat up, frantically looking around. We were still in the jacuzzi at my cabin. Even though it was just a premonition, I could still smell the fire and feel the invisible burns on my skin.

"You are burning up. What happened? You were screaming my name and reaching over the jacuzzi," she said. I got out of the jacuzzi, grabbing a towel off the shelf.

"Are you ignoring me?" she asked.

I walked out of the bathroom, I needed to cool off while my mind was racing. That fear of putting my feelings on the front line to get the short-end of the stick was tormenting me. Love brought bad luck into my life. How could I get Black Rose to open up to me when I had issues of my own? She appeared in front of me, blocking the doorway of the master bedroom.

She pointed her finger in my face. "Don't piss me off! I asked you a question and I want an answer," she said.

"I don't need to answer you, Rose, and you are blocking my way as if I can't walk through you."

She rolled her eyes while stepping to the side so I could enter the bedroom. I sat on the chaise in the corner of the bedroom near the window. My skin was burning up so I opened the window, letting the breeze from the lake come inside.

"Just let me cool off for a second."

She sat on the bed across from me. "You can't unlock a door to my heart then shut me out when I'm concerned about you. It makes me feel like it was pointless to open up to you," she said.

"I have issues, Rose. When I get close to someone, I start having visions of them leaving me. I have a dark past too…a very dark past," I shamefully admitted.

"What happened to you?" she asked.

"It's embarrassing as fuck to admit but I was at my lowest point."

"Tell me so we can fix each other starting now," she replied.

"Three months ago, I killed myself."

Black Rose chuckled. " Are you fucking with me right now?" she replied.

"No, I'm dead ass serious so just hear me out. I grew up suffering from depression and it caused me to isolate myself from the world, including my family. I hated being a warlock because I was different from everyone else in my father's pack. It drove me crazy, especially since I grew up with a twin who was a werewolf. The pack would go out hunting while I stayed behind reading the spell books my father gave me. Less than six months ago, I fell for a woman named Chancy who was a member of the wolf pack too."

Black Rose rolled her eyes and crossed her arms. "I guess there was a bitch you were in love with before me," she said with an attitude.

"Just chill out and let me finish."

"Go ahead and finish because I'm curious to know why you 'killed yourself' over a woman," she replied.

"She left me after she found out I cheated on her and got another woman named Jetti pregnant."

Black Rose's mouth dropped in shock. "What the fuck! I see that you are very fruitful giving your seeds away," she sarcastically said.

"I know it's a crazy story, but that depression I had from my youth came back ten times worse. I cheated because I had visions of her being with another man, a man that was a werewolf. Every time I thought me and her were on good terms, the visions came. When she took our daughter away from me, I couldn't take the pain anymore. I drank a potion to numb the pain, but it ended up killing me. My spirit went to the world of the afterlife and that's when the truth about me and Chancy came out."

"Wait, the world of the afterlife?" she asked.

"Yes, the afterlife. Going to that place made me a better man, it was just fucked up how much it took for me to see that I wasn't the problem."

"How when you couldn't keep your dick in your pants?" she replied.

"My triplet's spirit has been living in me since I was born. My father committed a sin so the gods figured he wasn't worthy of three sons. He died in my mother's womb and his spirit latched on to me. Anyway, the brother living inside of me was a werewolf and when I died, he was released. The gods thought I wasn't worthy of my life because I tried to commit suicide so me and him traded places. I spent days in the temple of the afterlife while he found his mate. He now lives in another relm with our parents."

Black Rose gasped, holding her chest. "Noooo, Akea. Don't tell me his mate was Chancy all along," she said.

"Yeah and Destiny was his daughter. It was his spirit that impregnated her when he possessed me. While I was in the temple of the afterlife, I found my purpose and was willing to accept the fate of me being dead, but I was released from that world with a second chance and became the man I was supposed to be. I told myself that love was no longer on my agenda. Shit, I was done with it after I got attached to a woman who was destined for someone else. Right after I took Nile from his mother, I had my new life figured out but then I met you. I know it was fate, but I'm bothered by the thought of you leaving me too."

"I won't leave you," she said. Black Rose sat on my lap and rested against my chest.

"I keep having these visions of you jumping into a fire. It doesn't show me why but all I know is that you gave up."

"What did I have on? Was I casket sharp as the humans say?" she asked.

I pushed her head away from my chest. "How can you joke about my pain?" I chuckled.

"I'm just asking because I wear vintage ass dresses that are worth a lot of money and I'm not jumping into a fire wearing my nice clothes."

"You had on a black dress with a fanned out train. It did look expensive but that's beside the point. All jokes aside, I'll feel let down if you choose death before me."

"I promise I won't but just know, I'm glad Chance or Chancy, whatever her name is, found her real soulmate. That bitch was stepping on my toes and didn't even know it," she replied. I cracked up while Black Rose mugged me. Her jealousy was adorable.

She climbed off my lap. "And you think I'm going to die and leave this beautiful man single? I'll be haunting you for the rest of your life if you give your pureness to someone else," she replied. I stood from the chair dropping my towel on the floor. She knew what I wanted without me asking. She climbed onto the bed and gripped the sheets with her back arched. My dick jumped when she spread her pussy lips, revealing the pink folds. She was already soaking wet with her essence sliding down her inner-thigh.

I'm one lucky ass muthafucka!

I grabbed a fist full of her hair; she moaned when I slapped her ass.

"Babyyyyy," she moaned when I put the head of my shaft in her flower. I took my frustration from that vision out on her pussy. Black Rose knew what she was doing when my name magically etched across her back in bold letters. She was marking herself as mine. I almost slipped and told her I loved her too, but I still felt it was too soon.

I'm sorry Grandma but I'm not going to stop seeing this beautiful creature. She is mine and I am hers.

Dyika

A week later...

"Jetti!" Baneet knocked on the pool house door and I almost dropped the potion I was drinking with Jetti's DNA.

"Hold on! I'm not dressed yet!" I said, waiting for the potion to kick in. I could hear Nile on the other side crying because it was time to be fed.

"We're werewolves, we see each other naked all the time," she said. I looked in the mirror and the results from the potion had kicked in, turning me into Jetti. Baneet knocked again, pissing me off because she was annoying. Nobody in their pack was likable, especially Monifa, the alpha's mate. Jetti really left a nasty impression on everyone and if I wanted to be a part of their clan, I had to clean it up. I had always wanted to be a mother, since the opportunity was stolen from me. Jetti's stupidity had her believing I was going to sacrifice the grandchild of a god just to break a spell that couldn't be broken. Like the saying went "never trust a witch" and when it was all said and done, I planned on permanently living as her.

I opened the door, letting Baneet into the pool house. She was wearing an expensive silk kimono and she had diamond bangles around her wrist and feet. She was on the thick side and had strong Native American features. From what I had learned about her, her mother was from a Native American tribe. She was a gorgeous girl, but too nosey for my liking.

"Are you okay?" she asked.

"Yes, I'm fine. I was taking a nap," I lied.

I took Nile from her so that I could breastfeed him. Baneet sat on the couch and I sat across from her. Akea was serious about not leaving me alone with Nile so either Baneet or Fiti watched me when I had him. I wondered if he harbored any secret feelings for Jetti since he wasn't allowing the men from the pack to sit with me.

"Did you hear about the dinner tonight?" Baneet asked.

"What dinner?"

"Akea is bringing Keisha over. He wants the pack to meet her. I think he's serious about her because I overheard Kanye telling Monifa that Akea spends a lot of time with her at his remote cabin. I also heard that Tiko is dating her friend but I haven't learned her name yet," she replied.

"He said nothing to me about that, he doesn't tell me anything if it's not about Nile."

"I know I should mind my business but me and you have always had a mutual friendship. I saw the struggles your pack was facing so I understand why Akea was your escape plan. With that being said, you need to fight harder for him. I know you care about him," she said. Baneet had joined our pack for a little while before rejoining Kanye's pack.

"Can you help me win him back?"

"I can try but it won't be easy. Akea is a stubborn dick head at times," she replied.

"Tell me about it, but I'm going to break through to him. How does this new woman look?"

"She's gorgeous from what I've seen. She's the one who brought him home the day he took Nile from you. They instantly hit it off and I think it's because she's a witch. Between me and you, Naobi doesn't approve of her so you might want to use that to your advantage," she replied.

"I'll keep that in mind. Maybe you should invite Naobi over for dinner."

"She and her mate are in Africa on a trip, but she'll be back in a week," she replied.

After I breastfed Nile, I patted his back so he could burp. He was the perfect baby and I wanted to protect him from the unfit Jettis and evil Black Roses of the world. That crazy monster Black Rose had cursed my womb, causing me to lose the only thing I had left of my husband, our unborn child. I would never forget the day she killed my husband in front of me. Those images played in my head every time I closed my eyes. Akea and Nile were the perfect duo to get back what I lost and hopefully it could mend my broken heart.

"We need to go shopping. I want you to look up to par when you meet Keisha. I'm not saying you look bad, but your clothes and shoes are outdated. The least you could do is use Akea's black card and splurge on yourself," she said.

This bitch here is lucky I don't rip her face apart!

"I'll keep that in mind but I want to prove to Akea that I don't need his money. I'm here for my family, not the lifestyle."

"Well, I'll go shopping for you once Fiti gets here. What are you? A size eight?" she asked.

"I think so, but I'll settle for a nice dress."

Baneet clapped her hands in excitement. "I can't wait to get you dolled up. Maybe we can braid your hair. I think Akea loves braids," she said.

"Is that how Keisha wears her hair?"

"From what I saw she has long thick braids and she looks gothic. You know the people that wear black lipstick and heavy eyeliner? So maybe we can put you in a nice black dress, killer stilettos and braid your hair," she said.

"Akea doesn't take me as the type that likes gothic looking women."

"Opposites attract," she replied.

I heard Akea's voice outside of the pool house, it sounded like he was talking to his brother. He sounded so happy which was unusual. Seconds later, he knocked on the door before coming in. I couldn't help but to admire the beauty of him. He was masculine of course, but it wasn't overboard. A lot of immortal men were over the top, especially when they wanted to prove their strength to others. Akea wasn't like that, he was magical but in a quiet way. He reminded me so much of my husband that I wanted to give my body to him. Unlike Jetti, I was going to get what I wanted.

"You can leave," Akea said to Baneet.

Baneet smacked her teeth. "Why? We're having girl talk," Baneet replied.

"She's not supposed to be comfortable here. She's only here to be a mother, not a family member or a friend," he said to her. Baneet stood from the couch with her hands on her hip.
. "She's like family whether you like it or not," she replied.

"Unfortunately she's not because once me and my woman have offspring together, all of this is a wrap. Nile can't stay on breastmilk forever so that family bullshit doesn't apply to us," he said.

"Wait, you got your new girlfriend pregnant already?" Baneet asked.

This won't be good if she is!

"Not yet but that time will eventually come," he replied.

"Can you not talk like that around me? Where is the respect?" I asked.

"I'm an honest man, Jetti. At least you have a heads up so you can deal with Nile having a stepmother," he replied. Baneet covered her mouth. Even I was shocked at his bluntness.

"Naobi won't approve of that," Baneet said.

"I'm a grown ass man, Baneet. My brother approves of it and he's the leader of this pack so that's what matters," he replied. Akea took Nile out of my arms. I caught a whiff of a fruity garden scent oozing out of his pores.

"Were you just with her and you have the nerve to put her scent on Nile?" I asked him. I wasn't necessarily jealous, but the way I saw it, Nile was my son and another woman's scent on him was disrespectful. It was Akea's day off from the jewelry store, but he hadn't been home all morning. It was four o'clock in the afternoon so he had been away for hours. He was dressed casually which meant he didn't take her to a fancy restaurant. He was wearing a sweatsuit and tennis shoes so I assumed he had spent all day at his cabin fucking her.

"Don't worry, I won't kiss him," Akea said, implying his mouth had been on her.

"Whew, this is oddly intense so I'm going to head out. Stay strong, Jetti," Baneet said. She rushed out of the pool house, closing the door behind her. Akea sat across from me while rocking Nile. Because of his gray sweatpants, I caught a glimpse of his huge dick print. He was the only warlock I knew that was hung like a werewolf. I couldn't deny the sex appeal.

"Can we go for a walk to get some air? I've been cooped up in this pool house for a week."

"Yeah, we can. I'll be outside while you get dressed," he said. I took off the bath robe I wore around the pool house to get dressed in jeans, a T-shirt and a pair of tennis shoes.

I rushed out of the pool house. "I'm ready!" I said in excitement. My smile was quickly replaced with a frown when I saw Monifa standing next to Akea with her babies in a carriage. She was on the thicker side too with dark brown skin and long dreadlocks that came down her back. She was also fashionable like Baneet, wearing cute, ripped jeans and a loose, tan, boho top with flat shoes. I noticed the wedding ring on her hand; the pack was very modern and didn't practice old fashioned living.

"I didn't know she was joining us," I told Akea.

"The babies always go for a walk together. Even though they are young, they can sense each other already and when they get older, they'll never be separated," Monifa said. Akea laid Nile in the carriage between Monifa's twins.

"I didn't mean it like that," I replied. I looked at Akea so he could cosign for me and get me out of the awkward situation but he didn't bat an eye.

"I'll be right back. Kanye needs help with the books," Akea said.

"I didn't hear him call you," I replied. There was no way in hell I wanted to be left alone with the evil bitch Monifa.

"We communicate telepathically. I thought you knew that," Akea said.

"You are right, I just didn't want you to leave," I replied, playing it off.

Akea walked away, leaving me with Monifa, who was mean mugging me. A smirk appeared across her face with a chuckle as if she were making jokes about me in her head. She pushed the carriage and I walked beside her. "It's a lovely day isn't it?" I asked to make small talk.
"Yes, it is," she replied.

We walked over a small wooden bridge and the scenery was breathtaking. Their landscape was radiant with healthy green grass and bright flowers. With each day I spent at the castle, I somewhat understood Jetti's greed. Their world was stress free, I even found myself a little jealous because they could live openly. My clan had been in hiding for so long, we hadn't experienced the modern world yet. Monifa sat on a bench underneath a cherry blossom tree; I sat at the end of the bench. Zaan and Fiti were walking through the garden holding hands. He kissed her on the cheek and playfully grabbed her ass. Every person in the pack had a mate and I had a chance to see their love for another. A tear escaped my eye while thinking of Ryul.

"What's the matter with you?" Fiti asked me.

"I enjoy watching people in love," I replied.

"Awww one day you'll find someone who cherishes you," she said. I wished she was on my side as much as Baneet was when it came to Akea. Fiti only sided with me when it came to being a present mother.

"That's only if Akea doesn't forgive me," I replied.

"Honey, Akea is in love and in case you haven't noticed, he's been floating through the house like someone put a love spell on him. You might want to start looking for a new boo now," Monifa said.

"I'll see you when you come into the house. I'm about to see what the fellas are up to," Zaan said to Fiti. He kissed her cheek before he walked away. Fiti fanned herself while blushing.

"I think I'm ready," Fiti said.

"Ready to smoke a blunt? Zaan has turned you into a pothead," Monifa laughed.

"Zaan told me that a couple that blows herbs together, stays together so I plan on smoking every time he does. But I'm talking about having a baby, I think I'm ready. We've talked about it and he's ready too," Fiti said.

These selfish women talk freely about birthing offspring as if everyone else has the gift to!

"Yayyyyy, let's fill the house up with our offspring. This land is too big for just the ten of us. Hopefully Zaan was sober when y'all had that conversation. You know he has his off moments," Monifa said.

"You know what, you are absolutely right. We talked about it after we smoked," she said.

"Speaking of babies, where is your daughter?" Monifa asked me.

"With my old pack," I replied.

"Typical Jetti. Leave her baby somewhere else so she can forget about her old life. Why is Nile more important than your other child? Last time I checked, your daughter's father was your actual mate. Why not love that child the same?" Monifa asked.

That selfish Jetti!

I jumped off the bench. "Why is that your business? Matter of fact, what is your fucking problem with me? You seem more angry with me than the man I share a child with! Get off my ass!" I yelled at her.

"I'm never going to let up on you, Jetti. I don't trust you and I have a feeling you are still up to no good. What mother leaves her baby behind to a wolf pack that can't take care of her? I hate that we all know Nile is a goddamn meal ticket but because he's a part of us, we have to accept you. And don't raise your voice at me again because I'll drag your ass through hell and back," Monifa replied. Her pupils changed to pitch black so I knew she meant business. She was a witch and werewolf hybrid, there was no way I could defeat her as Jetti. Only if she knew I was an ancient witch that had plenty of magic tricks up my sleeve.

"We should calm down," Fiti said.

"Yeah, you are right," Monifa replied.

"I apologize for yelling at you, but you don't know what I went through so don't cast judgment on my situation," I said. Monifa stood from the bench. "There's something else up with you. I can't put my finger on it just yet, but eventually I will and when I do, nobody can stop me from killing you," she said.

She pushed the carriage away with Nile still inside and I went the separate way, heading back to the pool house. That Monifa bitch had another thing coming if she threatened me again. Akea was walking down the walkway towards the pool house. I rolled my eyes at him because he was a coward. Monifa talked to me any kind of way because he allowed it.

"We need to talk...NOW!" I told him.

I opened the pool house door, leaving it ajar for Akea. There was a liquor cabinet near the bed. I opened the cabinet door in desperate need of a drink. I found a half empty bottle of weed infused vodka with Zaan's weed label on it. Akea snatched the bottle out of my hand after I put it towards my lips.

"You can't have this while breastfeeding, what the hell is wrong with you?" he asked.

"I'm sick of this!" I yelled.

"You might want to bring your voice down while talking to me. I'm not a child," he calmly replied.

"Monifa is always fucking with me!" I flipped over the couch in anger.

Akea sat on my bed and watched me vent about Monifa's snide remarks towards my past. I was slowly but surely becoming Jetti because of how much potion I had consumed. Akea resisting me was breaking my heart when at first, I felt nothing for him. Now here I was yelling at him because he couldn't stick up for me. I was losing myself because I had sacrificed my life to be a mother.

"Can you just calm down?" Akea asked. His tone was so soothing that I wanted to cry. Finally, he sounded sincere and understood the pain I was in as an unwanted guest. He grabbed my hand, pulling me on the bed next to him so I could sit down.

"I'll talk to her, but I can't make her respect you," he said.

"Your father is a god; shouldn't gods believe in forgiveness? Did he not teach you that people make mistakes? I'm practically begging you to forgive me."

Akea wiped the tear away from my eye. "I don't hate you, I just don't trust you. I'm over the situation and I look at Nile as a blessing so I do thank you for that. But you'd feel better if you didn't have feelings for me. I don't want you to like me, Jetti, but I can respect you a little more," he said.

"By not coming around me smelling like another woman I hope."

"I can't help that her scent is always on me and I'm not trying to hide it either," he said.

"What's the difference between me and her?"

Akea brushed his hand down his waves, I could tell he was getting annoyed with me. Still, I was wondering why he didn't love the mother of his child, despite her flaws.

"I fell in love with her at first sight but you were just a quick moment of passion. I can't even remember how your pussy felt, your facial expression while I was inside you or that tingling feeling people get when their souls connect through intimacy," he said.

Jetti must have a lousy twat! How in the hell can he not remember the details? She looks like a selfish lover anyway. Ugh, I'm disgusted to even have her pussy. I have to fix this and make him enjoy it!

"Fair enough, I'll back off for now."

Akea stood from the bed. "I'll be back, get some rest. You look flustered," he said. He walked out of the pool house; I stripped down naked before getting underneath the covers. Jetti had the most worthless and meaningless life that anyone could ever have. It was going to take more work than I thought to be by Nile's side forever.

****

"Turn around for me, let me see the front," Baneet said. I turned around, modeling the dress for her. She had gone shopping for me, and bought me a ridiculous amount of expensive clothes and shoes that I didn't ask for. I was wearing a short, black, mesh dress with ruffles. It revealed more skin than I was used to showing. Baneet had put braids in my hair along with gold braid accessories. It wasn't my style and the stiletto heels I was wearing were too high.

"You look fabulous," she said.

"I feel naked," I replied, pulling the dress down.

"That's a good thing," she said.

"So why aren't you showing much skin?"

Baneet was wearing an off-white, calf-length, dress that contoured to her body and had a cut out in the middle of her back, showing off her tribal markings.

"Jasiah won't approve of that," she said, referring to her boyfriend.

Baneet looked at the clock on the wall. "She should be here in ten minutes so let's go," she said. She pulled my arm, almost causing me to slip on the floor. "Be careful, Baneet! These shoes are too high!" I said, when she snatched me out of the door. The walk from the pool house to the castle was pretty far, my feet were starting to ache.

"You have on flats yet I'm dressed as one of those women who offers sex services at night."

"A prostitute?" Baneet asked.

"I'm not sure, but I think I should go back and put on clothes."

She smacked her teeth. "And hide this terrific body? Don't you want to make his woman jealous? She'll be on pins and needles once she finds out that Akea has a hot baby mama staying on the property. Trust me, even if he doesn't notice you, she will and it'll cause friction between them," she replied.

Moments later, we entered the castle through a side door. There were twenty humans inside the house, catering trays of raw meat. Akea was standing in the hallway, directing the people where to set the trays. As usual, he looked handsome in a collar shirt, pants and loafers. His diamond frame glasses gave him a different sex appeal. I couldn't take my eyes off him. Baneet nudged me. "Girl, stop drooling and play it cool. Akea isn't that sexy," she said.

"FYI, I was staring at the meat. It looks so fresh," I lied.

Tiko approached Akea. They were talking amongst themselves and whatever it was, had Akea smiling. I wondered if they were talking about the women they were double dating. Baneet nudged me. "Go over there," she said.

"And say?"

"Ask him where Nile is," she replied.

"He's with Monifa."

She rolled her eyes. "Duh, but he doesn't need to know you know," she replied.

I wanted him to see me, so I strutted over to them to spark a conversation and to also get Akea to notice my skimpy outfit. Tiko stopped talking when he saw me coming towards them. He was attractive too with a neatly trimmed goatee. He was also dressed in gold, silk garments and jewelry with black and red diamonds. Every man in the castle was good looking opposed to the shabby warlocks I was accustomed to. Akea's eyes roamed over my body, but I couldn't decipher if he was turned off or aroused because of his blank stare. I broke the awkward silence.

"Where is Nile?" I asked.

"Taking a nap with the twins. I thought you knew that," he replied.

"I'll go outside to see if they have arrived," Tiko said to Akea. They gave each other dap before Tiko headed towards the lobby.

"This look doesn't suit you. You used to be eccentric and fully covered, I'm trying to figure out what has changed," he said.

"I thought you were into the modern look."

"Please don't hold Nile while wearing those stripper heels. I don't want you falling while holding my son," he said. I looked back to see if Baneet was still watching because I was highly embarrassed, but she wasn't there. The bird brain had set me up yet again, putting me in a rabbit hole.

"Baneet wanted me to look presentable. I didn't have a choice but to wear this trashy outfit."

"Don't listen to Baneet, not even when she tells you how the weather is outside. She goes overboard, is extremely nosey and is always wrong," he replied. The door in the lobby was open so I could hear a car pulling up to the front of the castle. Akea looked at the clock on the wall. "Right on time," he said to himself. I followed him to the door; outside the door I could see Tiko hugging on a tall woman that looked familiar. I'd know those snake scale patterns on her head anywhere. My heart was racing and I thought I was going to be sick to my stomach. Akea walked down the stairs to greet his date. Black Rose, the evil bitch walked around her car to hug Akea. I didn't think the creature could smile.

"I missed you," she said to him. He kissed her while wrapping his arms around her. She looked so happy, so beautiful and pure. She looked like a person who hadn't tortured and slaughtered my people, causing us to hide in caves like bats.

"You saw me a few hours ago," Akea replied.

"A few hours is too long," she flirted while caressing his chin. He looked down at her with so much passion that I thought he was going to fuck her right there on top of her car. Monifa, Fiti, Zaan, Kanye, Baneet and Jasiah walked out of the study. Everyone but Baneet nonchalantly walked past me to greet Black Rose.

"Put on your game face," Baneet said.

"Your advice isn't working so let me handle my own situation. You've made me look like a headless chicken."

"A headless chicken?" she asked.

"Yes, a headless chicken also known as a circus clown or fool. Akea hates my outfit."

"He can't hate it that much if she's wearing something similar," she said. Black Rose was wearing a black leather tutu skirt with the jacket to match. Her platform heels gave her a few inches in height, and she wore it with fishnet knee high socks. I wanted to put her on blast and warn everyone about her, but then my cover would be blown. She shook everyone's hand, but Monifa went the extra mile and pulled her in for a hug.

"Don't mind me, I'm a hugger," Monifa said to her.

"I can get used to that," Black Rose sweetly replied.

"Come on," Baneet said, pulling me out of the house. I almost tripped, but she caught me.

"Calm the hell down!" I gritted.

I'm going to curse this bitch for being a nuisance!

Baneet practically shoved me into Akea after she pulled me through the small crowd.
"Hi, I'm Baneet, Akea's housemate and this is Jetti, Nile's mother," Baneet said. She held her hand out to Black Rose. Black Rose shook her hand, while looking at me and Akea. She looked to be caught off guard. That could be for two reasons; she was shocked to see Jetti. And she was shocked to see Jetti standing next to her boyfriend.

"Nice to meet you too, Baneet. This is my sister, Majestic," Black Rose replied. Majestic shook Baneet's hand while staring at me too. I wanted to hide since she knew Jetti was cursed. Her seeing me was a red flag and I had to figure out a way to convince her, I hadn't drank the potion.

"And since no one asked, I am Jetti, Nile's mother and I'm also a housemate as well," I spoke up. Black Rose shot daggers at Akea and he cleared his throat. "Housemates live in the same house, Jetti. You are temporarily living in the pool house which is a mile away from the castle," he said sternly.

"I don't know about y'all but I'm starving. I'm going inside," Kanye said. He grabbed his mate's hand, pulling her up the stairs.

"Yeah, I'm hungry too," Akea said. He grabbed Black Rose's hand and followed his brother up the steps.

"What are you in a rush for? You don't eat raw meat and your food isn't here yet," Zaan said, bursting Akea's bubble.

"Not now, Zaan," Akea gritted.

Zaan had unknowingly put Akea on the spot because he wasn't rushing in the house to eat; he only wanted to get away from me. It was clear he didn't tell Black Rose about me being on the property.

Baneet whispered in my ear. "See, she's pissed off. Akea is probably in the dog house right now. Do not let up, you have one up on her," she said. I planned on destroying her relationship with Akea to repay the demon for destroying my family. Her karma was coming back, plus more.

Black Rose

The dining room was the size of a basketball court and there was an upper level that overlooked the room. The feast table was covered with trays of raw meat, fruit and vegetables. It was supposed to be a moment to enjoy since it was my first time being introduced to Akea's brother and the rest of the pack, but Jetti was eyeing me from across the table. I knew for a fact that she drank that potion, especially since her cousin had approached me about it. What I couldn't wrap my head around was whose magic was strong enough to break my spell. I looked over at Akea who was plucking a piece of raw broccoli because his food hadn't come yet.

Did he break Jetti's curse? No, what am I thinking? He would've mentioned it to me. Should I tell him about it? Nah, I should wait it out since she probably didn't drink the potion. Did her cousin lie to me because she wanted a refund? Those damn scammers!

"So, Keisha, how old are you? Nineteen," Baneet asked. The room grew quiet, they seemed to be used to Baneet being in someone's business.

"I'm a thousand years old," I replied.

Akea's brother choked on his water and his mate patted his back. "Goddamn," he mumbled.

"Wow, you are antique," Baneet said. Jetti covered her mouth and snickered. I could tell they were close since Baneet was the only one that was talking to her. Majestic's eyes glowed; black snake skin was beginning to cover her face. She was in defense mode and ready to shift to protect me. I shook my head at her so she wouldn't ruin the dinner. I'd been insulted more times than I could count and my clan had said worse things; the little shade Baneet was throwing was cute.

"Age isn't a factor in our world," I replied.

"That is true, I'm wayyy older than Zaan, but it doesn't feel that way. Isn't it a blessing to stay twenty-one forever?" Fiti asked. She was a witch and so was Monifa. I could only imagine the look on Circa's face if he knew I was having dinner with them. It was awkward but I had to remind myself they weren't my enemy since they were a part of Akea.

"Yeah, my baby is older than me by a few hundred years. Ain't nothing wrong with having a lion," Zaan said.

"I think your slow ass means cougar, bruh," Kanye replied.

"Well, shit what's the difference? They are both feline leukemias," Zaan said.

"I think you just mean feline, bro," Akea replied.

"A feline leukemia? I've never seen that before," Fiti said.

"It's in the basement, underneath the couch. But it will only come to you if you lock yourself inside the basement with the lights off," Kanye replied.

"Really?" Fiti asked, pushing her chair away from the table.

"Yeah, take Zaan with you. He'll help you find it," Kanye replied.

"I'm always in the basement and I ain't never seen it down there," Zaan said.

"Come on, Zaan. Let's go look," Fiti said. She grabbed Zaan's hand, pulling him away from the table. The pack erupted in laughter after they left the dining room.

" They ain't coming back for two days. I bet Fiti will forget that she can teleport and stay locked inside the room," Kanye said.

"Are they ill?" Majestic asked.

"Naw, just high ranking potheads," Kanye said.

"You smoke too and act just like that sometimes so cut it out," Monifa giggled.

"I do have my moments but I always find my way back to you no matter what. Zaan got lost the other day in the library. He was high as fuck damn near in tears because he couldn't think straight," he replied. Monifa picked up her napkin to wipe off the speckle of blood that had dripped off his lips from the raw meat cube.

"Do you smoke, Keisha? We always blaze one after we eat," Kanye said.

"No, but there's a first time for everything, right?" I replied.

"How are you that old and never smoked before?" Baneet asked me. A hissing sound echoed throughout the dining room; the sound had come from Majestic.

"Chill out, Baneet," Akea said.

"I'm just saying, I find it hard to believe that someone her age has never smoked before," she replied.

"Is there ever a time where you're not a bitch? You're always on the wrong side of the fence when it comes to this pack. I thought you had changed but you are still back to your bullshit. Just be quiet!" Monifa told her.

"Oh come on, Monifa, you are only nice to Keisha because you hate Jetti. Since when have you gotten along with females outside of this pack?" Baneet asked.

"Keisha is Akea's new woman! Of course I'm going to welcome her with open arms, she's like family now," Monifa said.

"They have only been together for a week. How is she family?" Jetti asked.

"Chile, don't question me in my fucking house! You are just a guest so act like it," Monifa replied. I sipped my wine while being highly entertained. Monifa was my kind of woman, a true alpha female.

"Can you show me to the bathroom?" I asked Akea. He looked nervous but I had to speak to him in private. He should've prepared me for Jetti's drama. I was feeling attacked and it was embarrassing to have someone from his pack talk down on me. Akea got up from the table and I followed him out of the dining room. We stood in the hallway while there was still a commotion at the dinner table.

"I already know I fucked up," he said.

"Are you screwing her again?"

He grilled me. "Why would you ask me that?" he replied.

"Why didn't you tell me that she lived here? You said nothing about her and had me thinking she wasn't in the picture. I thought you were a single father, not having a live-in baby mama! Then she has her side-kick coming at me sideways! I'm warning you, I don't do well when I feel cornered."

"It honestly slipped my mind but when the time comes, the three of us will have to have that talk. I'm not hiding anything from you, Rose. It was a miscommunication on my end and it won't happen again," he said. His words were sincere, especially when he looked me in my eyes and spoke to my soul. How could I get mad at him?

"I hate that you are perfect and now I feel bad for speaking to you that way," I admitted.

"Bring your old ass here," he said, pulling me in for a hug. I playfully pushed him when he reached out to me. "Nope, stay away from my old ass body," I giggled. He hugged me anyway, landing kisses on my forehead. We'd been at it like rabbits over the past week and the slightest touch from him spiked my arousal. I broke away from him. "We need to go back inside so they won't think we're screwing around."

"Do you care about that?" he asked, kissing the nape of my neck.

"Yes, because I don't want them getting the wrong idea so soon. I can expose my wild side after they get to know me."

"Thank you for holding your composure with Baneet. Excuse my language but she can be a bitch most of the time. She's close to Jetti because she used to be in the same pack as her. Baneet was a traitor at one point but because her father and my father were like brothers, we forgave her. But the only reason she came back was because she was being used for our pack's money. So, just know a lot of her insults come from her past hurt," he said.

"We all come from a dark past but she better tread lightly before I turn her ass into a winter fur coat."

"Make sure I get a pair of nice house slippers with it," he said.

The cries from a baby came from behind the door across the hallway. "That's Nile, come on," he said. He opened the door but I didn't budge. I briefly saw Nile the first day I met Akea, but I didn't deserve to meet the young warlock as his father's lover. The thought of him becoming older and being hunted down by the elves caused me to feel guilty. Jetti rushed out of the dining room to check on her son. From where I was standing, I saw her pick up the baby; he was wrapped in a blue silk blanket. Nile stopped crying as Jetti rocked him and sang him a lullaby. I felt an emotion of sadness and grief. Being a mother was a feeling I was familiar with but I couldn't understand how. It wasn't possible when I had never had any children. Akea sensed my sadness. "Go ahead in the dining room. I'll be there," he said.

"Take your time," I replied.

"I don't trust that evil creature around our son, especially since he's a warlock," I overheard Jetti telling Akea. I stopped at the dining room door, processing what Jetti told Akea.

Does she know I'm a witch hunter? Who would have told her that? Was it someone from Sheldon's clan?

Thinking back to my run-in with Jetti's cousin, she had mentioned she joined Sheldon's clan. My mind began racing, there was a possibility that Jetti was a part of that clan too.

Maybe Jetti didn't drink the potion after Sheldon warned her about me. But why would Jetti's cousin risk her life over a potion she didn't drink?

I came up with a conclusion after thinking about Jetti, her cousin and Sheldon. I concluded that Jetti did drink the potion and someone could've been posing as her. I chuckled to myself while entering the dining room because Sheldon and his people couldn't fool me.

The pack was eating, drinking and cracking jokes. Majestic fit right in and she looked so happy and full of life. She wasn't allowed at Circa's table so it was her first feast with other people.

"We're going to the club tonight. You should come," Majestic said when I sat across from her.

"What's it called?" I replied.

"Medusa," she said.

"You'll have fun," Baneet said.

"My ass isn't too old to hang?" I replied with sarcasm.

"I apologize for that. I'll get better," she said.

Bitch please, Monifa probably threatened to kill your wanna be tough ass!

"Who is going?" I replied.

"Everyone but me and Kanye. We need the castle to ourselves," Monifa hinted. Kanye's smile widened and his eyes glowed. It was his way of blushing and I thought it was cute because Akea's eyes were the same way.

"Shit, can y'all leave now?" Kanye asked us.

"We're not finished eating and plus it's too early to go. Y'all just can't wait to do the nasty," Baneet replied.

"I'll be a happy man once I get to do the 'nasty'," Jasiah said. Baneet pinched him on the sly but I caught it.

"You are too young for that, baby brother, especially if there is a golden lake," Tiko said. I knew a lot of werewolves referenced the men in their pack as brothers, but Tiko and Jasiah were almost identical, the only difference was that Jasiah looked younger. Both of them had greenish-gray eyes with skin the color of chestnuts. Their cheekbones were also extremely high which was a look of royalty from another world.

"Well how old is he, Baneet? Are you a cougar too?" I asked her.

She rolled her eyes. "He's nineteen which is two years younger than me," she replied with an attitude.

"But what's a golden lake?" Majestic asked.

"Extremely wet pussy that can control the strongest warrior," Kanye said.
"We don't need to talk like this in front of guests," Baneet said.

"We're sexual beasts, why not? Sex is a part of our lives. I don't know why you're so stingy with it," Jasiah said. He downed another shot of whatever was inside the gold urn. He was getting drunk and Baneet was embarrassed.

"Damn it, Jasiah. That's no one else's business!" Baneet said.

"You talk about everybody's business but your own. This pack is like a family so why not tell everyone why you are wasting my time," he replied.

"Take the bottle away from him," Monifa told Tiko.

"Naw, don't do it, Tiko. Let the brother vent," Kanye said.

"I'll attack you if you say it!" Baneet yelled at Tiko.

"Akea is fittin' to be pissed off with us doing this in front of the company so maybe we should chill," Monifa said.

"Baneet still has feelings for Zaan. She called out his name while I was pleasuring her with my tongue earlier, but what really hurts is that no one told me that she and Zaan had history when I came from Anubi. It's fucking heartbreaking!" Jasiah said.

"Are feasts always this entertaining?" Majestic asked.

"No, but this pack damn sure is very entertaining," I replied.

"That's not true," Baneet shrieked.

"Are you calling me a liar?" Jasiah asked her.

"Fiti is like a sister to me. I would never cross her!" Baneet replied.

"You don't like her like that, you only tolerate her so it won't raise a red flag," Jasiah said.

"SHUT UP!" Baneet screamed at him.

"You know what, fuck you! I'm done being your rebound while you wait for Zaan to come to you," he said. Baneet shifted into a werewolf that was bigger than the typical male wolf. Her large animal knocked over the table; I caught a tray of raw rabbit meat before it hit the floor. She was a remarkable beast, with deep brown fur, red tipped ears and markings on her legs that she had inherited from her native ancestors. She growled while pouncing on Jasiah with her heavy paws. The rest of the pack jumped in to pull the huge beast off Jasiah.

"Get this crazy bitch off of me before I shift and kill her!" Jasiah yelled out.

"Get off his arm, Baneet! Jasiah's beast is still an adolescent!" Tiko shouted. Adolescent werewolves were untamable, ruthless and deadly. Dark brown and gray hairs were covering Jasiah's skin. His eyes glowed and his canine teeth extended as he howled. Blood splattered on the walls from Baneet tearing into his forearm. Akea barged into the dining room. "What the fuck is going on?" he asked. The pack was wrestling Baneet off of Jasiah.

"Baneet is trying to kill Jasiah," I responded. Monifa screamed like a banshee; the walls cracked into spider webs and the picture frames shattered on the floor. Baneet turned back into her human form, while holding her ears. "MY EARS!" Kanye shouted, holding his ears too. Monifa's screams were only affecting the werewolves' sensitive ears. They were on the floor, holding their heads. Monifa stopped screaming when Kanye fell against the wall, leaving a huge dent. The damage they were doing to their museum style castle was shameful.

"Damn, Monifa. You should've at least warned me," Kanye said. Majestic handed Baneet the table cloth to put around her naked body. I almost dropped the tray of rabbit meat when she snatched the table cloth from Majestic; she wrapped the cloth around her body before storming out of the room.

"I take full responsibility for ruining dinner so I'll clean everything up," Jasiah said to the pack. Akea massaged his temples, he was embarrassed and agitated. I grabbed his hand. "It's okay, Akea. Every family fights," I told him.

"They could've waited until your third visit," he replied.

"Are y'all still going to the club is the real concern?" Kanye asked.

"That's all you can think about at a time like this, bro?" Akea replied.

"Now, you two better not start," Monifa said to Akea and Kanye.

"I'm just saying that we need to be alone too sometimes," Kanye said.

"We'll be out of here soon as we clean up the mess," Tiko replied.

Akea picked up the fallen chairs. "Why did Baneet attack you?" he asked Jasiah.

"I called her out for still crushing on Zaan. Y'all should've told me that they shared a bed together. I didn't find out until she called me his name," Jasiah said.

"Baneet seemed happy with you so we didn't want to ruin it, but it was her job to tell you, bro," Akea replied.

"I thought I loved her," Jasiah sulked. He looked so heartbroken. Being honest was the key to a relationship but I wasn't honest with Akea. How could I tell him that I would have killed him had I not fell for him?
Tiko patted his brother's shoulder. "Next time, bite her back," he said.

Jetti came into the dining room, breastfeeding Nile. "What happened?" she asked.

"This is family business," Monifa replied.

"Aren't you going to say something, Akea? How come those two are getting more respect than me?" Jetti asked, referring to Majestic and me.

"Because they didn't come up here like they run shit," Monifa replied. Jetti was about to respond but Akea cut her off. "Don't make it worse," Akea told her. She eyed me down with her lip curled upwards in the corner. I traced my finger across my throat, threatening to slit her throat while mouthing the words "dead bitch walking."

I stood from the chair. "Babe, I'm ready for my tour of the castle. Can we stop at your bedroom first? I want to see if your bed is as comfortable as the one at your cabin," I said to Akea. He took the tray of rabbit meat from me. "Follow me," he said. Majestic nodded her head in approval when we locked eyes.

"Will you be okay down here?"

"Yes, Tiko wants to show me around too. Don't worry about me. Go ahead and enjoy your man," she replied.

I followed Akea out of the dining room. He held a piece of rabbit meat against my lips.

"I noticed you didn't eat much," he said as I chewed the meat. It was so delicious, I blushed. Akea fed me a few more pieces while we were standing in the hallway; he was always taking care of me.

"I couldn't eat because I was enjoying the jousting match."

"This ain't nothing compared to the feasts with my father and his pack brothers. It always turns into bloodshed," he replied. I picked up a rabbit's leg, holding it against Akea's lips.

"Fuck no I won't," he said.

"Just try it. You can't get sick and die from it."

He backed away. "I can't do it. The thought of eating slimy raw meat pains me," he replied. I ate the meat on the rabbit's leg, leaving nothing but the bone. Akea shook his head in disgust. "I can't stomach it," he said, walking up the stairs. I followed him, taking in the wall decorations. There were gold hieroglyphics drawn into the walls and on the railing of the stairs.

"I wonder if humans know there were black rulers in Egypt before they were displaced by the Romans and Arabs. It's good to see that the lost history still exists in your world."

"Humans are limited with their knowledge of the different worlds, but I'm not complaining. If they knew we existed, they'd be using us as army weapons," he replied. We made it to the top floor and there were statues at the end of the hallway of a man with a wolf's head. The statues were wearing heavy armor-like jewelry. I thought the jewelry store was decorated nicely but the castle held a lot of Akea's roots.

"Those statues are of my father's ancient form. He's the same height as the statues too, so what you see is identical to how he looks in his world," Akea said. I looked up at the statue; it had to be over ten feet. "He gets this big?" I replied, looking at the statue's feet.

"Yeah and he mated with my mother in this form when he impregnated her with me and my brothers," he said.

I gasped. "How did she take a man this big?"

"I heard she fainted," he chuckled.

"Your mother is the true warrior."

"Come on, I'm going to show you a picture of my parents," he replied.

We walked down the gold velvet runner, passing showcases of antique artifacts such as weapons, pharaoh jewelry, gemstone covered urns and clay vases encrypted in a language I couldn't understand. He opened a set of wooden double doors engraved with his initials. "This is my penthouse," he said. I walked into his man cave of black and red leather furniture. There was a computer monitor on the wall. "What's this?" I curiously asked.

"This is to operate my closet," he replied.

"Do you have a hidden place in the wall with superhero suits too?" I joked.

"Like Batman?" he asked.

"I think that's it. I'm not familiar with the names."

"I'm going to put this in the fridge," he replied.

He walked up the stairs to his kitchen area while I walked around his room. His bed was twice the size of my pool in my garden room. Above his fireplace was a picture of Akea and Kanye with a man and woman that could pass as their older siblings. They were all dressed in black silk garments and gold jewelry.

"Are they your parents?" I asked.

"Yeah," he replied.

"What are their names?"

He closed the fridge. "My father's name is Akua but we call him Goon. My mother's name is Kanya. They named us with names similar to theirs," he said. Akea's father was ruggedly handsome with bronze skin. His mother was a plus size woman with a wild deep brown mane and a youthful face. The picture looked recent, maybe a few years ago.

"Your father looks menacing, was he strict?"

"Yeah, he stayed on our asses. Kanye was always catching the most heat, but that's because alpha males bump heads a lot," he replied. He took off his shirt and shoes to get comfortable on the couch. "What are you doing? We haven't finished the tour."

"We'll be all night touring the house. What other room is more important than mine?" he asked.

"Jetti's room. I want to see how close she is to you."

He patted the couch so I could sit next to him. "I'm serious, Akea. You don't want me to do my own investigation."

"Do you want a magnifying glass too?" he smirked. I playfully flicked him and he vanished without warning.

"That's not funny! Stop playing games with me," I called out while scanning his place. A breeze caused my skirt to fly up, exposing my thong.

"I'm not in the mood to play games!" I lied. I was feeling giddy since the games we played with each other always lead to passionate and rough sex. I unzipped my jacket, freeing my bare breasts. Next, I took off my skirt and thong, leaving on my fishnets and heels.

"I'm feeling faint and I'm in need of someone catching me," I said aloud. The lights dimmed and the sound of waterfalls played out of the speakers from the wall. I sat on the couch, ready for Akea to pin my legs back and plunge into what he called my golden lake.

"You can show yourself now," I said. I parted my lips to pluck at my clit, preparing my center for Akea's girth. Thinking about him caused a trickle of nectar to spill onto his couch. I closed my eyes while biting my lip. "Ummm, Akea," I moaned.

"Goddamn, Rose," Akea said. I opened my eyes and he was holding a tray of food in his hands. "Don't tell me you left to get food," I said, feeling ashamed.

What if he thinks I'm crazy? Fuck it, I am crazy. I need him twenty-four-seven.

"Yeah, my brother told me the caterer for my food came. I should've warned you but I'm starving," he said. He sat the tray of food on the coffee table and it smelled atrocious. Eating seafood was like eating giant bugs.

"I didn't hear him call you."

"Our pack communicates telepathically, the same way you and Majestic do," he replied.

"How do you know me and her communicate that way?"

"Earlier, you and her were staring at each other without talking so I figured y'all were communicating," he said. He sat next to me. "I wonder why we can't communicate that way," he said.

"Probably because we're from two different worlds. Did you tell your pack the kind of creature I am? I noticed nobody thought it was odd that a 'witch' was eating raw meat."

"I only told them you come from a different world so your appetite is different. Speaking of food, should I push this to the side and please you?" he asked. I crossed my arms across my breasts. "Go ahead and eat so you can keep up. You need all the energy you can get. Did you see Majestic when you went to get your food?"

"She's in Tiko's room. Can they have offspring?" he asked.

"No and if it was possible, it would scare the shit out of me and I'm not easily scared."

"A werewolf and snake hybrid. Yeah, that sounds too out of this world. How come you never talk about offspring?" he asked.

"Because I've never been pregnant before. I'm assuming it's impossible for me to carry a child, but pregnancy for my kind is no fun anyway. Elves carry their children for twenty-four months but many die after birth because the air isn't pure and healthy from this world."

He sat his plate down. "Are you telling me your kind gives birth to two-year-olds?" he asked.

"Yes."

"Do you know how big a two-year-old is?" he replied.

"I'm aware."

"And you have to push out a walking human?" he replied.

"Our bellies will open like a flower when the child is born. But I've never seen a child born of my kind before, just heard stories."

Akea shook his head. "Your kind are warriors too," he said.

I laid across his lap and he massaged my scalp. "Can you dance?" I asked with my eyes closed. His strong hands running through my hair had me on the verge of going to sleep.

"Hell no and never tried. Can you?" he asked.

"You can't tell by the way I move my hips?" I flirted. Akea picked me up, positioning me on his lap. The butterflies were fluttering fast, causing me to quiver. "How do you expect me to eat while laying on me like this?" he asked. I kissed his buttery lips; his lips made the butter taste delightful. He grabbed my breast while we locked lips.

"What if they hear us? I'm not a quiet comer."

Akea shrugged. "We're used to it," he replied. He unzipped his pants, sliding the pants below his waist to free the one-eyed giant. "I lied to you," he said.

"About what?" I asked. My mood went from sugar to shit, thinking he was going to confess something I wasn't ready for.

"Not being here while you undressed, but I did go downstairs to get my food," he said. I pinched him and roared in laughter. "That's not funny, asshole! You had me thinking I got undressed and pleasured myself for nothing."

"I didn't think you'd fall for it so easily," he replied.

"That's because I let my guard down like you asked. What else have you lied about?"

He cupped my chin while moving my hair away from my face. "I was just kidding with you, Rose. Don't kill a brother," he said.

Someone barged into his bedroom. "I need to tell you about B..."

Jetti paused in shock from witnessing my naked body straddling Akea whose pants and boxer-briefs were pulled down. "You won't take him from me, bitch!" Jetti screamed. She leapt across the room, shifting into a dark brown werewolf with white spots. Her beast knocked me off of Akea's lap while her teeth sank into my neck. My nails sharped, slashing Jetti's face. An invisible force knocked us apart, my body soared across the room. I slid across his coffee table, knocking over the food. Jetti's beast angrily growled while pacing back and forth.

"I cannot let you two fight!" Akea said.

"Forgive me, my love, but nobody puts their hands on me!" I replied. Jetti's beast ran across the room, knocking over the couch to get to me. I pushed my legs off the table, back flipping in the air. She howled when I landed on her back, digging my nails into the neck of her beast. She fell on the floor, rolling her heavy body on top of mine. I wrapped my legs around her and sank my teeth through her flesh. She shifted back into her human form to get me off her. I rolled into a dresser, splitting it in half. I spat a chunk of her flesh onto the floor.

"BITCH!" she screamed. Both of us were naked and covered in blood.

"I'll be generous and fight you without magic," I told her.

"We need to sit down and talk about this!" Akea said, coming between us.

"SHUT UP!" Jetti and I said in unison.

We jumped over his head and our bodies collided. We fell onto his bed, cracking the head frame. Jetti pulled my hair while we wrestled. I dug my nails into her eyes and she screamed out for Akea.

"If I use my magic it'll hurt Rose. I'm sorry, Jetti, but you started it!" he said. Her anger heightened, she cocked back and slammed her fist into my face. I jabbed her in the nose, knocking her off the bed.

"How dare you choose this witch hunter over me?" she asked Akea. She got up from the floor in a daze.

"She's my soulmate, Jetti. I'm going to choose her over you every time," Akea replied.

"She's going to kill you! That's what she does, she hunts down warlocks because her stupid clan thinks everyone is responsible for their forest dying! I don't want her near my son because who knows, she could be wanting to kill him!" Jetti screamed.

"Show your real face because I know you aren't Jetti. I know that you drank that potion I made for you because your cousin came to me wanting me to re-do the spell. Unlike you, I don't need to hide who I am!"

"Hold up, what is she talking about, Rose? A witch hunter?" Akea asked.

"You question me but not her?" I replied.

"But my son is involved. Are you a witch hunter or not?" he asked.

"Yes, she is, Akea. From a clan called, Yubsari. She's the reason why the Amstid Clan is under your father's protection. She's the real enemy and just for the record, bitch, I didn't drink that potion. I gave it to someone to test because I didn't trust you. Don't believe me, Akea can check me right now!" Jetti said.

Akea plopped down on his love seat, he was stunned from the hard truth about my life. It was my chance to come clean and tell Akea about the life that I had escaped because I fell for him. "She's right, Akea. I've killed plenty of warlocks and I came to you because my clan wanted you dead. I was supposed to kill you but I couldn't."

Tears fell from my eyes and Jetti smiled. "Oh bitch, save the tears! You are a wicked creature and you plotted on Akea and my son!" she said.

"My grandmother warned me. She told me to cut you off but I couldn't. I understand you wanting to kill that other clan, but why me, Rose? You couldn't tell me that I had a target on my back? Is that why you couldn't meet Nile? Was it guilt?" he asked.

"Yes, it was guilt but I would never hurt a child. That's not me!"

"You can get out now and take that snake with you," Jetti replied. I looked at Akea and he couldn't look at me. "This is it, huh? You turn your back on me and side with that bitch that's lying about who she is?" I asked Akea.

He stood. "Go back to the pool house, Jetti," he told her.

"Why am I being kicked out when she's the traitor?" she asked.

"Because you are still a guest and should've knocked before coming into my room. You can leave and do it quietly," he told her.

"Fine!" she said.

She grabbed Akea's shirt, pulling it over her head. "Don't go to Nile, just leave the castle," Akea told her. Jetti sauntered out of his room; I couldn't wait to finish her off. My clothes were buried somewhere underneath the broken furniture, spilled food and blood. A black dress appeared over my body along with a wide brim hat and veil to hide my tears.

"Your grandmother warned you about me, huh?" I asked Akea.

"Would you trust your life around someone who wanted to kill you? I told you I didn't know Sheldon so you should've told me a week ago what it was with me and you. I wasn't in a position to fall for someone but I did and again, I get fucked over," he said.

"I left my clan for you! I killed someone just to have a way out so don't tell me shit. I'm not perfect!"

"I took Nile away from Jetti so he wouldn't be in a pack that could bring harm to him so what good am I if I allow you into my home where my son sleeps when you are a bigger threat to him? You don't have kids so you can't empathize with shit I'm saying," he replied.

"It sounds like your mind's made up so I'll see my way out."

"Yeah, let me walk you out," he replied.

That pain came back, worse than before. It shot straight to my heart, crippling me. I fell onto the floor. Blood was dripping out of my mouth and nose. "Rose, what's wrong?" Akea panicked. I coughed up blood; Akea rolled me over on my back. I wanted to tell him that love could kill me but death was how I survived. Sheldon's words echoed inside my head.

Love can be a blessing or a curse. Black Rose will pick her own medicine.

My vision became blurry while Akea was shaking me. "What's going on, Rose?" he panicked. My heart stopped beating and the last thing I heard was Akea calling out to me…

Dyika

I ran as fast as I could away from Akea's castle through the woods in Jetti's beast form. My jealousy had ruined the plan, but I couldn't take how happy that demon appeared to be with Akea. The love and lust she had in her eyes for him had to be taken away. I killed her spirit, something that I'd been wanting to do for a long time. Akea was stubborn and didn't forgive easily; he'd always distrust Black Rose for conning her way into his life.

Once I reached the stream close to Sheldon's cave, I shifted back to my human form to catch my breath. I dropped to my knees and splash water on my face to cool off from the long run. I noticed my skin tone was getting lighter; Jetti's serum was wearing off and I didn't have any left.

I came here at perfect timing.

I exploded with laughter thinking of Black Rose's tears. "I did it, Ryul. I finally hurt that bitch the way she hurt me. It felt damn good seeing her cry," I spoke aloud. I danced around, spinning and twirling underneath the moonlight.

"Victory is mine...victory is mine!" I cheerfully clapped. I stopped celebrating when I heard a cherry bush rustle.

"Show yourself!" I said.

Sheldon stepped out of the darkness with a basket of cherries he had picked from the bushes. That stupid owl was sitting on his shoulder with yellow eyes glowing at me.

"Was it worth it, Dyika?" Sheldon asked.

"What are you talking about?"

"Your week away from the cave," he replied.
"This isn't prison, Sheldon. I'm allowed to leave whenever I want to."

"That is true, but was it worth it?" he asked in a menacing tone.

"Was what worth it?"

He floated over to me. Sheldon rarely walked, he floated across the ground like he was a god. I hated being underneath his watch at times, but I knew he meant well. We had shared several nights together. I thought it would help me get over my mate, but it had made me miss him even more. Sheldon fell for me, but I turned a blind eye to it hoping he would stop caring about me.

"You must have forgotten that I keep tabs on you. What were you doing at Goon's son's castle?" he asked.

"I was helping Jetti. Her offspring has to be fed and since she's cursed, she can't be the mother she's supposed to be for her son."

"And you never thought how that would deceive the god's son that we need protection from? You are no kin to Jetti! I thought you'd be smarter than that, Dyika, but you betrayed your clan over a fantasy! You will never be the mother you want to be!" he replied.

"Instead of coming at me wrong, you need to be thanking me for ruining Black Rose. You know everything but didn't know she was sleeping with Akea so me being there was a blessing in disguise. Can't you see? The god you worship wanted me there to protect his son and grandchild from Black Rose. They needed me, especially Akea! That was fate!"

Sheldon's pupils turned dark as night; he slammed his cherry basket on the ground before grabbing the collar of my shirt. He slammed me against a tree. I wasn't one-hundred percent healed from Black Rose's attack so my body was still aching.

"AHHH!" I shrieked in pain.

"What the fuck did you do?" he asked, squeezing tighter while shaking me.

"I don't need to tell you! You aren't shit to me but a weak clan leader that had us hiding from Black Rose! Are you jealous that I hurt her and you couldn't? And the so-called wolf god should be thanking me for saving his son and grandson!"

"You didn't do anything but play a wolf in sheep's clothing. You just set us back and you need to fix it!" he replied.

"How should I fix what's already broken? Black Rose warned Akea that I'm an imposter too. He might be on to me so I can't go back!"

He dropped me on the ground. "What do you mean by being an imposter?" he asked.

"You thought I went to Akea as myself?"

"Didn't you go on Jetti's behalf as a friend?" he asked.

"I used Amstid's spell book," I admitted.

Sheldon kicked me; my ribs cracked from the impact. "You used my brother's spell book knowing that he used black magic?" he asked.

"What else was I supposed to do? I had to become Jetti in order to mother her child! I used her hair to create a potion that would give me her DNA so her child could be connected to me. I wanted to be a part of a family! Not some fucking clan that has caused me a lifetime of pain. When Jetti came to our cave, it was my chance to be free from all of you, especially you!"

"Amstid's spell book was created by a demon. My brother was a wicked man and so was Ryul. Your unborn child was taken away because of Ryul's sins. Black Rose didn't kill your child, it was Ryul. When will you understand that he wasn't pure? You are soul tied to a demon worshipper so your thoughts and actions will never be pure. I did all I could for you, I wanted to love you so you could let go of the darkness in your heart that your mate put there, but I realized that I can't save you," he replied. I fought back the tears, not wanting to believe that the Yubsari Warriors were innocent.

"Black Rose isn't innocent for what she did to Ryul. I will never believe it!"

"Black Rose was justified for what she did to Ryul and the many others she killed in the past. I can't speak on what she's doing now, but I do know they deserved it. I was there that day when Amstid and Ryul went to the elves world and it was the same day they turned into dark elves. They were normal magical creatures who lived in a beautiful world, way better than this one but we destroyed it. Amstid brainwashed Circa, filling his heart with hate. Like a coward, I sat back and watched because of the loyalty I had to my brother. You don't know shit, Dyika...NOTHING!" Sheldon yelled.

"I don't care about those animalistic creatures," I replied.

Sheldon whistled to alert his men. "You can spend eternity in the dungeon. I want to know what Jetster would do to you if she knew you were trying to steal her life. Do you not see the muscles she has now? She'll squash you like a tomato," he said. A clan of his people ran across the stream dressed in black hooded cloaks. They were Sheldon's top fighters.

"Throw her in the dungeon with Jetster! I even think he grew a few more inches and I'm certain that he's aroused for some fresh ass!" Sheldon told his people. I was frightened of being in the dungeon with Jetti; I would rather die than to constantly fight off an angry beast.

"I thought you loved me?" I cried to Sheldon.

"I felt something special for you, but unfortunately that Jetti spell is becoming permanent. I can't believe you let your beauty go just to become an average at best, deadbeat werewolf. Now I see why Akea fell into the drop-dead gorgeous witch hunter's trap," he chuckled. He signaled for his men to tie me up; in defense mode I shifted into a beast. I leapt over Sheldon's head, wrapping my arms around a tree to get as far away as I could. A spear flew past my snout when my large beast ran up the tree. My heavy weight was weighing the tree down so I jumped on another.

"GET HER!" Sheldon yelled. His owl flew above the treetops; a warlock threw a ball of fire at my beast from below. I howled when my paws caught on fire.

"Bring her ass to me, even if she's barbecued!" Sheldon shouted. I fell into the stream to put out the fire on my legs. My beast was wounded, but I kept running through the woods, panting from being out of breath. I wasn't used to my new body yet and was quickly becoming short winded. A swarm of giant wasps appeared with deadly stingers. I looked behind me; the wasps were coming from the warlock's mouth. I ran to a cliff and below was a river. I estimated that the cliff was two-hundred feet tall. The wasps covered my body, drilling their stingers into my flesh. My body was swelling up from the pain; I turned back to my human form. I screamed while in a fetal position. "I'll surrender!" I yelled. The wasps turned into dust particles. I grabbed a handful as Sheldon's warlock made his way to me. "Get up!" he ordered, while pulling me up. My body was covered in blood and puss filled bubbles from being stung almost to death. Sheldon and the rest of his warriors caught up to us.

"You did a great job, Mukato," Sheldon said to the warlock who had captured me.

"Of course, my leader," he replied.

"Fuck all of you!" I screamed. I threw the dirt into Mukato's eyes and he let go of my arm.

"Get her!" Sheldon shouted. The adrenaline to get away pumped through my veins while I jogged towards the cliff. A warlock ran after me, but it was too late. I was already falling to my death...

Akea

Two hours later...

*K*anye's massive black and gold haired beast followed Tiko's beast as we navigated through the woods to get to Black Rose's cabin. I had insisted we stay at the castle to figure out a way to cure Black Rose there, but Majestic said she needed her garden to revive her.

"We are almost there!" Majestic said. There was a lot of sadness in her voice, but she didn't hold a grudge against me for hurting Black Rose. Black Rose was bleeding internally and it was oozing from her mouth and nose; her dress was drenched in black blood. In the past, I had studied other immortals and learned that black blood was associated with demons. She was a demonic creature but how was she able to hide it through her smile? She wasn't a selfish lover and once I broke down her barrier, she had surrendered her heart to me.

"I will be happy when we get there, bro. I'm getting tired of feeling your nuts on my back and why are y'all so heavy?" Kanye asked. Even in his beast form we communicate telepathically.

"Bro, you are over a thousand pounds and stand taller than a horse. You can carry a killer whale on your back and you want to complain? You offered to come when I told you I could've come alone."

"I couldn't send you on a journey alone. We promised our father to stick together no matter what. I'm just clowning around with you so you can redirect your focus on something else. I can feel you sulking up there, your energy is very pitiful, bro," he replied.

"It's my fault that her heart stopped beating. I'm too fucked up to deserve Rose when I still have trust issues."

"Bro, you gotta stop wanting a perfect love and just see where her head is as far as you and Nile. You might as well see where it goes since you probably knocked her up. I understand why you were angry, you were only being a father concerned about bringing an enemy into the house. Shit, I can't believe I'm understanding your feelings. Aye! What if I'm a logical thinker because I haven't had any pussy in a while," he replied.

"You are never a logical thinker and why do y'all think I get everyone pregnant? I don't walk around passing out sperm like trick-or-treat candy."

"Because us werewolves only produce wolf serum when it's time to mate, but you, my brother, can make as many children as you want. Speaking of pregnancy, is Tiko smashing Reptile Girl? Their offspring would be some ugly muthafuckas when they get older. Gotta say older so our *god won't be upset for talking bad about peoples' babies,"* Kanye replied.

Tiko's beast came to an abrupt stop. Kanye accidentally bumped into him, almost causing Black Rose to slide out of my arms. "Why are we stopping? Our cabin is farther up, past that water well," Majestic pointed out. Tiko growled while sniffing the air; Kanye's beast picked up the scent too. Based on their growls and snarls, we weren't the only ones in the woods. Something swooshed past us behind the trees and I felt the vibrations on the ground—it was a large animal.

"SILVER!" Majestic called out.

"Black Rose's fox?" I asked.

"Silver must be Clifford the Big Red Dog cause I know a small ass fox didn't make the ground rattle," Kanye said.

"Yes, and please don't attack her. She's gentle," Majestic replied to me.

"Foxes are like the crackhead cousin to wolves. We don't fuck with them!" Kanye said.

"Chill out bro, damn. It's just a fox," I told Kanye.

"Foxes are territorial, genius! You should know that by all those books you read!" he replied.

"Come on, Silver. They aren't going to hurt you," Majestic said.

Silver came out of hiding in a crouching position while wagging its tail. The fox was almost the size of Kanye's beast, but slimmer in weight. The silver hairs in her black shiny coat looked platinum.

"Bro, my beast is fascinated but don't tell Monifa I admire the beauty of another woman," Kanye said.

"Silver isn't a shifter. She's just a magical fox."

"I've been catfished!" he replied.

"See, she's gentle," Majestic said, patting Silver's ear. Silver shrunk to a normal size fox; we were no longer a threat. She ran in a circle in front of Kanye; she was signaling him to play with her. Kanye's beast huffed when the fox licked his face.

"Do not tell Monifa about my little side chick," Kanye joked. If I wasn't in a bad mood, I would've been cracking up. Kanye was a jokester, even during odd times. Silver jumped on Kanye's back; she licked Black Rose's face while whimpering. Tiko's beast walked away, continuing the journey and Kanye followed.

A few minutes later, we approached a three-level cabin sitting in front of a cave. It was the only house in the woods surrounded by tall oak trees; the place looked lonely.

"I'm going to be honest, this place looks like it belongs to a humpback evil witch with a fat ass bumpy nose and no teeth who eats human-toe soup," Kanye said. Majestic hopped off Tiko's back. The front door of the cabin opened and the lights came on. "Someone's inside?" I asked, Majestic.

"No, the house greets Rose when she comes home. It's controlled by her garden," Majestic replied. I slid off Kanye's back, with my arms tightly wrapped around Black Rose's body. Silver ran up the steps of the cabin; she waited on the porch for us to enter.

"We'll be out here," Kanye said. He and Tiko sat in front of the house. I followed Majestic into the cabin; the inside of the cabin was like a flower shop with black antique furniture. I followed Majestic down a hallway, but a room caught my attention. Black Rose's psychic room was full of witchery items. She had witchery wreaths hung on the walls, skull heads decorated on her shelves, and a cabinet filled with potions. The shelf also had old-fashioned battle weapons such as shields, spears, katanas and khopeshes. The sword I had given her was on the wall by itself behind her desk.

"How do humans find this place?" I asked Majestic.

"Magic. This cabin can move anywhere accessible for humans. Sometimes, we stay in the same spot for a month before moving somewhere else. It just depends on Black Rose's mood," she replied.

Jetti was desperate enough to come to a witch's house for a potion to get me to fall for her? Question is, did she really drink it?

Majestic opened a door at the end of the hallway, it was the door to the cellar. I walked down the stairs, coming into an area that was the same as an outside garden. I could see the sky, stars and moon. Black Rose was more magical than I thought, she had held back a lot with me. Black butterflies and birds flew around her garden. I noticed a black rose bush covered in red blood.

"Her flowers bleed?"

Majestic shook her head. "Those are the souls that she collects to keep the garden. 'The blood of a soul will create a black rose'," she quoted. I was standing in a garden of souls. Black Rose was deeper than I thought and I had to accept her because it was too late to change her.

"Lay her in the pool, hopefully she'll wake up," Majestic said.

"Hopefully? You mean to tell me this might not work?"

Majestic began crying. "This never happened before but Circa warned her that she could die from love. Whatever curse Black Rose has doesn't want her to feel alive. She fell for you even though she knew this would be the outcome. She never had heart pains until she met you so this is new to me too," she said. Knowing that she had sacrificed her life to love me, made me feel worse than I did before. She was still breathing, but her heart wasn't beating. I took off my shoes before carrying her to her pond. The water was ice-cold but the room temperature was warm. Her dress and hat disappeared once her feet touched the pond water. I sat down with her back against my chest.

Majestic was still sniffling and wiping her eyes. She was trying to hold herself together to talk. "She wouldn't hurt a baby or a child no matter what they were. I'm not just saying this because I love her, but she has a soft spot for children. We've fought many battles together and Rose has never harmed a child," Majestic said.

"I overreacted and I see that more clearly now."

"I'll be back, I gotta make sure Tiko and Kanye are well hydrated," Majestic said. She left the garden room, leaving me with Rose. I looked around her garden and it looked familiar to the garden I had seen in my dream with Lyira, the only difference was that Lyira's garden was colorful. The connection was there, but I didn't know how to piece it together. I splashed her face with water to wash off the blood. Her eyes fluttered. "Rose! Can you hear me?" I asked, tapping her face. Her body was still limp, but she was trying to wake up. I dipped her body underneath the chilled water. Her eyes fluttered but she was still lifeless in my arms.

"Please forgive me for what I'm about to do to you."

I left her inside the pond underneath the water for the magic to work. Majestic came back into the garden room with towels. "You left her underneath?" Majestic asked.

"Stand back!"

My body rose from the ground while I was gathering energy. My adrenaline was pumping. "What are you trying to do?" Majestic asked. She was panicking but there was only one option to get Black Rose's heart pumping. Electricity the size of a bowling ball formed in the palm of my hand.

"You will hurt her! Electricity and water?" Majestic screamed. She ran towards me to stop me, but a blue magic shield blocked her. She pounded her fists against the shield. "Don't do it!" Majestic screamed.

"I'm not a fool! I know what I'm doing but this is the only way to revive her heart!" I cocked my arm back.

"NOOOOOO!" Majestic screamed.

I threw the ball into the pond. The electricity raised Black Rose's body from underneath the water. I got teary eyed watching her body twitch. "It's killing her!" Majestic screamed. Black Rose's body thrashed around inside the pond for ten seconds until the electricity seized. Her body was face down in the water; I jumped into the pond and turned her over. Her eyes shot open and she had a scowl on her face.

WHAP!

Black Rose slapped blood out of my mouth. "Get your ass off of me!" she yelled.

"What the hell did I do?" I asked, holding my mouth. She busted my lip.

"You broke up with me, jackass, and I'm going to kill Jetti with my bare hands," she said. Majestic ran to Black Rose after the shield went away. "You are back!" Majestic shrieked in excitement. Black Rose hugged her and kissed her on the cheek, meanwhile I was getting the cold shoulder.

"Escort that werewolf lover out of my cabin. Oh, and I need a glass of wine," Black Rose said.

"You really be on that bullshit sometimes," I told her. Black Rose climbed out of the pond; she was still staticky and her hair was all over the place. "Get out of my house. I will never forgive you for killing me," she said. Majestic was crying tears of joy while giggling at Black Rose. I knew she was going to wake up feisty. I got out of the pond and she was glitching.

"You turned me into a computer virus, Akea. I feel weird and you messed up my hair," she said. "Come here, Rose." I hugged her and felt a tiny shock. She didn't push me away, but she also didn't hug me back.

"I get it, Rose. I shouldn't have dismissed you like that."

"I'm going to go back upstairs and get that wine ready for you. Am I pouring Akea a glass too or no?" Majestic asked.

"No, he'll be leaving shortly," Rose replied.

Majestic left the garden room; Rose pried my arms away from her. She was getting teary eyed. "I hate you right now for embarrassing me. You let that crazy bitch see how vulnerable I can be. 'Never show your enemies your weakness.' That's how I lived and it's how I'll continue to live," she said.

"Do you want me to give you your space?"

"I don't want you here but I don't want you to leave. Does that make me weak?" she asked. A lone tear escaped her eye and I wiped it away. "I said some hurtful things tonight, but I do feel a way about you not telling me that I was involved in a beef between your people and whomever this Sheldon guy is supposed to be."

"I was going to protect you from Circa's people so I felt like I could handle it," she replied.

"Let me inside your head. I want to see glimpses of your past life."

"I can't allow you to see me as a monster. You don't need any parts of my past. That is my business," she replied.

"Our past makes us who we will be in the future. I want to help you."

"I don't need it for fucks' sake! You know what, just go! Get out of my cabin and return home to your ready-made family," she said. She was about to leave the garden room, but I teleported in front of her, blocking her.

"I can do that too," she said.

"I know I said I'd give you your space but let me hold you tonight."

"You think I want make-up sex so soon?" she asked.

"I can lay next to you without wanting sex. You've been taking advantage of *me* lately."

She crossed her arms underneath her breasts; she glitched again. "That's bullshit, I barely touch you," she lied.

"Bring your barcode ass over here," I said, grabbing her arm. "Look at me, Rose," I demanded. She kept her head straight ahead, looking at my chest since I was over a foot taller than her.

"No, because then the pain will be gone. It's easier to hurt now than waiting to get hurt. That way I won't be surprised when my heart breaks again," she replied. I tipped her chin so she could look into my eyes. "I did lash out on you, but you hurt me too. I can't take all the blame so at least meet me halfway."

"I can do that and I can also walk you halfway to the door," she replied.

"I'm not going to feed into your anger. I'll be in the kitchen getting the wine."

I walked out of the garden room. "You don't even know where it is!" she said.

"I'll figure it out."

Black Roses Grow in The Dark   Natavia

"I want you to leave," she said. Her tone was less condescending. Her voice had softened; she didn't want me to leave. I still decided to give her breathing room, but I wasn't going to leave her cabin so soon. I heard Kanye and Tiko's voices while I was walking up the stairs. Majestic served them wine as they sat on the couch with sheets wrapped around their bodies.

"How is Rose feeling?" Tiko asked.

"She's up, but I think that electricity has her riled up, so I'm going to sit out here until she cools off," I replied.

Majestic poured a glass of wine for me too. "My way of thanking you for helping Rose," she said.

"Appreciate it."

Tiko and Kanye were watching me while I held the wine glass to my lips. "I'm not really a wine drinker so you can have mine," Kanye said. He slid his glass across the coffee table. The wine was dark green and the consistency was a little thick. Tiko drank his in one gulp to get it over with; he didn't want to hurt Majestic's feelings.

"Go ahead, I made it," she said.

"Yeah, go ahead and drink up, bro. It's almost like your herbal smoothies you drink in the morning," Kanye said. Tiko was sweating bullets and his eyes were bloodshot red. He cleared his throat and patted his chest. "It's a lil' spicy, that's all, it tastes good, though. It has a very earthy flavor," Tiko told Majestic.

"You definitely put your snake eggs in there," Kanye said.

"I don't know what you mean," Majestic replied.

"It's like the saying 'you put your foot in it' meaning it tastes good," I lied. Kanye was being sarcastic as usual.

"Awww, thank you, Kanye," Majestic told him.

I tossed the drink back the same as Tiko had to get it over with. It was rich in flavor but also spicy with a fishy, iron and ginger taste. "The texture comes from slug mucus so it'll coat your stomach if it's too spicy," Majestic said. I swallowed my vomit.

"I'm ready to hunt," Tiko said. He stood up and almost lost his footing. He fell back onto the couch. I couldn't tell if he was tipsy or sick. Black Rose appeared in the living room in her elf form while wearing a black dashiki and her hair was still disheveled. She snatched the wine bottle off the table. Kanye and Tiko stared at her in confusion because they weren't aware of her creature; they thought she was a witch.

Gulp...gulp...gulp...

She finished the wine in a matter of seconds. "I think you need to rest," Majestic told Black Rose. "I've had enough rest," she burped.

"I think we should bounce," Kanye said to Tiko.

Black Rose sat on the couch next to me. "Bring me another bottle, Majestic," she said.

"Is that Yoda from Star Wars?" Kanye asked because of Black Rose's ears.

"Yoda? Really, bro?" I asked him.

"I'm an elf, Kanye. There I said it, the secret is out," Black Rose said.

"The little people that work for Santa Claus with the little green shoes?" he asked.

"Who is Santa Claus?" Tiko asked.

"A human folklore," Majestic replied.

"My kind isn't connected to Santa Claus. I'm a creature from a magical forest in another realm," Black Rose said.

"Monifa's voice is in my head telling me to come home so I should be heading back. I'll look out for Nile while you make sure Yoda, I mean Black Rose, is straight," Kanye told me. He stood from the couch and so did Tiko.

"I'm leaving too," Tiko said.

"Will I see you tomorrow night?" Majestic asked.

"Why tomorrow night? You should come back to the castle and let them be alone," Tiko replied.

Majestic looked at Black Rose. "I'll be fine. Go on ahead and maybe you two can still catch the club," Black Rose told her.

"I'll walk y'all out," I said, getting up. The wine made me feel a little woozy. "Are you straight, bro?" he asked.

"Yeah, come on."

I followed them outside on the porch. Silver was running around in front of the cabin with a dead raccoon in her mouth.

"Save me a piece my Nubian fox!" Kanye shouted out.

"Maybe I should stay with Rose," Majestic said. She was about to turn around to go back in the house but Tiko blocked her. "She only needs Akea right now. Let them get used to leaning on each other during these times," Tiko said.

Majestic breathed a sigh of relief. "I'm still not used to her sharing her feelings with someone else, but I am glad that she can experience it," she said.

Kanye shifted into his beast form to help Silver eat the juicy raccoon.

"I'm telling Monifa about your lil side chick since you want to call my woman Yoda. You are foul for that, bro!"

Kanye's beast looked up from the mangled raccoon. I would never get used to the sound of werewolves crushing their prey's bones. *"You wouldn't do that to me, bro. But*

Black Rose is short with those big ass ears, what else was I supposed to think?" he asked.

"Don't say it again, bro, and we're good."

"Aight, bro. Love you and goodnight," he said.

"Love you too, bro!" I called out.

I stayed on the porch until Kanye, Tiko and Majestic disappeared into the darkness of the woods. Silver brought what was left of the raccoon onto the porch. Black Rose came to the door naked. "Glad they are gone so I can be comfortable. I hate wearing clothes," she said.

She came outside and sat on the top step. She patted the space next to her. "You aren't going to gouge my eyes out are you?" I halfway joked. I didn't want to be caught off guard by her mood swings.

"I will if you don't sit next to me," she said. I sat next to her and she rested her head on my shoulder.

"I killed Jetti's cousin. I snatched her heart right out of her chest for coming to my home to retaliate against me because of the potion I gave Jetti. That's what I didn't want you to see. I have a very dark side and you are too pure to witness such evil," she confessed.

I looked up at the sky, stalling to find the words to say. "It's okay to regret me," she said.

"I don't care about Jetti's cousin or anyone else that you've killed in the past. If it's not me or my family you are after, I can't tell you who you shouldn't kill. It doesn't matter to me how you feed your garden, I just want to see you blossom."

Black Rose smiled. "You should be a poet. You have a unique way with your words that makes me feel special. You are a beautiful man inside and out," she replied.

"What was the potion for again?"

"To change her identity, I gave her what she asked for. She was desperate to live in a castle and go on shopping sprees. I don't think that woman is Jetti. I think it's a witch since they can shape shift," she said.

"But they can't produce breastmilk. Witches can change their appearances but not their traits. Are you sure her cousin wasn't trying to con you out of a refund? Jetti's pack are the biggest scammers in the area. That woman in the castle is Jetti for sure, I can tell by her desperate attempts to get back in good graces with my pack. Who was she supposed to turn into?"

"A man. She doesn't deserve to carry children," Black Rose replied.

"Bruhhh, that's cold as hell. Damn Rose, now that was fucked up. Nile would've had two daddies?"

She shrugged. "Isn't that what's in now? Same sex parents? Plus, she said you were taking him away from her. I had no idea the bitch was going to be in the picture," she replied. She grabbed my face and kissed my lips. "If she didn't drink the potion you can't be mad at me," she said, yawning.

"I'm not mad at all, but you need to rest. This day has been hectic."

"Let's sleep in the pond," she said.

"Sleep in the pond? I don't think I can do that, Rose. That's not in my nature."

"Anything can be a part of your nature if you learn to adapt. Try it, you'll wake up feeling refreshed with a clear conscience," she replied. She got up and went into the cabin, leaving the door open for me.

"Silver staying out?"

"Yes, she's nocturnal even though she's sleeping now," she replied.

I followed Black Rose into the cabin; her ass cheeks bounced as she seductively walked down the hallway. She was purposely flaunting her sexiness and signaling me to enter her.

"I know what you are doing."

"You must not know if you are all the way back there and not on me," she flirted.

She was startled when I popped up in front of her, scooping her in my arms. "You are fast," she replied.

"And I can beat a vampire in a race."

She laughed. "How far did you stretch for that reach?" she replied.

"I'm dead ass serious. I've fought bloodsuckers, werewolves, demons and mutant werewolves."

"Ohhhh, talk your shit," she replied, squeezing my cheek.

I carried her down to the garden room and into the pond. "You know, this garden follows me wherever I make my home. It's really a piece of me. This place is my serenity, a small portion of my world. No matter what time of day it is, it'll always be night time here," she said.

I sat her on a rock. "I know for sure I saw this garden in my dream, but it belonged to Lyira. My memory is legit, the only thing that's missing is the tree that sat near this pond."

Black Rose smacked her teeth. "I'm starting to feel some type of way that she gets to be in your dreams more than me," she replied. I took off my clothes before sitting in front of her. "I think she's your mother. My visions have steered me wrong in the past but now I'm confident about the meanings of my visions."

"I've never heard anyone speak that name before so it should tell you that maybe she's a figment of what I would be if I wasn't cursed," she replied.

"But she was pregnant, Rose. This woman had a mate that was an elf too. It was damn sure real and not just some fantasy."

"You are a warlock, Akea. You see things that are above the average imagination. I'm not saying you are wrong, but I never heard of this Lyira chick," she replied.

"The next time I have a dream, I'm going to do everything I can to see her face. I bet she's going to look like you because she's your mother."

Black Rose placed her finger over my lips. "I'm getting jealous so hush and lean back and relax. Have you ever fallen asleep floating above water?" she replied.

"No, but I'm assuming you want me to try it."

"Of course, come on," she replied.

She raised her legs above the water then leaned back. "Aghhh," she exhaled while floating. I floated next to her. "This is nice," I said, closing my eyes. I had never been on a water bed but I imagined this was how it felt. Black Rose started humming a song. The melody was high but soft. I considered telling her Lyira had the same voice, but I didn't want to bring her up anymore while we were meditating. I drifted into a deep sleep...

Eight hours later...

I woke up in the pond to the smell of something burning and Black Rose screaming. I teleported to the living room and smoke was coming from underneath a door in the hallway. I burst through the door. Black Rose was cooking burnt food on a wood burning stove. She was covered in flour and slaughtered chickens were spread across the kitchen floor.

"Get in there, bitch!" Black Rose yelled at a headless chicken covered in egg yolk and flour. The chicken was still moving and flapping its arms. She forced the chicken into a cauldron iron pot of overflowing boiling water. Little dark, twelve-inch, naked elves with rose shaped heads were standing on the counter cutting up, feta cheese, carrots, pickles and fish.

"Y'all have five seconds to get this right or else y'all are going back into the flower vase. Akea likes soul food, not spirit food. Chop…chop," Black Rose said, snapping her fingers. I leaned against the wall, quietly watching her boil a live chicken with its feathers still attached. Once she covered the pot, she dusted off her hands, smiling like she was proud of herself. It was the funniest, but cutest and most thoughtful thing a woman had ever done for me. An elf threw down his knife and wiped the sweat off his forehead. He was fussing in a squeaky and unfamiliar language.

"The closest way to a man's heart is through his stomach so pick up that knife and cut up that carrot or else I'm going to bite your head off," Black Rose fussed. She picked up a yam and sniffed it. "Candied yams should be sweet, right? Ugh, I left the candy at the store," she stomped her foot.

"Good morning, beautiful," I finally said. I couldn't take watching her torture herself anymore. She turned around. "I wanted to surprise you and fix you the meal your mother used to make for you. Go back to bed," she said.

"This is the greatest surprise of all. When will it be ready?"

"In two minutes so get out of the kitchen and let me and my little helpers create this amazing meal. I promise, you are going to love it," she said. She pushed me out of the kitchen door. "Don't come back in!" she shouted.

Dear Father, please watch over me as I eat the food Rose has prepared for me. I know it might send my spirit to her garden but I can't hurt this woman again. I'll eat every piece on the plate like a warrior as long as you watch over me. My magic can't help me out of this, so I turn to you and ask for your guidance. AMEN!

I sat on the couch and noticed she had the coffee table nicely set up with candles burning. A bottle of Majestic's wine was sitting in a bucket of ice. I bowed my head and said another prayer. "I am the son of Goon and a prince of Anubi. I can do this," I told myself.

"Akeaaaa, breakfast is ready," Black Rose sang.

She came out of the kitchen carrying a glass tray of food. The chicken was finally dead but it resembled a white mop. She sat the tray on the table and I tried my hardest to keep a straight face. The mac and cheese consisted of cooked noodles with feta cheese sprinkled over it. I couldn't identify anything else on the plate.

"I want you to be nice and full before you go home," she said.

The noodles are decent, I can eat that.

"Do you need salt or pepper?" Black Rose asked.

"No, beautiful, you already seasoned it with your love."

"I'll feed you," she said.

She sat on my lap. "What do you want first?" she asked.

"The noodles, give me all of it."

She scooped a spoonful of noodles; she almost shoved the spoon to the back of my throat. "Am I being too rough? I'm not used to being a mushy romantic," she said.

"Everything is perfect, but I'd rather eat you then come back to this later. The food isn't going anywhere. Well, I don't know about the chicken, but I need some of you," I told her. Distracting her with sex was the only way to get me out of eating the feathered chicken. I squeezed her meaty ass cheek; she blushed from my morning erection poking against her. After I swallowed the food, I kissed her neck.

"Ummm Akeaaa," she moaned. Her essence coated my leg and the warmth from her center caused me to crave her even more. Black Rose teleported to a bathroom, we were still in the same position while sitting on a toilet seat. The bathroom was surrounded by mirrors with vines from black roses along the walls. A hummingbird's wings buzzed in my ear while flying past my head. Black Rose slid off my lap leaving the flowery scent of her essence on my leg. It permeated the air. She grabbed a bar of what looked like handmade soap; she turned on the shower head. She stood underneath the water, letting the flour and egg yolk rinse off her naked body. Her body transformed to her elf form and the specs of water ran down her graphite skin. Her skin glistened like diamonds and her hair fell to her ankles from the weight of the water. It didn't take a genius to know that she was a goddess of her world. I joined her, grabbing the plumpness of her ass. She lathered my chest and I picked her up, pinning her against the wall. We fervently kissed; we were making up for our fallout the day before. Her sexy moans ringing in my ears swelled the tip of my dick. I sat on the shower floor with her still in my arms. She giggled when I turned her upside down. "What is this?" she asked. She wasn't familiar with the position which meant.

"Sshhh, just go with the flow."

I pulled her back, her knees rested on my shoulders. Her fat mound was at the tip of my nose. She gasped when I kissed her clit. I firmly gripped her waist, burying my face between her wet folds. Without having to tell her, she placed her mouth on my shaft. I snaked my tongue around her swollen bud; she rhythmically rotated her hips while backing it up to my mouth. My dick swelled, stretching out

Black Rose's mouth. "Shit, Rose," I groaned, fucking her mouth. Her pussy squirted on my chin. I flicked my tongue against her clit faster. "Babbyyyyy, right thereeeee! Fuckkkk you, Akeaaaaa!" she called out. Her cries weren't good enough, I wanted her to scream loud enough to crack the mirrors. My tongue planted a blue marble of electricity inside her pussy at the same time that I fucked her with my stiff tongue. I blew on her clit to activate the marble. Her nails dug into my legs, piercing through my flesh as her body wildly bucked like she was riding a bull. Her pussy glowed from the tiny jolt of electricity stimulating her G-spot. She fell over and I pulled her legs back to massage her clit. "ARGHHHHHHHHH!" she screamed while cumming. Her back raised off the floor when I entered her. I gripped a handful of her coils when her wet, tight walls gripped my girth. The stimulant planted inside of her was still causing orgasms.

"Akeaaaaaa...I love youuuuu!" she screamed. The mirrors cracked from her powerful cries and the floor rumbled while our bodies joined as one. A golden glow surrounded us, paining my eyes. After the glow subsided, the bathroom turned into the bed size flowers I saw in my dreams. I latched on to her neck, gently suckling her sensitive spot behind her ear. My thrusts were delicate; I slowly went deep. Her stomach raised against my abdomen when I entered her womb. She wrapped her legs around me, squeezing tightly while making love back to me. I raised my body away from hers to stare into her slanted black eyes. Her body rocked when I plunged into her flower.

Phap...phap...phapp...

Black Roses Grow in The Dark   Natavia

I thrust and wined. She put her legs behind her ears, propping her pussy up. "Babyyyy go deeperrrr. I need you in my soullll," she begged. I dived deeper taking her breath away. My dick swelled, causing her face to twist in pain. Black Rose was taking every inch of my magically enhanced fourteen-inch dick. I thanked the gods for creating a woman who could take my magic.

SOUL Publications

Circa

I had been searching the deep woods to find Black Rose's cabin for a week. Her magical cabin usually sat on moist dirt because of the garden needing its nutrients. I was getting closer; following her magically aroma had always led me to her. Her scent was strong to those who were connected to her. I jumped from a tree top, landing on my feet. Her flowery fragrant was getting stronger as I walked across a stream. I spotted a rotted deer carcass with a missing head. I followed the paw prints in the mudded area and it ended near a fox's den. The den was still warm with strands of silver hairs sticking out like a sore thumb. I picked up a strand to inhale the smell; the aroma was identical to Black Rose's garden. Silver spent most of her time in the garden so she carried the sweetness the same as her owner.

Black Rose's cabin must be close by. Silver frequents this area a lot.

I kept on walking, heading North where the scent was getting deeper with each step I took.

"AKEAAAA!" a familiar voice screamed.

I ran towards the noise, passing an old water well. The noise led me right to her cabin. Her scent was strong, strong enough to lure any man within a fifty mile radius. The house trembled and a gold lightning blared out of the windows. Since I was close by, I teleported into the cabin. On the table in the living room was a food tray covered in slop along with two wine glasses. Whimpers and sobbing was coming from the top floor. I jumped from the bottom step, landing on the top stair where the cries were coming from. My scythe appeared in my hand, in case Black Rose was in trouble. I crept down the narrow hallway and glass from the hallway mirror was scattered on the floor.

That warlock is going to die for hurting my Rose!

"UHHHHHH! UMMMM!" a man's voice bellowed.

I stopped at the door where gold specs of dust were coming through the cracks. "This your pussyyyy, murder it if you want! Just don't stop fucking meeee," Black Rose shouted. I snatched the door off the hinge and there it was, the vision Amstid had shown me a thousand years ago. Black Rose and the warlock were in a passionate moment. He was thrusting on top of her while tears fell from her eyes. The young warlock had the rose symbol on his neck and it fueled my anger even more because I was too late. I followed every rule to keep the future in my grasp but no matter what I did, I lost myself more and more. Not once did the warlock look up to find me standing in the doorway. He kissed Black Rose's tears away. "Ohhh I love you, Akea," she confessed. I hurled the scythe at them, the sharp end cut across the ceiling before it slashed open the warlock's face. He pulled out of Black

Rose and his manhood was dripping in her essence, the essence that belonged to me.

"What are you doing in my house, Circa?" Black Rose asked. Akea's face wound was already healing.

"Playtime is over, collect his soul so you can come back to me," I told her.

"You look familiar…very familiar," Akea said to me.

"Who gave you the authority to speak to me, little boy?"

"I told you that I'm done with the clan! What more do you want from me, huh? I'm sick of you! I'm sick of all of you!" Black Rose yelled.

"There's no need to pretend that you are on his side, Rose. His time is up so kill him like you promised. We might have taken a break from the fight but the war isn't over. Now, drain him so we can leave!" I seethed.

"That's the man I saw Lyira with in my vision," he told her.

He knows too much! This is the information I wanted to keep away from Rose. He has to die!

"Is Lyira my real mother?" Black Rose asked.

"Are you questioning me over the enemy?"

"With all due respect, Black Rose doesn't want to be in your clan anymore, bro. Why are you still standing here?" he asked.

"Just leave, Circa," she said.

"We've come too far to let this human come between us. I'm not leaving here until he's dead."

Akea chuckled. "Bro, you can't kill me or steal my magic. I'm not those other warlocks you have killed, I'm cut from a different cloth so you might as well squash this weird ass beef you have with me and let me continue seeing your daughter," he said. I wanted to cut his arrogant tongue out of his mouth and feed it to the maggots.

Black Rose grabbed a robe off the wall to cover her naked body. I couldn't pull my eyes away from the dips in her hips and busty chest. The love I had for her wouldn't allow me to leave her cabin, even if I had to die. She grabbed his arm, holding onto him tightly. Her eyes were filled with hatred against me and the only way I could get her to come to me was to tell her the truth.

"I'm not leaving here without my wife so kill me now," I confessed.

"The fuck did you just say?" Akea asked.

"Father, please stop! ENOUGH! Is this what you turned into? A creep that will say anything to make me feel and look bad. No father should lust after his daughter!" she yelled. I moved my hair away from my neck and ripped the neckline of my cloak so she could see the rose symbol.

"You aren't my daughter, Rose. You are my wife! Do you see this symbol? This is your symbol of love. This warlock isn't your mate! It's me, god dammit!" I yelled. Tears fell from my eyes as I relieved myself from the secret that I had harbored for ages. Sitting back and watching her be with other men has tormented me in more ways than one.

"You will do anything to keep me from being happy! Get out or else I'll forget you are my father and behead you. Please don't make me kill you because I will!" she said.

"You are Lyira, Rose, and we had a daughter. You suffer from memory loss. I had no choice but to move on, but I had to keep you close to me so I let you believe I was your father. The Amstid Clan killed our daughter when they cursed you. This is why I can't stop fighting and my hate for his kind will never go away," I replied.

Black Rose shook her head in disbelief. "You are only saying this because you caught me with a warlock. I won't believe anything you say from here on out. You are so dead to me. You are pathetic!"

"Your magic is the way it is because you were a goddess. A lot of things changed in you but your magic stayed the same. Explain where you get your abilities from if I'm your father?" I asked.

"If what you are saying is true about the rose marking, she's my mate too. You are her past, bro. I am her present and future," Akea said.

"Then we shall fight," I gritted.

Sports attire magically appeared over his naked body while I rushed him. I knocked him through the bathroom wall; we landed in the grass outside the cabin. The warlock hurriedly got on his feet; blue glowing orbs spun in the palm of his hands. I back flipped to stand on my feet.

Spiked whips with deadly hooks extended from my hands. "Unlike you, human, my magic doesn't come from spell books. You are not a true sorcerer."

"You are going to rethink that by the time I'm finished with you!" he said. The power orb came towards me like a jolt of lightning. I leaned back, with my head touching the ground, dodging the ball. The orb knocked over a tree. "I'm warming your old ass up!" he said.

Black Rose appeared between us. "I can't watch this fight," she said.

"It's not up to you so back away, Rose. This creep got to be dealt with! I'm going to rip his eyes out of his head so he won't have to lust after you again," the warlock said.

"Circa, this is the last warning! You need to leave my property now!" Black Rose said.

"Move out of the way, my love. I know you can't remember our past and the day the warlocks invaded our world, but I was the king of the forest. For ages I fought through blood, sweat and tears to get back what we lost. It makes my heart bleed to watch the son of the god who is protecting Sheldon's clan, make love to you. He's the enemy too, Rose!"

I swung my whip over her head and it wrapped around Akea's throat. Blood oozed from his neck from the claw hooks that were hooked in his skin. I wanted to take his head off. He hurled another orb that I couldn't dodge fast enough. The hot ball of fire went through my chest. I fell to the ground with a cannon size hole in my chest. Black Rose stood over me, pleading with her eyes for me to give up.

"You let him do this to me? What happened to you?" I asked, getting choked up from the blood clogging my throat. I was bleeding out as she watched. Akea pulled me up and leaned me against a tree. "This is a warning, Circa. You gotta bounce or I'll be forced to do something I really don't want to do," Akea said.

The hole in my chest was healing and the burn was becoming numb. "I'm unkillable too but I have my wife to thank for that," I replied, charging into him again. The young warlock slammed his fist into my face. I sank my teeth into his face to give him a permanent scar. The metal canines in my mouth burned his flesh. Black Rose knocked me off her mate with a blow from her fist. I got up with the warlock's blood dripping from my lips.

"Your father should've taught you some fighting lessons, boy! I've killed many warlocks with my bare hands! Squashed them like ants!" I boasted.

"I can kill you, though, so back the fuck away!" Black Rose screamed.

Akea got up and the veins in his neck were pumping. "Back away, Rose! This is a man's fight so don't defend me," he told her. She backed away with tears falling from her eyes. "I can't let you kill him either," she admitted. Akea floated off the ground above our heads. In a flash, he kicked me from mid-air. A bone from a cracked rib popped through my flesh, crippling me. He grabbed my cloak and jabbed me repeatedly in my face with his steel fist. Black Rose grabbed him. "You are going to kill him!" she screamed.

"Arghhhhh!" I shouted when he cracked my eye socket, damaging my eye. He stepped away from my body while I laid in the grass, bleeding profusely. His strength and power was stronger than the other warlocks but that was to be expected. He was the son of a god and highly protected.

"You want to start a war with me, bring it, muthafucka," he seethed. I couldn't sit up, the pain knocked me back down. My head was swelling like an elephant was stomping on me. I was losing my hearing but I could make out Black Rose's voice.

"I'm going to take him home and I'm coming right back so wait for me," she told the warlock. I couldn't hold on any longer, I passed out...

****

"Circa, can you hear me?" a woman's voice asked.

I opened my eyes. "Lyira?" I asked because my vision was blurry.

"It's Merci, Circa," she said.

She helped me sit up; I winced in pain from my bruised ribs. I was pissed off that I was waking up in the bed I shared with Merci and not the bed at Black Rose's cabin. I sat on the edge of the bed. "Why am I here?"

Merci kneeled in front of me. "You've been gone for a week and you come back to me like this? Who did this to you?" she asked.

"How did I get here?" I asked, ignoring her questions.

"I don't know, but someone left you on the doorstep an hour ago. Did Sheldon's people catch you while you were searching for Rose?" she asked.

Black Rose left me on the doorstep like a newspaper! That whore has no respect for her mate.

"No, I was attacked while crossing a werewolf's territory," I lied.

I couldn't dare tell her I let a young warlock kick my ass because he was stronger than me. My clan thought the best of me, but if word got out that I lost to a warlock, they'd lose faith in our clan.

"You have to let her go. She doesn't want any parts of our clan," she said. She touched my face and I smacked her hand away.

"Why do you care about me, Merci? You know I don't love you and I will never love you. The only reason you're being my wife is because you were the strongest female warrior out of the clan. By instinct, alpha females and males create a better foundation for their family. But now you are a weak woman who wants love and affection. You've lost your spark trying to love me; your light is dull."

She backed away from me in tears. "I'll go get a rag since your wound is still bleeding. You aren't healing as fast as you normally do. Did Black Rose attack you?" she asked. Merci dismissed everything I had said to her.

"Stop ignoring my honesty, Merci. It's okay to accept that our course has ended. I saw Black Rose before I was attacked and I told her the truth. I told her that she's Lyira. I still love her."

"Well if you loved her, why did you kill her and slit your daughter's throat?" she asked.

"I needed her blood to bring Lyira back! I made a sacrifice because of the love I had for her. That day, I chose my mate."

"But your mate came back as Black Rose. Lyira is dead, Circa! That innocent and pure goddess you love was replaced with a death seeking dark creature!" she said. I lunged towards Merci, knocking her over a love seat. My weak body fell on top of hers; I wrapped my hands around her throat, strangling her.

"I did what I had to do to save Lyira! You don't get to speak on that."

"Father!" Nayati screamed. I looked up and Nayati was standing in the doorway watching me strangle her mother. She wasn't my daughter, but I had raised her as mine. Merci was raped by a warlock when he came to our realm. Nayati was the enemy's seed, but I let her live because she was still a part of our world. I stepped away from Merci who was gagging for air. Nayati rushed to her mother to get her off the floor.

"Why are you treating Mother this way?" Nayati asked.

"Get her out of my sight."

"Who is Lyira? Is she someone you are having an affair with?" Nayati replied.

"Don't question your father, let it go," Merci responded weakly. My handprint had bruised her neck badly and I felt guilty for it. For years she had to deal with my temper and frustration because of the past choices I'd made. She only wanted to be loved, but I couldn't give it to her.

"I came up here to tell Father that the cab caught a flat tire, but then I saw him choking you and couldn't stay out of it," she said. Nayati's face had a permanent scar, she was practically lipless from Black Rose's curse. I could barely look at her; she was hideous and had the mouth of an old corpse.

"Tell your husband to fix it! Why do y'all act like invalids? Circa this, Circa that! Give me a goddamn break! You and your mother are on my ass like a tick on a deer!" I shouted.

"My husband can't even look at me because of what Black Rose did to my face! When are you going to handle her for dividing the clan? Zelda's parents still want justice and so do I for what that monster daughter of yours did to my marriage!" Nayati said.

"Nobody deals with Black Rose but me! I'll slaughter every single last one of you vermin if you touch her. How about you take your pitiful dweeb of a mother and put ice on her neck before I strangle you next. Now get the fuck away from my bedroom!" I shouted, kicking over a table. Nayati and Merci ducked when the table flew towards them and broke into pieces.

Nayati and Merci quickly left the bedroom. I limped to the mirror on the wall to look at my face. A piece of bloody cloth was around my head to cover my eye. I unraveled the bandage to inspect the damage to my eye socket. Findis knocked on the door. "Can I come in?" he asked.

"What is it, Findis?" My eye was swollen and bashed in. It looked like someone had beat my face with a sledgehammer.

"Who did that to you? Black Rose?" he asked.

"I caught that young warlock fucking Black Rose inside her cabin. That weakling knew about Lyira so I told Rose the truth about me and her."

"You told her everything?" he replied.

"I only told her who she was but not what happened to her."

I put the wrap back on my head; Findis went to the corner table to pour two glasses of whiskey. We sat in the living room area of the bedroom. Findis passed me the glass and I tossed it back. I needed the whole bottle to numb the pain.

"I think we should move in on Sheldon as soon as possible before Black Rose finds out what you did to her and her child. A woman like that scorned isn't safe for anyone; she can kill us before we succeed in the mission. If we survive, we can go far away from this place. We can make a new home in the Amazon Rainforest to start a new slate," he said.

"What about the wolf god that Sheldon worships? I couldn't defeat Akea, a young warlock, so imagine the strength and power his father possesses."

"It can also be one of Sheldon's ploys to keep us away," Findis said.

"Amstid predicted this, he said that his brother would outlive all of us because he would give his life to the wolf god. That wolf god is real and this will be a suicide mission without Black Rose."

"Then we will die as courageous warriors. We need to attack soon but I know you'll come up with a plan, you always do. We have to be a union without her because no matter how you feel about her, that's not Lyira anymore. Black Rose turned enemy when she killed Zelda to protect the warlock," he said. He finished his drink before he stood to leave. "How is Lark doing?"

"He and his family went to the market," he replied.

"How long ago?"

"This morning, they have been gone for nine hours," he replied.

"Did you check his headquarters to see if his belongings are missing?"

"No, I haven't. Do you think he left?" he asked.

"Go check and do it now, Findis! You are second in command so you should keep tabs on these things!" I shouted. He bowed his head. "I'll go look now," he said. He rushed out of my bedroom, shutting the door behind him. I went to the corner table, grabbing the whole bottle of whiskey to chug down. After I took the last sip, I smashed the bottle into the wall. Lark being gone for nine hours left a bad feeling in my stomach. He knew too much and I wondered if he had left to tell Black Rose the truth.

"He can't find her, he won't. I'm the only one who can scope out Black Rose," I said, pacing back and forth.

"HA!" a woman said.

I turned around, facing Lyira. She was sitting on my couch smiling at me. "You aren't real!"

"You've failed again, Circa," she laughed.

"And you got what you wanted, which is Black Rose knowing who she really is so you don't have to keep coming to me."

She walked over to me. "But that's not all that I want. What I really want is for her to kill you. As long as you are alive, I'll continue to eat away at your conscious until it drives you more insane than you are now. Your time is coming, my love, and when it does, you'll be begging for mercy or should I say, Merci?" she smiled.

I walked away from her. I put a cloak over my pants, ignoring her because it was all an illusion. She disappeared when someone knocked on the door. "Come in!" I said.

Zelda's father, Duke, came into the bedroom. He dropped to his knees in front of me. I threw my arms up in frustration. "What the hell is it now?"

"Sir, I'm begging you to follow the clan rules and bring justice for my daughter," he said.

"We can stop pretending now, Duke. Do you and your wife really think I can kill my wife...my *real* wife."

"She's not your wife anymore and we should treat her like we've been, which is like a regular clan member," he replied.

"Are you trying to tell me how to be a leader?" I asked, clenching my fist.

"No…no, sir, but I would like for you to honor the clan's rules. Zelda took on the mission you gave her because she wanted to be a top warrior. She died because of your orders and as a leader, you shouldn't want her death to be in vain," he said.

"Black Rose wasn't thinking clearly that day. That warlock has a spell on her. He's manipulating her, turning her against us. He's the one that should be punished."

"When will we attack?" he asked.

"Findis will be reporting to everyone soon so go wait in the practice for further word."

Duke clasped his hands together. "Thank you so much, sir," he said. He bowed his head again before getting off the floor. Lyira came back right after he left the bedroom. She was lying on my bed. "I should call you Circus instead of Circa because you are full of tricks. You'll deceive anyone to get what you want," she said.

"And you had a front row seat at my show so is it safe to say that you were the first to be entertained by tricks?"

"I wanted you dead that day. I sent Merci to kill you, to take off your head for allowing those demonic warlocks into my forest. Nothing has changed, my love, I still want you dead," she replied.

I left the bedroom to go to my study. Findis was running down the hallway, I could tell by the creases in his forehead that something had happened and he was worried. I opened the door to my study at the end of the hall so no one else could hear our conversation. I sat at my desk. "Shut the door," I said as soon as he came into the study.

"Lark, his wife and Blizzard are gone, but Glendan is still here," he said.

"Go trace them down and take Glendan with you because I know he knows something. Lark would never just leave his son behind so he must've refused to leave with his father."

"Lark and his family are fighters. It won't be easy to bring them back," he said.

"I don't want their bodies, just their heads. Kill Glendan too if he objects. We can make it a family reunion."

"I'll get right to it," Findis said. He turned the door knob to leave the room but I called out to him. "I can always count on you so don't let me down," I warned him.

"Of course I won't," he replied.

He closed the door behind him after he exited the room. I opened the drawer of my desk and retrieved a set of keys. I needed them to unlock the secret compartment in the wall where I kept Amstid's head. He coughed when I sat the box on the desk. "Eh, you almost look like me. Since we're both missing an eye, I'm assuming we can now see eye-to-eye," he joked.

I leaned back in my chair. "Now isn't the time to be joking. How can I kill the wolf god's warlock son?"

"My prediction must've come true. Did you find Black Rose with her legs spread for that handsome warlock? He's wayyy younger than you so I'm sure she enjoyed the stamina," he joked.

"Goddamn it, just tell me!" I banged on the desk.

"Kill him how you killed me. Chop his head off with a hatchet!" he said.

"It's that easy, huh?"

"No, because you'll summon his father if you do that. I have to admit, your clan are vicious Neanderthals but you can't challenge the wolf god, he'll eat you alive. I only showed you the future in exchange for a piece of your world and to screw every beautiful female creature in your forest. Your obsession to have power turned you into your own enemy. It's true, I did trick you but I didn't force you to do what you've done to your world. You were easily conned," he said.

I picked up the box, raising it above my head. "Put me down! I was resting!" he shouted. I slammed the glass box onto the floor and it shattered. His head gasped for air. I got up from my desk and stood over his head. "Helpppp meeeee," he said. I brought my foot down on his head and it splattered across the floor. I kept stomping on the remains while a grayish-green slime oozed between my bare toes. "I killed your ass twice so I already won."

I walked to my liquor cabinet, leaving slimy footprints across the floor. Lyira appeared inside my study while I was taking a shot. "You are sexually frustrated. You are so angry," she teased. She was sitting on top of my desk naked and taunting me. I missed the feel of her tightness, gripping me in a chokehold.

"I only lust after one woman."

"Lust is correct, but you didn't love me. You loved my body and the way it felt, that's all you saw in me," she said. I took another shot, blocking her out so she would disappear.

"When I said bring Black Rose home, I meant bring her to her past so she can find herself again. I wanted you to protect her from the enemy which is yourself. She's going to find out the truth since Akea can see glimpses of her past life. Go ahead and dig your grave, my love. She's going to avenge her daughter," she said. I was about to respond but she was gone again.

Tomorrow night we will attack the warlocks again even if it means I'll die. This war must continue, even if the wolf god comes to save his son.

Dyika

Knock...knock...

Baneet came into my room with a pitcher of water and meat cubes. I had survived the fall from the cliff the night before and made it back to Akea's castle, broken up and bruised. Sheldon had it wrong, it was meant for me to be in Nile's life, why else would I still be alive? I was nervous that he would come to the castle and blow up my spot, but I had nowhere else to go. Hopefully, he would think that I was dead because of the high fall. I sat up to devour the meat and drink the ice cold water. She sat my tray next to the bed and fluffed up my pillows.

"Thank you so much for this. I'm starving."

"Are you ready to tell me what happened to you?" she asked, sitting on the bed. Since I was feeling ill, Baneet moved into a guest room inside the basement of the castle to be closer to me. It was also easier to bring Nile to me versus being a mile away in the pool house. I grabbed the plate of fresh, raw deer meat off the tray.

"I went to hunt and was chased down by a pack of werewolves. I lost my footing and fell off a cliff. But forget about me, is Jasiah talking to you yet?"

"No, he went to the club last night and didn't come back until the morning. He smelled like another wolf so I know he was with someone else. I like him, but I'm familiar with Zaan. We grew up together. I didn't see Zaan's full potential until I saw how he treated Fiti. If it wasn't for me cheating with a wolf from another pack, me and him could've had pups by now. Fiti is talking about having his baby and it bothers me," she said.

"Life is too short to let someone you love be with someone else. Fight for Zaan before they have a baby together."

She let out a deep sigh. "I can't do that. I've learned that being conniving to hurt others will come back and bite you in the ass," she said. I swallowed the meat then flushed it down with ice water.

She's so stupid. Bless her heart!

"I've been here for seven hours and Akea hasn't come to see me yet."

"I wasn't going to tell you because you are in bad condition but he's in his penthouse with Keisha. She's moving in because some guy is after her," she said.

"WHAT!" I screamed.

"Kanye said she could stay for however long she wants. He's the pack leader so it's his call," she said.

"She's a witch hunter and I don't want her around my son! Shouldn't they confirm that with me?"

"No, because you are just a guest. Eventually, Nile won't need breastmilk anymore so Akea plans on cutting back the time you spend here," she replied. I got out of bed wearing Baneet's robe, which was too big. She grabbed my arm when I tripped over the bottom of the robe.

"Get back in bed," she said.

"How dare he do this to me?"

"Akea hasn't been this happy in a long time so I think you should let it go. I thought she was just someone he was kicking it with but him bringing her here just confirmed how he *really* feels about her," she said.

"What kind of bullshit is that? They've only known each other for what? Nine days?"

"My parents had pups a few months after meeting each other. You can't put a time frame on love. Anyway we're having a campfire at midnight, if you're up to it," she said.

"A campfire?" I repeated.

"Yes, it's fun. We sit around a bonfire in the yard and just relax and talk while drinking. It'll ease your mind," she said.

"How am I supposed to deal with Black Rose being there?"

"Ugh, I keep forgetting that's her nickname, but who cares if she's there?" she asked.

"You are the one who told me to fight for Akea and make Black Rose jealous so now you are siding with them? I thought we were better than that?"

She rolled her eyes. "Monifa ripped me a new asshole after dinner. The bitch can be crazy at times so I'm staying on her good side. I'm a lover, not a fighter. I need to keep this pretty face intact. Eat your food and relax. I'll tell Akea to bring Nile down here," she said. I climbed back into the platform bed, pissed off that Black Rose was easily forgiven for plotting against Akea.

"Do you know what she is? She's not a real witch, she's an elf!"

Baneet pulled the satin white sheets over my body. If only Akea was that attentive and caring towards me.

"Kanye told us last night," she said.

"So they know she's an elf witch hunter?"

"Yes, we are aware, but that was her past. You have a past too," she replied.

This silly minded hoe flip flops a lot. I have to be careful what I say around her!

I waited until she left the guest bedroom before I broke down in tears. Jetti was taking over my mind more and more each day. My hate for Black Rose was one thing, but Jetti's obsession over Akea was another. Jetti's thoughts, her memories and her anger had fully consumed me. Nile was supposed to cure my lifelong postpartum depression, but it was becoming less about him and more about Akea. I didn't think the potion would change me completely, but each day I strayed further away from Dyika.

I couldn't sit still anymore, so I got out of bed and caught the elevator to the fifth floor of the castle. When I got off on Akea's floor, a fox ran out of Akea's penthouse and down the hallway with a pair of socks in its mouth. I walked into the penthouse and there they were, in the kitchen. Akea was standing behind her with his arms wrapped around her waist, he was showing her how to work the smoothie machine. She was wearing one of his black, long-sleeve, button-up shirts. The shirt hung loosely off her shoulder, revealing a lot of her cleavage. Akea was shirtless and passion marks covered his chest. He didn't have the decency to hide that they were fucking each other.

"I don't think I want one. It's too much kale inside," she said about the smoothie.

"I'll take one since I need the nutrients to breastfeed," I interrupted.

"How do you feel?" Akea nonchalantly asked.

"I would've felt better if you were nursing me back to good health instead of Baneet."

"I heard you only had a few scratches and bruises. Werewolves are natural healers," he replied. Black Rose whispered something to him and he grabbed a shirt off a chair to cover up his chest. I came farther into the penthouse and sat on the couch. Nile was asleep in his bassinet and it pissed me off that he was even in the room with that evil bitch.

"Nile is asleep so you ain't gotta chill up here," Akea said.

"I got to keep an eye on him and make sure she doesn't snatch my son's soul," I replied.

Black Rose came out to the living room area and sat on the couch across from me. She patted the spot next to her for Akea to sit. He joined her on the couch; I couldn't take my eyes off his bulging dick print.

This psychotic bitch is getting his love and great sex!

"I think it's time we lay everything on the table because I don't think you fully understand what's going on between me and her. I shouldn't even be having this conversation with you because we only had one sexual encounter that led to you getting pregnant. I've been taking care of my responsibilities since Nile was born so what else do you need, Jetti? My parents didn't even barge into my room when I lived with them and they paid the bills. You are just a guest on this property, but you walk around this muthafucka like you are more than what you are," he said. His tone was calm and smooth but his words were harsh and uncalled for. I watched Black Rose, waiting for her to crack a smile but her face was emotionless.

"This isn't about you! It's about Nile being around a bitch that has hunted down his kind for centuries!"

"I've hunted those who deserved to die, but you seem to know a lot about me. Were you there when I killed members of the Amstid Clan?" she asked.

"No, I wasn't there but I know what I heard when I was at Sheldon's cave. My cousin, Gensin, joined Sheldon's clan and she wanted me to join her. While I was there, they talked about you so much that I probably know more about you than you know about yourself," I replied.

"I'm willing to call a truce since I'm not going anywhere," she bluntly stated.

I burst out laughing, this was a clown show and Akea was entertained. Black Rose was a monster, the type of monster that hid underneath a child's bed, waiting to suck out their soul as they slept. Her long, sharp, pointed, black nails were weapons and could easily harm Nile, but that was her plan. She was conning her way into my family to kill them.

"Let me in on the joke. I need a good laugh," Black Rose said.

"It's funny that Akea forgives you so easily but he's still upset with me because my pack stole jewelry from him and his brother. I've done a lot of things but I'm not a killer."

"I'm over that, Jetti. It's not about that anymore, I simply don't have feelings for you. I don't need you coming up here if I don't send for you. Nile is asleep so you can leave," he said. I got up from the couch and went over to Nile's bassinet, he smelled fresh with a hint of chamomile and lavender. His hair had grown into a curly little fro and his chubby cheeks were so kissable. I wanted to take him and get far away from his father, so I wouldn't be easily distracted by Akea and his love life. I wanted to be a better version than the old Jetti.

I kissed his cheek and his eyes opened. My presence woke him; he wanted to be fed. I picked him up, cradling him close to my chest. Akea went back to the kitchen while I sat in the rocking chair to feed Nile. Black Rose attentively watched me, her eyes watered as if she were in pain. She looked away when she saw me smiling at her.

I bet she's jealous that I'm breastfeeding. I doubt her evil womb can carry an innocent life. Sheldon said elves are infertile without their magical forest, I wonder if it's true.

"I hate to sound like a bitch but I heard your kind isn't fertile without their forest. It must suck not being able to conceive and give your mate a child. Nile deserves a sibling in later life," I said to provoke her. She giggled to mask her hurt but I knew it was a gut wrenching feeling, especially by the way she was watching me with Nile.

"I know what you are trying to do, you want me to attack you while you are holding your child so that I can look like the monster you want me to be, but it won't work. I actually enjoy watching you become a loving mother instead of swiping Akea's Visa card. It suits you," she said. Akea was looking at me like he was smelling cow shit. He hated my guts and there was nothing I could do about it. Black Rose got up and went into the bathroom.

"I don't know why you said that knowing damn well she's eventually going to be his stepmother. Once we take that step, she'll have access to all parts of me, including my son. Hopefully, by that time, you'll be mated with someone," he said. He poured what was inside the blender into two glasses.

I'll be gone to another country or probably on a deserted island far away from you and your elf!

"Drink this," he said, handing me the drink. I took the glass from him, purposely brushing my fingers against his on the sly. He didn't react to me touching him, he coolly walked away and knocked on the bathroom door. "Are you straight?" he asked Black Rose.

"Yes, just washing my hair!" she called out.

"Do you need help?" he replied.

"No handsome, I got it!" she shouted.

Their love was disgusting and should've been a sin; they both deserved to burn in hell. Akea sat at his desk near his bed then put on his glasses. He opened a textbook and began highlighting words from a notepad.

"What are you doing?" I asked.

"Studying," he replied.

"I thought you were taking a break to focus on Nile and your family business."

"I'm back to taking online classes now," he said.

Fucking nerd!

I finished the tart smoothie, sitting the glass on the windowsill. Nile was finished feeding so I held him up and patted his back to burp him. Black Rose was still in the bathroom and I wondered if it was because of me. I walked around the penthouse, rocking Nile in my arms.

"Broooo," Kanye knocked on the door before walking in the penthouse with the fox following him.

"I see you guys are just taking in anyone," I said.

Kanye grilled me. "Why is she talking to me, bro?" he asked Akea.

"Ignore her, she'll stop," he replied.

Assholes!

"I see Monifa isn't trippin' over Silver following you around," Akea said to Kanye while patting Silver's head.

"Nope, she's talking about how she thinks it's cute that we have a pet. The hell type shit is that? I thought she was going to get a little jealous, but naw, she likes Silver. What does a brother have to do to get some attention? I thought me and her were going to you know...hump like wild animals," Kanye complained.

"Give her some flowers, run her a milk and honey bath with roses then give her a massage with a happy ending. Where were you when Father was showing us how to treat our mate? He always showed our mother that he appreciated her, even on their bad days," Akea said.

"Yeah, bro, you are absolutely right. I've been going insane thinking Monifa was getting tired of me. I'm addicted to her, you know? I can't handle withdrawals," Kanye chuckled. The fox jumped on the couch, wagging its tail while still chewing on the pair of socks. Black Rose was turning the castle into an animal reserve.

"I'm going to go back to my room. I'll see Nile later," I announced. They were treating me like I wasn't there anyway.

"I'll take my nephew," Kanye said, grabbing Nile from me. I kissed Nile's forehead before leaving the penthouse. The elevator door was already open so I got on. I pressed the button to the basement as the doors were closing. It came to a sudden stop. "These people are too rich for this raggedy elevator," I said aloud while pressing the button. Suddenly, my hair was snatched back and someone slammed my face into the elevator wall. I fell on the floor, holding my bloody nose. Black Rose appeared in front of me in the form of her creature. Her nails were longer than before and her eyes were pitch black. I backed into the corner.

"I'll scream for help!"

"No, you won't, bitch. I want you to repeat what you said back there about me being infertile," she said. My heart was beating fast, where was Akea when I needed him?

"Get your crazy ass away from me!" I screamed. She backhanded me; my body slid across the floor in the fetal position. She grabbed a fistful of my hair, snatching my head back. "Say it!" she said. She held a knife across my neck and it was deja vu of the night she killed my mate.

"Go ahead and repeat it so I can kill you like I killed your cousin. I snatched her heart right out of her chest, I guess you can call it a heart attack," she said. Black Rose was known for her sinister wordplay during her attacks. She made a mockery out of death.

"I can't!" I cried.

She gripped my hair tighter and I could feel it ripping from my scalp. "That's a good man back there, Jetti. I'll kill myself before I hurt him, so can you imagine what I'll do to someone who fucks with him? I'll take their head clean off their goddamn shoulders," she gritted. She pressed the knife into my neck.

"I always start here," she said, pressing the knife behind my right ear. "Then I end up here," she said, dragging the knife to the left side of my neck without cutting me. "I call it a smiley face and smiley faces always make me happy," she said. She shoved me into the elevator door; a patch of my hair fell onto the floor.

"This secret will stay between us. A word to anyone and I'll kill your weak ass with my bare hands. Do you think I won't do it?" she asked. The elevator lights went out, it was pitch black. I felt around to press the emergency button, but I felt something wet on my hands.

"Get me out of here!" I banged on the walls. Seconds later, the lights came back on; it was a bloody massacre. Gensin's dead body sat in the corner of the elevator; she was naked with a giant hole in her chest. Black Rose appeared again, holding a heart in her hand.

"Wh...wh..." I couldn't get the words out.

"Do we have a problem, flea bag?" she asked. I felt something wet running down my inner-thighs—I had pissed on the elevator floor.

"I won't tell anyone so please leave me alone," I whispered. She snapped her fingers and Gensin was gone, even her blood and heart. Black Rose pressed the button to the basement. "You will clean up that piss so nobody else has to do it," she said. The elevator doors opened when it stopped at the basement. "Word of advice, make sure you can back up your snide remarks. Nothing is worse than a dog that's all bark and no bite. Hell, you are not even house trained," she said, looking down at the urine. She patted my head before she vanished. I took off the robe and cleaned off the elevator floor. Afterwards, I went into the guest room and climbed into bed in a daze while still holding the dirty robe in my arms. I couldn't believe Black Rose had the balls to torment me that way and inside Akea's home.

This can't be it! My husband didn't die for me to be a coward. I can't give up...I won't give up. Black Rose will not get the last laugh! I'm going to that bonfire like everyone and smile in the devil's face.

Black Rose

"Fill me up," I told Monifa. She poured a strong rum inside my glass, filling it to the top. Between Circa's lies and Jetti's rude mouth, I was on the verge of going crazy. How could a man I'd known for centuries claim I was his mate when I only knew him as my father? Whenever I thought back to the past, I always remembered the battles between Yubsari and Amstid, but I had no recollection of ever being a child. I thought my fogged memory was because I was cursed but now I was confused. To top it off, Circa claimed we shared a daughter. I tossed the drink back, to take my mind off the creep. "Slow down, that will turn you into a mummy," Fiti said, blowing smoke out of her mouth. I was in the bar and lounge area at the castle with Fiti, Monifa and Baneet. I was enjoying the warmth of being around a nurturing group of people despite Baneet's nosey ass. My stay was only temporary because Akea wanted to protect me from Circa's manipulation. I should've let him kill Circa but I wouldn't have been able to live with myself.

"That right there will have you twerking on the walls," Monifa said, referring to the rum.

"I don't know what that is," I replied.

"Whatttt? You got all that ass and don't know what twerking is?" Baneet asked.

"I think it's a dance move," Fiti said.

Baneet rolled her eyes at Fiti. If I was Fiti, I would've zapped her across the mouth.

"Soo, I see Majestic and Tiko have been cooped up in the room all day. I hope she doesn't swallow him whole," Baneet joked because Majestic was a snake.

"There's nothing wrong with swallowing your man's manhood. I swallow Zaan's all the time," Fiti threw out there. I couldn't help but laugh, especially at Baneet getting upset. She slammed her shot glass on the table.

"Enough of sex talk around me or else I'll go in heat," Monifa said.

"I'll be happy when you give Kanye some so he can stop moping around like a lost dog," Baneet said.

"Maybe you should screw Jasiah and stop worrying about everyone else," Fiti mumbled. "What was that?" Baneet asked.

"Can we just relax while the men are upstairs getting along? We have the best ancient rum in history so we should be enjoying it," Monifa said.

"How long are you staying with us?" Baneet asked me.

"Did Jetti put you up to asking me that? She could've asked me herself," I replied.

"I was just asking because you fit right in with our pack. We got a little bit of everything going on. We have werewolves, witches, a warlock, a snake, a fox and a dwarf. We're like the black version of Harry Potter," Baneet joked.

"Who is the dwarf?" I asked.

"I thought that's what Kanye said. I overheard him saying you put gifts under Christmas trees and you drive a sleigh. Is that not true?" Baneet replied.

"I apologize on Kanye's behalf. He smokes a lot and sometimes he hears things differently," Monifa said.

"Zaan said she was a troll and lives under a bridge," Fiti interjected.

"I don't expect anyone to know of my kind since we come from a very ancient world and not too many know we exist. I actually like it that way, especially when people try to come up with their own assumption of what I am," I said.

"Well, what are you?" Baneet asked.

"A woman, the same as you," I replied. She gave me a fake smile with an eye roll.

Monifa turned on the music with a remote and a singer named Jill Scott came through the surround speakers. The song was called, The Way.

"What time are we going to the bonfire? I need some air," Fiti said.

"At midnight," Monifa replied.

I looked at the clock on the wall above the bar and it was eleven forty-five. Silver ran into the lounge, standing on her hind legs so I could pet her. She happily wagged her tail, she was enjoying herself.

"Kanye wanted me to be jealous of her cute little self, but if she was a shifter, it would've been a different story. He tries to push my buttons but he keeps it PG-13," Monifa said.

"She likes hanging out with the beasts, but she doesn't have a desire to mate so it's innocent," I said. Silver ran out of the room, just as quickly as she came. Fiti slid off the barstool, smoothing out her linen pants. She was an ebony beauty with a slim body, small angelic face and big brown eyes. She didn't have much butt or breasts, but it was perfect for her. Her dreadlocks hung to her hips and she had hieroglyphic symbols on her neck. "I'll catch you girls later. I'm about to find Zaan so we can get in a quickie," she announced.

"We aren't going to see you for a few days then," Monifa said.

"I promise we won't get lost again. We leave sticky notes on the wall so we can find our way through the castle. We gotta quit smoking but it's hard," Fiti said.

"Wait, y'all are the ones leaving sticky notes on the wall with misspelled words? I should've known it was one of you," Baneet snickered.

"I do know one thing. I know how to spell 'Zaan's going to be my pups' daddy' correctly. I've been practicing all night," she said.

"Kudos to you, I'm happy for the both of you. I cheated on Zaan our whole relationship, so he needed someone to lean on to get over me," Baneet replied.

"That's nothing to brag about. You are making yourself sound like a jezebel," Monifa replied. Fiti vanished without warning anyone. I thought she would at least put Baneet in her place.

Baneet needs a good stabbing in the throat. I'll bet that'll stop her big mouth from talking.

"Potheads are so weird," Baneet said.

Jasiah stormed into the lounge and grabbed Baneet by her sweatshirt, jacking her up. "Not this again!" Monifa said.

"Where in the hell is the necklace my father gave to me? I know you did something with it!" he said to her. His eyes glowed and his teeth sharpened. I was silently hoping he would take a chunk out of her. "Get your hands off me!" Baneet screamed. Jasiah slammed her on the bar, knocking over the rum urns and glasses. I backed away so nothing spilled on my black, silk pants.

"You took it to hurt me! Now where the fuck is it?" he growled.

"I don't know!" Baneet shouted.

"Where is his necklace, Baneet?" Monifa asked calmly. It was just a normal day for her.

"I don't know! I could've swept it up by accident when I cleaned our bedroom," she said. Jasiah shoved her off the bar. "I want my shit put right back where you took it from! If not, I'm going to chew up everything in your closet and drawers," he said. She got up from the floor, ready to attack him, but Monifa stopped her.

"Just give it back to him," Monifa told her. Baneet snatched her arm away from Monifa. "He's the one who flaunted another female's scent in my face. Y'all don't think that was painful for me?" she asked.

"I don't care about any of that. Go ahead and find my necklace!" Jasiah snarled.

"It's underneath the mattress," she said with her head down. She was acting like a scolded child.

"I'll be moving my stuff out of your bedroom tonight so you don't have to worry about my things being in your way," he said. He apologized to us before leaving the lounge. Baneet picked up the urns and broken glass off the floor.

"We'll be outside," Monifa told Baneet.

We walked out, leaving Baneet to clean up the mess she'd made. Monifa took a deep breath. "I'm exhausted," she said.

"You should go to bed."

She chuckled. "I wish but I have two pups who drain my body. They are always so hungry. It's normal for baby werewolves to drink more milk than the average baby, but imagine feeding two," she replied.

"I'm sure it's worth it in the end. They'll grow up and eventually take care of you when you get older."

"The kicker is we stay young forever," she laughed.

I followed Monifa down a hallway and out of a side door which led to the backyard. There was a lake in their backyard with canoes and jet-skis. The land was bigger than I thought. I stepped outside, enjoying the late night breeze. Akea and Kanye got off an elevator with baby carriers.

"The babies sit next to the fire too?" I asked Monifa.

"Yes, but not too close. We bring them out because they love the night's sky too," she replied. The four of us walked towards the four tree logs they used for sitting.

Owwwwwhooooooooo!

The sound of a howling wolf came from the castle. "That's Tiko howling. Does he gotta let the whole world know he's shooting up Majestic's club?" Kanye asked.

"Like you and Monifa didn't howl. We used to hear y'all from the woods," Akea said.

"Yeah, that's when we were young," Kanye replied.

"That was like four months ago, bro," Akea chuckled.

"I think we're the only ones that's going to be out here," Monifa said.

"I'm cool with that. We need the quiet time anyway," Akea replied.

I sat on the log and Akea sat next to me. He took Nile out of the carrier and held him. His little eyes glowed, he was the perfect mixture of Akea and Jetti. "You want to hold him?" he asked.

"He's so small and fragile. I don't want to prick him with my nails."

"You won't, just hold him in the crook of your arm and underneath your breast. You nails won't touch him," he said. "Okay, but the minute I panic, take him away from me. I mean it, Akea. I love children but I've never touched one."

He stood up and placed him in the crook of my arm. "He feels like he doesn't have any bones and he's extra soft. What if I bend him?" I asked. I was beginning to panic. "Calm down, Rose. I'm not going to let you hurt him so trust me," he said. Nile rested against my arm while I held him.

"See, a piece of cake," Akea said.

Nile's eyes glowed again, they were beaming into mine as if he was looking into the windows of my soul. I stopped breathing when he turned into a little girl with a head full of black coils and pointed ears. She resembled me and someone else that I knew…Circa. She looked to be two years old and blood was oozing from her neck. I held my hand against her neck to stop the bleeding but it wouldn't stop. Her small body was ice-cold and her lips were blue—she was dead. I freaked out, holding onto her tightly while tears burned my eyes. "What did they do to you? Why are you so cold?" I asked. I was trembling trying to contain my emotions but they were exploding.

"ROSE!" Akea's voice snapped me out of my daydream. I looked up, Kanye, Akea, Monifa and Jetti were staring at me. I didn't know she had come outside. Tears were falling from my eyes and onto Nile's forehead.

"Get my baby away from her! She's insane!" Jetti said. I gave Nile to Akea before running to the lake. Once I reached the lake, I collapsed. I couldn't stop crying because I was so confused. That dead little girl belonged to me, I could feel it. I couldn't explain it or remember having her but I had a connection to her.

"How Circa! Howwwww!" I screamed. I felt a pair of hands around me and before I knew it, I was standing on the other side of the lake. Someone had teleported with me and I knew it wasn't Akea because their arms weren't as strong as his. I was still sitting in the grass and the person sat next to me as I wept. "I figured you needed to be away from everyone. Did Nile show you something?" the voice asked. I looked over and it was Monifa next to me.

"He's just a baby. How was he able to see through me when Akea couldn't?"

"You let your guard down because he's a baby; there's no need to have your guard up around a baby. He is too young to understand what's going on," she said.

"I don't remember her. I don't know her name...nothing. But I felt her and connected with her. Someone killed her; where was I? How could I not protect her?" I asked. I caught an excruciating headache while trying to remember the past—it gave me an anxiety attack. "Your nose is bleeding," she said. I held my arm against my nose to stop it from bleeding. Across the lake, I heard Jetti shouting at Akea. She was pointing her finger in his face while he was holding Nile. I couldn't make out what they were saying, but I heard her shout "punk bitch" at him.

"Your blood is very dark, did you come back to life from a sacrifice?" she asked. I looked at her trying to figure out why she would say that. "Don't mind me, I know about black magic. In my past life before I was reincarnated, I was an evil witch that practiced black magic from a demon's spell book," she said.

"I don't know anything," I replied, on the verge of tears again. Slowly, I was breaking down into small fragments. I couldn't hold myself together and most times I felt detached from the woman I used to be before Akea.

"I'm not much of a psychic, but memory loss could be from a rebirth. But not the kind of rebirth where there's a reincarnation, it's more of a ritual rebirth. What you did in your life before the rebirth, you will do the opposite after rebirth. We call it The Antithesis Curse," she said.

"Antithesis?" I repeated.

"Yes, it just means 'opposite'. If you were full of happiness, you'll be full of sadness in this life. This curse is very ancient, though, I mean over a thousand years old so an ancient witch or warlock must've performed the ritual," she replied.

This has Sheldon written all over it! Nothing is going to stop me from killing him this time.

"Is it reversible?"

"I'm sorry, but it's not. It's like a disease, you have to live with it. It can go into remission but anything can trigger that opposite side. I'm the same way, I have my moments where I still feel like my evil self from the past life. You got to make the best of it. Kanye keeps me grounded and when I have my bad days, he comforts me. Don't feel guilty for leaning on Akea when you have your bad days. Goon's sons can handle everything, they are built Ford tough," she said. I knew her words were meant to comfort me, but I realized I really didn't deserve Akea. Monifa rubbed my back while I continued to shed tears. Even though it was the past, the wounds were fresh so I was grieving as if it had just happened. I thought of Circa's confession. His hatred towards the Amstid Clan was because of the pain they had caused us. I had to go back to the Yubsari Warriors and help Circa kill all of Sheldon's people. It was going to hurt Akea so I didn't plan on telling him. I planned to make our last night together a moment to remember, before walking away.

"Are you ready to go back?" Monifa asked.

"Yes, we can."

We teleported back to the bonfire and the whole pack was outside. Jetti and Akea were still arguing. "She was trying to choke him! You saw it with your own eyes. She put her hand around his neck!" Jetti lied.

"How are you going to lie like that with a straight face? And your screaming is making my pups scream!" Kanye said.

"Mind your business. This is between mother and father. I didn't lay down with you!" Jetti yelled.

"Thank god because I would've been slapped the shit out of you!" Kanye replied.

I sat on the log next to Majestic. She was wearing Tiko's sweat clothes, they were too big for her, but what stood out was her smile. I couldn't tell her about going back to Circa because I wanted her to live her life away from me. She deserved to be happy and I was keeping her away from that.

"What happened? I just came out here and heard Jetti screaming about you trying to kill Nile," she said.

"Don't believe that bitch. She speaks nothing but nonsense but is as quiet as a snail when she's away from everyone else."

"I know she's lying. Look at her, she's so over the top," Majestic said.

"Take her to the pool house. She can't come back to the castle ever again. If she does, snap her neck and put her out of her misery," Akea demanded. I knew he was serious by the tone in his voice and the veins popping out of his neck. He was beyond pissed off. Tiko and Jasiah picked her up by her legs and arms to carry her to the pool house. It was hilarious, her body was in mid-shift but Tiko and Jasiah held her in a restraint that she couldn't shift out of.

"I apologize for that. I'll send her away tomorrow for good. I can't deal with her and I hate looking at her. I'll take being labeled as the petty father instead of having her in our faces any day. Fuck being a gentleman, I've tried too many times with her," Akea told Kanye.

"I hope your future children die in their mother's womb!" Jetti screamed while being carried down a hill.

"Such a bitch," Fiti said and everyone else agreed.

Akea sat close to me. "What did Nile show you?" he asked.

"I thought I saw someone I knew from the past but it was the rum I had that caused me to see things. Is he okay?"

"Yeah, he's fine but I feel like you aren't being honest with me. We can talk about it later, though," he said. I rested my head on his shoulder but kept my eyes on the bonfire. Nile was making baby noises but I couldn't look at him, I feared he'd show me something else.

"Why did y'all have to go across the lake to talk?" Baneet asked Monifa. Monifa shot Baneet a crazed look with glowing eyes. "I'm just asking, my heavens. Y'all act like I'm not a part of the pack," Baneet said.

"You act like you aren't a part of this pack! And how you are doing Jasiah is pretty fucked up. And the shade you have been throwing Fiti lately is petty. Your spoiled bratty attitude is overbearing," Monifa said.

"This is like deja vu. Y'all might not get along because y'all fathers were bro-enemies. Uncle Dayo and Uncle Izra fought at every family get together. It might just be a natural instinct," Zaan said.

"That's the smartest thing you've ever said, bro. I'm proud of you," Akea teased.

Baneet threw her arms up in frustration. "I'm not saying anything else. Fuck it!" she said.

"Since we're gathered here on this lovely night, I would like to announce that me and my mate will be launching our new weed line called, Akea's IQ," Zaan said. He went inside his pants pocket and pulled out a gold Ziploc bag. He took out a gold weed bud. "This right here is for people who need to be focused in school or at work, hence the name Akea's IQ. It enhances the mind, specifically the cerebello-parietal component and the frontal component which is where we gain most of our knowledge from. As you can see, I already smoked two joints of it," he said.

"Bro, did you just memorize the schoolwork I left on my desk?" Akea asked Zaan.

"Duh, that's why it's called Akea's IQ. Were you not listening, bro? Stay focused," Zaan said, pointing to his head.

"You are fittin' to get our black asses sued if it doesn't work. Go back to the drawing board and stay off my desk," Akea replied.

"About that, I think I accidentally smoked your thesis paper so I can memorize the words. I swear bro, I became an honor student smoking your homework. That's cool, huh?" Zaan asked.

"WHAT!" Akea shouted.

"My bad bro, I ran out of weed paper," Zaan shrugged.

"I memorized what was on the paper so don't worry, we'll write it over for you," Fiti nonchalantly said.

"Y'all can't even spell, don't worry about it. I memorized everything word for word," Akea replied.

"Exactlyyy bro. That's why we are naming it after you," Zaan said.

"I can't even say shit. I'm not even shocked, I actually expected the worst," Kanye said.

This is so bad. Poor Akea, my baby is always going through it. Hopefully when I'm gone, he can have the stress free life he deserves.

Tiko and Jasiah came back to the bonfire. Tiko sat on the other side of Majestic. The rest of the night turned out to be fun and it was filled with laughter and jokes like always. I was never going to forget this welcoming pack, especially Akea.

****

Akea came out of the shower with the towel wrapped around his waist. We were in the room alone since Nile was sleeping in the nursery with Monifa's pups. I was sitting in a chair next to the bedroom window, staring at the moon. I was thinking of a quiet way to slip out without being noticed.

"What's up with you, Rose? You've been quiet since that run in with Circa," he said.

"Nothing, I'm just tired. I'm not used to having much fun, so it easily wears me down."

"We're alone now so you can talk to me about what happened when you held Nile," he said.

"I'm fine, I promise."

He sat on the end of the windowsill. "I think it's about Circa. Don't worry about that creep, Rose. I gotcha and this pack is solid, they can't even reach you here," he said.

"It's not him, I promise."

"Is it about the daughter he said y'all have together, and how he was your mate before you had memory loss?" he asked.

"Circa was just being Circa. He is *very* manipulative. I don't want you worrying about me. I'm grown and can deal with everything that comes my way on my own."

"Your aura always gives you away. You are sad again," he said.

"I'm always this way."

"Maybe before you met me, but you were happy while you were cooking for me yesterday morning and plenty of times before that. We can sleep on it and talk about it when we wake up," he said. I got up from the chair and went to him. He kissed my hand when I caressed his beautiful face. "I'm fine, Akea. I promise I am."

He grabbed the waist of my silk pants, pulling me closer to him. I hugged him tight, resting my head against his chest. He picked me up and I wrapped my legs halfway around him. "Short ass legs," he joked. I bucked at him, pretending I was going to hit him. He kissed my fist. "Take your best shot," he said.

"You really don't want me to punch you, don't sleep on my small hands." Invisible hands were unbuttoning my silk blouse while Akea was cupping my ass cheeks. My blouse fell to the floor. I closed my eyes when Akea traced the outline of my nipple with his tongue. The center of my pants was soaked, especially since I was pantyless. "Should I stop since you had an exhausting day?" he asked.

"I'm always in the mood for this."

He sat in the chair next to the window with me on his lap. He ripped my thin pants right off my body. He suckled on my breast while kneading into my breast like dough. "Ohhh," I moaned. His magical hands were sending electrical bolts through my body. I unwrapped his towel, unleashing his dick.

"Ummmmm," his raspy voice moaned while I was working my hips down his girth. He bit his bottom lip and the vein in his neck was bulging; he was fighting the urge to cum too soon. He pulled my legs from underneath my body, placing them over the arms of the chair; with my legs spread so far apart, he was rock bottom in my pussy.

He bounced me on his dick while grinding his dick against my G-spot.

"This is my pussy, huh Rose," he arrogantly asked.

"YESSSS!" I cooed.

He cupped the bottom of my face, still thrusting. He had a pattern that always made me squirt. His strokes were slow but deep and when he'd go fast, he grinded.

"Uhmmm hmmm," Akea nodded while my pussy was throbbing. I buried my nails into his chest. "Let it go, beautiful," he coached because I was holding in the orgasm. He picked up my legs and threw them over his shoulders, letting them dangle over the chair. "AHHHHHHH!" I exhaled while he slammed me on his dick.

"Fuckkkkkk...this shit is so wet and tight!" he said. I had a loud orgasm. My pussy sounded like ocean waves washing up on shore. "I love youuuuu!" I screamed while erupting. He never told me back, but I wasn't expecting him to. Now I preferred it that way so it wouldn't be hard on him when I left. Nothing was worse than confessing your love to someone only for them to walk out of your life without an explanation. Our bodies floated from the chair, but Akea didn't miss a stroke. He laid on top of me when my back was pressed against the ceiling. The lights in the room dimmed; the only light inside the room came from the moon and stars. His ice blue eyes glowed and shadows of hieroglyphics appeared on the walls and ceiling. His fingers intertwined with mine while he held my arms above my head, making passionate love to me against the ceiling. The ceiling cracked from Akea's pounding. His chandelier fell on top of the glass coffee table.

"Don't look down, Rose. Look at me," he said. I looked into his eyes. "I lov—" I cut him off, by pressing my lips against his. A tear slipped out the corner of my eye, falling on top of his desk. I didn't want him to love me, the love being one-sided was better for his heart. His body jerked at the same time he gripped a handful of my hair. His breathing was fast paced and his dick was about to rupture my cervix from his orgasm. "AGHHHHH!" he moaned. I kissed his chin and he chuckled. "I'm supposed to be opening the store in a few hours. I probably won't make it," he said. He landed on the floor, I pushed my body off the ceiling and fell into his awaiting arms.

"Go to sleep while I shower."

"We usually shower together," he yawned. His eyes were back to their normal deep brown color, but they were also bloodshot red.

"I'm serious. Go to bed, Akea. I'll join you in twenty minutes."

He smacked my buttocks. "Aight, but hurry up. Watch out for the glass, I don't want you cutting your feet," he said.

"I will."

I watched him get in bed and underneath the sheets. He went right to sleep when his head hit the pillow. "I'll clean this up for him." I zapped the pile of glass with my wand and it disappeared; the chandelier appeared back on the ceiling seconds later. Afterwards, a hooded cloak appeared on my body with a pair of combat boots. I wanted to kiss Akea goodbye but didn't want to wake him.

"Thank you for being you, my love." I laid a single black rose on the pillow where I would've slept had I stayed. It was late, the castle was quiet and I didn't want to alert anyone so I teleported to the outside of the castle's gate. "Bye Majestic, take care of Silver for me," I said as if she could hear me.

Circa better give me all the answers I need! I'm not playing any more games with him!

****

I walked down the hallway of Circa's home. The feast room was loud and Circa's deep voice resonated through the hallways. I opened the doors and the room got quiet. Circa was sitting at the head of the table with a cloth wrapped around his head, covering his eye. I walked past the evil glares. Zelda's father threw his goat wine on me. "TRAITOR!" he yelled. He raised his hand to hit me, but an axe plunged through his skull, splitting his head in half. His dead body fell forward, face down in a tray of meat. Circa was a fast weapon thrower, no one ever saw it coming.

"Black Rose is off limits and if anyone touches her, they'll have to deal with me! A spell was cast on her to make her betray this clan but as you can see, she's back to normal," Circa said. He walked around the table and wrapped his arms around me. "You just made me the happiest man. I missed you, Lyira," he whispered.

"When are we going to attack the wolf god's son who made her kill Zelda?" a warrior named, Artie, asked.

"What is he talking about, Circa?" I asked.

Circa ran his fingers through my hair. "Akea will die tonight for what he did to you. He brainwashed you," he replied.

"I've come here to kill Sheldon and his people! Akea is off limits!" I screamed.

"As you can see my fellow warriors, her mind is still poisoned from the spell he cast on her. Akea is carrying out his father's orders by protecting Sheldon's clan. He poisoned our best warrior to weaken us, but we can't allow the disrespect anymore! Not only did he weaken her mind, but he raped her! Those warlocks are rapists and take what they want from our women!" Circa shouted. He was getting his men riled up. "What are you doing?" I gritted. "I'm making you look innocent and if you want to know the truth about me, you and our daughter, you might want to play along. I will not look weak in front of my warriors," he whispered in my ear.

"I want his fucking head!" someone shouted.

"We will not mourn Duke's death. He knew of this spell Akea cast on Black Rose but he attacked her anyway. He's a coward and should be burned!" Circa ordered. His men dropped down to their knees, worshipping him. "We are sorry for doubting Black Rose," they said.

"All is forgiven. Eat and drink up. I have to talk to Black Rose alone," Circa told his men. He grabbed my hand, pulling me out of the feast room and into the hallway.

"Why did you lie on Akea? He doesn't know Sheldon, never seen his face. Is this what's been happening since I've been gone? You've been lying to make yourself look like a great leader?"

"Yes, Rose. I've been lying to protect your image. You think I want them knowing you fell in love with the enemy? That isn't a good look but I'm willing to forgive you if you never leave me again," he pleaded.

"What was our...our daughter's name?" I asked. Asking a man that pretended to be my father about our daughter was making me lightheaded. It left a bad taste in my mouth, but I had to know about the little girl that shared mine and his looks.

"Her name was Baccara," he said.

I got weak in the knees, but Circa caught me before I hit the floor. Akea had brought me three dozen of the rare roses that were named after my daughter.

"But why, Circa? Why was she killed and I was cursed? Was she a sacrifice for a ritual?"

"I don't know, I only know I found the both of you lying in your garden with Sheldon, Ryul and Amstid standing near y'all bodies. But you weren't dead, you woke up a different woman. I killed Amstid, but Ryul and Sheldon escaped through the portal they had opened to our world. We had to leave the forest because the ritual killed the forest. Can't you see why I fight for us? Akea is the enemy because his father is protecting Sheldon. He's just like them, Rose," Circa said.

"I believe you, Circa, but I can't believe that Akea or his father are like them. His father raised great sons who accepted me with open arms, regardless of what I am. We will take care of Sheldon as planned, but Akea is off limits."

Circa angrily punched a hole in the wall. "FUCK!" he shouted.

"I can go alone to take care of Sheldon," I told him. He grabbed my arm when I walked away. "Wait, Rose," he said. I snatched my arm away from him. "What?"

"I'll leave the warlock boy alone under one condition," he said.

"What is it now?" I asked, getting annoyed.

"We start over. Me and you belong together. I'll send Merci and Nayati away," he said.

"You will exile your own daughter? You are really disgusting!"

"She's not my daughter, she belongs to Ryul. Merci was raped when they stormed into our forest. She's nobody to me. I've waited a thousand years for us to be together, that's why I kept you close, hoping you'd notice me as your mate," he said.

"I can't see you as my mate, but I will be by your side to defeat Sheldon."

Merci and Nayati stormed down the hallway when they saw me. "I hope damn well she's being punished for what she did to me, Father," Nayati said.

"I need to speak to you in our bedroom now!" Merci said to Circa.

"What did we talk about? Didn't I tell you I need my space?" Circa asked her with a raised eyebrow. Merci clenched her jaw and her fist, I could tell she was getting sick of Circa's authoritative behavior.

Nayati stood in front of us with her arms crossed. "Stand down, Nayati. I'm not in a good mood. I will kill you this time," I warned her.

"Mother, can you scold her?" Nayati asked Merci.

"Her father can scold her. It's not my duty to scold a grown woman," Merci said.

"It's late and you two need to be in bed. We're having a man's feast," Circa replied.

Merci grilled me. "You are a fool for coming back," she said.

"Upstairs Merci!" Circa yelled.

SOUL Publications

"Black Rose isn't in trouble for Zelda and what she did to me?" Nayati asked.

"Get your daughter, Merci, and take her upstairs," Circa said.

"My husband won't look at me because of her!" Nayati said, stomping her feet.

"Let your father talk to his daughter. They have a lot of catching up to do, hopefully she'll be punished soon," Merci said. She rolled her eyes at me, before she grabbed Nayati and escorted her down the hallway.

"This isn't over, Black Rose. You'll pay for what you did to me and my marriage!" Nayati screamed.

Why would Merci tell me I shouldn't have come back? These broads get crazier by the second. I came here to finish a mission, not to be a happy family.

"I broke things off with Akea so stay away from him. That's all I can give you."

"I'll take that. I can wait another thousand years for you as long as you stay away from him," he said.

"Where can I sleep for the night?"

"Follow me," Circa said.

I followed him all the way to the fourth floor. The hallway was vacant but spotless. I had always stayed in my cabin instead of in the home with Circa and others, but I would've relapsed and gone back to Akea if I would've gone to my cabin. The memories of him and my cabin were fresh and I wanted to keep him off my mind. Circa opened a door to a room with a shower and bed with clean sheets. "You can work your magic to spruce it up," he said.

"It's only for the night," I replied walking into the guest room. I slammed the door in his face before he could get out a word. "Goodnight, my love," he said from the other side of the door. I laid across the bed, staring at the ceiling. I relived the moment when Akea had me on the ceiling, ready to confess his love to me.

If you would've met me as Lyira, I know we could've lived happily ever after. You deserve the best version of me, but she's dead. I no longer want you to catch me if I ever fall. I don't want you to save me at all. I've been in the dark for so long, I've learned to grow without the sun. I am Black Rose, Akea, the flower of sadness, death and mourning. I hope you find someone who can live with the same confidence as you...

A tear slipped out of my eye while thinking of the only way to release myself from the curse and soon I would be free...

Akea

*T*he morning sun beamed through my bedroom window, stinging my eyes. I stretched my arms and legs. "What time is it, Rose?" I asked her.

I didn't get a response. Rose rarely slept so I figured she'd be up. I sat up, looking around the room; a single black rose was lying on the pillow next to where I slept. Someone knocked on my door.

"Bro, Nile is up!" Kanye said. I could hear Nile crying at the top of his lungs from the other side of the door.

"Come in!" I said, pulling the sheet over my manhood. He came into my bedroom, covered in blood. Nile's blanket was covered in blood too. "You keep doing this bro. You know I don't like deer blood on my floor."

"I just got in from hunting when Monifa told me to bring him to you. Baby boy is hungry, but Jetti is on her way up here. You don't want her in here, right?" Kanye asked.

"Fuck no, tell her to stay in the pool house. I'll take Nile to her after I get dressed."

"We gotta be at the store in two hours so hurry up," he said. He laid Nile on my bed then headed towards the door. "Aye, did you see Rose this morning? She's not in here."

"Naw, but Monifa said she had a lot of rum last night; she might be in one of the bathrooms. You know how females don't like taking care of their business around anyone, they gotta shit in private," he said.

"Yeah, you are right."

"We gotta leave soon and be on time so don't be long," Kanye reminded me. I waited until he left and took Nile to the bathroom and bathed him. He was still screaming at the top of his lungs.

"Hellooooo," Jetti said, coming into my penthouse.

"Wait in the living room!" I shouted.

Kanye must not have seen her coming up because she's not supposed to be in here.

I held Nile's head back to wash the blood out of his hair. Kanye's pups were always covered in blood to get a taste of it until they were old enough to hunt.

"He keeps forgetting Nile isn't a werewolf," I said while scrubbing the blood out of his hair. His cries got louder. "I'm almost finished lil' man, just give me a second."

The bathroom door slid back. I was naked and Jetti was standing in the doorway, with her eyes glowing at my morning wood. It wasn't a good look, especially if Black Rose caught us.

"GET OUT!"

"Oh my god, why is he bleeding?" Jetti asked, rushing to the tub style sink I had put in for Nile. "You thought I was joking about you being in here?"

"I heard him screaming and besides, it's past his feeding time and I got worried. Is he hurt?" she asked.

"No, it's just deer blood. Now get out."

She left the bathroom, closing the door behind her. I grabbed a towel and wrapped it around Nile's body. Before I left the bathroom, I put on a robe. Jetti was sitting on the couch, topless and dying for my attention. I gave Nile to her without looking at her chest.

"You know I have a woman and you purposely do this so I can look at you," I chuckled. Jetti was one big ass joke that wasn't funny.

"My body is just as perfect as hers so why not?" she asked.

"I want you to pump your breast milk after you finish feeding him. After today, you are only allowed to come twice a week. Not only are you disrespectful to me, you are disrespectful to the entire pack."

"But-"

I cut her off. "I don't want to hear it. You brought this on yourself. We had a deal anyway, before he was born that I was going to raise him alone, but I thought you changed and we could co-parent, but you are still unfit. The fake concern about his well-being is over the top. And the obsession you have for Black Rose thinking she's going to kill him is exhausting."

"Where is Black Rose now?" she replied.

"Why?"

Jetti cracked a smile. "You must not know," she said.

"Know what?"

"That she left. I was in the woods hunting when I saw her leaving. Her words were, '*Bye Majestic, take care of Silver for me.*' That sounds like someone leaving for good, right?" she asked.

"You are psychotic. She doesn't have a reason to leave when she's safer around me."

"We should wait and see then but I prayed on it last night. I asked our God to give me a sign if I should stay and fight for you and Nile or walk away. And guess what? He moved her out of our lives. Why keep a woman who doesn't want to be kept?" she asked.

"Those words don't mean shit. She could've gone for a walk."

Jetti hysterically laughed, pounding the couch with her fist. "AH HA HAAAAA!" she shouted. "You are a smart man, Akea. Don't be a fool over love. Black Rose left Majestic and Silver here because they are better off without her. I bet she's out and about right now, slaughtering the last of the Amstid Clan. Nobody can stop a witch hunter who has unfinished business," she said.

I looked back at the black rose lying on my pillow. Jetti was a liar, but her story wasn't too far-fetched. Thinking back to what transpired yesterday, it made sense. The fight with Circa, her cries when she held Nile, and lastly, her cutting me off when I was ready to confess my feelings to her. She became distant after Circa bombarded his way into her cabin.

"Where does Sheldon live?" I asked Jetti.

"I don't know," she replied.

"But you said you met him and he talked about Black Rose."

"Why would you go there and get involved? Black Rose is more than capable of defeating Sheldon. Stay out of it, it isn't your fight," she replied.

"I'll figure it out."

"Okay fine, I'll tell you what I know. Sheldon moves his clan around in fear of the elves. He doesn't stay in one spot but when I met him with Gensin, he mentioned going somewhere west. This was a week ago so he's long gone," she said. Someone knocked on the door, my penthouse was everyone's favorite spot it seemed.

"Good morning, Akea. It's Naobi, are you decent?" she asked.

Jetti almost tripped, putting Nile in his bassinet. She was moving fast, putting her shirt on backwards. "Come in!" I told Naobi.

She opened the door. "I hear my great-grandchild was fussy this morning," she said.

"I'll see you when you get back. I feel embarrassed that I don't have enough clothes on," Jetti said, looking disheveled. She bowed to my grandmother on her way out of the bedroom.

"Why is she walking around with those tiny shorts? Did I interrupt something?" she asked.

"Not at all, how was your trip?"

"It was lovely. It's always a pleasure visiting the motherland," she replied. She went to the bassinet and kissed Nile's cheek. "He's getting chunky. Jetti is feeding him well," she said.

"That's the only reason why I've been dealing with her bull, but I hate her being here."

"That is why it's important to have offspring with someone you love. It makes the foundation more solid. By the time I realized that, your father was grown and having his own children. But what's a lesson learned if it doesn't teach you anything?" she asked.

"While you were away, I had a chance to learn more about Black Rose. I know you had your doubts but I took it upon myself to find out."

She sat across from me, crossing her legs. My grandmother's presence was still of a Queen. I was on the verge of changing the subject but I already had her full attention. "Go on, Child. What did you learn?" she replied.

"She's a cursed witch hunter and could have possibly tried to kill me but she didn't. I fell for her and she fell for me too. I'm going to continue seeing her and the pack is cool with it."

"The first thing I heard from Baneet's mouth when I walked through the front door was that someone was living in here with you. I already know you chose your own path without my guidance. But what I want to know is why your aura is off? I'm feeling sad, angry, and regretful energy from you while talking about her. Did she hurt you like I knew she would?" Naobi asked.

"Dang Grandma, why would you say it like that?" I asked, feeling worse than before.

"I knew that woman was battling something dark the moment I saw her. People like her are incapable of being in a genuine relationship. She left you didn't she?" she asked.

"I think she did and it's pretty fucked up that she didn't give me a chance to tell her that I love her. She's not a bad person though, she knows how to laugh, smile, joke and love. Grandma, I need a favor," I said.

She waved her hands and shook her head. "Nuh uh, I won't find her for you. If it's meant to be she'll come back. If you chase something, it runs from you so the answer is 'no'," she said.

"I was going to ask you if you can find a man named Sheldon for me. He's a warlock that has something to do with Black Rose's curse. She said, Father, is protecting him and his people from her clan."

"I can't get involved in the King's business. That's a sin in Anubi. What your father and that man have going on is between them. Stay out of it, Akea," she said sternly.

"I only want to know more about Black Rose's past. A man that she knew as a father confessed that he was her mate, but she doesn't remember that part of her life. Black Rose has memory loss and I feel like she can be easily manipulated since she doesn't remember anything. She was once a goddess named Lyira. That woman is more than just a dark soul, she's a goddess, a creator of her world."

"No matter what, Akea, she will never remember her past life so if you discover the truth, what difference will it make? This isn't your fight, sweetheart. Your fight is living your best life and keeping Nile protected," she replied.

"Just say you don't want me with her," I said, getting up. I was done talking to the only person who could help me.

"I'm afraid that finding out the truth will hurt you too. My best advice to give you is don't go digging for gold and you end up with a skeleton. Now, go get ready for work. I'm going to be here all day watching my great-grandbabies," she said.

I didn't respond to her; I picked up the rose Black Rose left me and put a glass cloche over it on my nightstand to protect it. Afterwards, I proceeded to get ready for work. I was so full of rage that my energy broke all the glass inside the bathroom, putting numerous cuts on my skin.

I can get cut a thousand times and it still won't hurt as much as Black Rose leaving me for another man.

****

Two hours later, I was riding in the backseat of Simon's limo with Kanye. We were on our way to the jewelry store. He was smoking Zaan's weed and the smoke was getting in my eyes. I pushed the blunt away when he passed it to me.

"Bro, are you tripping about Rose? She might just be out with Majestic and Tiko. They left this morning too. It's only been seven hours since you saw her," Kanye said.

"Whatever bro," I replied.

"Mannnn, for the life of me I don't know why the Gods won't let you be happy. We keep going through this. You think it doesn't hurt me too, bro? I hate when you get like this. I'll find Black Rose for you soon as we get off from work if it'll help you feel better. Hit this, it'll ease the stress," he said.

"Naw, I'm straight. Appreciate you trying to make me feel better but I'll deal with it. I'm good, Kanye. And you might be right, Black Rose might be with Majestic. They *are* inseparable," I lied. I wasn't in denial about Black Rose leaving me, I just didn't want anyone constantly asking me how I was doing. Shit, I didn't even want to think about her because it would send me looking for her.

Simon pulled up in front of our store. "We got it from here, Simon. You don't have to let us out," Kanye said.

Simon rolled the partition down. "Are you sure?" he asked, looking back at us.

"Yeah but hit this. I got more for your wife's cataracts, just let me know how much you need," Kanye said, passing Simon the blunt. Simon domed the blunt, nodding his head in approval.

"Whewww weeee," Simon exhaled.

"Yeah, that shit tough ain't it?" Kanye asked.

"Always; I'll see you young men shortly," Simon said.

We both gave him dap before getting out of the limo. Two men got out of a pick-up truck parked in front of the store. Both men were dressed in black cargo pants and shirts with combat boots. They looked like military men. One guy had dark brown dreadlocks and the other had long silver dreadlocks. I noticed their sharp ear tips and realized they were elves.

"We're here to speak with Akea," the one with the silver dreads said.

"I'm Akea, what's up?" Kanye asked.

"Can we go inside?" the man replied while anxiously looking around.

"Is everything alright?" Simon asked, getting out of his limo. Simon was a veteran and was always strapped.

"Get back in the limo, Simon," I replied. He was reluctant at first, but he got back inside the limo and watched us.

"Yeah, we're good. It ain't nothing we can't handle," Kanye said.

"We're looking for Black Rose. I heard she's with you so we've been waiting here for you all night. This is urgent. My name is Lark and this is my son, Blizzard," the man with the silver hair said. Blizzard was grilling Kanye, I'm assuming because he thought Kanye was me.

"Did Circa send y'all here?" I asked.

"No, he doesn't know we're here. Listen, I have no quarrel with you but Black Rose needs to know the truth. I'm tired of fighting and just want to take my family away and live like a decent person," he replied.

"Come inside," I said.

"Bro, you're trippin'. They could be setting us up," Kanye said.

"I'll take the blame but I think they're here on Rose's behalf."

"You better be right," Kanye replied.

He scanned the keycard against the panel. The gates in front of the doors lifted so the doors could open. I let Kanye go in first and waited for Lark and Blizzard to enter the jewelry store so I could lock it back up.

"Our customers will be here in ten minutes so make it quick," Kanye said with a growl.

"Are you sure you are Akea? We're looking for the warlock Black Rose is with," Lark said.

"I'm Akea," I admitted.

Kanye was trying to protect me in case they came to hurt me, but I had to protect him too so no harm could come his way. Blizzard grilled me while crossing his arms. He was a few inches taller and thought that was enough to intimidate me.

"You got a problem with me?" I asked Blizzard.

"Matter of fact I do. I'm trying to see what Black Rose sees in your geek ass," he said, referring to my glasses.

"You must be mad you couldn't hit it, huh?" I replied and he clenched his jaw while balling his fist. "Yeah, that's what it is bitch boy," I said.

He stepped in my face and Kanye shoved him back. "Watch it, Peter Pan ears. You don't want to get your throat chewed out so chill out and respect our business!" Kanye barked.

"Be respectful in someone else's territory, Blizzard. This isn't the place or time to let jealousy consume you," Lark told his son.

"My apologies," Blizzard gritted.

"Now can we get down to business? The clock is ticking," I said.

"Circa's got to be stopped. I can't kill him, but Black Rose can. Her magic can defeat his weapons," Lark said.

"I'm assuming you know more about her curse," I replied.

"Yes, I do but I want to show you so you can explain it to Rose. I know Circa sent his men to come after me and my family so we won't be here long. I know too many of his secrets so I'm worth more dead than alive," Lark said.

"How can you show me?" I asked.

"I'm willing to lend my body to you so you can see my memories," he replied.

"Wait, Father. You trust a warlock getting inside your head? He might kill you," Blizzard said.

"Shut up, Son. This is the only way," Lark said.

"Keep an eye on him while I speak to Lark in private," I told Kanye.

"Are you sure about this?" he replied.

"I'm certain about this. I think it's time Black Rose finds out the truth."

"Five minutes, bro. If I don't see or hear you, I'm coming to get you under any circumstance," Kanye said.

"No doubt," I replied.

I told Lark to follow me in the office on the first level. "Will Blizzard be okay staying behind with your brother? I know he can be a little ill mannered sometimes," Lark nervously chuckled.

"Yeah, he's straight as long as he doesn't do anything that'll get him killed."

He looked around, admiring the statues and jewelry cases. "Beautiful place. Looks better in real life than inside the globe," he said as I opened the office door. "What globe?"

I gestured for him to take a seat on the couch and unbuttoned my suit jacket before sitting down myself. "Amstid's globe. He predicted everything that was going to happen between you and Black Rose, well Lyira. Amstid knew Circa's fate so he bribed him with changing his destiny with Black Rose," Lark said.

I poured him a glass of cognac that was on the center table. He was nervous and I wanted him to relax.

"Thank you," he said, throwing back the shot back. "Ahhh, refreshing," he let out.

"In other words, Circa was supposed to die a long time ago?"

"Correct. He was supposed to be beheaded for not following our goddess' orders. He let outsiders into our world. Anyway, Amstid promised Circa he could change fate so instead of him dying he'd live in exchange for a portion of our forest. The thing is, fate didn't change anything except Circa still being alive and Lyira as Black Rose. Even as Black Rose, she was destined to meet you. Circa decided to claim her as his daughter to keep control over her. He hated that she wanted to kill him and be with someone else. He has a crazed love and hate obsession over her," he said.

I hope I don't turn out like that crazy muthafucka! Black Rose is an addiction, though. I'm going insane thinking about her and trying to keep it under control.

"Who cursed Black Rose? It sounds like Amstid only instigated the situation."

"Circa killed her garden with salt," he replied.

"Salt?"

"It was a poison salt, something Amstid made. It destroyed her garden which is Black Rose's second heart. Circa's stupid ass didn't know that the forest would suffer from it later on. I'm a coward for not saying anything and sticking by him but he was like my brother. He had a good heart until Amstid came along, showing him the future. Back then, we didn't know anything about sorcery, we only knew of magic. I had no clue what Circa was doing," Lark said, getting choked up. I poured him another drink and he tossed it back.

"Go ahead, look into my soul and you'll see everything I saw that day, even the death of Black Rose's little girl," he said.

I was getting sick to my stomach but I had to see it through to protect Black Rose. Lark flinched when I grabbed his head. "Steady yourself so I can see back that far," I coached him. A blue beam shot from my eyes through Lark's to look into his soul. His eyes widened and his body froze as if he saw a ghost. I vanished completely into Lark's mind...

A Thousand Years Ago...

The moon in Black Rose's world was different from our moon. Her moon was pink and the night sky was a deep purple with gold stairs. There were two men on unicorn horses, standing behind Circa in the grove part of the forest. Lark was one of the men but the other man was a stranger. I was a spirit of the future, but I wished like hell I could kill Circa right there. He was arguing with a short and stubby man wearing a cloak with a three pointed star on his medallion. Behind him was an army of warlocks, about fifty of them. More were coming out of a portal with weapons.

"This wasn't the plan, Amstid! I poisoned my mate's garden to let your people get a portion of the forest, not the whole forest! I'm still the king and you will follow my orders!" Circa shouted.

Amstid laughed sinisterly. "You never should make a deal with a warlock, you might get more than you bargained for, now bring us the women or we'll take them by force. Think of the future, our kind could create with whatever your kind is will make a stronger union. Better yet, bring me your mystical goddess, I still haven't gotten a chance to see her in person, yet. We only want to have fun with her. I bet she's tight and wet for us," Amstid said, pulling out a sword. The portal was piling up with more warlocks. I didn't know that many existed.

"We can't defeat all of them by ourselves! We're outnumbered," Lark said. He blew through a horn to alert the others in the forest for help.

"I'm going to take your head for conning me. I poisoned my pregnant mate for nothing? You conned me to steal our women?" Circa asked.

"We're the Amstid Clan, the pirates of different realms. This forest will just be another memory of the past so we can do this the hard way or the easy way. You'll bring the women here or we will search for them," a man wearing the same medallion as Amstid said. His eyes were black as night, his teeth were sharp and needle thin, and he had carvings on his forehead. He was ugly and looked demonic.

Amstid laughed. "Don't scare him, Ryul. Try to be a little nicer," he said to the gremlin looking man.

"We are going to win this war, Amstid. Don't underestimate my people," Circa threatened.

"Sheldon, go and find that goddess of his," Amstid ordered a young man wearing a dark brown hooded cloak. Sheldon had the same carvings on his head as Ryul along with the same medallion. I saw the innocence in his eyes and hesitancy to follow Amstid's orders. Sheldon stepped away from Amstid.

"Why can't we just leave them alone? Maybe we can send them out and keep their forest but why should we kill them?" Sheldon asked Amstid.

"Do it or else I'll kill you myself. How can you be a part of this clan and wear that medallion of honor but can't slay the enemy?" Amstid asked him.

Sheldon ran towards the portal to leave, but Ryul knocked him to the ground with the scabbard of his sword. Amstid spat on Sheldon's face then kicked him in the ribs while he was on the ground.

Sheldon is innocent and his soul isn't dark like the others. That's why my father is protecting him. Black Rose thinks he's the enemy.

"I'm ashamed you are my brother!" Amstid yelled at Sheldon, kicking him again.

A stampede of elves riding on unicorns arrived with weapons. There were just as many of them as Amstid's people. Circa proudly poked his chest out.

"This is the Yubsari Clan and we don't back down from a fight. You should've kept your promise and now you have to die!" Circa yelled, turning around to face his people. "These men are the reason our goddess has fallen ill. They trespassed on our land to rape our women. So, tonight we will honor Lyira and kill the men that poisoned her! We will fight to the death of us!" He shouted.

"He's lying! He poisoned the goddess and offered us a portion of the forest!" Amstid shouted.

"The king wouldn't do that to our goddess!" A male elf shouted out and the rest agreed.

"I'm going to take your fat head and use it as a souvenir!" Circa yelled at Amstid. He charged into Amstid, knocking him on the ground. The army of elves clashed into Amstid's clan. I was in the middle of a bloody massacre. Weapons were flying through the air, slicing warlocks heads off.

"Go to Lyira and protect her!" Circa yelled out to Lark. I followed Lark when he ran away from the battle. Children were hiding underneath the flowers.

"Go hide! NOW!" Lark told the children. A little boy ran away, but he didn't make it far. A chakram sliced his small body in half. It was the first time in my life, seeing a child no older than five gruesomely murdered.

The little girl cried out to the little boy. "Don't scream, just keep quiet until the noises stop," Lark told her. She nodded her head and ran back underneath the bush. Lark ran across a stream and passed a village of tree houses. He got to Lyira's garden and she was lying in the grass while holding her stomach.

"I have to hide you," Lark said, kneeling next to her. I felt helpless that I couldn't help her. Her garden had withered and her pond water was brown. Her garden looked nothing like the garden I saw in my dream. Lyira pushed him away when he comforted her.

"You, Findis, and Circa betrayed me. You knew what he was doing and didn't do anything to stop him. I thought highly of you," Lyira said. She coughed up blood and the veins in her skin were protruding.

"Please forgive me. I promise, I'll fix it," Lark sobbed.

"The garden is the heart of the forest and soon, the poison will spread. Our home...our magic from the forest will never be the same. I wish I can fight, but I can't so you should go and salvage what is left," she replied. A liquid ran down her legs and veins stretched across her swollen belly like tree roots. She let out a piercing scream. My hand went through her body when I tried to comfort her.

"We have to go somewhere safe to give birth to your daughter. I'll take you," Lark said. He picked her up and a force knocked him over, causing Lyira to fall to the ground with blood flowing down her legs.

She screamed when her stomach opened, resembling a blossoming flower. Lark got up to go to her but was knocked over again. His body was lifted from the ground then slammed into a tree. I scanned the garden to see who was telekinetically attacking Lark and it was Amstid.

"This must be the goddess," he said while Lyira was giving birth.

"Do what you want to me but don't touch my daughter!" she said.

"That depends on whether she looks like you or not," Amstid said, circling around Lyira. He was watching her the same way as someone would watch their pet dog give birth to puppies. She was nothing to him but a foreign creature to use for sexual desires.

"Your beauty is rare. Never seen anything like it. No wonder the big fella kept you hidden," Amstid said.

"Get away from her!" Lark yelled.

Lyira was in pain; I could see it in her face. She was also weak and couldn't defend herself. Amstid kneeled next to her and caressed her face.

"I want you right here and now," he told her. A dagger formed in Lyira's hand while he was groping her breasts. "Ahhhhh!" he howled when she twisted the dagger in his eye. Circa came to the garden covered in blood.

"Kill him now!" Lark yelled. His body was folded in half from being tossed into the tree.

"You can't kill me! You need me!" Amstid said right before Circa cut his head off with his scythe.

Lyira stopped breathing after she gave birth. Her daughter laid next to her on the ground and her stomach was back to normal without a mark in sight. "Lyira! Wake up, I'm sorry!" Circa said, shaking her.

A tall man, the same man I saw moments ago with Circa, came to the garden carrying a bloody sack. "A lot of our people are dead," he said.

"I don't care about that right now, Findis. Lyira is dead!" Circa cried while holding on to her body. Their daughter was trying to stand but she fell. She was two years old, but the size of a six-month old baby. Findis picked up Lyira's daughter.

"A lot of our women were raped and killed. We have nothing now," Findis said.

"This is my fault. I've failed my people," Circa sobbed.

"You said Amstid showed you his sorcery that can bring back the dead. Where's that globe you wanted from him? Will it show you how to save her?" Findis asked.

"Don't use anything from them! It's all wicked," Lark said, snapping his body into place. Circa went into Amstid's knapsack and pulled out a spellbook made out of a human's face. The eyeball on the book winked.

"That's a demon's spellbook muthafucka's! Y'all don't know what those spells are made of!" I yelled. They were ignorant to that kind of sorcery Amstid was into.

A warlock came into the garden. He saw Amstid's head on the ground and was ready to make a run for it. Circa teleported, standing in front of the warlock. "Read this book and see how I can bring my mate back," Circa said to him.

"Will...will you...free me?" he stuttered from fear. Circa kicked the warlock in his leg, snapping it back. He fell onto the ground, screaming. Circa dragged him to Lyira by his cloak then dropped the spellbook next to him. The warlock checked Lyira's pulse. "Her body is in shock but she's not dead. If she dies, the curses in this book won't work," he said.

"Well, hurry up and figure it out!" Circa said.

The warlock's hands shook uncontrollably while he flicked through the pages. "If you want to save her, I'll need an innocent life to sacrifice. Something pure, like her," the warlock pointed at Lyira's daughter.

Lark ran over and pushed Circa, "Don't do it!" Lark said before Circa shoved him to the ground.

"Are you lying to us?" Findis asked the warlock.

"You can hang me if I am. I'm telling the truth and we are running out of time," the warlock said.

"She can be our next goddess. Let her live, I'm begging you not to sacrifice her. She was just born!" Lark said. Circa took his daughter out of Findi's arms while the warlock prepared the ritual. He used a stick to carve a circle in the dirt around Lyira's body.

SOUL Publications

"She won't remember this night. Her memory will be lost forever," the warlock said.

"That's even better," Circa replied.

"Let me die...I sacrifice myself. Let our daughter live, Circa. I'm begging you to let her live. Give her to me...give me my daughter!" Lyira screamed with the little strength she had left. She was going in and out, but she was alert.

"I'll spend the rest of my life avenging her death, but I rather you live," Circa said. He slit his daughter's throat with a knife while she had a smile on her face from watching a butterfly fly past...

Back to the Present...

"Akea!" Kanye called out to me. I was crying like a baby while balled up on the couch when I came out of Lark's head. My stomach was in knots, forcing me to throw up on the carpet. "What did you do to my brother?" Kanye yelled at Lark.

"He saw the truth," Lark replied. I was dry heaving from emptying my stomach.

Kanye patted my back. "I can't see her past anymore. I won't do it again, I can't do it again! That beautiful little girl...Lyira...the little boy. It's sick!"

"I can't get it out of my head either," Lark sobbed.

"You weak muthafucka!" I charged into him.

"Get off of my father!" Blizzard shouted, grabbing on to me.

Kanye slammed Blizzard through the glass table. "Calm down Tornado, this is a one man fight," Kanye told Blizzard.

I choked Lark. "You aren't a real man! You are a fucking coward! You didn't do enough!" I yelled. I picked him up, slamming him through the wall. "Where does Circa live? I'm going to kill him and that Findis muthafucka too. You were supposed to die protecting your goddess! The woman that gave y'all a world to live in!" I punched Lark in the face, busting his nose.

"Go ahead and kill me! I haven't been the same since that night. Do it!" Lark sobbed.

"Don't do it, bro," Kanye said.

"I gotta do it. He deserves it and he knows he does," I replied. I twisted his neck, turning his head backwards. His son caught his dead body before it hit the floor.

"Whyyyy? He told you the fucking truth! I knew we couldn't trust y'all warlocks! My mother is expecting us to meet her, what in the fuck do I tell her about her husband, huh?" Blizzard asked with tears running down his face.

"My bad bro, but we can't have you telling anyone what happened," Kanye told Blizzard.

Blizzard pulled out a knife but Kanye's canines were already tearing through his neck. Blood squirted on my body and on the walls. Kanye's teeth crushed his throat, killing him instantly. Blizzard's dead body fell on top of his father's. I took off my suit jacket, shirt and under shirt because I was covered in blood.

"How in the hell did we catch two bodies at our place of business? You could've let him walk away now look, my good suit is covered in blood," Kanye said.

"You don't know what I saw. Circa killed his daughter while she was smiling at a fucking butterfly flying past her head. She was a baby, Kanye. A happy and innocent baby that didn't know what was going on! Lark didn't do anything, he bitched up. He ain't no real warrior anyway, fuck him and his son."

Kanye gave me a dap hug. "I feel you wholeheartedly, you did what you felt was right. I support you in every way, except I'm not cleaning this up so work your magic and get rid of these bodies," he said.

"We gotta close the store for the day. I need to find Rose and this isn't about her leaving me. She's been in the dark for too long and she needs to know the truth about her past, the *real* truth. I don't want you to come with me, I plan to ride solo."

"How are you going to find her? She could be out of the state," he said.

"Majestic might know where she went to. She has to know something."

"Shidddd, I'm coming too and so is the rest of the pack, well, except the women. We ain't fittin' to let you go into the lion's den. I know you got your Doctor Strange magic going on, but every superhero has a weak moment. You need a team to carry you in case you start slacking," he said.

"You just gotta be in my business bro, no matter what."

Kanye shrugged. "We're twins so of course," he replied.

"We're triplets," I reminded him.

"I keep forgetting about that fool. Shit, he's in another world anyway. It's just me and you here, Twin. But get your magic on and clean these bodies up. I have to activate the alarm so we can leave," he said.

I can't wait to get my hands on Circa! I'm going to slit his throat, the same way he did Lyira's daughter.

Dyika

I was in Baneet's room, peeking out of the door to steer clear of Naobi. The potion I drank to become Jetti was thorough, but it could still be revealed that I was an imposter. The ancient Anubian without a doubt would've seen my visions had I stuck around her longer.

"What are you doing?" Baneet asked. She was standing in the mirror putting on her earrings. She was wearing tight jeans that hugged her curves, a tight jean shirt with her breasts spilling out and a pair of nude pumps.

"I'm steering clear of Naobi. I don't want to leave while she's walking through the halls."

"Why not? Did you do something wrong?" she asked, spraying on perfume.

"I'm not dressed appropriately. She's old fashioned and might think lowly of me."

"I have plenty of clothes in my closet but you can't be in here for too long. Akea doesn't want you in the castle. He told Tiko and Jasiah to snap your neck if they catch you in here and they'll do it. They were trained to be killers and I'm not just talking about killing to eat. Jasiah would probably eat you alive. His beast is crazy," Baneet said.

"Akea didn't mean that. He was acting that way so Black Rose wouldn't feel insecure. Trust me, Akea doesn't want me dead. Earlier, when I was in his room, he said we could work it out since Black Rose left him."

Baneet crossed her arms. "Ummm, I don't believe that. I don't always agree with him but I know he doesn't want you. He wants Keisha, Black Rose, hell whatever her name is, he wants *her*. Don't be in denial anymore. If I can stop living in the past, so can you. You don't love him, you are just jealous of Black Rose and you'll do anything to hurt her. That's how I was with Fiti and now I'm ready to apologize to her. You should do the same, apologize to Akea and Black Rose and be cordial with them," she shrugged. She said it as if it wasn't a big deal. Baneet was really pissing me off.

"Ohhhh, I get it. You are friends with Black Rose now?"

"She didn't do anything to me and besides, I don't want to anger Monifa. The bitch is crazy. And to be honest, I miss Jasiah sleeping next to me. I'm done playing games and now I'm ready to win my man back so if he comes in here and finds you, I can't help you," she said.

"Are you freaking serious right now? You'll let him kill me?" I shrieked.

She shrugged. "I mean, what can I do? He's ten times stronger than me," she replied.

"I hope you end up miserable and if I was still a witch, I would put a spell on you. A spell that'll chew away your flesh and eat out your wicked and conniving heart!"

"What do you mean if you were still a witch? Are you saying you are someone else?" she replied.

"Don't get above yourself, I meant if I was a witch. Don't put words in my mouth!"

"Get out of my room! We aren't friends anymore anyway. Your drama is getting exhausting and no longer entertaining," she said. She grabbed my hair and dragged me towards the door. I slapped her face, scratching her with my sharp nails. Blood dripped on her shirt from the wound marks on her face. "This is Jasiah's favorite shirt of mine and your poor ass ruined it!" she yelled. I heard Akea's voice in the hallway.

What is he doing back so soon? He never gets off work this early.

I looked at the clock on Baneet's wall and it was two o'clock in the afternoon. He was gone for three hours. I panicked so he wouldn't see me. "Hide me!" I told Baneet.

"Fuck you! Fend for yourself from now on! I'll never nurse you back into good health again," she said, shoving me out of her room. I fell into a statue of Bastet and the glass statue shattered across the floor. Kanye and Akea stared at me with venom in their eyes.

"I'm not the only one who breaks things in this castle."

"But we live here and can replace what we break," Kanye said.

"We'll worry about her later. We gotta find Majestic," Akea replied.

"She's in Tiko's room. I heard them walking down the hallway thirty minutes ago," Baneet said.

"Is it because you want to know where Black Rose went? I told you she and her people are monsters!" I yelled loud enough for everyone to hear me. They needed to know Black Rose was a demonic elf.

"I'll be a happy man when you kill this woman. I'll give up sex for the rest of my life if you snap her neck," Kanye said. Jasiah got off the elevator wearing sweatpants and covered in blood.

Baneet fixed her hair and poked out her breasts for his attention, but he didn't look her way. "It must be an emergency if y'all came home early," he said to Akea and Kanye.

"Yeah it is; tell Zaan to meet us by the door in ten minutes. We're going to Circa's house," Kanye said.

"Who is Circa?" Jasiah asked.

"A man that cursed Black Rose and killed her daughter. We'll explain more later, but Akea can't go alone so we're going with him," Kanye replied.

"Like hell he'll go to save that bitch!" I said, standing up.

The doorbell rang.

"I'll get it," Baneet said. She threw her hips side-to-side to catch his eyes.

He grabbed her arm. "Stay here, I'll get it," Jasiah told her.

"Our gate is closed so who is ringing our bell?" Kanye asked. He sniffed the air. "I don't smell another wolf, it must be a human," he said. Kanye followed Jasiah to answer the door.

Baneet's nosey ass followed them. "Wait for me," she said.

Akea walked down the hallway and I followed him. "You want to save a bitch like Rose when she has her own people? You didn't come to save me when I was starving with my old wolfpack!" I screamed at the back of his head. That was Jetti speaking out, she felt like Akea abandoned her. He ignored me as always, pretending I was a spirit.

"Get back here!" I said, grabbing his arm.

In a flash, he had me by the throat. My feet dangled off the floor and his eyes were glowing. I've seen him angry many times, but he never went as far as putting his hands on me.

"I want you out of my life and if killing you is the only way, so be it!" he said. I clawed at his arms, while gasping for air. My eyes were ready to pop out of my head as he strangled me.

A familiar voice called out to Akea. The man was standing with Kanye, Jasiah, and Baneet. I was praying that it was a dream but he found me.

"Sheldon?" Akea asked. Sheldon bowed his head at Akea.

"I'm your father's messenger and he sent me here to guide you correctly," Sheldon said.

"I hope he didn't send you here to stop me from killing Circa. This is my war, no one else's," Akea said. He still had his hand around my throat. I was going limp, barely hanging on to life.

"He knew you'd say that. He said that you are a man now and will make your own choices and he won't stop you. I'm only here to be his eyes and ears. Before I follow you on this journey, I will have to ask you to release that woman. She's a prisoner of mine," Sheldon said.

"A prisoner? You mean we've been housing a fugitive?" Kanye asked. I shook my head at Sheldon, begging him not to rat me out.

"Yes, she's an imposter," Sheldon said. Akea dropped me on the floor.

"I knew that bitch was a snake!" Baneet lied.

"An imposter?" Akea repeated.

"I thought she was dead after the fall from the cliff. She would've been captured if I knew she was alive. That woman right there is Dyika, the wife of Ryul. She used demon magic to become Jetti, who is also a prisoner of mine for killing one of my men," Sheldon said.

"He's l...lying," I panted. I could barely catch my breath.

"Black Rose was telling the truth and I didn't believe it. This woman was able to breastfeed. She was just like the selfish Jetti I knew. There wasn't one flaw to think otherwise," Akea said.

"Jetti has transformed completely into a man and she no longer has her usual thoughts. Dyika siphoned her memories and traits to become her," Sheldon said.

Kanye gasped. "Nile's mother is a man?" he asked. Akea rubbed his temples while falling against the wall in shock.

"Well, is she handsome?" Baneet asked.

"Extremely handsome," Sheldon chuckled to make light of the situation.

"This world is very interesting," Jasiah said.

SOUL Publications

"I'm Nile's mother!" I said, patting my chest. "You can't abandon me! He's used to me now. It's Black Rose's fault anyway, she conned Jetti into taking that potion. I'm the victim here! That bitch killed my husband and child so I had no choice! I wanted back what was taken from me and being Jetti was the only way," I cried. Everyone stared at me as if I had gone insane.

"You aren't his mother and will never be! Black Rose will be his mother after I marry her so your crazy ass can kick rocks. And just for the record, I saw your husband. I saw everything that happened the night Black Rose was cursed. Ryul, that ugly gremlin deserved that death! They were killing children, raping women and Ryul, was in the midst of it. Black Rose was a goddess, and your people are also to blame for what she'd been through," Akea said.

"She knows Ryul was wicked. Love had her in denial. She never believed he or their demon child deserved to die. I tried to love this woman and help her see that there's a better way to live. Even now, I still feel for her but I love my new meaning to life even more. I won't let her get away with what she's done or beg for forgiveness on her behalf," Sheldon said.

"That was deep. She had real love right in her face but she chose to chase someone else's man. What a shame," Baneet said.

"You would know firsthand," Jasiah replied.

Monifa, Zaan, Fiti, Tiko and Majestic came from the other end of the hallway.

"What is he doing here?" Majestic asked, referring to Sheldon.

"I'm here on behalf of the Wolf God. Nice to see you too, my nubian serpent," Sheldon said.

"Where is Rose? I've been looking for her all morning. Did he do something to her?" Majestic said. She was frantically looking around for Black Rose.

"Black Rose returned to Circa and I need you to show me where he lives. He's the one who cursed Rose and killed their daughter," Akea replied.

"Black Rose isn't Circa's real daughter? I know his other daughter belongs to Ryul. I've never seen the goddess of the forest so I didn't know it was Black Rose all along," Sheldon said.

"Stop spreading lies on my husband! He didn't have any children!" I screamed.

"Your husband was a rapist dummy," Akea said.

"What did I miss?" Monifa asked, looking confused.

"This Jetti is a fake, the real Jetti is a man, Black Rose was a goddess in her past life and the man that's supposed to be her father is really her baby daddy. The baby daddy killed their daughter and used her for a ritual that turned Black Rose dark," Kanye blabbed.

Monifa gasped. "My poor Rose," she said.

Poor Rose my ass! She deserved it all!

"Who is the bald guy?" Zaan asked.

"He's Goon's messenger," Akea replied.

"We need to leave...like right now! I know Circa, I bet he's tormenting Black Rose. She was vulnerable yesterday and I know how she gets when she's defensive," Majestic said.

"Watch her Monifa, make sure she doesn't leave your sight but keep her alive. She's a prisoner and Sheldon will be back for her," Kanye said.

"Stay here with the ladies," Akea told Zaan.

"What the hell bro. I can fight too," Zaan replied.

"You're too high and this is a serious mission. Stay here and we'll be back," Akea said. The others got on the elevator and Akea vanished into thin air. I got up from the floor and ran down the hallway to get Nile and leave.

Black Rose will never mother my son! I'll kill him if I have to save him from her!

I burst through a swing door, entering another section of the castle that was the library. Monifa appeared in front of me. "Where are you going sis?" she asked.

"Fuck you!" I screamed. I ran in the opposite direction, bumping into Fiti. There were only two doors in the library and they were both blocked. I was trapped and the only way out was to burst through the window.

SOUL Publications

"We will catch you if you jump through that window," Fiti said.

"I expected more from you since you were nice to me. We could've been friends," I replied.

"Nahh, never friends. You are fucking with the wrong family," she said.

Monifa tackled me onto the floor, our bodies rolled into a bookshelf. Fiti casted a bubble around the shelf to keep it from falling on Monifa. Jetti's beast was a weak beast, I could barely defend myself when being attacked. I clamped down on Monifa's arm, she howled before catching me with a mean left hook that knocked me off her. My canine tooth slipped down my throat.

"You still got it," Fiti told her.

"Of course, now we can put her into a deep sleep until the pack comes back," Monifa said. I was seeing stars from that vicious blow. Fiti sprinkled witch dust all over my face. I fell asleep in a matter of seconds.

Black Rose

An hour later...

"Come out and eat something." Circa knocked on my door.

I've been in the same room and spot since I arrived at Circa's home. I didn't have an appetite; I had slipped into a crippling depression. Every time I closed my eyes, I would see the face of the little girl in my arms. It angered me that I couldn't remember her but was still connected to her.

"I'm not hungry," I replied. I rolled over to face the wall. Akea's scent was still on my body and I didn't care to wash it off.

I wanted to die to get rid of the ugly soul inside of my body. Tears slipped from my eyes while I silently wept.

"Lyira," Circa whispered. How could I answer a name that I wasn't familiar with?

"Don't call me that!" I yelled.

"You aren't answering to Black Rose," he said.

Black Roses Grow in The Dark Natavia

"Go away Circa. I'll come out when you're ready to defeat Sheldon."

"I want to see your face and hold you while we mourn our angel together. She had your smile and your eyes, and I see it every day when I look at you. Being next to you is the only way I can feel her presence," he said. I kept quiet, hoping that he'd go away, but he teleported in my room. He touched me around the waist, and it sickened me. I sat up in bed and Circa had a plate of rabbit meat in his hand.

"Don't you ever in your life touch me like your name is Akea. You are my father, my adoptive father since we aren't blood related. I don't remember the past with you being my mate so give me my space and stop coming on to me! It's perverted! Let your wife, Merci, comfort you. Let me think in peace!" I screamed at him.

"I can't refrain myself from acting like your mate! You chose me out of everyone in our forest because I busted my ass to get you. I brought you a rabbit every day, helped you comb your hair, fed you the finest fruit and I kept the snakes out of your garden. You hated snakes back then and I killed every last one for you. We made love next to your pond every night and you fell for me. You stamped me with your rose, because you loved me," he said.

"That's not me. The only man that is stamped with my love is Akea. I fell in love with him at first sight, the moment I heard his voice. He's the only man I will ever love and if I was pure, I would bear all of his children. His pack is loving, family oriented, and safe. I've spent a thousand years with this clan and nobody has ever hugged me and told me *'it'll be okay.'* I'm hurting right now and the only thing you've done is talk about yourself!"

Circa threw the plate of rabbit meat against the wall. "I'm not comforting you while you cry over another man! I'll die before I ever do that!" he yelled.

"You were never going to tell me about the past. You weren't going to say a fucking a thing until Akea pointed out that he saw you with Lyira. Come to think about it, you had Nayati and Zelda keeping tabs on me the moment his name was mentioned. You immediately took me off that mission and appointed it to Zelda who is a horrible fighter! You knew Akea was going to find something about my past."

Circa's eyes glowed and his jaw clenched in anger. He struck me in the face, knocking me onto the floor.

"Fuck you!" he yelled.

I got so used to pain that it no longer hurt me. He was ready to strike me again when Findis came into the room.

"We located Lark's truck outside of the warlock's jewelry store but there's no other sign of them," he said.

"Those damn traitors! What were they doing there?" Circa asked.

"I don't know," Findis shrugged.

I burst out laughing. "Old losers lost their hunting skills. No wonder you need me," I said.

"Watch your mouth!" Circa warned. He raised his hand to strike me again, but I caught his arm.

"I'll break it off your shoulders! Try me bitch!" I kicked him between the legs; he fell over holding his dick.

"The rules haven't changed since you came back. You cannot hit the leader!" Findis barked.

"Or what?" I asked.

"Argggghh," Circa groaned. A clan member came to the doorway of the guest room.

"What happened to our leader?" he asked.

"I tripped over the bed! Goddamn it! Who told you to come to this room?" Circa asked.

"Majestic is here to see Black Rose," he said.

"That snake isn't allowed in my grass or in my home. Take her head off!" Circa replied. Findis helped him off the floor and he was still wincing in pain.

I teleported to the front of the door. Two clan members had their spears against Majestic's head. "What are you doing here?" I asked.

"Circa doesn't want any snakes near his home," Glendan said.

"I wanted to see her face one last time. I'll be quick," Majestic said with her arms up. She was in mid-shift, her body was covered in black snakeskin and she talked with a hiss because of her fangs.

"You have a minute," Glendan said. I locked eyes with Majestic to communicate with her.

"Get out of here...Now! Akea discovered the truth. Circa killed your daughter and cursed you. He's a traitor! Sheldon is innocent. The pack is waiting for you near the graveyard. They want you out of here before they attack," she said.

"That sick bastard! After I came here, I had a feeling he did something to me and my daughter, but I didn't expect it to be this! Tell the pack this is my fight and to return home! Leave me here! It's about to get ugly so save yourself!"

"Are you two just going to stand here and look at each other?" A clan member asked.

"I have an eerie feeling about this," Glendan said. He raised his weapon to strike Majestic. I jumped on his back, driving a dagger through his skull. "Ahhhhh!" Glendan yelled.

His brain matter dripped down my dagger while I twisted it into his head. The other member grabbed me to pull me off, but Majestic bit him with her poisonous fangs. Circa appeared in the hallway with his clan of men.

"Drop him Rose!" Circa yelled. I jumped off Glendan's dead body and he fell to the floor.

"It was you who did this to me!" I screamed.

SOUL Publications

"Let me guess, your warlock boyfriend sent that snake here to tell you that? Are you this weak Rose? Do you trust the enemy? It was their sorcery, not mine. The proof is in your face and you still can't see it!" he said.

"He saw your future with Akea and he hated it. You were meant to be with Akea, Rose, regardless of who you became. This is *your* life and you can love that man freely because he is yours," Majestic said.

Circa pointed at Majestic, "Torch that bitch!" he yelled at his men.

My wand appeared, turning into a staff. "Nobody touches her!" I warned his men. I jabbed the staff into the floor of Circa's home, causing a whirlwind.

"You believe a snake over me?" Circa asked with tear-filled eyes.

"The only snake is you! You deserve to die for the shit you did to my fucking child! For years, I thought it was the curse that was giving me an empty feeling. That lost feeling was because you took something precious from me! You robbed me of motherhood so how dare you pretend to be the victim! I'm going to take everything from you today...EVERYTHING!"

"You wouldn't dare because I own you!" he yelled back.

The floors cracked from the magic of the staff, causing an earthquake. "Get them now!" Circa shouted at his men.

They were knocked over like bowling pins from the impact of the wind. I grabbed my staff and pulled Majestic out of the house. The wind grew stronger, bursting the windows out of Circa's home and blowing away the roof. Majestic hugged me.

"Don't do that again! How can you leave and not tell me? I'm mad at you but I'm happy we caught you in time," she said. The trees in the surrounding area uprooted from the ground to grow legs.

"Go find cover before a tree stomp on you. I got this!" I told her. Majestic ran for cover while the tree roots were snapping from the ground.

A giant burst through the roof of Circa's house. "URRGHHHHHH!" he roared.

He was thirty feet tall with a wart nose and his breath smelled like a sewer as he shouted. Wild forest dogs with spiked hair and killer trolls with sharp sticks emerged from the tornado. They were the spirits of the magical forest that died with Lyira.

"The Yubsari Clan will die today for what they did to our home! Kill them all but leave Circa to me. Bring him to me alive!" I shouted to the forest creatures. A man wearing a hooded black cloak surfed through the air on a wood board, carrying blue balls of energy in his hands.

Is that my Akea?

The man swooped in, landing in front of me. He uncovered his head, revealing himself. It was Akea, the man that I loved more than life.

"I'm happy and mad at the same time. Why did you come here to get hurt? Me and Majestic kick ass by ourselves," I said.

Akea looked around as the creatures came towards Circa's home. "My pack don't roll like that, we're going to fight regardless of how big your army is," he said.

The trolls were jumping one of Circa's men, stabbing him with their sticks. "Get them off of me!" he screamed.

Nayati ran to him, stabbing the trolls with her daggers. An elf ran towards Akea with a spiked club; a black and gold giant werewolf tackled the elf, by his throat. The beast overpowered the elf, mauling him to death. I saw the beast's blue eyes—the beast was Kanye. Findis shot a fire arrow at Kanye but missed. Akea slammed a ball of electricity into Findis's chest, causing him to backflip in the air.

"Stop this Rose!" Merci said from behind me.

"I bet you knew of my daughter, didn't you?"

She circled around me in a fighting stance. Merci was holding two katanas and I noticed they were covered in a powder. Whatever it was, Circa used it on me before.

"I was raped because of you. You sent me away while you stayed in your garden and didn't come to me. I was your top warrior back then and I gave my life to you but I was also a teenager. My innocence was stolen from me that day and the only person who comforted me was Circa. He was my first love but all he talked about was your beauty. You should've never come back and now you will die!" she said. She leapt into the air then dived into me with her swords pointing at my chest.

I caught the swords and they burned my hands like I knew they would. I bit Merci's cheek off, spitting the chunk of flesh on the ground. She lost her katanas after I knocked her down. She got up rushing to me. I elbowed her in her face, causing her to stumble.

"Show me what you got, Mother! Bring it bitch!" I screamed. She did a front flip while pulling out a dart from her boot. A rose shaped dagger shot from the palm of my hand, piercing through her throat. Merci slid across the grass and into a wild dog that was mangling an elf to death. The dog turned its attention to Merci.

"Leave her!" I told the dog.

It ran off, attacking someone else. The giant was eating an elf's leg and the walking trees were stomping on Circa's men. Nayati ran to Merci to help her off the ground. I walked over to Merci who was lying on the ground with the dagger stuck in her throat.

"AHHHHH!" Nayati screamed when I stomped on the dagger, drilling Merci's neck to the ground. She was gurgling on her blood. "STOP!" Nayati cried. I stomped on it again and again until Merci's neck was crushed. Blood poured from her eyes. "Rest in piss bitch!" I spat. Nayati tackled me, digging her nails into my face.

"You are going to join your daughter bitch!" Nayati seethed. Majestic's serpent tackled Nayati and wrapped her body around her. "FATHER!" Nayati screamed when Majestic licked her face.

"Eat her! Swallow that bitch whole!" I said. Nayati's bones cracked from the snake squeezing her tightly.

Circa ran through the battle on a horse, using his poisoned scythe to kill the forest creatures. I crouched while my body shifted into a barghest. My heavy paws thumped against the ground, running underneath the giant's legs. I jumped on Circa and his scythe went through my chest.

"Give it up, Lyira. I know your weakness," he said, while I laid on the ground. The weapon was burning my insides, paralyzing me. "I always outsmart you, I know how you think! I took your soul back then and I'll do it again," he said. He yanked the weapon out of my chest. "I'm going to kill you this time!" he yelled. The giant picked him up to eat him. Circa sliced open his stomach and a rancid smell covered the land. He continued wielding his weapon, dropping the big giant to his knees. I shifted into my human form and was covered in blood. My body was sizzling in pain.

"DIE!" Circa yelled at the giant who was still alive and tried to eat him.

Akea came over to me, helping me up. He was drenched in blood. "Are you hurt?" I panicked.

"Don't worry about me right now," he replied.

Findis limped towards us missing an arm and half his face gone, exposing his skeletal muscle. A werewolf or a wild dog must've gotten to him. Findis threw a chakram towards us.

"AKEA!" I screamed. I was too weak to use magic, and the chakram was sharp enough to slice Akea in half.

The chakram cut through a tree and then a pack of wild dogs eating the dead elves. It was getting close to Akea's head. Silver caught the chakram in mid-air like a frisbee just before it could harm him. Akea ran away from what was left of Circa's home, but then suddenly he collapsed.

"Akea! What happened? Talk to me!" I said. Black veins were spreading across his skin and his lips were turning black. Someone poisoned him.

"I'll bounce back, just give me a minute," he whispered. Tears fell from my eyes, but I was too weak to help him.

"Why would you come here anyway!" I yelled at him. He coughed up blood. Kanye's beast ran to his brother, he was bloody too but didn't appear hurt. He pushed Akea's head with his snout to get him up. Kanye shifted into his human form.

"Stop playing, Akea! Wake up," Kanye shook him. Akea's eyes rolled to the back of his head. I pulled up

Akea's cloak to look for the wound. He was cut in his torso, down to his ribcage. The wound was turning black.

"NOOOOO BROOOO!" Kanye cried out. I put my mouth against his wound and sucked out the poison.

Akea saved me while he was barely clinging onto life. The poison burned but I couldn't stop until he was saved. Akea's wound was beginning to heal, and his skin was feeling warm again.

Kanye sat him up. "I almost killed you for scaring me, bro. Can you see?" Kanye asked while holding up two fingers.

"Yeah, I was jumped by trolls. They mistake me for someone else. Those lil' fuckers whipped my ass. Shit, I almost had Findis after I took his arm off," Akea said.

"I should punch you for scaring me," I threatened Akea. My wound was healing too, and the poison was wearing off.

An elf ran towards us. "Y'ALL ARE DEAD FOR KILLING MY BROTHER!" he screamed. Tiko and Jasiah's beasts tackled him from behind. "ARHHHHHH! GET OFF ME!" he yelled. They pulled on his body, tugging him back and forth until he ripped apart.

"BLACK ROSE!" Circa shouted across the yard. My wand came back to me like a boomerang. A black dress with a long train hugged my body and a veil covered my face.

Silver and Majestic joined us; they were out of breath from the long battle. Akea got up from the ground. Circa and Findis walked across the yard and through the gate over the dead bodies. The spell was wearing off, the trolls, and wild dogs turned into ashes as the trees went still. It was just us left against Circa and Findis. My wand turned into a knife so that I could slit his throat.

Circa spat blood on the ground, "Nice dress," he said.

"I'm dressed to kill; you know how that goes. I might not be the goddess of the forest anymore but I'm still the goddess of death."

"Want to know why I saved you?" he asked.

"This muthafucka is fittin' to lie again," Akea said.

"Hush it boy!" Findis pointed at him.

"We'll jump your big ass," Kanye said. Findis dragged his thumb across his throat, threatening to kill him.

"I saved you so I could watch you suffer in which you have. See, you can kill me but at the end of the day, Rose, I've won the war. I damaged you. I turned you into a monster. It's painful to love ain't it? That's because you're not supposed to. Love won't come easy for you. So come and kill me. I've succeeded in the mission," Circa chuckled.

Findis's smirk was quickly wiped away when a spear pierced through his forehead from behind. He fell face forward next to Circa's boot; Sheldon killed him. Circa attacked Sheldon and choked him. Akea hurled a ball of blue fire at Circa, knocking him off Sheldon.

"I'm going to beat his ass again!" Akea said, running to Circa. He and Circa went at it, throwing punches at each other.

"Fuck him up Akea!" everyone cheered. I was waiting for the final moment to swoop in and kill Circa.

"Punk bitch!" Akea yelled at Circa. He upper cut Circa, breaking his jaw.

Circa tackled Akea. "She belongs to me!" Circa yelled.

Akea picked up a dagger and took out Circa's good eye. He repeatedly jabbed his eyeball. Circa fell to the ground. Akea lifted him by the hood of his cloak while Circa was on his knees. I walked over to him. He sniffed the air and smiled a bloody grin.

"Ahhhhh, the scent of flowers. You are close to me, aren't you?" he asked. It was silent, everyone was waiting for me to kill him. I fought back the tears because killing him wouldn't solve anything. Even in death, he would still have control over me.

"I'm waiting," Circa laughed.

"What are you waiting for, Rose? Kill him so we can go home," Akea said. His voice was as soothing as the day I met him, but his fate was with Lyira. I could only flourish in the darkness of my heart. I didn't want to live anymore since I couldn't live for myself. How could I give myself to Akea when Circa still had chains around my neck. It wasn't fair for Akea to only have a piece of me when all he did was give me all of him. I was in his way of true love and happiness, he deserved better than that.

The knife slipped from my hand. "Do it, Rose," Akea said.

"I can't do it. This is what he wants," I replied.

"I'll do it myself," he said before cutting Circa's throat, going straight through his jugular vein. Circa's limp body fell to the ground.

"We can go home now," Akea said, reaching out to me.

"I can't live like this Akea! I'm dying on the inside after knowing this was his plan to control me. I will no longer give him the satisfaction."

To the left of me was a grass fire, my only escape. "I'm sorry, Akea. Live strong for me," I told him. I teleported quickly so no one could stop me.

"ROSE!" Akea shouted as my dress went ablaze. I closed my eyes, letting my body burn until there was nothing left. A tear fell from my eye as I heard Akea's cries.

"ROSE!" he screamed.

Dyika
Epilogue

Two years Later...

I sat in the corner of the prison with unbreakable shackles around my ankles. My days consisted of writing Akea's name in feces on the wall. I wanted to die instead of living in the dungeon for the rest of my life. The door to the dungeon opened, someone was coming down the stairs to bring me food. I haven't bathed in two years or worn a piece of clothing—I lived like a wild beast. A man banged on the dungeon bars with a plate of raw meat. He slid the plate underneath the feeding slot. I was being treated like an animal at the zoo. Matter of fact, the animals in the zoo lived better than me.

"Sheldon wants you to eat," he said in his deep baritone.

The tall and nice-looking muscular man looked familiar. "Jetti?" I laughed. The man snarled from being offended which caused me to laugh harder. I dragged the heavy chain across the dungeon when I went to the door.

"Give me my life back! How dare you serve me food after you wanted me to live your miserable life. I want to get out of here and go to Akea! I deserve to be in that castle and inside his warm king-size bed!" I yelled. The curse was tormenting me while Jetti had a chance to be someone else with a better life. She lost her memory the same as Black Rose because of that demon spellbook. I wanted the same experience they had from the spell instead of battling two different people inside my head. Jetti was restless for not having the luxurious life she wanted and so was I for not having my child

"Eat your food while it's fresh," he calmly stated.

"You don't remember anything? We were a team! You owe me your life so break me out of here. Remember your cousin, Gensin? Black Rose ripped her heart out. She showed me Gensin's dead body. Why aren't you getting mad? We can help each other get revenge, Jetti. We both can free Nile of the evil things Akea exposed him to."

"My name is Ordell and it means *'beginning'*. I'm thankful that the Gods have blessed me with a new life and maybe they'll bless you too if you let go of my old spirit," he replied.

"New life my ass! You are cursed! The Gods didn't do shit for you, moron!" I screamed.

"Yes, they have, and I worship them every day," he calmly said.

Sheldon appeared next to Ordell. "Go upstairs Young Leader and get ready for today's teachings," Sheldon told him. He bowed his head at Sheldon before he went upstairs.

Sheldon looked at me in disgust. "You look like shit, literally," he said.

I pulled on the bars. "Get me out of here so I can be with my family!" I cried.

"Akea and Nile don't need your shitty and crazy ass in their lives again. They are doing fantastic without you. You are stuck here for the rest of your life. This is the only way to keep you from Nile because you will never give up. You are demonic and you belong in this hell. Now eat your food, Dyika or Jetti, whichever crazy one you are today," he chuckled. I picked up the plate of meat and threw it against the wall.

"A person who opens a demon spell book will always end up either dead or insane. You have to reap what you sow and live by the book that you opened. This is your tombstone," he said. He went into his cloak's pocket and got a single black rose.

"BASTARD!" I yelled when he dropped the rose through the bars. He walked away while whistling. "I'm going to kill you!" I yelled.

Sheldon slammed the door after he left the dungeon. I screamed, kicked and cried at being a prisoner for eternity. "AKEAAAAAA!" I sobbed but nobody heard me, nobody cared.

This was my life forever…

Akea

"Hey handsome," a woman said to me. She wrapped her arms around my neck to dance with me.

"I'm good," I told her. She rolled her eyes before strutting away.

"Damn bro, she was stacked," Jasiah said.

I looked at my diamond face watch and it was almost three o'clock in the morning. We had a private section inside the strip club and to be honest, it wasn't my style.

"Bro, you are only twenty-three. You don't have to be a prude," he said.

"I'm not impressed by ass and titties. My magic can create women that look like this for free."

"Thinking about Rose, huh?" he asked.

"I'm thinking about going to bed!" I shouted over the rap music.

Jasiah had a leather *Christian Dior* man bag filled with money and was giving it all away. We had enough money to last us a lifetime, but it didn't deserve to be wasted. Jasiah has a long way to go when it comes to spending unnecessarily.

"Aight come on!" Jasiah said.

He grabbed his man bag and I finished my drink before leaving. The bouncer gave us a head nod when he lifted the rope so we could leave.

"Aight my brother, be easy," Jasiah told him. He gave the bouncer a fist pound before we walked down the stairs. Simon was leaning against our limo, smoking a cigar when we exited the club.

"Already?" Simon asked because Jasiah normally leaves the strip-club at six or seven in the morning.

Jasiah patted my shoulder. "Old man here doesn't like going out," he said.

"Ain't no place like home," Simon replied.

He opened the backdoor to the limo; there was a line of women calling out to us. "We want to party with y'all!" one said.

"Next time ladies," Jasiah replied.

"Yo, get in the car, damn," I said.

SOUL Publications

I pushed him into the backseat then got in after him. "Party poopers!" a different woman called out while Simon was closing the door.

"Baneet is going to kill you," I chuckled.

"Aye, I look and don't touch. But, I'm single and so is she. We do the nasty here and there but bro, she just ain't my type of woman anymore. I was a lil' young when I met her and not fully experienced, but I ain't gotta settle with her. A mate is a big responsibility and I'm not there yet," he said. Simon got into the driver's seat and pulled off.

"Yeah, don't rush it. Love can hurt and it ain't for the weak."

He yawned. "I'm taking my time. I might settle down when I'm forty, I have plenty of years left," he said. He closed his eyes and fell asleep. A jazz song played on the radio.

"Turn that up, Simon!" I said.

"Will do," he replied.

I went into the weed stash in the compartment on the door and found three blunts. I lit the blunt to relax and enjoy the city lights and tall buildings while looking out the window. We passed a florist shop with *Black roses for sale* sign in the window. That day kept playing over and over in my head of Black Rose burning herself. I should've known what she was going to do when I saw that long train black dress, it was the same dress she wore in my premonition.

Time flew by fast while I was thinking about my Rose. Simon was already driving up the driveway of our castle.

"Wake up!" I told Jasiah who was snoring.

"Damn, we're home already?" he asked, discombobulated.

"Yeah, now come on."

Simon was ready to get out to open the door for us. "I got it from here, Simon," I told him.

"Alrighty then, you two have a good night," he replied.

The front door of the castle swung open, and Baneet came outside wearing a robe. She was pissed off like always. "Is he drunk? Did he sleep with one of those nasty ass strippers?" Baneet asked me.

"Naw, I don't sleep with them. Want to go hunting?" Jasiah said. I already knew what he was hinting at.

"Don't wake the kids up with y'all's howling," I said.

"Did you have fun?" Baneet asked.

"Hell no," I replied, walking up the stairs. I closed the front door after I walked into the foyer.

The blunt I smoked was kicking in and I was too high to make it up the stairs or to the elevator. I vanished, reappearing in my penthouse. Nile was asleep in my bed with a bedtime book next to him. The bedroom light came on and stung my eyes.

"I said be here by one o'clock, Akea. Not four in the morning," Black Rose said.

"Sshhh," I told her before Nile woke up.

Rose sniffed my clothes. "You smell like perfume," she said with an attitude.

I kissed her forehead. "Do you want to smell that too?" I asked, pointing to my dick.

She smacked her teeth. "Do I have a reason to?" she replied.

"I was messing with you."

"I missed you," she said. I picked her up and she wrapped her legs around me.

"How much?" I replied.

"Enough to want you inside me," she said.

I carried her to the bathroom, locking the door behind me. Nile was at an age where he was getting into everything like opening the doors and catching me and Black Rose sexing. I sat her on the counter; she took off my shirt and unbuckled my pants. She reached into my boxer-briefs, grabbing my erection. I still couldn't believe she was in my life after the horrid scene I witnessed. Every morning I'd search for her when she wasn't in bed thinking she left me again.

I moved a braid away from her face. "I love you," I told her. She scooted to the edge of the counter.

"I love you too. Through the fire and back," she said.

"Bro, why would you bring that up? Goddamn Rose, you think it's funny? Kanye was calling you Freddy Krueger for a whole year straight and he still does it sometimes. I'm ready to take a shower. Thanks for ruining the moment," I told her.

She fell out laughing, almost slipping off the sink. "Babe, don't be like that. We gotta laugh to keep from crying. You saved me from that fire and I healed perfectly fine. I'm still here so it's okay to joke about it. Comere and let me kiss you," she said, puckering her lips. I pecked her lips while untying her robe.

"Say what you want but that day will never be funny. Your dark humor is going to get your ass in trouble one day."

She waved me off. "You get to see your parents tomorrow after two years. Are you excited?" she asked. I took off my pants and boxer-briefs.

"Yeah, I want to know the big surprise Sheldon said they have for us."

"How about you give me my big surprise," she said.

She was stroking my manhood. I cupped her neck while kissing her. She moaned, putting my dick against her wet entrance. I spread her legs wider so I could fit. Her pussy was tighter than a snake's grip. She rocked her body against my pelvis.

"I've been aroused all night, waiting for you to return home," she said. She fell against the mirror when I hit the back of her pussy.

"Don't run now, Rose," I gritted. I pushed her flexible legs back, folding her to take every inch I had to give.

"Right thereeeee! Shit, Akeaaaaa. Ohhhhh," she moaned. I heard glass breaking which meant Nile was up. Black Rose pushed me out of her. "I was ready to bust," I said.

She hopped off the counter and picked up her robe. "His magic is getting stronger day by day. He can barely sleep," she said.

"Naobi said he's an early bloomer. It's normal for him to experience night spells in his sleep."

I put on my boxer-briefs and followed Black Rose out of the bathroom. Nile was floating upside down in the air. His body was glowing with a blue hue but he was still asleep. The lamp by the bed was on the floor. He had to sleep with us for night floating, equivalent to night walking just in case he floated into a chandelier or something. I floated to him, catching him before he hit the chandelier.

He woke up rubbing his eyes. "Daddy, juice," he said.

I put him down and he ran into the kitchen. "See, you should've been home earlier. He wakes up around this time every morning," Rose said.

She went into the kitchen to get his juice. I sat at the kitchen island and watched her with Nile. It wasn't my plan to force motherhood on Black Rose, but it came naturally for her which made me extremely grateful.

"Mommy, I'm thirsty," Nile said, pulling on her robe.

"Give me one second," she replied. She was bent over in the fridge to get his sippy cup. "Got it," she said.

She handed him his sippy cup of homemade juice. "Thank you," he replied. Black Rose picked him up and they sat at the kitchen island across from me.

"I'm nervous about meeting your parents for the first time. What should I wear? Do I need to dress like Naobi with wrap dresses?" she asked.

"Just be yourself and I promise it'll work out," I assured her.

Nile was drawing symbols on the table with his finger. I looked at the drawing; the drawing was a silhouette of a rose. "Good job Nile," she clapped.

"Smart boy. Give me a pound," I said. Nile held out his fist; he chuckled when we bumped fists.

Black Rose yawned. "It's your turn to stay up with him while I get my beauty rest," she said. She got off the barstool.

"Don't go to sleep. Stay up with us."

"I have flowers to plant in a few hours," she said. She was talking about collecting the souls for the garden. Without the forest, her cursed garden lived off the blood of human sacrifices.

"Is it 'bring your man to work day' yet?"

She giggled. "You really want to see me take people's souls?" she asked.

"You can snatch mine."

She pecked my lips. "Good night," she replied. She left the kitchen area to get in bed.

"It's just me and you, Nile," I said. He got off the barstool to get his toys out. "Daddy, come on," he said.

He wanted to race cars. I sat on the floor next to him. He looked more like his biological mother each day. Dyika was a prisoner for eternity and Jetti became Jetster with no memories of being a woman with offspring. Either way, I was content that Nile wasn't attached to either of them anymore.

"Rrrrrrmmmmmmm," Nile said while we raced cars on the rug. His car crashed into mine.

"BOOM!" I shouted.

I played with Nile until the sun came up. We eventually fell asleep on the couch.

****

Sheldon's Cave...

Sheldon, his people, and the pack were gathered inside his cave where he held his lessons. His setup was the same as a church. Eventually, he became a family friend that we'd see once a month whenever he had to relay a message. There were an estimate fifty people sitting on the stone benches in his cave. Sheldon stood in the middle of the cave with his owl perched on his shoulder. My father was supposed to be arriving through a portal from his realm. It's going to be another few years before we see him since the portal opens every few years. Nile was sitting on Black Rose's lap playing with an action figure; she was nervously shaking her leg.

I put my hand on her thigh. "Relax," I told her.

"What about my clothes? How do I look?" she asked.

"We are all wearing a cloak. I promise you have nothing to worry about."

"I'm going to be so mad at you if they are mean to me. I promise I'm going to kick your ass," she threatened. Majestic, Tiko, Kanye's twins, Jasiah and Baneet were sitting in front of us. Zaan, Fiti and their one-year-old son Zafi were sitting behind us. He was named after his parents.

"Bsssp, Akea," Zaan whispered.

I turned around. "What?"

"You think Sheldon wanna cop some smoke?" he asked.

"I don't know, ask him. Why are you asking me?" I replied.

"Because I don't like talking to him. He's creepy as fuck and that bird keeps looking over here," he said. I looked at Sheldon's owl and it was asleep.

"Yo, you are high."

"Help a brother expand his clientele," he said.

"You gotta get over your fears and ask him yourself."

"Where is Monifa?" Black Rose asked Majestic.

"She and Kanye went hunting, well more so like humping," she replied. Majestic and Silver were also an addition to the pack. They were the only family Black Rose had left after the battle with Circa. Tiko was sprung over Majestic, so it was only right she joined the pack. They couldn't have offspring for being different species, but they were great godparents.

"The portal is opening!" Sheldon shouted. The black stone wall behind him beamed with a golden light. The people in the front rows were beating their drums.

"My nerves are so bad. I might need to use the bathroom," Black Rose said.

She was antsy and sweat beads covered her forehead. "Look on the bright side, beautiful. At least you can ask my mother how to cook," I said.

"I thought you loved my cooking," she replied.

"The food don't be cooked but we can worry about that later."

Kanye and Monifa snuck in. He sat next to me. "What did I miss?" he asked. He had something wet around his lips and in his chin hair.

"Bro, wipe your mouth off. Don't kiss Ma on her cheek when you see her or else we are going to be beefin'."

Kanye looked dumbfounded. "What's wrong with my mouth?" he asked.

"Oh shit," Monifa said. She scrubbed Kanye's face with the sleeve of her cloak.

"The portal is opening now," I nudged Kanye. Everyone covered their eyes from the bright light. The drumbeats grew louder and faster. I was excited and ready to run to my parents like I was Nile's age. The brightness got dull, and I could make out the gold and black silk garments my father was wearing. My father's pack was back. Everyone respectfully bowed their heads to welcome them home. My mother was holding two little girls whose dresses were identical to hers. Sheldon was giving him a long welcome home, but I couldn't ignore the twins with glowing ice-blue eyes.

"Wait a minute. Did our parents have more children?" Kanye asked.

"Yeah, it seems that way to me. They look the same age as our kids. I'm not ready for little sisters. What if they get boyfriends when they get older?" I replied.

"And we will kill them. They better get used to being single like Venus when she gets older," he said. Venus was Kanye's daughter's name.

"I hate to cut this ceremony short, Sheldon, but I got to see my boys," my father said to Sheldon.

"Everyone can leave the room while the king speaks to his family," Sheldon announced. Everyone but our pack exited the cave, including Sheldon. We got up to go to our family but everyone beat me to it. I was holding Black Rose's hand while walking her to greet them.

My mother hugged me. "My baby," she cried, kissing my face. I hugged her back.

"I'm not a baby anymore."

"You'll always be my baby. Look at you, Akea. You look so mature now and I see you are getting thicker around the arms," she replied.

My father rushed to me, picking me up off the ground. He was squeezing the life out of me. "You are squeezing him too tight, Goon," my mother said.

"Hush, Kanya. I missed my boys," he said.

"I can't...I can't breathe!"

My father released me. My mother noticed how nervous Black Rose seemed as she stood next to me with Nile. "Don't be shy, sweetheart, come over here," my mother said with her arms out to Rose. She walked into my mother's embrace. My mother hugged her and Nile.

"My son is very lucky to have a beautiful woman like yourself," my mother said to Rose.

"Thank you," Rose shyly responded.

"I'm proud of you, Son. You have a beautiful family," my father said.

"I did it with your guidance," I replied. His beard had grown out from the last time I saw him, and gold covered his canine teeth. The wolf medallion around his neck had blue diamond eyes and his silk suit was tailored.

"I see Anubi switched up their dress code. Y'all went from wearing wrap skirts to suits. Now, I gotta start an Anubian men's clothing line. This shit is fly, Pops," I said.

"Watch your mouth Akea," my mother scolded.

"The boy is grown, Kanya. Look at him, he has a son and a mate now. He can say what he wants," my father replied. I spotted Kanye through the crowd holding the twin girls that resembled us when we were babies.

"I'm assuming the surprise is our sisters," I said.

"Yes and their names are Egypt and Pharaoh. Egypt is just like you, Akea. She's magical. I can't wait for you to teach her how to use her gift," my mother said.

"I can't wait either, we need more sorcerers in this family," I replied.

"I'm going to take Rose and Nile to meet everyone. I'm too excited about your family," my mother said. Black Rose looked at me for help; she was a nervous wreck.

"You'll get used to it and no time," I told her.

"We're family now, Rose. You're in good hands," my father told her. My mother pulled Black Rose through the crowd while holding onto Nile.

"You aren't going to see your mate for a while. Kanya has been talking about her new daughter-in-law all night," my father said.

"How long are y'all here for?" I asked.

"Until the moon rises," he replied.

Kanye and our triplet, Djet joined us. I gave Djet a dap hug. "Are you ready to make the big move and come stay with us?" Kanye asked him.

He shook his head. "This world is too fast for me. I'm afraid of it," he replied. Djet was an introvert and wasn't used to a fast-paced world.

"Where is your mate?" Kanye asked him.

"She's due any day now, so I'm hoping I make it back home in time," Djet proudly said.

"What are y'all having?" Kanye asked.

"We're having two boys. I can't wait," he replied.

"Goddamn, y'all in Anubi running a twin marathon? Something in the water?" Kanye asked.

"We're strengthening the family tree," our father chuckled.

"It's triggering my anxiety. Why should our children and baby siblings be the same age?" Kanye asked him.

"I'm still young and so is your mother. I'll leave the rest to your imagination. But I will say, our world is peaceful, and we don't have anything else to do but spend time with each other. The next time we visit, expect a football team," he said.

"Y'all started a reunion without me?" Naobi said while approaching us. She hugged our father then Djet. "It's been a while," Naobi said.

"Two years feels like a long time. But at least I can get a good night's sleep knowing that everyone is doing well for themselves," our father said.

I searched the crowd looking for Black Rose. She was standing next to my mother laughing with her and Monifa. She blended into the family like I knew she would.

I mouthed the words, "I love you." She blew me a kiss before directing her attention back to my mother.

"With all the grandchildren and great-grandchildren, I'm curious to know how their lives will be. The journey never ends," Naobi said.

"I don't want to think about it," Kanye said.

"I never know how it'll end but I know there's always a new beginning," our father said, and we agreed.

The End...Just for Now.

To stay up to date with Natavia's paranormal reads join:

Natavia's Magical Unicorns and Beastly Beauties Paranormal Reads

Books to read for the backstory of Akea's family…

Beauty to his Beast
Beauty to his Beast 2
Beauty in the eyes of his Beast

Beasts: New Chapter
Beast 2: A Mate's War
Beast 3: Unleashed

Available for Pre-order soon

SOUL Publications

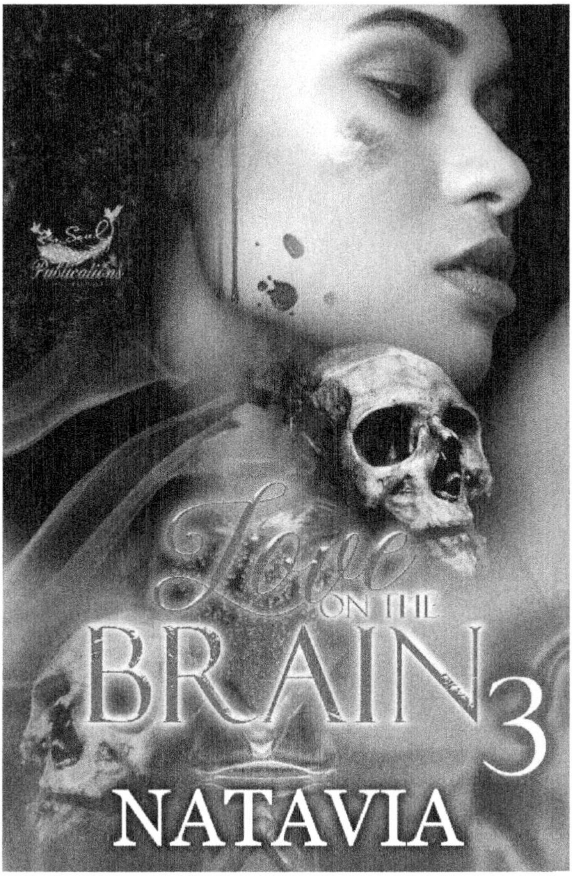
Love
ON THE
BRAIN 3
NATAVIA

Printed in Great Britain
by Amazon